YOU HAVEN'T
TO DESERVE

YOU HAVEN'T TO DESERVE

A GIFT TO THE HOMELESS
FICTION BY 21 WRITERS

Jane Hill
Editor

Task Force for the Homeless
Atlanta, Georgia

Published by
TASK FORCE FOR THE HOMELESS
363 Georgia Avenue, S.E.
Atlanta, Georgia 30312-3027

Printed in the United States of America

1st printing 1991

Library of Congress Catalog Card Number: 91-66430

ISBN 0-9628530-2-X

Book development and production management by Bookmark.

Jacket design by Jim True. Jacket painting by Benny Andrews.

This book was printed by Arcata Graphics Book Group, Martinsburg, West
Virginia on 50# (400 ppi) Amherst Tradebook Natural Paper provided by
Georgia-Pacific Corporation, Communication Papers Division, Atlanta,
Georgia. Endleaf is 80# Sandstone Proterra Felt Recycled Premium Paper,
provided by Hopper Paper Company (Georgia-Pacific Corporation). Jacket
paper and printing were provided by Phoenix Color Corp., Long Island
City, New York; case materials were provided by Holliston, Kingsport,
Tennessee.

Text was set in Palatino by RKS Resources, Inc., Atlanta, Georgia; cover
typography was provided by Typo-Repro Service, Atlanta, Georgia; color
separations courtesy Magna Graphic, Orlando, Florida.

Distributed by Longstreet Press, Atlanta, Georgia.

*"Home is the place where when you have to go there,
they have to take you in."*

*"I should have called it 'something you somehow
haven't to deserve.'"*

Robert Frost
"The Death of the Hired Man"

Contents

Acknowledgments

Melanie Smallie of Bookmark joins me in thanking the writers and book suppliers whose generous contributions made this book possible. We are pleased to acknowledge them here.

A special note of thanks to the contributors who donated their honorarium to the homeless: Tina McElroy Ansa, Michael Bishop, Emily Ellison, Paul Hemphill, Rebecca Hill, Mary Hood, Greg Johnson, Terry Kay, Eugenia Price, Ferrol Sams, Anne Rivers Siddons, Alice Walker, and Philip Lee Williams.

We are especially grateful to the following individuals and companies for donating their time and services to this project: Jim True; the entire staff of RKS Resources; Joyce Jackson and Ray Chafin of Typo-Repro Service, Inc.; Cody Cox of Magna Graphic; Eddie Owens, Wayne Masters and Kathy Coston of Arcata Graphics Book Group; Brad Ripple of Georgia-Pacific Corporation; Louis LaSorsa of Phoenix Color; Don Lee and George Clark of Holliston; and the staff of Longstreet Press.

We also wish to thank the folks at the Task Force for the Homeless, particularly Sally Doornbos and Anita Beaty, for their enthusiasm and assistance.

And finally, we'd like to thank our many friends and colleagues for their encouragement and support of this project: Bob Hill, Larry Smallie, Jane and Tom Keene, Stan Robinson, Tony Sylvester, Joy Wesson, Jan Smyth, Rebecca Sherrill, Lee Hornsby-Dodds, Keith Gribble, John Dodds, Joey Salle, and all the members of the Success Group.

Introduction

Several years ago, while I was still a graduate student at the University of Illinois, I was asked to be on a panel with literary folks. Our topic of discussion was approaches to teaching Twain's *Adventures of Huckleberry Finn*, one of the two or three greatest novels ever produced by an American author.

The other panelists were all what we graduate-student types called "real" teachers, meaning that they had their degrees, jobs, and insurance as we know it—all luxuries that graduate students can only aspire to. I was nervous. But not nervous enough to keep my mouth shut when perhaps the most prestigious of the other panelists attacked the ending of *Huck Finn*.

Attacking its ending is fairly common critical stuff—I had referred to the history of such attacks in my own presentation. But one point in his assault genuinely upset me, enough that I forgot my "place" and spoke right out.

He said the ending was grievously flawed for him because Jim, the runaway slave with whom Huck casts his lot, can be freed just by Miss Watson's scribbling a generous note on her deathbed. The triviality of that note really, really irritated the prestigious critic.

Without even thinking, I blurted out that I thought that what bothered him was precisely Twain's point: it should *bother* us that a human's life could hang on such a trivial thing as a deathbed note scribbled in the moment before one meets her maker. That was the problem with slavery as an institution—it trivialized humanity, humanness.

When I first suggested the quote from Frost's poem "The Death of the Hired Man" as the title for this anthology, a number of folks reacted negatively because they thought the phrase "you haven't to deserve" awkward—hard to say and to remember. I've worked in the book business

long enough to take their comments seriously. I really, really thought
about it.

But I decided to stick with the title, largely for the same reasons I
spoke up in Mark Twain's defense about that trivial piece of paper. I
think Frost's sense of what home is—"something you somehow haven't
to deserve"—is dead-on accurate, even if the language doesn't slip effortlessly off our sound-byte-trained tongues.

And I've read enough Frost to know that he could have written just
as telling a definition in the simplest, clearest grammatical construction
possible, if he'd wanted to. So I like to think of his language-rich brain
sorting through the possibilities and coming to rest upon a phrase that
said what he meant with just enough awkwardness to make us pause,
to make us think and struggle—to show us how the hired man and
the good folks who contemplate his fate in the poem felt. The language
gives us the experience, and the language fits. This particular experience
is hard to take and give.

There's a stereotype of the artist as temperamental, shut off from reality,
even frivolous. But when Georgia's literary community was asked about
this project, their response—as evidenced by what you hold in your hand—
disproves that stereotype.

The writers included in this anthology not only agreed to participate
but also embraced the idea with such warmth and generosity and fervor
that they transformed—through talent and craft—a good idea into a thing
of beauty and truth.

In my initial request, I asked the writers to send any piece of fiction
they chose. The subject matter needn't be directly related to the issue
of homelessness; the work needn't present a didactic message of any
kind. I asked good writers for good fiction. Period.

What I got was, indeed, good fiction, and because good fiction almost
always touches on the mysterious essence of our humanness, in a magical
and serendipitous way the book speaks eloquently to Frost's definition
of home: its awkwardness and compassion and beauty and truth.

The twenty-one writers gathered here have made the book's subtitle—*A
Gift to the Homeless*—literal truth. The richness of their creative talent
is a great gift, indeed, for us all. That gift demonstrates better than
anything else could that the distinctions between us are far less important
than the links.

If you know the work of these women and men already, *You Haven't
to Deserve* will be a reunion of sorts, a gathering of old friends. If you
don't know them and their work, what fine new friends you are getting
ready to meet!

The world is big, and its problems often seem overwhelming. Once, years ago, during the time when Vietnamese refugees were fleeing on boats that hardly deserved that name, I saw Joan Baez on *Donahue*, trying to inspire good, hard-working, middle-class Americans to care about their Vietnamese neighbors.

A woman in the audience stood at one point and told Joan Baez that she'd really, really like to do something but she didn't understand what she could do. Furthermore, when she tried to discuss it with her friends, tried to figure out what they could do, her friends asked her to change the subject, talk about something less depressing, more about their lives.

Joan Baez looked at her, smiled, and said, "Get new friends."

How lucky we all are to have twenty-one such wonderful friends as the writers in this book. How lucky that they have given us all the chance to do one small concrete thing for those of us who are just now without what we haven't to deserve. We can buy this book and help the homeless. We can read it and help ourselves. We are lucky.

—Jane Hill
Atlanta, Georgia
August 1991

YOU HAVEN'T
TO DESERVE

from JESSIE AND JESUS AND COUSIN CLAIRE

Raymond Andrews

Lord, Jesus was stumped! What in the world had she done to bring out the "shotgun" in the Pretty Girl? Had the Pretty Girl wanted to kill her? Why was the Pretty Girl mad at her? It was enough to make her cry—later. Right now she was too baffled to boo. She wanted to be the Pretty Girl's friend—even though she'd been told on that long-ago and sorrowful day that the Pretty Girl had been the cause of her Candy Man getting killed. She hadn't understood why anyone would've wanted to kill such a good person—a person she hadn't been able to imagine doing anything to make someone even think of killing him. And then, the idea of someone as pretty as the Pretty Girl doing such a thing, or being the cause of it, she, as the years went past, found harder and harder to believe.

These passing years found her back following many of the same trails she and her ma had blazed throughout the area much earlier. Out on the trail again, she, in the very beginning, had often thought of going up to knock on someone's door and ask for work and a room. But she was deathly afraid of people. Her ma and the Candy Man had been the only two souls she'd never been afraid of and now they both were dead. After taking her in following her ma's death, the Candy Man had at first wanted to turn her, who had nobody and nowhere to go to, over to the authorities whom, he tried his best to assure her, would see she got a good home. Her answer to this was to head back to the trees . . . a move stopped only by his letting her stay with him, the only person once her ma died (and whose burial he personally saw to) that she felt she could trust.

In the beginning, the Candy Man had wanted her to meet and associate with children in her own age group, she being fifteen when she came to live with him. Lord, she tried. But everybody just laughed at her because of her name and because of the facts that she'd never before lived in a house or been inside a school. But in much less time than a year she'd learned to cook, clean, and care for the Candy Man's house, he'd told her, just as good as or better than any other house was taken care of in the neighborhood of Thompson Town, where they lived. And as far as school was concerned, her ma had taught her how to read from her frazzled old romance magazines, and she felt she was just as good or even better at reading than anybody in her class or in the school. But most of all everyone had made fun of her because of who her ma had been. "Gal, the ol' crazy cracker chick with the nigger baby," she'd often heard her ma and herself referred to as. She'd loved, and deeply missed, her ma, who'd been a good ma who had loved her right back. Her pa she hadn't known, but her ma had often told her he was the first man who had ever been good to her and always referred to him as being "a nice colored gentleman." She hadn't wanted to be around any of these hate-minded people, and thus her whole life at the time came to center on the Candy Man and on doing for him—up until the day she'd gone to the doctor, where she found out she was pregnant with his baby and hurried happily back home to find the law . . . and, Lord, a dead Candy Man.

She'd cleaned up the Candy Man's house and left, carrying her few belongings in a plastic bag and wearing the pretty new winter blue dress he had just bought her the day before his death—the one she wore to the doctor when she found out the happy news about the baby and the one she'd worn ever since. She'd also left crying, wanting, needing to talk to the Pretty Girl, whom Thompson Town folks had told her he'd been with when her pa killed him. She'd wanted to know from the Pretty Girl why did her Candy Man, the only person besides her ma who had ever treated her kindly, have to be killed? Or she'd just wanted *somebody* to talk, or cry, to. But after walking all the way from Appalachee out to the country and seeing the big pretty house the Pretty Girl lived in, she knew she wouldn't, didn't, know how to talk to such a person living in such a house. That, Lord, is when she came back home to the woods.

She didn't go to the Candy Man's funeral because she felt even his family hadn't liked her. On the day of the burial, she stayed in the woods . . . not coming out until sundown to go to the cemetery, where she slept the night and cried on the Candy Man's grave.

During her first year back to the woods she'd kept pretty close to the Mitchell Dairy Farm because of her expectant baby. Here at night she could leave the forest and walk just a few yards to gather and eat fresh, raw vegetables from the family garden of the Mitchells' farm helper—the "Milking Man," she called him—and fruit from the trees making up the orchard in back of the dairy's huge barn. And, of course, pecans from the big tree in the front yard. All healthy food, she felt, to nourish her and her coming baby. Besides, she deep-down believed, because of the Pretty Girl and her pa being responsible for her Candy Man's death, his son had the *right* to eat free from the family Mitchell's land.

When that first winter of her being back to the forest came and all the vegetables, fruits, and nuts were no more, she lived solely off the dairy cows' milk, drinking it straight from the teat. To ensure her baby good health, she refused to eat out of the garbage, even though she just knew the Pretty Girl's garbage was better than most. Nor, when in the woods, unlike her ma, could she bring herself to kill and cook any of the forest's wild game. She considered them all, from the harmless fish to the poisonous snakes, to be her friends who just like her were just trying to survive. Nor did she steal farmers' animals or fowl for food—only (the Mitchells') vegetables, fruits, and nuts, and always only a few at a time so that she felt they wouldn't be missed. Soon she'd become such a familiar nighttime figure moving through the garden and orchard, beneath the pecan tree, and around the barn that the Mitchell Dairy Farm's two families' dogs became her friends, their barks quickly replaced by wagging tails for her. If the Pretty Girl's big and nice German shepherd didn't come meet her at night out by the barn upon her exiting the forest, she automatically suspected the animals of being somewhere close to the Mitchells' house with its owner. Thus she knew these weren't the nights to go gather pecans from beneath the big pecan tree in the front yard.

It was in the barn's big, fodder-filled hayloft where her baby was born that spring. The birth occurred sometime between midnight and daylight, she in the dark of the loft delivering the baby herself, with her teeth chewing through the umbilical cord. Having spanked a cry out of the baby and yet unable to see it in the dark, she slowly and surely ran her hand all over its tiny body, caressing and exploring its head and face, counting each finger and toe to make sure they were all there, checking between its legs where she felt a penis and sac, and rummaging around back to make sure the butt had its hole. Satisfied that everything was accounted for and in place, she left her baby temporarily to descend the ladder to the ground floor with the empty quart tin she'd kept among her belongings for this special occasion. No warm water being available in the barn, she roused awake one of the cows down there and after getting it on its feet and eating the feed left in the evening before, began milking it until her can was nearly full. Returning to the loft, she washed her baby in the warm milk, dried it with the lone towel from her plastic bag of belongings, and nursed it from her breasts for the first time before, finally, wrapping it in the towel to sleep. Then she went back down the ladder to bathe herself with cold water from the faucet located inside the barn. Climbing back up to the loft, she had the intention of resting awhile to regain her strength before taking the baby to her day place in the woods, thus leaving just ahead of the Milking Man, who arrived at the barn before dawn each and every morning. Instead, exhausted and still weak, she fell quickly to sleep.

Then, suddenly, her eyes popped open to stare right smack dab back into a bigger pair looking out of a head peeking over into the loft at the now-wide-awake mother and still-sleeping baby on their haybed. She and the Milking Man just stared at one another wordlessly for several long moments until, finally, his head popped down out of sight. She lay listening to his feet descending the ladder, waiting until they cleared the last rung before making her move. But before she, yet-sleeping baby in one arm and plastic bag of belongings looped around the other, could reach the loft's opening to escape the barn, she heard someone coming up the ladder. The sound froze her in her tracks. The Milking Man's head popped back up through the opening—followed by his right hand . . . carrying a gallon waterbucket nearly half-filled with fresh milk and holding a tin dipper. Setting the pail down gently over into the loft, the Milking Man didn't say a single word but gave her a look telling her she didn't have to run and that it was all right for her to stay. Then he was gone back down the ladder. Only to return about a half-hour later. This time he brought and left at the edge of the loft's opening a large cardboard box before disappearing from view again. Walking over slowly and looking into the box, she reached in and began taking out still-warm containers of food: biscuits, grits, scrambled eggs, fried ham, coffee, butter, jelly and sugar, along with salt and pepper shakers, a fork, knife, and spoon. Lining the bottom of the box were several items of baby clothing, diapers, safety pins, and a quilt. Later, while enjoying her first home-cooked meal since returning to the woods, she sat that early morning crying in her grits.

Every morning before the crack of dawn, the Milking Man would climb the hayloft ladder to leave a cardboard box containing enough food for her for the day, at the same time taking away the box from the day before with its empty containers washed the previous night by her in the dark under the barn's water faucet. The two never spoke to one another, but every morning when the Milking Man's head popped up into the loft she would be awake with a smile for him and the look in his big warm brown eyes told her he knew she appreciated and thanked him with all of her heart for everything he was doing for her and her baby. When the weather was nice, which it was most of that spring, summer, and fall, immediately after eating and while the Milking Man was busy at this work, she would descend the ladder with her baby and belongings and sneak out the barn's back door, walk through the orchard, and reach the woods before sunup. Here she would remain until the lights went out in the Mitchells' house that night, whereupon she would return to the loft. When the weather was too bad for the baby to go out into, she would remain as quietly as possible in the loft. Fortunately for her, during this period her baby had been one who didn't cry very much. At first she was deathly scared he might be too noisy and the two of them would be discovered by the Pretty Girl or her pa and thrown out of the barn, especially if they found out her baby was the Candy Man's. Or, worse, they would be arrested and turned over to someone she would be afraid of. But during a brief period that first year the baby did cry quite often at night. Whenever this happened she always tried to make sure the morning after that she was out of the barn and back into the woods before the lights in the Mitchells' house went on. One morning she didn't quite make it.

The baby had cried most of the night and didn't fall asleep until just shortly before dawn. Not wanting to interrupt his sleep by picking him up, she decided to chance staying in the barn a bit longer than her usual time that morning—Lord, long enough to hear and then, through a crack between the floorboards of the loft, see the Pretty Girl come into the barn early that morning. Hardly breathing from fright, she watched the Pretty Girl walking around down below looking all over the barn as if in desperate search of something . . . or somebody. Not finding it down there the Pretty Girl looked up at the loft . . . then started up the ladder. Here the Milking Man stopped his work to holler out at her to leave the barn right away because he had a very sick cow on his hands and no one, especially young'uns who were full of all kinds of children diseases, was to touch *anything* the cow ate . . . even the hay up in the loft . . . but himself. At this bit about the hay, the Pretty Girl stopped halfway up the ladder . . . but started back down only when the Milking Man told her the name of the sick cow. Yet after reaching the floor and pleading with him to let her back to see the sick cow, whom they called "Ol' Mag," he refused her and the Pretty Girl left the barn pretty mad. The Milking Man went back to his cows and she quickly got her baby and belongings and left out the back way for the woods.

She was concerned about the sick cow herself, but she didn't know, nor could she tell, which one ailed. Nor from her view through the floorboards over the next several days did she ever see the Milking Man below attending to a sick cow.

The older her baby got, the less time she spent in the barn, preferring the pine-needled beds of the forest during the warm months over the hot hayloft. The Candy Man had once told her that while he was in the Army and stationed overseas in France, a Frenchwoman, upon learning the name he was best known by among his friends back home, began calling him "Le Bonbon." So sweet did his name sound to Jesus that she decided immediately to give it to her Candy-Man baby the day she found out she was pregnant.

Le Bonbon was her whole life. The older he grew the more he looked like his pa—the hair of the same generous-sized curls, those dimples ever teasing the corners of his mouth into a smile, and, Lord, those green eyes. He didn't at all look like her, whose skin, according to her ma, was the dark color of her pa's and whose thin, tight features she got from her ma. And like her pa was supposed to have been, she was all seriousness, with no sense of humor whatsoever, unlike her ma, who knew how to laugh. There came those times when she thought about whether or not she should put Le Bonbon in a schoolhouse where he would grow up and have a life more like other children. But remembering how she had been treated by those "normal" children and knowing how mean and hateful they would be to her son once finding out who his ma was made her feel extremely protective and not want to think about his ever leaving her. Meanwhile, from books the Candy Man had bought her, which she still kept among her few belongings, she, like her ma had done her, taught him how to read.

The older the Pretty Girl got the more time she seemed to spend at home, especially in and around the barn and farm—a situation eventually ending Jesus's and Le Bonbon's barn days and sending them to live full-time in the woods. However, unlike her ma had done with her, she didn't roam throughout the region with her child. She never strayed too far from the Mitchells' land, from whose garden, orchard, and dairy she deeply felt her son had a right to feed. So strongly did she feel about this that she refused to take anything from any other farm, or house, in the area.

Then, Lord, came the day of the Pretty Girl's husband's funeral. When the burial services ended most of the cars left the church early, going back towards town. Thinking all of the funeral cars had gone, Jesus, holding Le Bonbon's hand, had just exited the forest at the Oconee River Bridge and the two of them were about to cross over to the other side of the road and into the woods when, suddenly, a car shot around the curve leading onto the bridge. It was the Pretty Girl's car. This was the second time she'd been on the bridge when the Pretty Girl came speeding by. The first time she hadn't been able to take her eyes off the Pretty Girl's face as she shot past. But this time her eyes were able to catch a fleeting glimpse of the face of the child sitting beside the Pretty Girl on the front seat of the car as it blurred past . . . but not so much of a blur that she wasn't able to see the child's face and tell that it was even prettier than the Pretty Girl's. Lord, that's the very instant it struck her that she knew now what in life she wanted for her son, Le Bonbon. Long after the car had gone she yet stood on the bridge staring after it while holding her son's hand thinking that, having been the cause of his pa getting killed, the Pretty Girl now *owed* her son. *Owed* Le Bonbon her pretty little girl.

But, she knew, first she had to ready her son. He was a good boy but despite his obedience she, as the years slipped past, could strongly sense beneath his quiet and calm facade a growing curiosity about life other than the way they lived it. She now, convinced of not wanting her son to roam the woods with her until she died like her ma had done with her, right away started preparing him for his future. She began by attempting to teach him the ways and habits of the world of the "normal" people. Thus, for the next two years the two of them competed with the local raccoons and possums throughout the area in raiding garbage and trash cans and dumps. But instead of looking for food for the belly, they were searching for fuel to feed Le Bonbon's mind, printed matter. Few books were ever found but newspapers, magazines, and, Lord, *TV Guides* were plentiful, all of which she fed her son to read and study to learn to be "normal." When not reading, he would be brought by her out of the forest up to the edge of the trees where, without their being seen, she would point out to him the Mitchells' big house and barn. Occasionally the Pretty Girl would be spotted and, Lord, she just *loved* looking at the Pretty Girl, who was always so immaculately dressed. Not a hair or string did the Pretty Girl ever have out of place, even when she wore overalls. Her slender and shapely body carried clothing like it had been painted on her. Jesus wished she was as beautiful . . . and as important . . . as the Pretty Girl.

Then whenever she and her son saw the Pretty Girl's Pretty Little Girl she would whisper sweetly to Le Bonbon, "If you keep reading and learning all them books and papers we keep getting for you, then one day you'll be jes as smart as the Pretty Little Girl there." Without a word he would squeeze her hand and just keep staring at the big house and barn . . . and the car, and most times two of them, sitting in the front yard. He, she knew, was a good boy and would someday do what his ma wanted for him.

Now, Lord knows, she didn't want the Pretty Girl mad at her. Especially not mad enough to come after her with a shotgun again. She was sure the Pretty Girl was mad at her because of how she was always dressed. She had some other clothes, given to her by the Milking Man (though she couldn't help but feel the good man's wife, whom she'd seen only once and at a distance, was the one chiefly responsible for him giving her and Le Bonbon all the food and clothing he'd given them without a single word of complaint at her over the years) but didn't like not wearing the last dress the Candy Man had bought her. But now she would change that by wearing around her body the beautiful, colorful quilt given her by the Candy Man, and dress, she felt, in a manner more befitting the ma of Le Bonbon.

Tomorrow, Thanksgiving Day, would be the tenth anniversary of the burial of the Candy Man. She and Le Bonbon would, after dark, go and put flowers on his grave. Then, she had firmly and finally decided, on the day after that she would take her nine-year-old Le Bonbon out of the woods to the Mitchells' barn before daybreak to see the Milking Man who'd always been so good to both of them and ask him would he let her son help him do the milking. (The little boy who looked to her to've been near Le Bonbon's age and whom she'd seen at the dairy from afar was always in the company of the Pretty Girl's pa and never seemed to help the Milking Man. She was never quite sure who this little boy belonged to.) This way, she figured, her Le Bonbon would eventually get to know the Pretty Little Girl . . . who, when they got old enough, he would court . . . then *marry* . . . then live with in the big pretty house . . . then she and her son wouldn't have to live in the woods any more . . . because he and the Pretty Little Girl would let his ma live in the barn . . . Yes, Lord, the Pretty Girl *owed* the Candy Man's Le Bonbon her Pretty Little Girl . . .

WILLIE BEA AND JAYBIRD: A LOVE STORY

Tina McElroy Ansa

When Willie Bea first saw Jaybird in The Place, she couldn't help herself. She wanted him so bad she sucked in her bottom lip, cracked with the cold, then she ran her tongue so slowly over her top lip that she could taste the red Mabelline lipstick she had put on hours before. He looked like something that would be good to eat, like peach cobbler or a hot piece of buttered cornbread.

She had just entered the bar clutching her black purse under her arm and smiling to try to make herself look attractive among the six o'clock crowd of drinkers and dancers and socializers, every one of them glad to be done with work for the day. He was there at the end of the bar in his golden Schlitz uniform sharing a quart of Miller High Life beer with a buddy. Willie Bea noticed right away how he leaned his long frame clear across the bar, bent at the waist, his elbows resting easily on the Formica counter. There didn't seem to be a tense bone in his lean efficient body.

"He look like he could go anywhere in the world," Willie Bea thought as she followed her big butt friend Patricia as she weaved her way to a nearby table already jammed with four of her friends, two men, two women. "If somebody put him in a white jacket and a flower in his buttonhole, he could pass for an actor in a Technicolor movie."

As the jukebox started up again, playing a driving Sam and Dave number, he looked around the bar, picked up his glass of beer and headed toward her table with his chin held high over the other patrons. When he smoothly pulled up a chair to her table and straddled it backwards, Willie Bea crossed her stick legs and pinched her friend Pat's thigh under the table to give her some Sen-Sen for her breath.

"Hey, Little Mama, you got time for a tired working man?"

She had to remember to wipe the uncomfortable moisture/spittle from the corners of her mouth with her fingertips before she could respond to him.

She still felt that way, four years after they had started going together, when she looked at him.

Nothing gave her more pleasure than to be asked her marital status with Jaybird around.

"Willie Bea, girl, where you been keeping yourself?" some big-mouthed woman would shout at her over the din of the jukebox at The Place. "I ain't seen you in a month of Sundays. You still living with your aunt, ain't you?" This last asked expectantly with pity.

Willie Bea would roll her shoulders and dip her ears from side to side a couple of times in feigned modesty.

"Naw, girl, I *been* moved out of my aunt's," Willie Bea would answer. "I'm married now. I live with my . . . *husband*."

The old horse's big mouth would fall open, then close then open as if she were having trouble chewing this information.

"Husband? Married??!!"

"Uh-huh. That's my *husband* over there by the jukebox. Naw, not him. My Jay is the tall light-skinned one, the one with the head full of curly hair."

Willie Bea never even bothered to look at her inquisitor when she pointed out Jay. She could hear the effect the weight of the revelation had had on the woman. And Willie Bea only glanced smugly at the old cow as she raced around the bar nearly knocking over her chair to ask her friends and companions why no one told her that skinny little shiny-faced Willie Bea had a man.

"I thought she was sitting there mighty sassy looking."

Even Willie Bea would have admitted it: most days, she did feel sassy and it was Jaybird who made her so. He burst into the bathroom while she was in the bathtub and pretended to take pictures of her with an imaginary camera. He teased her about flirting with Mr. Maurice who owned the store on the corner near their boarding house when the merchant sliced her baloney especially thin the way she liked it.

Now, she really thought she was cute, with her little square monkey face and eager to please grin, a cheap jet black Prince Valiant wig set on the top of her head like a wool cap with her short hair plaited underneath and a pair of black eyeglasses so thick that her eyes looked as if they were in fish bowls.

Jaybird had done that to her. He even called her "fine," an appellation that actually brought tears to her eyes made huge and outlandish by the Coke-bottle thick glasses.

"Fine." It was the one thing in life Willie Bea longed to be. She had no shape to speak of. She was just five feet tall and weighed about ninety pounds. But she did her best to throw that thing even though she had very little to throw.

"If I had me a big old butt like you, Pat," she would say to her friend, "y'all couldn't stand me."

The pitiful little knot of an ass that she had was her sorrow, especially after noticing from Jaybird's gaze that he appreciated a full ass. His favorite seemed to be the big heart-shaped ones that started real low and hung and swayed like a bustle when the woman walked. Many mornings, Jay lay in bed watching Bea move around the room getting dressed and thought, "Her behind ain't no bigger than my fist." But he didn't dare say anything, even as a joke. He knew it would break her heart.

But since she knew she didn't have a big ass, she did what she had done since she was a child when someone told her what she was lacking: she pretended she did and acted as if her ass was the prize one in town. The one men in juke joints talked about.

Wherever she went—to the market, to work cleaning houses, to The Place, downtown to shop—she dressed as if she had that ass to show off.

She wore tight little straight skirts that she made herself on her landlady's sewing machine. Skirts of cotton or wool or taffeta no wider than twelve inches across. Not that wide really, because she wanted the skirt to "cup" if possible under the pones of her behind and to wrinkle across her crotch in front. Using less than a yard of material and a Simplicity quickie pattern she had bought years before and worked away to tatters, she took no more than an hour to produce one of her miniature skirts.

On Sundays, when the house was empty of other boarders or quiet from their sleep, Willie Bea used her landlady's sewing machine that she kept in the parlor. The steady growl of the old foot-pedal-run Singer disturbed no one. In fact, on those Sundays she and Jaybird went out and she did no sewing, the other tenants of the large white wooden house felt an unidentified longing and found themselves on the verge of complaining about the silence.

Willie Bea looked on the ancient sewing machine, kept in mint condition by the genial landlady who always wore plaid housedresses and her thin crimpy red hair in six skinny braids, as a blessing. She didn't mind that the machine was a foot-propelled model rather than an electric one. It never occurred to her to expect anything as extravagant as that. For her, the old machine was a step up from the tedious hand-sewing that she had learned and relied on as a child. With the waist bands neatly attached and the short zippers eased into place by machine, her skirts had a finished look that would have taken her all night to accomplish by hand.

Many times, she felt herself rocking gently to the rhythm she set with her bare feet on the cold iron treadle to ease a crick in her stiff back before she realized that she had been at the job nonstop all afternoon. Just using the machine made her happy, made her think of men watching her at the bus stops in her new tight skirt and later, maybe, these same men letting some sly comment drop in front of Jaybird about her shore looking good.

She imagined Jaybird jumping in the men's faces, half-angry, half-proud, to let them know that was his *wife* they were talking about. Just thinking of Jaybird saying "my wife" made her almost as happy as her being able to say "my husband."

She loved to go over in her head how it had come to pass, their marriage. They had been living together in one room of the boarding house at the top of Pleasant Hill for nearly three years, with him seeming to take for granted that they would be together for eternity and with her hardly daring to believe that he really wanted her, afraid to ask him why he picked her to love.

As with most of his decisions, movements, he surprised her.

One evening in August he walked into their room and said, "Let's get married." As if the idea had just come to him, his and original. She responded in kind.

"Married? Married, Jay?" she said, pretending to roll the idea around in her head a while. Then, "Okay, if you want."

It was her heart's desire, the play-pretty of her dreams, being this man's wife.

She bought stiff white lace from Newberry's department store to make a loose cropped sleeveless overblouse and a yard of white polished cotton and sewed a tight straight skirt for the ceremony at the courthouse.

When they returned to their room for the honeymoon, Willie Bea thought as she watched him take off his wedding suit that no other man could be so handsome, so charming, so full of self-assured cockiness . . . and still love her.

He was tall and slender in that way that made her know that he would be lean all his life, never going sway-backed and too fat around his middle like a pregnant woman. He was lithe and strong from lifting cases and kegs of Schlitz beer all day long, graceful from leaping on and off the running board of the moving delivery truck as it made its rounds of bars and stores.

Once when he had not seen her, Willie Bea had spied him hanging fearlessly off the back of the beer truck like a prince, face directly into the wind, his eyes blinking back the wind tears, a vacant look on his face. His head full of curly hair quivering in the wind. The setting sunlight gleamed off the chrome and steel of the truck giving a golden-orange color to the aura that Willie Bea felt surrounded him all the time.

Overcome by the sight, Willie Bea had had to turn away into an empty doorway to weep silently over the beauty of her Jaybird.

Jaybird even made love the way she knew this man would—sweet and demanding. When her friend Pat complained about her own man's harsh unfeeling fucking, Willie Bea joined in and talked about men like dogs. But first, in her own mind, she placed Jaybird outside the dog pack.

"Girl, just thank your lucky stars that you ain't hooked up with a man like Henry," Pat told her. "Although God knows they all alike. You may as well put 'em all in a croker sack and pick one out. They all the same. One just as good as the other. Just take your pick."

"Uh-huh, girl, you know you telling the truth," Willie Bea would answer.

"Why, that old dog of mine will just wake any time of the night and go to grabbing me and sticking his hand up my nightdress. He don't say nothing, just grunt. He just goes and do his business. I could be anything, a sack of flour, that chair you sitting on."

"What you be doing?" Willie Bea asked in her soft sing-song voice even though she already knew because Pat always complained about the same thing. But she asked because she and Pat had grown up together, she had been Pat's friend longer than anyone outside of her family. And Willie Bea knew what a friend was for.

"Shoot, sometimes I just lay there like I *am* a sack of flour. I thought that would make him see I wasn't getting nothing out of his humping. Then I saw it didn't make no difference to him whether I was having a good time or not. So, now, sometimes I push him off me just before he come. That makes him real mad. Or I tell him I got my period.

"Some nights, we just lay there jostling each other like little children fighting over a ball. I won't turn over or open up my legs and he won't stop tugging on me."

"Girl, both of y'all crazy. That way, don't neither of you get a piece. That's too hard," Willie Bea said sincerely.

"Shoot, girl, some nights we tussle all night." Pat gave a hot dry laugh. "Henry think too much of hisself to fight me for it, really hit me up side my head or yell and scream 'cause with those little paper sheer walls, everybody next door would know our business. So while we fighting, it's real quiet except for some grunts and the bed squeaking."

Then, she laughed again. "I guess that's all you'd be hearing anyway."

Willie Bea tried to laugh in acknowledgment. Once Pat told her, "Shoot, girl, I've gotten to liking the scuffling we do in bed better than I ever liked the screwing."

That made Willie Bea feel cold all over.

"It's like it make it more important," Pat continued. "Something worth fighting for. Some nights when he just reach for me like that, it's like he calling me out my name. And I turn over ready to fight.

"I would get somebody else, but they all the same, you may as well pick one from the sack as another. But look at you, Bea. You just agreeing to be nice. You don't believe that, do you?"

"I didn't say nothing," Willie Bea would rush to say. "I believe what you say about you and Henry. I believe you."

"That ain't what I mean and you know it. I'm talking about mens period."

"I know what you saying about men."

"Yeah, but you don't think they all alike, do you?" Pat asked.

Willie Bea would start dipping her head from side to side and grinning her sheepish closed-mouth grin.

"Go on an admit it, girl," Pat would prod.

After a moment, Willie Bea would admit it. "I don't know why he love me so good."

Then Pat would sigh and urge her friend to tell her how sweet Jay was to her . . . in bed, at the table, after work. Especially in bed.

Willie Bea balked at first, each time the subject came up. But she always gave in, too. She was just dying to talk about Jaybird.

Most women she knew held the same beliefs that Pat did about men. They sure as hell didn't want to hear about her and the bliss her man brought her. She had found they may want to hear about you "can't do with him and can't do without him" or how bad he treat you and you still can't let him go. All of that. But don't be coming around them with those thick window-pane eyes of hers all bright and enlarged with stories of happiness and fulfillment. Those stories cut her other girlfriends and their lives to the quick.

But her friend Pat, big-butt Pat, urged Bea to share her stories with her. Sometimes these reminiscences made Pat smile and glow as if she were there in Willie Bea's place. But sometimes they left her morose.

Willie Bea, noticing this, at first began leaving out details that she thought made Pat's love pale in comparison. But Pat, alert to nuances in the tales, caught on and insisted Willie Bea never leave stuff out again if she was going to tell it.

And Willie Bea, eager to tell it all, felt as if she were pleasing her friend as much as herself. So she continued telling stories of love and dipping her ear down toward her shoulder in a gay little shy gesture.

"When Jaybird and me be doing it, he has this little gruff-like voice he uses when he talks to me."

"Talk to you? What y'all be doing, screwing or talking?" Pat would interrupt, but not seriously.

"He say things like, 'Is that all? That ain't all. I want it all. Uh-huh.'"

At first, Willie Bea was embarrassed disclosing these secrets of her and Jaybird's passionate and tender lovemaking. But Pat seemed so enthralled by her stories that Willie Bea finally stopped fighting it and gave herself over to the joy of recounting how Jaybird loved her.

Pat never told Willie Bea that many of the women at The Place talked under their breaths when Jaybird and Willie Bea came in together.

"He may sleep in the same bed with her, but I heard he put an ironing board between 'em first," some said.

"He can't really want that little old black gal. He just like her worshipping the ground he walk on," another would add.

Pat knew Willie Bea would have tried to kill whoever said such things. But even Pat found it hard to believe sometimes that her little friend had attracted Jaybird.

Mornings, Pat watched Willie Bea step off the city bus they both took to their jobs, her too pale dime store stockings shining in the early light, her narrow shoulders rotating like bicycle pedals in the direction opposite the one she sent her snake hips inside her straight skirt and thought how changed her friend was by the love of Jaybird. Now, that walk is something new, Pat thought as the bus pulled away from the curb.

Willie Bea, who lived two blocks above Pat, got on the bus first, then alit first when she got near the white woman's house she cleaned five days a week. Pat stayed on until the bus reached downtown near the box factory where she worked. They rode to and from work together nearly every day.

So the one evening when Pat wasn't on the bus when she got on returning home, Willie Bea began to worry about her. All that one of Pat's co-workers on the bus said when Willie Bea asked was, "She left work early."

I wonder if she's sick, Willie Bea thought.

She was still thinking about her friend when the bus began making its climb up Pleasant Hill. I better stop and see 'bout her, Willie Bea thought.

She was still standing with her hand near the signal wire when the bus slowed to a stop in front of the cinder block duplex where Pat lived and Willie Bea saw the gold of a Schlitz beer uniform slip back inside the dusty screen door of her friend's house.

The bus driver paused a good while with the bus door open waiting for Willie Bea to leave. Then he finally hollered toward the back of the bus, "You getting off or not?"

Willie Bea turned around to the driver's back and tried to smile as she took her regular seat again. When she reached her boarding house, she was anxious to see Jaybird and ask him who the new man was working on the beer truck. But he wasn't home.

She sat up alone on the bed in the boarding house room long after it grew dark.

Willie Bea didn't know how long she had been asleep when she heard the rusty door knob turn and felt a sliver of light from the hall fall across her face. Jaybird almost never stayed out late without her or telling her beforehand.

"You okay, Jay?" she asked sleepily.

He only grunted and rubbed her back softly. "Go back to sleep, Bea," he said. "I'm coming to bed now."

Willie Bea lay waiting for Jaybird to say something more, to say where he had been, to say he saw her friend Pat that day. But he said nothing.

Willie Bea tried her best to keep the image of her Jay in her mind without the glint of his gold uniform shining in her eyes, but she couldn't keep it out. And when he did finally slip into bed, it felt as if an ironing board was between them.

LIFE REGARDED AS A JIGSAW PUZZLE OF HIGHLY LUSTROUS CATS

Michael Bishop

Your father-in-law, who insists that you call him Howie, even though you prefer Mr. Bragg, likes jigsaw puzzles. If they prove harder than he has the skill or the patience for, he knows a sneaky way around the problem.

During the third Christmas season after your marriage to Marti, you find Howie at a card table wearing a parka, a blue watch cap with a crown of burgundy leather, and fur-lined shoes. (December through February, it is freezing in the Braggs' Tudor-style house outside Spartanburg.) He is assembling a huge jigsaw puzzle. The Braggs give him one every Christmas. His challenge is to piece it together, unaided by drop-in company or anyone else, before the Sugar Bowl kick-off on New Year's Day.

This year, the puzzle is of cats.

The ESB procedure being administered to you by the Zoo Cop and his associates is keyed to cats. When they zap your implanted electrodes, cat-related memories parachute into your mind's eye, opening out like fireworks.

The lid from the puzzle's box is Mr. Bragg's—Howie's—blueprint, and it depicts a population explosion of stylized cats. They are both mysterious beasts and whimsical cartoons. The puzzle lacks any background, it's so full of cats. They run, stalk, lap milk, tussle, tongue-file their fur, snooze, and so on. There are no puzzle areas where a single color dominates, a serious obstacle to quick assembly.

Howie has a solution. When only a handful of pieces remain in the box, he uses a razor blade to shave any piece that refuses to fit where he wants it to. This is cheating, as even Howie readily acknowledges, but on New Year's Eve, with Dick Clark standing in Times Square and the Sugar Bowl game only hours away, a man can't afford to screw around.

"Looking good," you say as the crowd on TV starts its rowdy countdown to midnight. "You're almost there."

Howie confesses—complains?—that this puzzle has been a "real mindbender." He appreciates the challenge of a thousand-plus pieces and a crazy-making dearth of internal clues, but why this particular puzzle? He usually receives a photographic landscape or a Western painting by Remington.

"I'm not a cat fancier," he tells you. "Most of 'em're sneaky little bastards, don't you think?"

Marti likes cats, but when you get canned at Piedmont Freight in Atlanta, she moves back to Spartanburg with your son, Jacob, who may be allergic to cats. Marti leaves in your keeping two calico mongrels that duck out of sight whenever you try to feed or catch them. You catch them eventually, of course, and drive them to the pound in a plastic animal carrier that Marti bought from Delta, or Eastern, or some other airline out at Hartsfield.

Penfield, a.k.a. the Zoo Cop, wants to know how you lost your job. He gives you a multiple-choice quiz:

    A.   Companywide lay-off
    B.   Neglect of duty and/or unacceptable job performance
    C.   Personality conflict with a supervisor
    D.   Suspicion of disloyalty
    E.   All, or none, of the above

You tell him that there was an incident of (alleged) sexual harassment involving a female secretary whose name, even under the impetus of electrical stimulation of the brain (ESB), you cannot now recall. All you can recall is every cat, real or imaginary, ever to etch its image into your consciousness.

After your firing, you take the cats, Springer and Ossie (short for Ocelot), to the pound. When you look back from the shelter's doorway, a teenage attendant is giving you, no doubt about it, the evil eye. Springer and Ossie are doomed. No one in the big, busy city wants a mixed-breed female. The fate awaiting nine-year-old Jacob's cats—never mind their complicity in his frightening asthma—is the gas chamber; today, though, you are as indifferent to the cats' fate as a latter-day Eichmann. You are numb from the molecular level upward.

"We did have them spayed," you defend yourself. "Couldn't you use that to pitch them to some nice family?"

You begin to laugh.

Is this another instance of Inappropriate Affect? Except for the laughing gas given you to sink the electrodes, you've now been off all medication for . . . you don't know how long.

On the street only three years after your dismissal, you wept at hoboes' bawdy jokes, got up and danced if the obituaries you'd been sleeping under reported an old friend's death.

Once, you giggled when a black girl bummed a cigarette in the parking lot of Trinity United Methodist: "I got AIDS, man. Hain't no smoke gonna kill me. Hain't time enough for the ol' lung cee to kick in, too."

Now that Penfield's taken you off antipsychotics, is Ye Old Inappropriate Affect kicking in again? Or is this fallout from the ESB? After all, one gets entirely different responses (rage and affection; fear and bravado) from zapping hypothalamic points less than 0.02 inch from each other.

Spill it, Adolf, Penfield says. What's so funny?

Cat juggling, you tell him. (Your name has never been Adolf.)

What?

Steve Martin in *The Jerk*. An illegal Mexican sport. A joke, you know. Cat juggling.

You surrender to jerky laughter. It hurts, but your glee isn't inappropriate. The movie was a comedy. People were *supposed* to laugh. Forget that when you close your eyes, you see yourself as the outlaw juggler. Forget that the cats in their caterwauling orbits include Springer, Ossie, Thai Thai, Romeo, and an anonymous albino kitten from your dead grandparents' grain crib on their farm outside Montgomery. . . .

As a boy in Hapeville, the cat you like best is Thai Thai, a male Siamese that your mama and you inherit from the family moving out. His name isn't Thai Thai before your mama starts calling him that, though. It's something fake Chinese, like Lung Cee or Mouser Tung. The folks moving out don't want to take him with them, their daddy's got a job with Otero Steel in Pueblo, Colorado. Besides, Mouser Tung's not likely to dig the ice and snow out there. He's a Deep South cat, Dixie-born and -bred.

"You are who you are," Mama tells the Siamese while he rubs her laddered nylons, "but from here on out your *name* is Thai Thai."

"Why're you calling him that?" you ask her.

"Because it *fits* a cracker Siamese," she says.

It's several years later before you realize that Thailand is Siam's current name and that there's a gnat-plagued town southeast of Albany called, yeah, Ty Ty.

Your mama's a smart gal, with an agile mind and a quirky sense of humor. How Daddy ever got it into his head that she wasn't good enough for him is a mystery.

It's her agile mind and her quirky sense of humor that did her in, the Zoo Cop says, pinching back your eyelid.

Anyway, Daddy ran off to a Florida dog-track town with a chunky bottle-blonde ex-hair dresser who dropped a few pounds and started a mail-order weight-loss-tonic business. He's been gone nine weeks and four days.

Thai Thai, when you notice him, is pretty decent company. He sheathes his claws when he's in your lap. He purrs at a bearable register. He eats leftover vegetables—peas, lima beans, spinach—as readily as he does bacon rinds or chicken scraps. A doll, Mama calls him. A gentleman.

This ESB business distorts stuff. It flips events, attitudes, preferences upside-down. The last shall be first, the first shall be last. This focus on cats, for example, is a *major* distortion, a misleading reenvisioning of the life that you lived before getting trapped by Rockdale Biological Supply Company.

Can't Penfield see this? Uh-uh, no way. He's too hot to screw Rockdale Biological's bigwigs. The guy may have right on his side, but to him—for the moment, anyway—you're just another human oven-cake. If you crumble when the heat's turned up, great, zip-a-dee-zoo-cop, pop me a cold one, justice is served.

Thing is, you prefer dogs. Even as a kid, you like them more. You bring home flea-bitten strays and beg to keep them. When you live in Alabama, you covet the liony chow, Simba, that waits every afternoon in the Notasulga schoolyard for Wesley Duplantier. Dogs, not cats. Until Mouser Tung—Thai Thai—all the cats you know prowl on the edges of your attention. Even Thai Thai comes to you and Mama, over here in Georgia, as a kind of offhand house-warming gift. Dogs, Mister Zoo Cop, not cats.

Actually, Penfield says, I'm getting the idea that what was in the *forefront* of your attention, Adolf, was women. . . .

After puberty, your attention never *has* a forefront. You are dive-bombed by stimuli. Girl's faces are billboards. Their bodies are bigger billboards. Jigsawed ad signs. A piece here. A piece there. It isn't just girls. It's everything. Cars, buildings, TV talking heads, mosquito swarms, jet contrails, interchangeable male callers at suppertime, battle scenes on the six o'clock news, rock idols infinitely glitterized, the whole schmear fragmenting as it feeds into you, Mr. Teenage Black Hole of the Spirit. Except when romancing a sweet young gal, your head's a magnet for all the flak generated by your media-crazed century.

"You're tomcatting, aren't you?" Mama says. "You're tomcatting just like Webb did. God."

It's a way to stay focused. With their faces and bodies under you, they cease to be billboards. You're a human being again, not a radio receiver or a gravity funnel. The act imposes a fleeting order on the ricocheting chaos working every instant to turn you, the mind cementing it all together, into a flimsy cardboard box of mismatched pieces.

Is that tomcatting? Resisting, by a tender union of bodies, the consequences of dumping a jigsaw puzzle of cats into a box of pieces that, assembled, would depict, say, a unit of embattled flak gunners on Corregidor?

Christ, the Zoo Cop says, a more highfalutin excuse for chasing tail I've never heard.

Your high school is crawling with cats. Cool cats, punk cats, stray cats, dead cats. Some are human, some aren't.

You dissect a cat in biology lab. On a plaster-of-Paris base, guyed upright by wires, stands the bleached skeleton of a quadruped that Mr. Osteen—he's also the track and girl's softball coach—swears was a member of *Felis catus*, the common house cat.

With its underlying gauntness exposed and its skull gleaming brittle and grotesque, this skeleton resembles that of something prehistoric. Pamela van Rhyn and two or three other girls want to know where the cats in the lab came from.

"A scientific supply house," Coach Osteen says. "Same place we get our bullfrogs, our microscope slides, the insects in that there display case." He nods at it.

"Where does the supply house get them?" Pamela says.

"I don't know, Pammie. Maybe they raise 'em. Maybe they round up strays. You missing a kitty?"

In fact, rumor holds that Mr. Osteen found the living source of his skeleton behind the track field's south bleachers, chloroformed it, carried it home, and boiled the fur off it in a pot on an old stove in his basement. Because of the smell, his wife spent a week in Augusta with her mother. Rumor holds that cat lovers hereabouts would be wise to keep their pets indoors.

Slicing into the chest cavity of the specimen provided by the supply house, you find yourself losing it. You are the only boy in Coach Osteen's lab to contract nausea and an overwhelming uprush of self-disgust; the only boy, clammy-palmed and light-headed, to have to leave the room. The ostensible shame of your departure is lost on Pamela, who agrees, in Nurse Mayhew's office, to rendezvous with you later that afternoon at the Huddle House.

"This is the heart," you can still hear Osteen saying. "Looks like a wet rubber strawberry, don't it?"

As a seven-year-old, you wander into the grain crib of the barn on the Powell farm. A one-eyed mongrel queen named Sky has dropped a litter on the deer hides, today stiff and rat-eaten, that Gramby Powell stowed there twenty or more years ago. Sky one-eyes you with real suspicion, all set to bolt or hiss, as you lean over a rail to study the blind quintet of her kittening.

They're not much, mere lumps. "Turds with fur," Gramby called them last night, to Meemaw Anita's scandalized dismay and the keen amusement of your daddy. They hardly move.

One kitten gleams white on the stiff hide, in a nervous curl of Sky's furry belly. You spit at Sky, as another cat would spit, but louder—*sssphh! sssphh!*—so that eventually, intimidated, she gets up, kittens falling from her like bombs from the open bay of a B-52, and slinks to the far wall of the crib.

You climb over the rail and pick up the white kitten, the Maybe Albino as Meemaw Anita dubbed it. "Won't know for sure," she said, "till its eyes're open."

You turn the kitten in your hands. Which end is which? It's sort of hard to say. Okay, here's the starchy white potato print of its smashed-in pug of a face: eyes shut, ears a pair of napkin folds, mouth a miniature crimson gap.

You rub the helpless critter on your cheek. Cat smells. Hay smells. Hide smells. It's hard not to sneeze.

It occurs to you that you could throw this Maybe Albino like a baseball. You could wind up like Denny McClain and fling it at the far wall of the grain crib. If you aim just right, you may be able to hit the wall so that the kitten rebounds and lands on Sky. You could sing a funny song, "Sky's being fallen on, / Oh, Sky's being fallen on, / Whatcha think 'bout that?" And nobody'll ever know if poor little Maybe Albino has pink eyes or not. . . .

This sudden impulse horrifies you, even as a kid, *especially* as a kid. You can see the white kitten dead. Trembling, you set the kitten back down on the cardboardy deer hide, climb back over the crib rail, and stand away from the naked litter while Sky tries to decide what to do next.

Unmanfully, you start to cry. "S-s-orry, k-kitty. S-s-sorry, Sk-sky. I'm r-r-really s-sorry." You almost want Gramby or Meemaw Anita to stumble in on you, in the churchly gloom and itch of their grain crib, to see you doing this heartfelt penance for a foul deed imagined but never carried out. It's okay to cry a bit in front of your mama's folks.

I'm touched, Penfield says. But speak up. Stop mumbling.

For several months after your senior year, you reside in the Adolescent Wing of the Quiet Harbor Psychiatric Center in a suburb of Atlanta. You're there to neutralize the disorienting stimuli—flak, you call it— burning out your emotional wiring, flying at you from everywhere. You're there to relearn how to live with no despairing recourse to disguises, sex, drugs.

Bad drugs, the doctors mean.

At QHPC, they give you good drugs. This is actually the case, not sarcastic bullshit. Kim Yaughan, one of the psychotherapists in the so-called Wild Child Wing, assures you that this is so; that antipsychotics aren't addictive. You get twenty milligrams a day of haloperidol. You take it in liquid form in paper cups shaped like doll-house-sized coffee filters.

"You're not an addict," Kim says. (Everyone at QHPC calls her Kim.) "Think of yourself as a diabetic, of Haldol as insulin. You don't hold a diabetic off insulin, that'd be criminal."

Not only do you get Haldol, you get talk therapy, recreational therapy, family therapy, crafts therapy. Some of the residents of the Wild Child Wing are druggies and sexual-abuse victims as young as twelve. They get these same therapies, along with pet therapy. The pets brought in on Wednesdays often include cats.

At last, Penfield tells an associate. That last jolt wasn't a mishit, after all.

The idea is that hostile, fearful, or withdrawn kids who don't interact well with other people will do better with animals. Usually, they do. Kittens under a year, tumbling with one another, batting at yarn balls, exploring the pet room with their tails up like the radio antennas on cars, seem to be effective four-legged therapists.

One teenage girl, a manic-depressive who calls herself Eagle Rose, goes ga-ga over them. "Oh," she says, holding up a squirmy smoke-colored male and nodding at two kittens wrestling in an empty carton of Extra Large Tide, "they're so soft, so neat, so . . . so *highly lustrous.*"

Despite Kim Yaughan's many attempts to involve you, you stand aloof from everyone. It's Eagle Rose who focuses your attention, not the kittens, and E.R.'s an untouchable. Every patient here is an untouchable, that way. It would be a terrible betrayal to think anything else. So, mostly, you don't.

The year before you marry, Marti is renting a house on North Highland Avenue. A whole house. It's not a big house, but she has plenty of room. She uses one bedroom as a studio. In this room, on the floor, lies a large canvas on which she has been painting, exclusively in shades of blue, the magnified heart of a magnolia. She calls the painting—too explicitly, you think—*Magnolia Heart in Blue.* She's worked on it all quarter, often appraising it from a stepladder to determine how best to continue.

Every weekend, you sleep with Marti in the bedroom next to the studio. Her mattress rests on the floor, without box springs or bedstead. You sometimes feel that you're lying in the middle of a painting in progress, a strange but gratifying sensation that you may or may not carry into your next week of classes at GSU.

One balmy Sunday, you awake to find Marti's body stenciled with primitive blue flowers, a blossom on her neck, more on her breasts, an indigo bouquet on the milky plane of her abdomen. You gaze at her in groggy wonderment. The woman you plan to marry has become, overnight, an arabesque of disturbing floral bruises.

Then you see the cat, Romeo, a neighbor's gray Persian, propped in the corner, belly exposed, so much like a hairy little man in a recliner that you laugh. Marti stirs. Romeo preens. Clearly, he entered through a studio window, walked all over *Magnolia Heart in Blue*, then came in here and violated Marti.

My wife-to-be as a strip of *fin de siècle* wallpaper, you muse, kissing her chastely on one of the paw-print flowers.

You sleep on the streets. You wear the same stinking clothes for days on end. You haven't been on haloperidol for months. The city could be Lima, or Istanbul, or Bombay, as easily as Atlanta. Hell, it could be a boulder-littered crater on the moon. You drag from one place to another like a zombie, and the people you hit up for hamburgers, change, MARTA tokens, old newspapers, have no more substance to you than you do to them, they could all be holograms or ghosts. They could be androids programmed to keep you dirty and hungry by dictating your behavior with remote-control devices that look like wrist watches and key rings.

Cats mean more to you than people do. (The people may not *be* people.) Cats are fellow survivors, able to sniff out nitrogenous substances from blocks away. Food.

You follow a trio of scrawny felines down Ponce de Leon to the rear door of a catfish restaurant where the Dumpster overflows with greasy paper and other high refuse. The cats strut around on the mounded topography of this debris while you balance on an upturned trash barrel, mindlessly picking and choosing.

Seven rooms away from Coach Osteen's lab, Mr. Petty is teaching advanced junior English. Poetry. He stalks around the room like an actor doing Hamlet, even when the poem's something dumb by Ogden Nash, or something beat and surface-sacrilegious by Ferlinghetti, or something short and puzzling by Carlos Williams.

The Williams piece is about a cat that climbs over a cabinet—a "jamcloset"—and steps into a flowerpot. Actually, Mr. Petty says, it's about the *image* created by Williams's purposely simple diction. Everyone argues that it isn't a poem at all. It's even less a poem, lacking metaphors, than that Carl Sandburg thing about the fog coming on little, for Christ's sake, cat's feet.

You like it, though. You can see the cat stepping cautiously into the flowerpot. The next time you're in Coach Osteen's class, trying to redeem yourself at the dissection table, you recite the poem for Pamela van Rhyn, Jessie Faye Culver, Kathy Margenau, and Cynthia Spivy.

Coach Osteen, shaking his head, makes you repeat the lines so that he can say them, too. Amazing.

"Cats are digitigrade critters," he tells the lab. "That means they walk on their toes. Digitigrade."

Cynthia Spivy catches your eye. *Well, I'll be a pussywillow*, she silently mouths. *Who'd've thunk it?*

"Unlike the dog or the horse," Coach Osteen goes on, "the cat walks by moving the front and back legs on one side of its body and then the front and back legs on the other. The only other animals to move that way are the camel and the giraffe."

And naked crazy folks rutting on all fours, you think, studying Cynthia's lips and wondering if there was ever a feral child raised by snow leopards or jaguars. . . .

Thai Thai develops a urinary tract infection. Whenever he has to pee, he looks for Mama pulling weeds or hanging out clothes in the backyard and squats to show her that he's not getting the job done. It takes Mama two or three days to realize what's going on. Then you and she carry Thai to the vet.

Mama waits tables at a Denny's near the expressway. She hasn't really got the money for the operation that Thai needs to clear up the blockage, a common problem in male Siamese. She tells you that you can either forfeit movie money for the next few months or help her pay to make Thai well. You hug Mama, wordlessly agreeing that the only thing to do is to help your cat. The operation goes okay, but the vet telephones a day later to report that Thai took a bad turn overnight and died near morning.

Thai's chocolate-and-silver body has a bandage cinched around his middle, like a wraparound saddle.

You're the one who buries Thai because Mama can't bring herself to. You put him in a Siamese-sized cardboard box, dig a hole under the holly in the backyard, and lay him to rest with a spank of the shovel blade and a prayer consisting of grief-stricken repetitions of the word please.

Two or three months later, you come home from school to find a pack of dogs in the backyard. They've dug Thai Thai up. You chase the dogs away, screeching from an irate crouch. Thai's corpse is nothing but matted fur and protruding bones. Its most conspicuous feature is the bandage holding the maggoty skeleton together at its cinched-in waist.

This isn't Thai, you tell yourself. I buried Thai a long, long time ago, and this isn't him.

You carry the remains, jacketed in the editorial section of the *Atlanta Constitution*, to a trash can and dump them with an abrupt, indifferent thunk. Pick-up is tomorrow.

One Sunday afternoon in March, you're standing with two hundred other homeless people at the entrance to Trinity United Methodist's soup kitchen, near the state Capitol. It's drizzling. A thin but gritty-looking young woman in jeans and sweatshirt, her hair lying in dark strands against her forehead, is passing out hand-numbered tickets to every person who wants to get into the basement. At the head of the outside basement steps is a man in pleated slacks and a plaid shirt. He won't let anyone down the steps until they have a number in the group of ten currently being admitted. He has to get an okay from the soup-kitchen staff downstairs before he'll allow a new group of ten to pass.

Your number, on a green slip of paper already drizzle-dampened, is 126. The last group down held numbers 96 to 105. You think. Hard to tell with all the shoving, cursing, and bantering on the line. One angry black man up front doesn't belong there. He waves his ticket every time a new group of ten is called, hoping, even though his number is 182, to squeeze past the man set there to keep order.

"How many carahs yo ring?" he asks. "I sick. Lemme eah fo I faw ouw. Damn disere rain."

When the dude holding number 109 doesn't show, the stair guard lets number 182 pass, a good-riddance sort of charity.

You shuffle up with the next two groups. How many of these people are robots, human machines drawn to the soup kitchen as you may have been, on invisible tractor beams? The stair guard isn't wearing a watch or shaking a key ring. It's probably his wedding band that's the remote-control device. . . .

"My God," he cries when he sees you. "Is that really you? It is, isn't it?"

The stair guy's name is Dirk Healy. He says he went to school with you in Hapeville. Remember Pamela van Rhyn? Remember Cynthia What's-her-name? When you go down into the basement and get your two white-bread sandwiches and a Styrofoam cup of vegetable soup, Dirk convinces another volunteer to take over his job and sits down next to you at one of the rickety folding tables where your fellow street folk are single-mindedly eating. Dirk, who, as far as you're concerned, could be the Man in the Moon, doesn't ask how you got in this fix, doesn't accuse, doesn't exhort.

"You're off your medication, aren't you?" Your hackles lift. "Hey," he soothes, "I visited you at Quiet Harbor. The thing to do is to get you back on it."

You eat, taking violent snatches of the sandwiches, quick sips of the soup. You one-eye Dirk over the steam the way that, years ago, Sky one-eyed you from her grain-crib nest.

"I may have a job for you," Dirk says confidentially. "Ever hear of Rockdale Biological?"

One summer, for reasons you don't understand, Mama sends you to visit your father and his ex-hair dresser floozie—whose name is Carol Grace—in the Florida town where they live off the proceeds of her mail-order business and sometimes bet the dogs at the local greyhound track.

Carol Grace may bet the greyhounds at the track, but at home she's a cat person. She owns seven: a marmalade-colored tom, a piebald tom, three tricolor females, an orange Angora of ambiguous gender, and a Manx mix with a tail four or five inches long, as if someone shortened it with a cleaver.

"If Stub was pure Manx," Carol Grace says, "he wouldn't have no tail. Musta been an alley tom in his mama's kitty litter."

Stroking Stub, she chortles happily. She and your mother look a little alike. They have a similar feistiness, too, although it seems coarser in Carol Grace, whom your balding father—she calls him Webby, for Pete's sake—unabashedly dotes on.

A few days into your visit, Carol Grace and you find one of her females, Hedy Lamarr, lying crumpled under a pecan tree shading the two-story house's south side. The cat is dead. You kneel to touch her. Carol Grace kneels beside you.

"Musta fell," she says. "Lotsa people think cats are too jack-be-nimble to fall, but they can slip up too. Guess my Hedy didn't remember that, pretty thing. Now look."

You are grateful that, today, Carol Grace does the burying and the prayer-saying. Her prayer includes the melancholy observation that anyone can fall. Anyone.

Enough of this crap, Penfield says. Tell me what you did, and for whom, and why, at Rockdale Biological.

Givin whah I can, you mumble, working to turn your head into the uncompromising rigidity of the clamps.

Adolf, Penfield says, what you're giving me is a cat juggling.

Alone in the crafts room with Kim Yaughan while the other kids in Blue Group (QHPC's Wild Child Wing has two sections, Blue and Gold) go on a field trip, you daub acrylics at a crude portrayal of a cat walking upside down on a ceiling. Under the cat, a woman and a teenage boy point and make hateful faces.

"Are they angry at the cat or at each other?" Kim asks.

You give her a look: What a stupid question.

Kim comes over, stands at your shoulder. If she were honest, she'd tell you that you're no artist at all. The painting may be psychologically revealing, but it refutes the notion that you have any talent as a draftsman or a colorist.

"Ever hear of British artist Louis Wain?" Kim says. "He lived with three unmarried sisters and a pack of cats. His schizophrenia didn't show up until he was almost sixty. That's late."

"Lucky," you say. "He didn't have so long to be crazy."

"Listen, now. Wain painted only cats. He must've really liked them. At first, he did smarmy, realistic kitties for calendars and postcards. Popular crap. Later, thinking jealous competitors were zapping him with X-rays or something, the cats in his paintings got weird, really hostile and menacing."

"Weirder than mine?" You jab your brush at it.

"Ah, that's a mere puddy-tat." Then: "In the fifteen years he was institutionalized, Wain painted scads of big-eyed, spiky-haired cats. He put bright neon auras and electrical fields around them. His backgrounds got geometrically rad. Today, you might think they were computer-generated. Anyhow, Wain's crazy stuff was better—fiercer, stronger—than the crap he'd done sane."

"Meaning I'm a total loss unless I get crazier?" you say.

"No. What I'm trying to tell you is that the triangles, stars, rainbows, and repeating arabesques that Wain put into his paintings grew from a desperate effort to . . . well, to impose order on the chaos *inside* him. It's touching, really touching. Wain was trying to confront and reverse, the only way he could, the disintegration of his adult personality. See?"

But you don't. Not exactly.

Kim taps your acrylic cat with a burgundy fingernail. "You're not going to be the new Picasso, but you aren't doomed to suffer as terrifying a schizophrenia as Wain suffered either. The bizarre thing in your painting is the cat on the ceiling. The colors, and the composition itself, are reassuringly conventional. A good sign for your mental health. Another thing is, Wain's doctors couldn't give him antipsychotic drugs. You, though, have access."

"Cheers." You pantomime knocking back a little cup of Haldol.

Kim smiles. "So why'd you paint the cat upside-down?"

"Because *I'm* upside-down," you say.

Kim gives you a peck on the cheek. "You're not responsible for a gone-awry brain chemistry or an unbalanced metabolism, hon. Go easy on yourself, okay?" Dropping your brush, you pull Kim to you and try to nuzzle her under the jaw. Effortlessly, she bends back your hand and pushes you away. "But that," she says, "you're going to have to control. Friends, not lovers. Sorry if I gave you the wrong idea. Really. Really."

"If the pieces toward the end don't fit," Howie tells you, "you can always use a razor blade." He holds one up.

You try to take it. Double-edged, it slices your thumb. Some of your blood spatters on the cat puzzle.

———————

A guy in a truck drives up to the specimen-prep platform and loading dock behind Rockdale Biological Medical Supply. It's an unmarked panel truck with no windows behind the cab. The guys who drive the truck change, it seems, almost every week, but you're a two-month fixture on the concrete platform with the slide cages and the euthanasia cabinet. Back here, you're Dirk Healy's main man, especially now that he's off on a business trip somewhere.

Your job is both mindless and strength-sapping. The brick wall around the rear of the RBMS complex, and the maple trees shielding the loading dock, help you keep your head together. Healy has you on a lower dosage of haloperidol than you took while you and Marti were still married. Says you were overmedicated before. Says you were, ha ha, "an apathetic drug slave." He should know. He's been a hotshot in national medical supply for years.

"We'll have you up in the front office in no time," he assured you a couple weeks ago. "The platform job's a kind of trial."

The guy in the truck backs up and starts unloading. Dozens of cats in slide cages. You wear elbow-length leather gloves, and a heavy apron, and feel a bit like an old-timey Western blacksmith. The cats are pieces of scrap iron to be worked in the forge. You slide the door end of each cage into the connector between the open platform and the euthanasia cabinet, then poke the cats in the butt or the flank with a long metal rod until they duck into the cabinet to escape your prodding. When the cabinet's full, you drop the safety door, check the gauges, turn on the gas. It hisses louder than the cats climbing over one another, louder than their yowling and tumbling, which noises gradually subside and finally stop.

By hand, you unload the dead cats from the chamber, slinging them out by their tails or their legs. You cease feeling like a blacksmith. You imagine yourself as a nineteenth-century trapper, stacking fox, beaver, rabbit, wolf, and muskrat pelts on a travois for a trip to the trading post. The pelts are pretty, though many are blemished by vivid skin diseases and a thick black dandruff of gassed fleas. How much could they be worth?

"Nine fifty a cat," Dirk Healy has said. That seems unlikely. They're no longer moving. They're no longer—if they ever were—highly lustrous. They're floppy, anonymous, and dead, their fur contaminated by lethal gas.

A heavy-duty wheelbarrow rests beside the pile of cats on the platform. You unwind a hose and fill the barrow with water. Dirk has ordered you to submerge the gassed cats to make certain they're dead. Smart. Some of the cats are plucky boogers. They'll mew at you or swim feebly in the cat pile even before you pick them up and sling them into the wheelbarrow. The water in the wheelbarrow ends it. Indisputably. It also washes away fleas and the worst aspects of feline scabies. You pull a folding chair over and sort through the cats for the ones with flea collars, ID collars, rabies tags. You take these things off. You do it with your gloves on, a sodden cat corpse hammocked in your apron. It's not easy, given your wet glove fingers.

If it's sunny, you take the dead cats to the bright part of the platform and lay them out in neat rows to dry.

Can't you get him to stop mumbling? Penfield asks someone in the room. His testimony's almost unintelligible.

He's replaying the experience inwardly, an indistinct figure says. But he's starting to go autistic on us.

Look, Penfield says. We've got to get him to verbalize clearly—or we've wasted our time.

Two months after the divorce, you drive to Spartanburg, to the Braggs' house, to see Jacob. Mr. Bragg—Howie—intercepts you at the front gate, as if apprised of your arrival by surveillance equipment.

"I'm sorry," he says, "but Marti doesn't want to see you, and she doesn't want *you* to see Jake. If you don't leave, I'll have to call the police to, ah, you know, remove you."

You don't contest this. You walk across the road to your car. From there, you can see that atop the brick post on either side of Mr. Bragg's ornate gate reposes a roaring granite lion. You can't remember seeing these lions before, but the crazed and reticulated state of the granite suggests they've been there a while. It's a puzzle. . . .

As you lay out the dead cats, you assign them names. The names you assign are always Mehitabel, Felix, Sylvester, Tom, Heathcliff, Garfield, and Bill. These seven names must serve for all the cats on the platform. Consequently, you add Roman numerals to the names when you run out of names before you do cats:

Mehitabel II, Felix II, Sylvester II, Tom II and so on. It's a neat, workable system. Once, you cycled all the way to Sylvester VII before running out of specimens.

As a fifth grader in Notasulga, you sit and watch a film about the American space program.

An old film clip shows a cat—really more a kitten than a cat—suspended to a low ceiling by its feet. It's a metal ceiling, and the scientist who devised the experiment (which has something to do with studying the kitten's reactions to upside-downness, then applying these findings to astronauts aboard a space station) has fastened magnets to the cat's feet so that they will adhere to the metal surface.

The scientist has also rigged up a pair of mice in the same odd way, to see if they will distract, entice, or frighten the hanging kitten. They don't. The kitten is terrified not of the mice (who seem to be torpid and unimaginative representatives of their kind), but of the alien condition in which it finds itself. Insofar as it is able, the kitten lurches against the magnets, its ears back, its mouth wide open in a silent cry. On the sound track, a male voice explains the import and usefulness of this experiment.

No one can hear him, though, because most of the other kids in Miss Beischer's class are laughing uproariously at the kitten. You look around in a kind of sick stupefaction.

Milly Heckler, Agnes Lee Terrance, and a few other girls appear to be as appalled as you, but the scene doesn't last long—it's probably shorter than your slow-motion memory of it—and it seems for a moment that you *are* that kitten, that everything in the world has been wrenchingly upended.

"I know it *seemed* to you that evil people were trying to invade and control your thoughts," Dr. Hall, the director of Quiet Harbor, tells you. He pets a neutered male just back from a visit to the Gerontological Wing. "But that was just a symptom of the scrambled condition of your brain chemistry. The truth is . . ."

Fatigued, you slouch out the rear gate of Rockdale Biological. Your apartment—the three-roomer that Healy provided—is only a short distance away. A late-model Lincoln town car pulls alongside you as you walk the weed-grown sidewalk. The tinted window on the front-seat passenger's side powers down, and you catch your first glimpse of the raw-complexioned man who introduces himself as David Penfield. An alias? Why do you think so?

"If you like," he says, "think of me as the Zoo Cop."

It's a permission you don't really want. Why would you choose to think of a well-dressed, ordinary-featured man with visible acne scarring as something as *déclassé* as, Jesus, the Zoo Cop. Is he a detective of some sort? What does he want?

The next thing you know you're in the car with Penfield and two other tight-lipped men.

The next thing you know you're on the expressway and one of the Zoo Cop's associates—goons?—has locked the suction-cup feet of one of those corny Garfield toys on his tinted window as a kind of—what?—mockery? rebuke? warning?

The next thing you know you're in a basement that clearly isn't the soup kitchen of Trinity United Methodist. The next thing you know you're flat on your back on a table. The next thing you know you don't know anything. . . .

. . . Marti's body is stenciled with primitive blue flowers, a blossom on her neck, more on her breasts, an indigo bouquet on the milky plane of her abdomen. You gaze at her in groggy wonderment. The woman you one day marry has become, overnight, an arabesque of disturbing floral bruises.

"Marti," you whisper. "Marti, don't leave me. Marti, don't take my son away."

Penfield, a.k.a. the Zoo Cop (you realize during your descent into the puzzle box), isn't a real cop. He hates you because what you've been doing for Healy is vile, contemptible, *evil*. So it is, so it is. He wants to get Healy, who hasn't been around this last week at all, who's maybe skipped off to Barbados or the Yucatan or Saint-Tropez.

Penfield is an animal-rights eco-terrorist, well-financed and determined, and the ESB zappings to which he and his associates are subjecting you are designed to incriminate, pinpoint, and doom old Dirk and *his* associates, who obviously deserve it. You too. You deserve it too. No argument there. None.

Christ, Penfield says, unhook the son of a bitch and carry him upstairs. Dump him somewhere remote, somewhere rural.

You visit the pound for a replacement for Springer and Ossie, gassed three or four years ago. The attendant tells you there are plenty of potential adoptees at the shelter. You go down the rows of cages to select one. The kittens in the fouled sawdust tumble, paw, and miaow, putting on a dispirited show.

"This one," you finally say.

"Cute." The attendant approves. Well, they'd fire her if she didn't. The idea is to adopt these creatures out, not to let them lapse into expendability.

"It's for Jake, my son," you tell her.   "His asthma isn't that bad.   I think he may be growing out of it."

"Look at my puzzle," Howie says, yanking the razor blade away from you.   "You've bled all over it . . ."

from EASTER WEEKEND

David Bottoms

L ately the old man had begun to feel his age, first in the joints of his hands and feet, then in his knees and hips and elbows. Then out of these joints the pain backed up into his bones—a cold pain that spread slowly and wouldn't go away. It stiffened him in the morning and only faded when he lay out in the grass on the side of a hill or the slope of the riverbank and soaked in the afternoon sun. But today the pain seemed to have moved from his bones deep into his muscles, and though the afternoon was more than half over and the sun sizzled in the sky, he still felt the dull cold.

It was sleeping in the damp, he knew that. But he didn't know what to do about it. He wasn't going down to the camp. Not with Kenny gone. George was down there, sure, and you could trust George all right. But he was as black as an old tire, and when some of those others started drinking hard, they didn't like him for it. Also, you just couldn't tell how long he'd be around. Maybe you'd wake up in the middle of the night and he'd be gone, and there you were, alone with a pack of wild dogs.

He reached up to his neck and pulled the earphones back over his head. A crow came out of the pines and swooped low over the river. Or *was* it a crow? It was black, but it didn't fly like a crow. Sometimes he thought his eyes were going too. His ears were still good. He could hear in the quiet of the night the far-off hoot of an owl, bark of a dog, the smallest wind in the trees, the slightest creak in the rusty gate of a grave plot. But sometimes he thought his eyes were going because they wanted to blur the edges of things. But maybe they weren't. Maybe they were just tired and it really was a crow. Anyway, he liked to sit here on the riverbank and look down over the tracks at the muddy water easing off under the bridge. The trees across the river were full of birds, and some days you could see a few fishermen huddled up on the far bank under the trellis, sitting on folding chairs and plastic coolers, watching their floats bob on the water, patient as Job.

He punched the button on the Walkman and voices cut in halfway through a song. *Out of Egypt I have traveled through the darkness dreary, over hills and valleys and across the desert sand.* It was a good song, the piano not too bouncy, but he wished a woman were singing it. Next time he was down at that store, he'd try to find a tape with a woman, a soft voice to put the real spirit into it, a voice you could wrap up in like a quilt and close your eyes and see good pictures of what she was singing about. Somewhere in those walls of plastic boxes he knew there must be one, a voice like that, a woman's voice. But it wasn't like you could ask the lady at the counter. It wasn't like you could ask her to climb down off that stool, to walk around those big stacks of red and white Bibles and show you where it was.

The singing trailed off and the last note of the piano died. Static blared in his ears and he turned down the volume. An organ started up, slow and deep, then violins. He turned it back up. The sweet notes trembled and deepened. *There's a land beyond the river that they call the sweet forever and we only reach that shore by faith's decree.* The husky quartet voices singing smooth and rich. And he turned it up again, lay back on the grass of the bank. That song was one of his favorites, and he loved to close his eyes to it and watch the white doors of the chapel open up again, to walk down the concrete aisle between the rows of folding chairs, the clean-shaven men holding in their hands the red paper hymnals but not reading from them, only holding them open and singing by heart, following the wheeze of the tiny organ, the red-haired woman in front of the pulpit, following her voice, the voice that wrapped up all their voices in its softness and warmth.

Amazing the way music brought things back. Sometimes he could hardly remember his name, and now he was looking at her face as though he stood right in front of her, looking at those red curls on her forehead, dark curls the color of ripe apples, then the deep brown of her eyes, the thin wrinkles under those eyes, the tiny scratch of a scar at the corner of her mouth, watching her smile over the congregation as her right hand traced the rhythms of the song in the thick air of the chapel.

He liked watching her hand flutter like a white moth over the page of the hymnal, rising, zagging, falling. It was writing some kind of message on the air, words you could see being written but couldn't read. It spelled something invisible that touched the eyes of the congregation, lit up their faces, and came out of their mouths as song.

Lately this was the memory the gospel music brought him. Sometimes there were other pictures too—the building of roofs and the tacking down of shingles, the tractors plowing the fields, the shirtless convicts clearing the woods with axes. He remembered vividly the spark of the blade on the grindstone, the swing jarring back through the handle. These were all from the same time, he thought, because the same music brought them back. Of course, there were other memories he could still call up, but they were from other times and needed different kinds of music.

Something rattled in the grass beside him and he opened his eyes to the blue sky above the river. A shadow crawled over his face.

"Hey, Pop?" the man said.

It was all right. It was George, and you could trust George.

"Hey, Pop, where you been at?" He was a large black man in a dirty T-shirt and jeans. His face was wide, his eyes bright and full of life, his mouth upturned a little at the corners.

The old man switched off the tape player. "Different places, I guess. You seen Kenny?"

"No. Figured you run off after him."

The old man frowned. "He didn't run off nowhere, I guess."

"You don't know nothing about that. He run off, that's all. Hey, you got you some new music? You better quit stealing them tapes, they gonna put you in the jailhouse."

The old man gazed up at the black face.

"Come on," George said. "We gonna walk up to the Krystal."

"Go where?"

"Eat something. You eat yet?"

"No, I don't guess."

George kicked the feed sack lying on the ground beside him. "I got maybe two dollars already. We can walk on up here to the Krystal, maybe find some more on the way."

"Two dollars?"

"Right at it. I ain't counted 'em."

The old man sat up and took off the earphones. One thing about George, he was a hard worker. He didn't mind breaking a sweat, and there wasn't any meanness in him either. Only it wasn't like Kenny. Sometimes George talked a lot and couldn't tell what to say and what not to. He didn't mean any mischief in it, he just couldn't tell what not to say. Kenny could keep your secret though. You could tell Kenny anything at all, and it was just like telling it to a tree.

"Maybe you oughta put it down on the guitar?"

"I'd as soon eat."

"What is it today, Pepsi or Coke?"

"Pepsi, I reckon. Ain't been too many Coke."

The old man pushed to his feet and stood up slow. The pain in his back flared a little but eased when he straightened up. He rubbed his arms and the backs of his hands. Not too long ago, if you wanted to, you could make a decent meal pretty easy just by walking the side of the road. But it was all cans now. Nobody drank much out of bottles anymore. And you just had to get too many cans together. Nothing to be made of that. It was a whole lot easier now to walk downtown

at night and lift tapes out of parked cars. If they were in good shape,
you could take them down to the pawnshop on Broadway and Joel T.
would give you fifty cents apiece for them. Sure, that was a little harder
than it used to be too, so many people locking their cars now, but you
only had to find one unlocked and you could generally get four or five
dollars' worth. Only George wouldn't do that. It didn't matter that
it was easy and not too risky. Or that you weren't really hurting anybody.
No, that didn't matter to George. It was against the law, and he wouldn't
have any dealings with it. He'd rather stand on the street corner, singing
and playing for spare change. Maybe that was okay for George, but
everybody couldn't sing and play music.

"You oughta put it on the guitar," the old man said again.

"Not today. I can't eat no guitar, and I ain't eat much lately. How
'bout you?"

The old man's stomach growled. "Yesterday. I eat some soup, I
think, some crackers too. You been drinking?"

"Not much." George started up the long hill. "Come on. Let's eat
us some burgers."

A crow cawed out of the graveyard behind him and flew over the
river. The old man watched it disappear above the pines. That one
was a crow, all right. He turned and saw that George had already started
up the hill and into the gravestones, the bag thrown over his shoulder.
A pain rolled through his stomach. Eating wasn't a bad idea.

With the sun coming at it from the west, a sharp light flared off
the walls of the Krystal. The old man liked the way it lit the glass
front, turned the white tiles into ivory. It was like something from an
old story he couldn't quite recall, something you dream about but never
expect to see. And he liked the bright cars parked around it. They
were pretty, with the sun gleaming off their windshields and hoods,
but they also meant a crowd. And a crowd meant good food, and that
made him hungrier. He looked up the highway and down, waited on
the traffic, and followed George across. From the edge of the parking
lot, he could just catch the aroma of meat and onions steaming on the
grill.

Coffee and hamburgers were good, but he hoped they had enough
for French fries too. It was like George said, though. It depended on
what kind of mood Mr. Taylor was in. If he hadn't been at the bottle
and maybe had gone to church last week, he'd be feeling his charity.
He'd take what they had then and give them whatever they wanted.
There were still good people around, people who'd spare you something
when you needed it. The trick, though, was not to take advantage of
them. Too many folks just wanted to take advantage, get what they
could now and never think about anybody else, never think about future

time. It wasn't hard to blame a man for tightening up if he thought you were taking advantage of him.

As they crossed the parking lot, the heat from the asphalt baked up through his shoes. But he lived for the heat. It was the best thing about Macon—the vicious summer heat, the hammering sun most people found joyless on the cooler days, torture on the rest. To him it felt good, though, especially now in the parking lot, where the trapped warmth felt like liniment seeping into the soles of his feet. How could his joints ache in weather like this? He was old, that's all. He was old and beginning to feel it.

George was moving quickly toward the side of the building. The old man stepped up his pace and followed him around to the back.

"You let me talk to him," George said. He stepped up to a white door and knocked twice. Nothing, so he knocked again, louder.

The old man shifted his weight from leg to leg and thought about the hamburgers steaming on the grill, three or four rows of thin tasty patties steaming in onions, square buns lined up behind them. They made a good picture in his head, but he hoped there was enough in George's bag for French fries too.

The door swung half open and a tall kid in a white apron stared out at them. His face was long and homely, and he had a Band-Aid covering the bridge of his nose.

"Yes sir," George said. "We looking for Mr. Taylor."

"He ain't here today."

"Ain't here?"

"That's what I said, ain't it?" The boy scrutinized the old man, then George. "He didn't come in. He's sick."

"Well," George said. "He usually take these drink bottles here and give us something to eat. He take 'em down to the Kroger, I think, and—"

"I don't know nothing about no bottles."

"Well, listen here, you could put 'em—"

"Look, them bottles is between you and him. He ain't told me nothing about 'em."

"But listen here, you—"

"No, you listen. I ain't got time for this, and I don't want no sack fulla bottles."

George put his hand on the door and pulled it toward him. "How come you treat a man like that, huh?"

"Get your hand off that door," the boy said.

"We trying to tell you something, you don't even let us say it. Mr. Taylor, he take these bottles down—"

"Get your damn hand off the door or I'll call the cops."

George dropped the hand and backed up a step. "Hey, we just trying to tell you something here. We just —"

"Look, boy, listen good. I don't want no goddamn bottles. So get on outta here, you smell like shit." The door slammed.

George stared for a few seconds at the small red letters that spelled Employees Only. He knocked again.

The old man rubbed his knuckles. The heat felt good rising up through his shoes, but the sun wasn't helping his hands. "It's okay," he said. "He don't understand, that's all."

It was a shadow like the hunched back of a cat edging across the top of the dumpster, then, as Connie eased the Volkswagen down the alley, it turned into the head and shoulders of a man. Connie brightened his headlights, watched the guy squint in the glare and try to shade his eyes with his hands. The man reeled backward a little, then turned away from the light, but as Connie edged the car past him, he turned again and leaned back over the top of the dumpster.

The parking lot of the Waffle House opened at the end of the alley. Two cars and a truck were parked near the door and another car parked in the back of the lot under a streetlight. That one was Rita's, a yellow '71 Plymouth Duster she'd bought at a police auction. Actually, Connie had picked it out for her. The body needed some work and the seats needed recovering, but the engine and the transmission were solid.

Connie pulled in next to it and cut the lights and ignition. He eased the door open and glanced over his hood at the front fender of the Duster. It wasn't really so bad, but she ought to get it fixed before it rusted any more. He thought about garages for a second, then walked back toward the end of the alley. Something rattled out of the dark, then banged loud.

"Hey, you all right in there?" Connie stepped into the alley. It was a long tunnel with no light at the end. "You all right?"

"Lid fell. That's all." The voice seemed to float up out of the dark, low and hoarse.

"You all right?"

"I didn't hurt nothing."

Connie walked toward the voice until the faint outline of a head showed above the dumpster. "What the hell you doing back here?"

"I ain't hurting nothing. I look like I'm hurting something in here? I look like it?"

Connie looked hard into the darkness. "I didn't say you was, did I? I said what you doing back here?"

The man stared at him for a minute. He was a short man, and thin, but he had broad shoulders for his size, and he wasn't stooped over.

He looked old, but it was hard to tell just how old. He pulled some paper off a sandwich he was holding. "I ain't bothering you."

"I didn't say you was, buddy. I thought maybe you fell."

The old man brought the sandwich up to his face and smelled it, then he took a bite and chewed it slowly, staring out at nothing.

"Hey, you get that thing outta that goddamn dumpster? Hey, don't eat that shit."

The old man swallowed and held up the sandwich for Connie to see. "Ain't nothing outside a man that goes in him can defile him. What comes out is what defiles him."

Connie watched him take another bite of the sandwich. "Throw that shit away and let's go on in here and get something to eat."

The bum didn't say anything.

"Come on," Connie said. "Let's go."

"Ain't no money in this belt, mister. Not a dime. You think I got some money?"

"Did I ask you that? Throw that shit away and let's go on in here and get some food."

The old man sized Connie up, both hands holding his find. He stood that way for a few seconds in the dark of the alley, then dropped what was left of the sandwich and stepped away from the dumpster. "Well, okay. You want me to, I won't say no."

Connie had thought the odor belonged to the garbage, but halfway down the alley he knew it belonged to the bum too. When they stepped into the parking lot, he saw what he'd more or less expected. The guy was filthy—beard and shoulder-length hair matted and greasy, and more wrinkles than Connie had ever seen cut into one man's face. His shirt was buttoned all the way up to his neck, but it hung open in a long tear down his chest, and his jeans were caked with dirt and oil, both knees ragged. The only thing clean about him was his shoes, new white high-tops that glowed in the streetlight.

A hot wind came up off the street and blew across the parking lot. Connie walked a step or two behind the bum, watching him swing his arms from side to side, walking hard into the wind that pushed back his hair and flapped the ragged front of his shirt. When they reached the front door, the bum pulled it open and waved Connie through.

The air conditioner felt good, and Connie stood for a moment inside the door, letting the cool air work under his shirt. It was bright and clean in the Waffle House, and he liked the way the orange seats glowed under the big globe lights. All the Formica tabletops shone like polished wood, and the front of the refrigerator mirrored the room in buffed aluminum. Even the floor shone, and the whole place smelled of coffee.

Only one booth was occupied, the middle booth against the left wall — three men hunched over bacon, eggs, and waffles. One of them looked over at Connie. He chewed a few times, slowly, then swallowed. "Hey, get that rat outta here. We're trying to eat some supper."

Something shot through Connie, but he caught himself, didn't say anything, only stood there staring. When the man went back to his food, Connie walked over to the counter and picked out a stool. The old man sat down on the other side of him.

Rita came out of the back with a tray of salt and pepper shakers, eyes glowing, hair burning red under the big lights. She smiled when she saw him, but let the smile fall when she noticed the bum. "Connie, he with you?"

"Looks like it."

"Well, William won't like it if he sees him in here." She bent down and set the tray under the counter. "He had to run him off once today already."

"Where's he at?" Connie said.

"Went home to check on his dog, but be ought to be back in here any minute." She spread two menus on the counter in front of them. "Let's eat up and roll."

"When did William get a dog?"

"Yesterday. He got a puppy from the pound."

"What's he want with a dog?"

"How do I know? Got tired of living alone, I guess. A dog's about the only thing that'd put up with him."

"Hey, Rita." The man in the booth pushed a paper napkin across his mouth. "I'm trying to eat my damn supper. And I don't like to eat with rats. If I wanted to eat with rats, I'd go down to the dump."

Connie turned on his stool and sent him another glare. He was a big balding guy in a yellow golf shirt, but most of his size was fat. "Listen," Connie said, "you don't have to talk like that."

"Is that right?" the guy said. "And I don't have to eat my supper with rats either."

"You don't watch your mouth, sport, you're liable to be eating it through your asshole."

The two other men looked up then, suddenly interested, and the fat guy across the table pointed his fork at Connie. "Don't give me any shit, friend, 'cause I ain't in the mood for it."

Rita threw her hands in the air. "Okay, boys. We can't have any trouble in here."

"We ain't starting no trouble," Connie said. "We're just trying to get something to eat."

"Come on," Rita said, "just look at him. And his clothes smell. You wanna get me fired? William'll be back in here any minute." She looked at the old man. "Why don't I fix you something good to go, and you can eat it in the parking lot?"

"We don't eat in parking lots," Connie said.

"Damn, Connie," she said, "you can't eat in here either. Not till you get him cleaned up. You're gonna get me fired."

Connie frowned at her and shook his head. Then he looked again at the man on the stool beside him. She was right. He looked like he hadn't bathed in months. And he smelled awful. But there was something else about him too, something sad and almost fragile. His hair and beard were a rusty gray that made his face look brittle. His eyes were gray too, and the wrinkles sagging under them gave him the look of a bad hangover.

Connie slapped his hand on the counter. "Come on," he said to the old man. He frowned again at Rita and slid down off the stool. The bum followed him out.

They stood outside by the phone booth while Connie stewed. He didn't know who'd pissed him off more, the guy in the golf shirt or Rita. He looked back through the window and saw her staring at them. That wasn't like her, turning them out like that. That wasn't like her at all.

Headlights and taillights moved in four lanes up and down Riverside, and Connie gazed into the crowded parking lot of the S&S Cafeteria. Maybe they'd just go over there and eat. Get serious. Who was he fooling? Not with the old man looking like that. Still, there were dozens of places on Riverside. It was all fast food and gas stations, bars and motels. But that wasn't the problem. He knew that. He just didn't like being told where he could eat and where he couldn't.

"We could've got it to go," the old man said. "We could've eat in the parking lot."

"I don't eat in parking lots. You don't neither."

The old man ran his fingers through his beard. He studied Connie and smiled. "Hell, I don't mind."

"Listen, buddy, I don't eat outside unless I'm at a goddamn picnic." He flapped some air under his shirt. "And I don't go on no picnics when it's this fucking hot."

"I eat anywhere. I don't mind."

"Come on," Connie said.

"Where we going?"

Connie turned the corner of the building and headed across the parking lot, the old man a step or two behind him. When he got to the Volkswagen, he unlocked the door on the passenger's side.

"Where we going?" the old man said again.

"We ain't going nowhere. We're there." He pulled the front seat down, rummaged in the back through some packages, and found what he was after. He handed the shirt, still folded and pinned, to the old man. "Here, try this thing on."

"What's that?"

"It's a shirt. Belongs to my brother."

The old man turned the shirt over in his hands. "That's real nice," he said. "I like blue. It's blue, ain't it?"

"Yeah, it's blue all right. And make sure you get all the goddamn pins out. I can't have you stabbing yourself."

He held the shirt up to the streetlight. "That's real nice. I appreciate it. You don't think your brother'll mind?"

"Carl? Naw, he's a sweet guy. He'd want you to have it. He's got tons of shirts."

The bum pulled the pins out of the shirt and tossed them into the darkness. He unbuttoned his old shirt, slipped out of it, and let it fall to the pavement. His chest was hairless, thin and yellow in the streetlight, ribs showing all the way to his nipples. He kicked the old shirt under the car and slipped into the new one. It swallowed him, only the tips of his fingers sticking out of the sleeves.

"Roll 'em up," Connie said. "It'll be fine."

"This is real nice. I can't remember nothing nicer."

"You got a comb?"

"I don't think so. I ain't got much."

Connie nodded. "Me neither, old man."

"Well, it says not to take much, don't it? No bread, no bag, no money in your belt."

"What?"

The old man didn't say anything, only stared out into the darkness at the edge of the parking lot.

"What'd you say?" Connie said.

But the bum was off somewhere, his eyes glazed and empty, his fingers nervously rubbing the backs of his hands.

"Hey," Connie said, "you all right?"

"Nice shirt." The bum smiled at him.

Connie reached into his pocket and came out with a red comb. "Here, see what you can do with that hair."

The old man took it and smiled again. He dragged it a few times through his hair and beard, wincing as he jerked out the greasy tangles, then he wiped it on his pants and held it out to Connie. "Much obliged."

Connie looked at the comb in the bum's hand. "You keep it," he said. "I got another one."

"You sure?"

"Yeah, go ahead and keep it. I got tons of combs."

They walked back across the parking lot toward the three cars and the bright glass corner of the Waffle House. Connie was still a little angry, but he was trying to shake it. It really wasn't Rita's fault. It was the jerk in the golf shirt. He'd spooked her, and she was afraid of losing her job. Besides, he needed her apartment for a while, he needed a cool shower and a beer. Maybe a movie on TV, something to give it all a rest.

"Listen," he said. "When we get back in there, you go on in the bathroom and wash your face. I'll square it with Rita."

"Okay, I can do that. I can wash my face."

Connie turned his head and looked at the old man. "Hey, what's your name, anyhow?"

"Pop, that's what they call me. That's good enough."

"Pop what?"

He shrugged. "It don't matter. Pop's good. There's a bunch I forgot, but don't none of it matter all that much."

"Well, my name's Connie. Connie Holtzclaw."

They turned the corner of the building and Connie jerked back the glass door. As soon as they stepped in, he pointed the old man to the right and pushed him toward the men's room. No one looked up from the booth, but Rita gave them a stare from behind the counter.

Connie walked over and sat down on a stool. "He's got a clean goddamn shirt on, and he's going in the bathroom to wash his face."

"Smart guy, huh?"

"Smart enough."

Rita looked at him for a few seconds, then she checked the three men in the booth. "Okay. But you all sit here on this side. I don't need any trouble in here tonight."

"Fine with me," Connie said. "I don't wanna sit with them assholes anyhow."

She glanced again at the three men across the room. "So where'd you pick him up?"

"He was back there in the alley going through a dumpster."

"Looking for something to eat?"

"And found it too. Can you believe that?"

She nodded. "I fixed him something last week. There were three of 'em hanging around out there, all beat up, noses bleeding."

"Who beat 'em up?"

"How would I know? Maybe they beat each other up. They were just hanging around out there on the sidewalk. William ran 'em off, but they came back. Panhandling, I suppose. Anyway, he was one of 'em. Finally, I just fixed 'em something to eat. It seemed like the best thing to do."

"Maybe that's why he came back."

"Well, I can't adopt anybody. I was afraid William might call the cops. I don't like to see people get locked up."

"Who does?" he said. "But at least they feed 'em."

"Maybe."

"Sure they do. They got to. And they don't feed 'em bad neither. They give 'em solid meals. Good food mostly. And they got a roof over their heads and a soft place to sleep. Where else they gonna find a deal like that?"

She rolled her eyes. "I don't care if they give 'em a steak and a king-size bed. I don't like to see anybody locked up in a cage. You lock animals up in cages."

"I'm just telling you it could be a hell of a lot worse. And you ain't worrying night and day about some asshole stabbing you for your shoes."

"People get killed in prison all the time."

"Bums like him don't. Not unless they piss somebody off. Besides, a city jail ain't a prison, the cops watch out for 'em."

Rita looked past him toward the door. "Well," she said. "Looks like we just talked a couple up."

Connie heard the door open behind him. Two policemen came in, one big and middle-aged, streaks of gray in his temples, the other about average and a few years younger, his hair as black and neat as his uniform. They nodded toward Connie, walked over and sat down in a booth next to the three men.

"You boys want some coffee?" Rita said.

The big cop held up two fingers. "Black."

Connie looked at Rita and raised his eyebrows. "You mind if I use your place for a little while tonight?"

"What's wrong with your place?"

"My TV's busted. There's a fight on."

"You're not taking *him* over there, are you?"

"Shit no. I ain't adopting him neither."

"Well, how am I supposed to know?" She took a pad and pencil off the register and slid them into the pocket of her apron. "I've seen you do crazier things. How do I know what to expect when you stroll in here with somebody like that?"

"I ain't asking to move in. I just wanna watch a fight."

"I don't want anybody else over there."

Connie held up his hands, then let them fall on the counter. "I ain't taking nobody else over there. Hell, I just wanna watch a goddamn prize fight. Hey, you ain't got somebody over there, do you? You ain't seeing that asshole again?"

"Don't be crazy. I just cleaned the place up, that's all. And I got my stuff out. I don't want anybody messing with it." She reached under the counter and brought up a brown leather purse.

"Well, I won't mess with it," he said. "I don't ever mess with your art stuff, do I?"

"Not much you don't. I came home one time and you had it scattered all over the place."

"That was Carl. It wasn't me."

"Well, I don't like it. That's personal stuff. And I don't appreciate you taking him over there. You know that." Rita took a key off a big ring of keys and laid it on the counter. "I'll be home a little after twelve. You still be there?"

"I doubt it. I got things to do. You got any beer in the fridge?"

"I don't think so." She nodded toward the restrooms. "Here he comes. You all take that far booth. I'll be over there in a minute." She stashed the purse back under the counter, picked up a coffeepot, and walked over to the policemen.

Connie turned on the stool and saw the old man standing by the door. He looked a little better, but not a lot. There was too much that just wouldn't wash away in the men's room of the Waffle House. He picked up Rita's key and put it in his pocket. He pointed toward the wall and a booth, and the old man turned and sat down.

"Well," Connie said, sliding into the seat across the table. "You look a little sharper. Look sharp, feel sharp."

"I used all the towels. You don't think she'll get mad, do you? There really wasn't all that many left."

"Forget it. They got plenty. We're the ones that pay for 'em."

"I wouldn't want her to get mad. She's a pretty nice lady. She give me a hamburger once."

"I wouldn't worry about it." Connie slid a menu in front of the old man. "Give it a close look, buddy. Anything you want."

The old man picked it up, and in the good light Connie noticed the backs of his hands. Between the first and middle knuckles of his right hand someone had tattooed the word LOVE, one blue letter on the back of each finger. On the left, it was HATE. The letters were crude and faded. He'd seen that somewhere before, but he decided not to ask.

"I think I'd like another one of them hamburgers." The old man scratched his beard and stared down at the menu. He read the left side, then the right. He flipped it over and looked at the back. "Or a couple of 'em, maybe, if that'd be okay."

"How 'bout some French fries?"

"Sure."

Then it came to Connie, and he pointed to the old bum's hands. "Bruce Springsteen."

"What?"

"Bruce Springsteen, rock 'n' roll singer. He's got a song about them tattoos."

The old man turned his hands over and looked at his fingers. "I don't hear much rock 'n' roll."

"Me neither," Connie said. "Rita, she does."

"Yeah, I remember them. Got 'em from a guy a long time ago. He had some just like it, I think. He seen it in a movie or something. Bunch of us got 'em all at the same time. I don't watch no movies neither."

The three men in the booth stood up and dropped a few bills onto the table. The fat one in the yellow shirt looked over toward Connie and the old man, then pulled another bill from his wallet and dropped it beside his plate. "Here's a little extra, Rita. Get the place sprayed."

Connie studied him as he walked by the counter for a toothpick, but he didn't say anything. He didn't need to start anything with two cops in the place, not with everything going on with Carl.

When the three men got to the door, the guy in the yellow golf shirt smiled. "See you later, rat boy."

Connie took a breath, trying to check his anger. "Count on it, sport. Me and you."

The fat guy stopped and turned, his lips tightening around the toothpick. He tugged at the front of his belt, walked over to the booth, and tapped his finger on the edge of the table. "You think that scares me, neighbor? You really think that scares me? I know who you are, I seen you fight. Trust me, it don't scare me."

Connie looked at the diamond signet ring choking the man's little finger, the black hair climbing up to his knuckles. "I ain't much concerned, mister. Maybe you ain't got sense enough to be scared."

"I seen you fight that Hugo kid in the Coliseum. He busted your fucking face. You was a *bum* in the ring." He frowned at Connie, then he pointed at the old man. "You see that? That's what you was in the ring, asshole. And that's what you are now."

Connie felt himself flush. He glanced at the old man, whose face was as white as milk, then clenched his jaws and stared back at the face nodding above the yellow shirt. "Mister, I ain't done nothing to you. And I don't know what your problem is. But somebody's liable to be carrying your fat butt outta here. I don't care if there's two cops over there or not."

"Tough talk, punk."

Connie looked past the man to the other side of the room. The cops were watching them now, waiting for it to start. Rita stood beside them, holding a pad and a pencil. There was a familiar look on her face, an expression of distress moving toward genuine fear. Connie clenched his jaws tighter and took a breath, then reached behind the napkin holder for another menu and opened it in front of him.

"That's what I thought," the fat man said. He rocked back on his heels. "Big words from the tough guy."

"Come on, Bill," one of the others said from the door. "Let's get outta here before he talks you to death."

The guy rapped his knuckle on the table.

Connie ignored him, buried himself in the breakfast specials.

The fat man gave him one last look. He took the toothpick out of his mouth and dropped it onto Connie's menu. "Asshole," he said, then turned and headed for the door.

Connie shook the toothpick into the ashtray and watched them walk to their truck, a black Chevy Blazer. It had a sharp dent in the front bumper and a Confederate flag decal in the lower right corner of the windshield. He watched them back out of the parking space and pull onto Riverside. He stared until their taillights disappeared in the traffic.

"You been in fights?" the old bum said.

"A few. I was a welterweight."

"I been in fights, too." The old man hooked a finger into the corner of his mouth, pulled back his upper lip, and showed his bare gum. "I didn't much like it."

"Me neither. I didn't much like it neither. So I guess we got something in common."

Rita walked over and flipped a page on her order pad. "Thanks for not starting it," she said, a little shaky. "I thought you'd punch him for sure."

"He ain't worth it."

She looked at the old man. "What's it gonna be, mister?"

"His name's Pop," Connie said. "Pop, this is Rita."

"Pleased to meet you," the old man said.

She scratched the pencil across the top of the pad, her hand still trembling slightly. "So what's it gonna be?"

"I'd like me one of them hamburgers like you fixed before."

"Two of 'em," Connie said. "Two for him and two for me. All the way. And a couple of hash browns." He looked at the old man. "You want hash browns or French fries?"

"Hash browns is good. Coffee's good too, black. Or milk."

"Bring us two coffees and a glass of milk."

She brushed her hair off her forehead, wrote it down on her pad, and walked back to the counter.

The old man looked even smaller now, framed by the orange plastic seat. Connie leaned toward him. "Where you from, pal?"

"Lots of places. I don't know." He took a napkin from the holder and unfolded it in his lap. "I don't wanna make no mess. You tell me if I'm making a mess. I wanna do this right."

"You ain't making a mess." Connie smiled at him. "You got any people anywhere? You got a wife?" He looked into the old bum's eyes. There was pain there, but also something else. An openness, a gratitude, maybe.

The old man shook his head. "I might have, maybe, long time ago. I can't remember much."

"Brothers and sisters?"

"Well," the bum said, "who does the will of God's my brothers and sisters. Ain't that what they say?"

"I don't know about that, but I got a brother, Carl. He mostly does what he wants to. That's his new shirt you got on."

"That's right. But he don't mind, you said so."

"I ain't got nobody else. My folks are dead."

"My folks too, I reckon," the old man said. "But I don't remember 'em. I know I had some though."

Connie smiled again. "I remember mine good enough. My daddy was a drunk. He killed my mama in a car wreck."

The bum shook his head. "That's too bad. I used to be bad to drink too. It ain't no good for you."

Connie watched the lines deepen in the old man's face. "Wasn't much good for him, that's for sure, or nobody around him."

"Clouds you up too much."

"I don't worry about it, though. I ain't the only one it ever happened to. I got this buddy, Jeff Willett, he's a trainer. His old man's a real bad drunk. Can't do nothing for himself. Can't fix a meal. Can't even boil an egg. Got shot up in the war, so he gets a government check. Spends it all on the booze. In a lotta ways that's worse."

The old man folded his hands on the table. "What war's that?"

"World War Two, I guess. Got shot up somewhere in Italy."

"I was in that war." He nodded slowly and rubbed his knuckles. "On this boat that went all over these islands. I remember some of that real good. These islands wasn't nothing but jungles, jungles all over 'em." He tilted his head a little to one side, then looked back at Connie. "He takes care of him, huh?"

"Jeff? Sure he does. A guy oughta take care of his folks. But there ain't no sense in that kinda drinking. And Jeff, hell, he works all the time, and he ain't got nobody to help him."

"But you got a brother." The old man cracked his knuckles. "And brothers is good to have, ain't they?"

"Yeah, he just about raised me." Connie propped his elbows on the table and thought about that. "Carl's a little crazy sometimes, but he took care of me. Out in Montana they tried to put me in this foster home. Carl wouldn't have it. He snatched me up. That's when we come down here. Well, we went to Atlanta first, but that wasn't for long." He thought about Carl standing over him in the lodge, what he said about not fucking this up. No, he wasn't going to do that. And then he thought about the boy, about hitting him, and it made a sickness turn in his stomach. How could he have lost control like that? And to hit a kid whose hands were cuffed, a kid who didn't weigh a hundred and twenty pounds soaking wet. It was awful. It was like hitting a woman.

"Montana?" the old man said. "I think I been there." Then a sadness came over his face. He pulled at his beard. "Brothers is good to have, all right. That's why it's one of the signs."

Rita came over with two coffee cups and a pot of coffee. She set the cups on the table and poured, then she walked back to the counter and brought the glass of milk.

"What signs you talking about, buddy?"

The old man picked up the glass and drank the milk down in three long swallows. He wiped his mouth carefully with the napkin. "I ain't got none on me, do I?"

Connie shook his head. "What signs you talking about?"

The old man's eyes went distant again. "I don't know. It's a lot I don't remember. Brother'll deliver up brother, ain't that it?" He picked up his coffee cup and took a sip. "Hot coffee. Good though."

Connie watched him blowing into the cup. "Hey, you used to be some kinda preacher or something?"

"Naw, I ain't no preacher. But I used to be a lotta things. Most of it I don't remember. Don't much matter."

"Yeah? What kinda things?"

"Who knows? I been to all over."

Connie took a sip of his coffee. He could smell the hamburgers sizzling on the grill. If they made him this hungry, he could imagine what they must be doing to the bum. "So where you live?"

"Here and there."

"Yeah? Well, where you sleep?"

"I slept down by the river last night. Down in the cemetery. It's real restful down there with the river going by. There's six or seven others got a little place down by the tracks. I don't hang out with them, though."

"Rose Hill?"

"I don't know. I guess. Whatever's the one down there by the river."

Rita took two plates of burgers and fries to the booth where the cops were sitting, then she hurried back and flipped the burgers on the grill. The smell of beef had completely filled the place, a thick, juicy aroma.

"Any time now," Connie said. "William, the manager, he ran off and left her by herself. Got him a dog yesterday, went home to feed it."

"I like dogs," the old man said. "I had me a good dog one time. Dogs is good company."

"Yeah? What kind was it?"

"I don't know. Just a big white dog. Smart though. Got run over by a car, I think."

Connie thought of Montana and the two German shepherds his father had brought home to watch the garage and the junkyard beside their house. He remembered the sign his father hung on the chain-link fence. Big black letters you could read all the way from the road: BEWARE: BAD DOGS, MEAN KIDS, GROUCHY WIFE. But it wasn't true, not all of it, anyway. Not the part about the wife. All that shouting in the house, and she never raised her voice. The kids, maybe, were another thing. But then, Connie didn't guess he was any meaner than most other kids. Still, there was Carl. And he nearly justified the whole sign. Maybe Carl figured that having a brother around was cheating him out of something. He was ten years older, so maybe he'd gotten used to being an only child. Connie really didn't know. He only knew that Carl was always trying to punish him for something, for being alive, it seemed like. And it never was much better with the folks. Maybe Carl had wanted to punish them, too, for having another kid, for bringing a stranger into the family.

"No, he didn't," the old man said. "A man shot him. That's what it was, a man shot him for getting into something. It was this other dog got run over by the car."

"What other dog's that?" Connie said.

The old man looked puzzled for a second. "This other dog. Bird dog. I don't know, don't matter."

When Rita brought the hamburgers, they ate without talking. The old man took careful bites and wiped his mouth after each sip of coffee. Connie enjoyed the way he chewed, slow and deliberate on the right side of his mouth, and the way the wrinkles under his eyes moved like ripples on a pond. He guessed the old guy must be missing more teeth than he showed. But he got it down, and he enjoyed it. Connie was glad he had done that for him. Bite by bite, the second burger followed.

Rita came by and poured more coffee. The old man leaned down and blew over his cup.

"Y'all okay?" she said. "Anything else?"

"How 'bout it?" Connie asked him.

The old man shook his head.

Connie looked up at Rita. "Nope, we'll just finish the coffee."

She figured up the check and laid it on the table, then she walked over to the register to ring out the policemen.

The big cop said something to her and nodded toward Connie and the bum. Connie couldn't hear what it was but it made him a little nervous. He didn't like cops talking about him. He sat up in his seat and took a sip of his coffee. Out of the corner of his eye he caught the cop walking toward the booth.

"You're Connie Holtzclaw, ain't you?"

Connie turned. "So?"

The cop coughed into his fist, then cleared his throat. "So I just wondered, that's all."

Connie took a sip of his coffee. "Sure, that's my name."

"Seen your brother lately, Connie?"

"Carl?"

"He's your brother, ain't he? You ain't got another one, do you?"

The cop was about fifty or so. His nose leaned a little to one side like it had been broken, and he had a gray five o'clock shadow. Connie studied his face, his cool blue eyes. "Naw, I ain't seen him in a while."

"How long's a while?"

"This here's his shirt," the old man said. "It's a nice one, ain't it? He don't mind, though, he's got tons of 'em."

The cop looked at the old man and grinned. "That's right, dad. It's a real nice one." He looked back down at Connie and the grin faded. "How long's a while, kid? Yesterday? Today?"

"I ain't seen him in a week or so. We went down to the Hagler fight, big screen down at the Coliseum. I ain't seen him since then."

The cop picked at his thumbnail. "Where'd the shirt come from?"

"Had it in my car."

"That's right," the old man said. "I seen him get it right out of the back seat. He had a bunch of stuff back there."

The cop turned back to Connie. "Carl usually keep his clothes in the back of your car?"

"It was a present," Connie said. "Only I ain't seen him lately to give it to him."

The cop raised his eyebrows and nodded. "You see your brother," he said, "you give him a message. You tell him Tommy's looking for him."

"Tommy who?"

"Don't give me any shit, kid. I'm trying to do your brother a favor. You tell him to give Tommy a call real quick. Make everything a lot easier in the long run."

Connie took another sip of his coffee. He looked up at the cop. "I ain't planning on seeing him no time soon."

The cop nodded. He sucked a tooth, glanced at the old man, then stared at Connie. "Ain't you on parole?"

"I might be."

"Burglary or something like that, wasn't it?"

Connie frowned. He could feel himself tensing. "Could be."

"Anybody on parole don't need to get run in. You know that? If I was on parole, I wouldn't wanna get picked up for nothing. A kid on parole might just get sent away for a while."

"I ain't doing nothing to get run in for."

The cop shot a slight smile at his partner standing at the register, then turned back toward Connie. "Listen, I ain't trying to be tough but sometimes a wiseass don't have to do nothing. You hear what I'm saying? Sometimes things just happen. Some guys just got shit for luck." He ran his thumbs under his service belt. "You give Carl the message. Tommy ain't too pissed off yet, he's still willing to work things out."

The cop nodded to his partner and headed for the door. Connie watched them push through and disappear into the parking lot, then he finished his coffee in a long gulp.

After a moment the old man said, "You been locked up?"

Connie saw something different in the bum's expression now. In his eyes there was a softness, not an emptiness. "Once," he said.

"I been locked up lots of times. I don't mind. It's a roof and a hot meal. What'd you get locked up for?"

"They said I took some money."

The old man took a slow sip of his coffee. "Who from?"

"Some woman in south Macon. I used to go around to people's houses, spray for bugs. Some woman said I took some money from her, took it out of her pocketbook."

The old man tugged again at his beard. "How come she say that?"

Connie thought for a second. Why lie to a bum? "'Cause I took it."

"It's generally got to do with money, don't it? I ain't got no money, don't much like it. Too much of a temptation."

Connie smiled. "You don't like money, huh?"

"Not much. I like what it buys, all right. Just don't like what it does. Makes folks mean. They want too much or they get too much, and it makes 'em do things. I seen people do awful things for money. Things they wouldn't even think about doing for no other reason. I don't much like it. It sours 'em, makes 'em mean."

"Well, I like it a lot."

"Most do. It's the human heart."

"Human heart?"

"That's it. Outta the human heart comes the evil thoughts, the fornications, thefts, murders. I forget what all else. Nothing good though."

"Well, I ain't never murdered nobody, pal. But I admit I thought about it once or twice."

"Who ain't?"

Connie reached into his back pocket and pulled out his wallet. He flipped the check over and laid two bills on top of it.

"I'm obliged," the old man said.

Connie gave him a look. He took a ten out of his wallet and pushed it across the table. "You take this, okay? I don't care if you like it or not."

"I'm obliged already."

"You take it. And don't spend it on the booze."

"Booze ain't no good for you," the old man said. "Booze ain't no good at all. Clouds you up. Clouded me up a long time ago. I can't remember nothing no more. Don't have nothing to do with it now. Nothing at all."

Rita started wiping off the table where the cops had been. She had a good pair of legs, and Connie liked what the uniform did for her when she bent over. Thinking about anybody else seeing her that way made him ache. He knew they did, though. He knew what every guy who came in the place dreamed about. Then he thought of the kid lying naked on the mattress, his little sausage of a cock standing straight up. What was he dreaming about? It was too much. He wished Carl would give him back his clothes. "Good for you," he said. "Too much of anything'll cloud you up. Where you headed for tonight?"

"Back to the graveyard, I reckon."

"You got someplace down there outta the weather?"

"I got me a place. Good place. Them others is down on the tracks by the river. They get a little rowdy sometimes. I don't like it when they get too rowdy, so I got me a place of my own."

"What others is that?"

"Hobos. They come in and out on them freights. But I got my own place. Kenny showed me where it was. He come in on the freights, too, but he's gone now. Them others, they killed him and throwed him in the river. Don't nobody know about my place now but me. They done killed Kenny."

"Killed him?"

"Knocked him in the head, I think. Kenny, he had him some money and he had a gold watch, too, a pocket watch, belonged to his daddy. Some of them others down there's pretty bad to get rowdy. I got some stuff, but I ain't got no watch." The old man rubbed his fingers and the backs of his hands.

"What you want a watch for?"

"I don't want no watch. A watch won't tell you nothing worth knowing. I got me some other stuff though. I do all right. Got me a flashlight and a lantern. Got me one of them bedrolls. You know, the kind you get in and zip it up. Sleeping bag, I guess. Man give it to me the other day. Got him a store downtown that's fulla that stuff. Give me these shoes, too. I do all right. I might not look like it, but I do all right."

"What store was that?"

"I don't know. Downtown. He seen me walking down the street, feet poking outta my shoes. Took me right on in that store and give

me these ones I got on. I reckon I thanked him pretty good 'cause that's
when he give me the sleeping bag."

"Some people are all right," Connie said.

"Sometimes they are, sometimes they ain't. It's a mix. I seen a bunch
of 'em, and it's a real mix." The old man drank the last of his coffee
and wiped his beard. "And that's the problem, ain't it?" He wadded
his napkin and dropped it on his plate.

"What's that?"

"The problem with folks. You gotta trust somebody, don't you? I
mean, if you can't trust nobody, then what's the use? You take Kenny.
I thought I could trust Kenny, and then he went off and got hisself killed."

"How you know they killed him?"

"I know things. I got ways."

"Well, you just gotta be careful, that's all. You can't take no chances
with people. Better safe than sorry."

The old man nodded and looked down at his cup. "I reckon. And
sometimes that ain't nearly enough. You can't trust nobody, then what's
the use in anything?"

"I'm going your way," Connie said. "I'll give you a lift."

They stood by the wrought-iron fence and looked down past the trees
over the dark hills sloping toward the river, rolling hills shining dull
with white marble catching the first of the moon—marble tablets and
crosses, angels with broad wings, huge gray mausoleums, brick-walled
terraces of granite and marble grave slabs. The old man had not wanted
to use the main entrance of Rose Hill Cemetery, so Connie had parked
the car across the street at a closed Shell station. Sometimes a patrol
car would drive by and slow down past that entrance, and sometimes
it might even drive through, and the old man didn't want to be seen
going in or out. It didn't happen often, he said, but sometimes. And
he didn't want to take the chance.

In what moonlight shone on the front of the gate, Connie could read
OAK RIDGE 1840. It was a huge, cream-colored brick wall with three entran-
ces built into it, two smaller ones on either side of a large one wide
enough for a carriage path. There was a strange, unconforming beauty
about it that Connie couldn't quite explain, the same beauty the darkness
brought to everything he saw—the huge marble mausoleum with E. ELKIN
carved on the front, its blue stained-glass windows covered with bars,
the charcoal trees backing away toward the road, even the old man leaning
over the fence—all the imperfections somehow darkened away.

Standing there, gazing out over the cemetery, the old man looked
proud of what he saw, as though coming to it was coming to something
of his own making, or at least his own discovery. He scanned the rows
of tombstones and the narrow, concrete carriage paths winding around

the hills, and Connie thought of the battlefields of Montana, of standing
with his father and staring down the falling ridges toward the Little
Bighorn River. He studied the old man as he turned his head slowly
from side to side, taking in the whole graveyard. On his face was an
expression of cautious fascination. Maybe that was what it felt like to
gaze down into that valley at the river and the trees and the endless
lodges of the Sioux.

"Hey, you know who Custer was?"

The old man's stare wandered out among the stones. "I heard of
him."

"I went to his grave once."

"Where's that?"

"Montana."

"I been there, I think."

"Yeah? When was that?"

"Who knows? I been everywhere once." The old man turned and
glanced at Connie. He stared back out over the cemetery. "That Mr.
Custer," he said, "he wasn't too smart, I guess."

Connie followed the old man's gaze into the middle of the graveyard,
where the hills broke into terraces of stone. "Oh yeah? How come?"

"Should've minded his own business. Left them people alone."

"I don't know," Connie said. "Might be a little more complicated
than that. My daddy used to tell me things about it. He used to read
a lot on it. I read some on it too. I don't guess Custer really liked
killing them Indians, women and babies and all."

"I don't know. Maybe he did, maybe he didn't." The old man paused.
He didn't turn away from the graveyard. "I don't reckon them bums
much minded killing Kenny."

Connie smiled. "It ain't the same thing. I'm talking about fighting
a war here. I'm talking about a general in the U.S. Army who was
trying to fight in a war."

"And this man Custer, he didn't like killing them Indians?"

"Probably not. Sometimes a man figures he's got to do something
even if he don't like it."

"That's what your daddy said?"

"I don't know. I guess."

"Well, that's okay if it's the right thing to do." The old man put
a leg up, climbed over the fence, and started walking out through the
graves.

Connie climbed over after him and followed him onto a carriage path.
On his left he passed a huge mausoleum that said DANNENBERG 1910
over the doors and just beyond it a marble angel or a woman. From
the top of the hill the graveyard opened up into a huge series of desolate
and gentle hills. It was all very beautiful—the layers of shadow the

moon cast over the stones and terraces—but sobering too. Connie liked the stillness of it, the deep, quiet emptiness.

The path sloped downhill past terraces of smaller stones—obelisks, crosses, marble tablets and slabs surrounded by black wrought-iron fences. Connie tried to take it all in, to put his finger on the way the darkness made it beautiful, dimmed everything toward perfection, but the old man walked quickly and it was all he could do to keep up. Then halfway down the hill the old man stepped into the shadow of a giant oak and stopped behind an obelisk. The lettering was faint, but Connie could make out the word PIERCE.

From here he could see a large part of the cemetery. Up on the far hill to his right was the tile roof of the office and the top of the main gate into Rose Hill, and just in front of that stood a huge mausoleum, all gray in the moonlight. From there the cemetery tumbled in hills toward the river—a dense scattering of monuments and mausoleums, occasional patches of oak and cedar black against the hills.

"How come you asked me about that man Custer?"

"No reason, I just thought of him. I remembered going with my daddy to the place where he died."

"Where's that?"

"Southeast Montana, not far from Wyoming. Little place called Hardin, on the Crow reservation. Hard On, that's what they called it."

"That's where you was from?"

"Naw, we lived way over on the other side of the state. My daddy took us down there one time on a trip. He souped up a car for somebody, or something like that. But I was born in Texas. My daddy, he used to run stock cars, but he smashed up and couldn't do that no more. I was about two or three, I guess. That's when we moved to Montana. His brother had a garage up there."

"I been to Montana," the old man said. "I'm just about sure of it. And I know I been to Texas. I remember lots about Texas. East Texas, awful hot and dusty." He looked off to his left, down a carriage path that ran along the top of the ridge. "That girl that makes them hamburgers, she something special to you?"

"That's right."

He nodded his head, still staring down the carriage path. "I believe I like her. I believe she's all right. You gonna get married?"

"Maybe."

"How come maybe? You don't want to?"

Sometimes Connie thought that was all he wanted. "Yeah, I want to."

"She don't want to then?"

A little fear went through him. He didn't want to think about that. "Well, you can't just get married. You gotta have something, you know. You gotta make a living."

"You don't make a living?"

"I will. I ain't worried about it."

"I fell for this woman once. She had that red hair too. I remember she was good at singing."

"Yeah?" Connie said. "What kinda singing?"

The old man looked at Connie, his face half hidden in the shadow of a low branch. "You know a song goes, *There's a land beyond the river?*"

"Nope."

"Good song. *There's a land beyond the river, that they call the sweet forever.* That kinda singing. She was good at it."

"I don't know that one."

"I don't remember much, but I remember them songs. Some of 'em all the way through. Most of 'em was about rivers. I remember that too. Singing about, that's what rivers are for. She said that, I think. There's another one goes, *I'll meet you in the morning by the bright riverside.* She liked singing about rivers. That's what rivers are for. She said that."

"And all this time," Connie said, "I just thought they was for fish to live in."

The old man slapped his thigh. "You don't know too much, do you?"

"I never said I did."

"I know it. That's one of your good points. And you give me a shirt and bought me something to eat, so that's two more."

"And rivers ain't for fish to live in?"

"I never said that neither. I see 'em down here every day catching fish. Not right down by the graveyard, but down there under the bridge. I'm gonna get me some fish hooks and some line. Fish is good to eat."

Connie looked down into the graveyard rolling off toward the river and thought of his father standing knee-deep in a trout stream, his line whipping back behind his head and out into the water. "Trout," he said. "Trout's what's good. I was just about raised on trout."

The old man laced his fingers together and cracked his knuckles. "Catfish. Ain't no trout in that river."

"I was talking about Montana."

"Catfish is good too, though. But then you gotta get you a knife to clean 'em with. And a frying pan to cook 'em in. One thing always leads to another, don't it? You can't get away with having just a little something, one thing always leads to something else. Either have it all, or don't have nothing."

Connie looked up toward the main gate, the huge brick arch over the entrance to the cemetery. He couldn't see it clearly, but it seemed to be open. He thought then about Carl. This might be just the place Carl was looking for. It was deserted enough, and from a couple of these hills you could see just about the whole graveyard. Then he remembered hitting the boy, the jolt of anger, his fist balling, then the jolt again and the sharp rap to the face, the blood running from the boy's nose. That was an awful thing to do, and he was sorry for it. But he had to show him he meant business. He had to show him he could do what needed to be done. He wasn't going to let Carl down again. One thing the old man said was true. If you can't trust anybody, what's the use? And Carl was trusting him not to fuck this up. Everything else aside, Carl was still his brother and Carl was trusting him, and he wasn't going to let Carl down. "What's beyond that far hill over there?"

"More hills, more graves."

"How many?"

"'Bout as many as you're looking at now. Maybe more."

Connie let the thought settle in his head. This might be just the sort of place Carl needed. Pick the right time and this could be perfect. "Listen, I got to get rolling, pal. I got places to be."

"Not yet," the old man said. "You follow me on down here a piece. I got something for you."

"Naw, I really got to go now. I got —"

"You come on. It ain't far. I'm gonna show you my place. I got some stuff and I got something for you." The old man walked ten or fifteen yards down the narrow carriage path, then stopped and looked back over his shoulder. "You come on. It won't take long."

Connie started after him. "Then I got to go, all right?"

"You come on."

The trees hanging over the path made a wide awning and they walked under it, the old man a few yards ahead of Connie. They were walking lower into the valley now, along the side of a ridge. A hundred yards down the path the bricked walls of the terraces rose higher than Connie's head, and to his right the valley deepened. All around them tall marble gravestones stood up out of the hill, but Connie could read only a few names—LAMAR, BACON, ELLIS, and at the foot of a marble woman in a long flowing robe, the name BOZEMAN.

Then the valley dropped off steeply into a stand of thick hardwoods and brush. On his left Connie noticed the concrete wall of a terrace scratched with graffiti—a rough swastika buried under a peace symbol, the breast and hips of a headless woman, a star with a circle around it, the word AMAZONS. Vandals. A beautiful place—the hills, the statues, the terraces—and somebody had to fuck it up. He hated that. Then, near the end of the wall, testimonies to another need, dozens of names and initials—CT LOVES BIG T, Liz/Jeri, STEVE DIES FOR GAIL.

Connie hurried his steps. They were walking now toward the point of the ridge, and halfway into the curve that would take them there, he could see on that point four or five huge marble monuments tucked among the oaks and magnolias. Forty yards short of those trees, the old man turned to his right and started to climb down a steep hill.

The half moon floating low over the tops of the far pines threw a bridge of dull gold on the river. It shimmered in the current but hung in place, as though it were anchored on both banks. The railroad tracks ran along the near bank, and just where they entered the trees at the far edge of the cemetery, a small fire burned.

"That's them," the old man said, climbing down the hill, holding on to scrub brush and the low limbs of oaks. "Tramps, hobos. That's yard speed down there. They come in on them freights."

Connie followed him down, half stumbling and half sliding, holding on to whatever he could find. "What they want a fire tonight for? I'm sweating like a pig."

"Bums always got fires. Someplace to hang out."

At the bottom of the hill the land flattened into a wide triangular gorge—grassy banks on two sides and on the third the graveyard sloping down to the river. A narrow creek ran out of the far bank and down the middle of the gorge, and beyond the creek, huge brick and marble crypts were cut into the face of the bank.

"Up this way," the old man said.

Connie followed him up the gorge and into a thicket of brush and small trees. They seemed to be moving toward the point where the two sides of the gorge converged, but in the thicket the moon was no help. Connie could barely see the back of the old bum's shirt weaving through the brush. After thirty yards, the old man got down on his knees and waited for Connie to catch up. They crawled another ten yards through thick undergrowth.

The old man motioned with his hand. "You wait a minute here," he said. He pulled back a large magnolia branch heavy with gray blossoms and crawled under it.

Connie squatted on his heels. He could hear the creek rustling through the gorge and what he thought was the river whispering along the foot of the hill. From the woods across the river a bird made a funny call, then everything was quiet, only a slight wind rustling the brush. Connie sat still where the old man had told him. It was an eerie place, quiet and almost totally dark. Then a strange hiss and glow came into the branches, a circle of gold in the dark foliage, bright and flaring, and in the closer leaves of the magnolia branches he could see the delicate green network of veins.

The light dimmed some and steadied, and the hiss faded. "Come on in here," the old man said.

Connie pulled back the branches to find more branches. He pulled those down and faced a hole in the earth, the mouth of a cave burning orange. But it wasn't a cave. He knew that from the bars, stubs of iron bars jagging the mouth like rusty teeth.

"You come on in here, it's okay. Watch them bars, though, they'll scratch you bad."

Connie crawled under the branches. It was a round hole about four feet wide and it opened into a short passageway. He swung a leg between the stubs, lowered his head and climbed through.

"Come on in here, boy. This is a good place, ain't it?"

The passageway opened up into a fairly large room with a shallow pit in the center and a tall domed ceiling. Connie thought of a large igloo, only the walls were clay, and in the lantern light they looked almost pink. In the middle of the floor the old bum's sleeping bag lay on a mattress of folded newspaper, beside it the lantern, a black plastic flashlight, a few paper bags, and a metal box.

"I cleaned it up a lot," the old man said. "Used to be lots of broke bottles and stuff. But it's all right, now."

"You know what this is, don't you?" Connie said.

The old man gave him a quick glance, then looked down at his things scattered across the floor. "I ain't in nobody's way. I reckon it's been empty a good while."

Connie stood up and stretched his back. "Any spiders in here?"

"I ain't seen none."

"I don't much like spiders. Bugs is one thing, but I don't like spiders. I seen a lot of 'em too, spraying up under houses and all."

"Well, I ain't seen no spiders."

Connie examined the walls. "You ever wonder who was in here or what happened to 'em?"

"Ain't no telling. Somebody probably moved 'em off. But that was a long time ago. I bet don't three people in this whole town even know about this place now."

The hole was already closing in. Connie stretched again and took a deep breath. The air smelled like a basement or the inside of a well. "Could be," he said. "This place is hid good enough."

"That's right. Can't see it from nowhere, and nobody's got no reason to be prowling around back here."

"How'd you find this place, anyhow?"

"Kenny showed me. This is his lantern here."

"The guy that got killed."

"That's right. I already told you about Kenny." The old man shook his head. "He was a good boy."

"How you know they tossed him in the river?"

"They might have. He had him some money. He said they was after it, them tramps down at the river."

"Maybe he just pulled out. Caught one of those freights."

"Not without his lantern and his flashlight, he didn't. He wouldn't go off without his stuff. Kenny, he was sort of a hippie, but he wouldn't run off without his stuff."

"Ain't no more hippies, pal."

"Well, you take Kenny, he was what's left of 'em, I guess. He had a mouth harp, and he wore one of them rags on his head. And then he had him this long yellow ponytail. Pretty nice boy, liked to tell stories about things. He was good at telling stories."

"What kinda stories?"

"Oh, this and that. Where he'd been and all. He'd been all over. Me too, I guess. Only I can't remember much about it no more. Kenny, he was sharp, he could tell it all." The old man sat down on the sleeping bag and crossed his legs under him.

"How long you been sleeping in here?"

"I don't know. Not long. Cozy ain't it?"

"Too cozy for me," Connie said. "Like being locked up in a closet."

"You got somewhere else to sleep, though. I ain't."

Connie didn't say anything, only tried to imagine sleeping in the dark surrounded by these walls, this ceiling and floor, tried to imagine what it would be like to be sealed up in this place, the stuffy air going to absolutely nothing. He didn't like the thought.

"Sit down," the old man said.

"I'm all right." Something moved on the wall behind the old man's head. It moved again and disappeared into his shadow. "You sure there ain't no spiders in here?"

"I ain't seen none."

"I don't like spiders. My brother, when I was five or six, he used to put spiders in my bed. Sometimes I'd wake up in the middle of the night with a spider crawling on my face."

"Ain't no spiders in here," the bum said. "Sit on down. It ain't so bad. Keeps the rain off. And when you go to sleep you don't worry about nobody knocking your skull in with a rock. Beats jail too. You can come and go when you take the notion."

Connie shook his head. "I don't like jail neither."

"Aw, jail's all right," the old man said. "I been in a lot worse places. You just can't leave when you want to, that's all. But sometimes I think one place is about as good as another."

Connie looked over at the old man. "I appreciate the tour, pal, but I really gotta go now."

"Hold on a minute here."

"No, I really —"

"Naw, wait a minute. I got something to give you." The old man reached across the dirt floor and picked up the metal box. It was a small red box, the kind fruitcakes come in, but a lot of the paint had chipped off and it was rusting. He pried off the top and dug around inside. "Here," he said, holding out his hand.

Connie opened his palm and felt the old bum drop something into it. He held it down toward the lantern. It was a coin, a dirty one. And maybe an old one, too, but the date was worn smooth. He tilted it toward the lantern. On one side was the picture of a bearded man in an odd helmet, on the other an eagle sitting on top of a big shield. The eagle had seven stars over its head. Most of the writing was worn away, but what was left looked foreign. "What is this thing?"

"I don't know. I had 'em a long time. Ain't nothing special. I got three of 'em. I'm giving you this one."

"Where'd you get it?" Connie said, still turning the coin over in his hand, studying the details.

"Who knows? It was a long time ago. Maybe it was your place, Montana. I believe I had them pieces most all my life. Used to carry 'em in my pocket, then I got scared I'd lose 'em."

"I bet it wasn't Montana."

"Some other place then. It doesn't much matter. Texas, California, Hawaii, Mexico, South America."

"Yeah," Connie said. "Looks like something foreign. Probably ain't worth much, but you can't never tell. Can't see what it's made out of, but it don't weigh much. Ain't gold or silver, that's for sure."

"Yeah, I know that."

"It's old, though, so you might be able to sell it at a pawn shop or something."

"Nope, it ain't worth nothing."

"You know that for a fact?"

"It ain't worth nothing, but you take it anyway. Take it for a lucky piece, or a memory piece, or whatever."

Connie rubbed the coin in his hand. He nodded.

The old man leaned back against the clay wall, his face almost pink in the lantern light.

AMERICAN HISTORY

Judith Ortiz Cofer

I once read in a "Ripley's Believe It or Not" column that Paterson, New Jersey, is the place where the Straight and Narrow (streets) intersect. The Puerto Rican tenement known as El Building was one block up from Straight. It was, in fact, the corner of Straight and Market; not "at" the corner, but *the* corner. At almost any hour of the day, El Building was like a monstrous jukebox, blasting out *salsas* from open windows as the residents, mostly new immigrants just up from the island, tried to drown out whatever they were currently enduring with loud music. But the day President Kennedy was shot there was a profound silence in El Building, even the abusive tongues of *viragoes*, the cursing of the unemployed, and the screeching of small children had been somehow muted. President Kennedy was a saint to these people. In fact, soon his photograph would be hung alongside the Sacred Heart and over the spiritist altars that many women kept in their apartments. He would become part of the hierarchy of martyrs they prayed to for favors that only one who had died for a cause would understand.

On the day that President Kennedy was shot, my ninth-grade class had been out in the fenced playground of Public School Number 13. We had been given "free" exercise time and had been ordered by our P.E. teacher, Mr. DePalma, to "keep moving." That meant that the girls should jump rope and the boys toss basketballs through a hoop at the far end of the yard. He in the meantime would "keep an eye" on us from just inside the building.

It was a cold gray day in Paterson. The kind that warns of early snow. I was miserable since I had forgotten my gloves and my knuckles were turning red and raw from the jump rope. I was also taking a lot of abuse from the black girls for not turning the rope hard and fast enough for them.

"Hey, Skinny Bones, pump it, girl. Ain't you got no energy today?" Gail, the biggest of the black girls, who had the other end of the rope, yelled. "Didn't you eat your rice and beans and pork chops for breakfast today?"

The other girls picked up the "pork chop" and made it into a refrain: "pork chop, pork chop, did you eat your pork chop?" They entered the double ropes in pairs and exited without tripping or missing a beat. I felt a burning on my cheeks and then my glasses fogged up so that I could not manage to coordinate the jump rope with Gail. The chill was doing to me what it always did; entering my bones, making me cry, humiliating me. I hated the city, especially in winter. I hated Public School Number 13. I hated my skinny flat-chested body, and I envied the black girls who could jump rope so fast that their legs became a blur. They always seemed to be warm while I froze.

There was only one source of beauty and light for me that school year. The only thing I had anticipated at the start of the semester. That was seeing Eugene. In August, Eugene and his family had moved into the only house on the block that had a yard and trees. I could see his place from my window in El Building. In fact, if I sat on the fire escape I was literally suspended above Eugene's backyard. It was my favorite spot to read my library books in the summer. Until that August the house had been occupied by an old Jewish couple. Over the years I had become part of their family, without their knowing it, of course. I had a view of their kitchen and their backyard, and though I could not hear what they said, I knew when they were arguing, when one of them was sick, and many other things. I knew all this by watching them at mealtimes. I could see their kitchen table, the sink and the stove. During good times, he sat at the table and read his newspapers while she fixed the meals. If they argued, he would leave and the old woman would sit and stare at nothing for a long time. When one of them was sick, the other would come and get things from the kitchen and carry them out on a tray. The old man had died in June. The last week of school I had not seen him at the table at all. Then one day I saw that there was a crowd in the kitchen. The old woman had finally emerged from the house on the arm of a stocky middle-aged woman, whom I had seen there a few times before, maybe her daughter. Then a man had carried out suitcases. The house had stood empty for weeks. I had had to resist the temptation to climb down into the yard and water the flowers the old lady had taken such good care of.

By the time Eugene's family moved in, the yard was a tangled mass of weeds. The father had spent several days mowing, and when he finished I didn't see the red, yellow, and purple clusters that meant flowers to me from where I sat. I didn't see this family sit down at the kitchen table together. It was just the mother, a red-headed tall woman who wore a white uniform—a nurse's, I guessed it was; the father was gone before I got up in the morning and was never there at dinner time. I saw him only on weekends when they sometimes sat on lawn chairs under the oak tree, each hidden behind a section of the newspaper; and there was Eugene. He was tall and blond, and he wore glasses. I liked him right away because he sat at the kitchen table and read books for hours. That summer, before we had even spoken one word to each other, I kept him company on my fire escape.

Once school started I looked for him in all my classes, but P.S. 13 was a huge, overpopulated place and it took me days and many discreet questions to discover that Eugene was in honors classes for all his subjects; classes that were not open to me because English was not my first language, though I was a straight-A student. After much maneuvering I managed "to run into him" in the hallway where his locker was—on the other side of the building from mine—and in study hall at the library where he first seemed to notice me, but did not speak; and finally, on the way home after school one day when I decided to approach him directly, though my stomach was doing somersaults.

I was ready for rejection, snobbery, the worst. But when I came up to him, practically panting in my nervousness, and blurted out: "You're Eugene. Right?" he smiled, pushed his glasses up on his nose, and nodded. I saw then that he was blushing deeply. Eugene liked me, but he was shy. I did most of the talking that day. He nodded and smiled a lot. In the weeks that followed, we walked home together. He would linger at the corner of El Building for a few minutes then walk down to his two-story house. It was not until Eugene moved into that house that I noticed that El Building blocked most of the sun, and that the only spot that got a little sunlight during the day was the tiny square of earth the old woman had planted with flowers.

I did not tell Eugene that I could see inside his kitchen from my bedroom. I felt dishonest, but I liked my secret sharing of his evenings, especially now that I knew what he was reading since we chose our books together at the school library.

One day my mother came into my room as I was sitting on the window sill staring out. In her abrupt way she said: "Elena, you are acting 'moony.'" *Enamorada* was what she really said, that is—like a girl stupidly infatuated. Since I had turned fourteen and started menstruating my mother had been more vigilant than ever. She acted as if I was going to go crazy or explode or something if she didn't watch me and nag me all the time about being a *señorita* now. She kept talking about virtue, morality, and other subjects that did not interest me in the least. My mother was unhappy in Paterson, but my father had a good job at the blue jeans factory in Passaic and soon, he kept assuring us, we would be moving to our own house there. Every Sunday we drove out to the suburbs of Paterson, Clifton, and Passaic, out to where people mowed grass on Sundays in the summer, and where children made snowmen in the winter from pure white snow, not like the gray slush of Paterson, which seemed to fall from the sky in that hue. I had learned to listen to my parents' dreams, which were spoken in Spanish, as fairy tales, like the stories about life in the island-paradise of Puerto Rico before I was born. I had been to the island once as a little girl, to grandmother's funeral, and all I remembered was wailing women in black, my mother becoming hysterical and being given a pill that made her sleep two days, and me feeling lost in a crowd of strangers all claiming to be my aunts, uncles, and cousins. I had actually been glad to return to the city. We had not been back there since then, though my parents talked constantly about buying a house on the beach someday, retiring on the island—that was a common topic among the residents of El Building. As for me, I was going to go to college and become a teacher.

But after meeting Eugene I began to think of the present more than of the future. What I wanted now was to enter that house I had watched for so many years. I wanted to see the other rooms where the old people had lived, and where the boy I liked spent his time. Most of all, I wanted to sit at the kitchen table with Eugene like two adults, like the old man and his wife had done, maybe drink some coffee and talk about books. I had started reading *Gone with the Wind*. I was enthralled by it, with the daring and the passion of the beautiful girl living in a mansion, and with her devoted parents and the slaves who did everything for them. I didn't believe such a world had ever really existed, and I wanted to ask Eugene some questions since he and his parents, he had told me, had come up from Georgia, the same place where the novel was set. His father worked for a company that had transferred him to Paterson. His mother was very unhappy, Eugene said, in his beautiful voice that rose and fell over words in a strange, lilting way. The kids at school called him "the hick" and made fun of the way he talked. I knew I was his only friend so far, and I liked that, though I felt sad for him sometimes. "Skinny Bones" and "Hick" was what they called us at school when we were seen together.

The day Mr. DePalma came out into the cold and asked us to line up in front of him was the day that President Kennedy was shot. Mr. DePalma, a short, muscular man with slicked-down black hair, was the science teacher, P.E. coach, and disciplinarian at P.S. 13. He was the teacher to whose homeroom you got assigned if you were a troublemaker, and the man called out to break up playground fights, and to escort violently angry teenagers to the office. And Mr. DePalma was the man who called your parents in for "a conference."

That day, he stood in front of two rows of mostly black and Puerto Rican kids, brittle from their efforts to "keep moving" on a November day that was turning bitter cold. Mr. DePalma, to our complete shock, was crying. Not just silent adult tears, but really sobbing. There were a few titters from the back of the line where I stood shivering.

"Listen," Mr. DePalma raised his arms over his head as if he were about to conduct an orchestra. His voice broke, and he covered his face with his hands. His barrel chest was heaving. Someone giggled behind me.

"Listen," he repeated, "something awful has happened." A strange gurgling came from his throat, and he turned around and spit on the cement behind him.

"Gross," someone said, and there was a lot a laughter.

"The President is dead, you idiots. I should have known that wouldn't mean anything to a bunch of losers like you kids. Go home." He was shrieking now. No one moved for a minute or two, but then a big girl let out a "Yeah!" and ran to get her books piled up with the others against the brick wall of the school building. The others followed in a mad scramble to get to their things before somebody caught on. It was still an hour to the dismissal bell.

A little scared, I headed for El Building. There was an eerie feeling on the streets. I looked into Mario's drugstore, a favorite hangout for the high-school crowd, but there were only a couple of old Jewish men at the soda-bar talking with the short-order cook in tones that sounded almost angry, but they were keeping their voices low. Even the traffic on one of the busiest intersections in Paterson—Straight Street and Park Avenue—seemed to be moving slower. There were no horns blasting that day. At El Building, the usual little group of unemployed men was not hanging out on the front stoop making it difficult for women to enter the front door. No music spilled out from open doors in the hallway. When I walked into our apartment, I found my mother sitting in front of the grainy picture of the television set.

She looked up at me with a tear-streaked face and just said: *"Dios mio,"* turning back to the set as if it were pulling at her eyes. I went into my room.

Though I wanted to feel the right thing about President Kennedy's death, I could not fight the feeling of elation that stirred in my chest. Today was the day I was to visit Eugene in his house. He had asked me to come over after school to study for an American history test with him. We had also planned to walk to the public library together. I looked down into his yard. The oak tree was bare of leaves and the ground looked gray with ice. The light through the large kitchen window of his house told me that El Building blocked the sun to such an extent that they had to turn lights on in the middle of the day. I felt ashamed about it. But the white kitchen table with the lamp hanging just above it looked cozy and inviting. I would soon sit there, across from Eugene, and I would tell him about my perch just above his house. Maybe I would.

In the next thirty minutes I changed clothes, put on a little pink lipstick and got my books together. Then I went in to tell my mother that I was going to a friend's house to study. I did not expect her reaction.

"You are going out *today*?" The way she said *today* sounded as if a storm warning had been issued. It was said in utter disbelief. Before I could answer, she came toward me and held my elbows as I clutched my books.

"*Hija*, the President has been killed. We must show respect. He was a great man. Come to church with me tonight."

She tried to embrace me, but my books were in the way. My first impulse was to comfort her, she seemed so distraught, but I had to meet Eugene in fifteen minutes.

"I have a test to study for, Mamá. I will be home by eight."

"You are forgetting who you are, *niña*. I have seen you staring down at that boy's house. You are heading for humiliation and pain." My mother said this in Spanish and in a resigned tone that surprised me, as if she had no intention of stopping me from "heading for humiliation and pain." I started for the door. She sat in front of the TV holding a white handkerchief to her face.

I walked out to the street and around the chain-link fence that separated El Building from Eugene's house. The yard was neatly edged around the little walk that led to the door. It always amazed me how Paterson, the inner core of the city, had no apparent logic to its architecture. Small, neat, single residences like this one could be found right next to huge, dilapidated apartment buildings like El Building. My guess was that the little houses had been there first, then the immigrants had come in droves, and the monstrosities had been raised for them—the Italians, the Irish, the Jews, and now us, the Puerto Ricans and the blacks. The door was painted a deep green: *verde*, the color of hope, I had heard my mother say it: *Verde-Esperanza*.

I knocked softly. A few suspenseful moments later the door opened just a crack. The red, swollen face of a woman appeared. She had a halo of red hair floating over a delicate ivory face—the face of a doll—with freckles on the nose. Her smudged eye makeup made her look unreal to me, like a mannequin seen through a warped store window.

"What do you want?" Her voice was tiny and sweet-sounding, like a little girl's, but her tone was not friendly.

"I'm Eugene's friend. He asked me over. To study." I thrust out my books, a silly gesture that embarrassed me almost immediately.

"You live there?" She pointed up to El Building, which looked particularly ugly, like a gray prison with its many dirty windows and rusty fire escapes. The woman had stepped halfway out and I could see that she wore a white nurse's uniform with St. Joseph's Hospital on the nametag.

"Yes. I do."

She looked intently at me for a couple of heartbeats, then said as if to herself, "I don't know how you people do it." Then directly to me: "Listen, honey. Eugene doesn't want to study with you. He is a smart boy. Doesn't need help. You understand me. I am truly sorry if he told you you could come over. He cannot study with you. It's nothing personal. You understand? We won't be in this place much longer, no need for him to get close to people—it'll just make it harder for him later. Run back home now."

I couldn't move. I just stood there in shock at hearing these things said to me in such a honey-drenched voice. I had never heard an accent like hers, except for Eugene's softer version. It was as if she were singing me a little song.

"What's wrong? Didn't you hear what I said?" She seemed very angry, and I finally snapped out of my trance. I turned away from the green door and heard her close it gently.

Our apartment was empty when I got home. My mother was in someone else's kitchen, seeking the solace she needed. Father would come in from his late shift at midnight. I would hear them talking softly in the kitchen for hours that night. They would not discuss their dreams for the future, or life in Puerto Rico, as they often did; that night they would talk sadly about the young widow and her two children, as if they were family. For the next few days, we would observe *luto* in our apartment; that is, we would practice restraint and silence—no loud music or laughter. Some of the women of El Building would wear black for weeks.

That night, I lay in my bed trying to feel the right thing for our dead president. But the tears that came up from a deep source inside me were strictly for me. When my mother came to the door, I pretended to be sleeping. Sometime during the night, I saw from my bed the street-light come on. It had a pink halo around it. I went to my window and pressed my face to the cool glass. Looking up at the light I could see the white snow falling like a lace veil over its face. I did not look down to see it turning gray as it touched the ground below.

THIS HEAT

Pam Durban

In August, Beau Clinton died. He was playing basketball in the high-school gym and when his bad heart set him free he staggered and fell, he blew one bloody bubble that lingered, shimmering, until it burst, sprinkling blood like rust spots, all over his pale face. The school phoned Ruby Clinton but they wouldn't say what the trouble was, just that Beau was sick, in trouble, something—it was all the same trouble—and could Ruby or Mr. Clinton come right down. "Isn't any Mr. Clinton," Ruby snapped, but the woman had already hung up the phone. So she figured she'd best go down to see what he'd done this time, her son who looked so much like his sorry father, Charles Clinton, it was all she could do sometimes to keep from tearing into him.

Ruby walked down the hall working herself up for the next showdown with Beau or the principal or whoever crossed her. No one made her angrier than Beau. She could get so angry that bright points of light danced in front of her eyes. Of course it didn't matter, not at all; she might as well rave at the kudzu, tell it to stop climbing on everything and choking it, hauling it down under those deadly green vines. A woman with a worried face directed Ruby to the clinic room and Ruby quickened her step. But when she got there, a man blocked the doorway. "You can't go in there," he said. Ruby didn't answer and she didn't stop. She was used to plowing past men such as he, and she knew her strength in these matters. There were things in this life that wouldn't give, that was a fact, but you put your shoulder against them and you shoved anyway.

"The hell you say," Ruby said. "If he's having one of his spells I know what to do."

"He's not having one of his spells," the man said. "I'm afraid he's dead."

She squinted and watched while the man collapsed into a tiny man and then grew life-size again. She had a steady mannish face, and when something stunned her that face turned smooth and still, as if everything had been hoarded and boarded up back of her eyes somewhere. Younger, she'd had a bold way of memorizing people, but that look had narrowed until she looked as if she were squinting to find something off in the distance. She'd been what they call *hot-blooded*, a fighter, all her people were fierce and strong, good people to have on your side. There was once something of the gypsy about her—a lancing eye and tongue and the gypsy darkness shot through with a ruby light. But that seemed like a long time ago. Now, at the time of Beau's death, Ruby was thirty-two, but she looked worn and strong. Her face had settled into a thick heavy grain like wood left lying outside since the day it was first split from the tree.

She'd gone there ready to scream at Beau, to smack him good for whatever he'd done, to drag him away from a fight one more time—he'd sat right there and heard what the judge had said—or from playing ball— he'd heard the doctor say that he was not to move faster than a walk if he wanted to live through the summer. She'd gone there ready to smack him, breathing harshly through her nose. She still had faith in the habit of hitting him—it roused him for a second or two, raised him out of the daze where he lived most of the time—a numb sort of habit that began as pressure behind her eyes and ended with the blunt impact and the sound of the flat of her hand landing hard against his skull.

The words she would have said and the sound of the blow she'd gone ready to deliver echoed and died in her head. Words rushed up and died in her throat—panicked words, words to soothe, to tame, to call him back—they rushed on her, but she forgot them halfway to her mouth and he lay so still. And that's how she learned that Beau Clinton, her only son and the son of Charles Clinton, was dead.

From then on it was just one amazement after another. She was amazed to find the day just as hot and close as it had been when she'd gone inside the school building. Everything should have been as new and strange as what had just happened. But the dusty trees stood silent against the tin sky, and below, in the distance, Atlanta's mirrored buildings still captured the sun and burned. Then the word *dead* amazed her, the way it came out of her mouth as though she said it every day of her life. "Well, that's what they tell me," she said to Mae Ruth as her sister sat there, hands gripping the steering wheel, exactly the way she'd been caught when Ruby dropped the word onto her upturned face. Then she was surprised by her sister's voice, how it boiled on and on shaped like questions, while Ruby breathed easily, lightheaded as a little seed carried on the wind. It was the most natural thing in the world that Beau should be dead; it had never been any other way. She patted her sister's hand: "That sneaky little thing just slipped right out on me," she said, chuckling to herself and wiping her eyes with the back of both hands. And her heart gave a surge and pushed the next wave of words out, as though she were speaking to Beau himself, come back from the dead to taunt her: "That sneaky little bastard," she said, "goddamn him."

Mae Ruth drove like a crazy woman—running red lights, laying on the horn, heading back toward Cotton Bottom at sixty miles an hour, gripping Ruby's wrist with one hand. "We got to get you home," she said.

"You do that," Ruby said. It would be nice to be back there among the skinny houses that bunched so close together you could hear your neighbor drop a spoon. She could slip in there like somebody's ghost and nobody'd find her again. That was the comfort of the village—the tight fit made people invisible. Too many people with too much trouble lived here, and everybody had gotten in the habit of going around deaf and blind just so they could have some peace now and again. She could hide there and never come out again, the way Old Lady Steel did after her kid got run over by a drunk: rocking on her porch day and night, cringing anytime tires squealed, and crying out at the sight of children in the street. That was a good use for life, she thought. She just might take it up like so many of the rest of her neighbors. They saw something once, something horrible, and it stuck to their eyes and the look of it never left them.

When they turned onto Rhineheart Street, Ruby sat up. "This ain't right, Mae Ruth, you took a wrong turn somewhere," she said anxiously. Her gaze never left the road that ran into a lake of white light, a mirage. In the glare, her street looked like a familiar place that had been warped. Then there was her house and the neighbors three deep on the narrow porch because somehow the news had gotten loose and run home before her. And she saw that the glare, the mirage, was a trick of the light on the windshield and she sat back and said, "Oh, now I get it. Fools you, don't it?" And she chuckled to herself. Someone had played a fine joke and now it was revealed.

The place where Ruby lives is called Cotton Bottom because of the cotton mill and because it's set in a low spot, a slump in the earth. The streets there run straight between the mill on one end of the place and the vacated company store on the other. In February when the weather settles in and the rain falls straight down, the air turns gray and thin, and there's silence as though the air had all been sucked into the big whistle on top of the mill and scattered again to the four corners of the earth. But in the summer, this place comes alive: the kids all go around beating on garbage-can lids, the air is so full of their noise you couldn't lose them if you tried, and the heat is so heavy you drag it with you from place to place.

The other border of this place is an old city cemetery with a pauper's field of unmarked graves on a low hill. Ruby used to go there between shifts or after work if it was still light and sit and listen to the wind roughing up the tops of the trees. They were the biggest trees she'd ever seen—oaks, some with crowns as wide as rooftops. Sometimes she thought of the roots of the trees, and it gave her a funny cold knot in the pit of her stomach to think of the roots and the bodies down there all mixed up together, the bones in among the roots, feeding the trees. She sat very quietly then, listening, as if she might catch that long story as it begins below the ground, as it rises and ends in the wind, in the tossing crowns of the oaks, in the way they sigh and bend and rise and lash the air again.

By eight o'clock the morning after Beau's death the sun looked brassy, as though it had burned all day. You had to breathe in small sips for fear you'd suck in too much heat and choke on it. Everybody was busy mopping at themselves, blotting their upper lips, women reaching back, lifting their hair and fanning their necks. Ruby didn't question how the night had passed; she watched while the sweating men struggled and pushed Beau's coffin up the narrow steps. And as she watched them coming closer she had one of her thoughts that seemed to come out of nowhere: Who is that stranger coming here?

She must have mumbled it to herself, because Dan Malvern and Mae Ruth both leaned over at the same time to catch what she'd said. "You'd think that'd be the easy part," she said, nodding toward the men with the coffin. Her arms hung at her sides; her face was slack, red and chafed-looking; her feet were planted wide to keep her upright. When they passed with Beau's coffin, her mouth went dry and her knees gave a little and Dan squeezed her arm and whispered: "Ruby, you hold on now." His warm breath on her ear annoyed her.

She tried not to listen to the rustling of the undertakers, the way they whispered as they fussed with the casket. They opened the casket and draped an organdy net from the lid to the floor and arranged it in a pool around the legs of the coffin stand and it all seemed to be happening beyond glass somewhere. The open lid was lined with shirred white satin—the richest cloth she'd ever been close to, that was for sure—gathered into a sunburst. Below it her son rested on his cushions with that stubborn look stuck to his face as though he were about to say No the way he did: jutting out his chin and freezing his eyes and defying the world to say to him Yes. "I never believed it," she said, and the words were cold drops in her ears, "not for a minute, and now look." And with that, a heaviness in her chest dragged on her, she turned on the people close by and said: "What was the way he should've come, tell me that? What other road could he have gone, why doesn't somebody tell me?" She grabbed Mae Ruth's arm.

"Be strong, darlin'," Mae Ruth said, from somewhere close beside her ear. "You got to be strong now."

She sank into the chair they had guided her to. It seemed that she'd been strong forever and in everything. Just after Beau was born sick she'd been strong in her faith. It had leapt on her one day like something that had been lying in wait getting ready. Afterwards, she'd gone about preaching the Word to anyone who'd stand still long enough to hear. That's when Charles Clinton had left for the first time. But the Lord had stayed, yes He had. He sent His mighty spirit down to fill her where she stood inside the Holiness Lighthouse Tabernacle over on Gaskill Street. He slung her onto the floor and filled her some more till she was so full of His spirit it pressed out against the walls of her chest, the walls of her skull, till she thought it might tear her open, trying to get free. She'd swooped down on her neighbor's houses after that night— praying, singing, weeping for all who lived there sunk in the sin and error of their ways, their sin a pressure building inside her as if it were her sin too. On Sunday, she sang the hymns with the force and flatness of a hammer hitting a rock, and on Wednesday evenings at prayer meeting, she beat the tambourine so hard that no one could stand close to her.

Then she'd been strong at work in the mill. First, she wielded the sharp razor, slashed open the bails so the cotton tumbled out. She roughed up the cotton and set it going toward the other room to be wooed and combed straight into fiber. They took note of how she worked and she was promoted to spooler. She stood beside the machines until she thought the veins in her legs might burst. She worked there yanking levers, guiding the threads as they sped along from one spool to the next. You had to yank the levers because the machines were old and balky, but the habit of it became the same as its action and the habit felt like fury after awhile. The threads flew by, never slowing, drawing tighter, flying from one spool to the next, the separate strands twisting, making miles of continuous threads for the big looms in the room beyond. The noise could deafen a person. The machines reared up and fell forward in unison and grabbed the fiber with metal claws and twisted the strands and rose and grabbed and fell again in rhythm all day and all night. The machines crashed like sacks full of silver being dropped again and again until she couldn't think, she could only watch the threads as they came flying out of the dark door and caught and flashed around the spools and flew out the other door.

For years she went to work during the day and at night she went to prayer meetings or to church singings. Later, when the Lord had eased up on her, she'd been with a bunch of women praying together one night when something ugly had come into their midst, something that smelled like burnt hair, and she'd stepped to the front like she knew just what to do. She'd been strong for them all and she'd led them in raising their voices louder in God's praise, every fiber set against the thing that had entered and filled the room right in the middle of prayer.

She'd known right away that whatever it might be, it was between this thing and Beau that she needed to stand. "Don't be afraid," she said. She made *quiet down* motions with her hands and she said: "You know, it comes to me to say there isn't nothing strange under the sun, not good and not bad either one. There is this thing we call the Devil and that old Devil turns things inside out and upside-down just that quick. Why, he spins you around and turns you around and scares you into thinking that he's stronger than anything you can call on, ain't that right?" And that, she told them, was the work this Devil was appointed to do on this earth.

But the work didn't stop there, oh no. The work went on working and people began to call themselves shameful and ugly before God. You could see it all the time, she told them, in the sad empty eyes around you. And the end of the work came when people turned into living tombstones over their own lives, when people hid their faces from one another; then the work was finished, she told them. "Now you've all seen it happen," she said. "Every single one of us in this room's seen it happen. But the way I figure it, we got to go one better than that. We got to stand up and say 'All right then, I got something for you better than what you got for me.' That's what we're all put here to do on this earth, and we can't ever let each other forget."

But that all seemed to have happened in another lifetime, in another country, a long time ago. Now there was this: the undertakers finished their business and left the house. Ruby dragged the reclining chair right next to the steel-gray coffin and eased herself down, feeling like a bag of flesh with a cold stone at the center. The coffin looked cold and shiny as coins, and her mind wandered there, counting the coins.

The green vinyl of the chair arms stuck to the back of her arms, and she saw the looks go around the room from Mae Ruth to her aunts, to Granny Brassler and the rest of them. Looks and sighs that flew around the room, passing from one to another, but she didn't care. She knew what they were thinking; she'd thought the same herself many a time about someone else: they were worrying that all the fight had gone out of her and wondering what they would do with another one to feed and wipe clean. In the village, that's the worst that can happen. "I'm here to stay," she said, "don't want no bath, don't want no supper, so don't start on me about it, just tend to your business and let me tend to mine."

She thought of that business and how she'd learned it well. To work, to live you had to be angry, you had to fight—that much she remembered. Her father had fought for his life, for all their lives, the time half the mill walked out, and the mill police came muscling into their house on fat horses. She could still see the door frame give, see her father's arm raised, all the veins standing up, before he brought the stick of stove wood down hard across the horse's nose. That was what life was for— fighting to keep it. That's how she'd been raised. All the good sweet passion and flavor of life soured if you just let it sit. Like milk left out, it could spoil. You had to be strong.

She smelled her own exhausted smell, like old iron, leaving her. Some-one had drawn the curtains across the front window. Someone wiped her face with a cloth. They bent over her one after the other. "Ruby, trust in the Lord," someone said. The thought rolled over her.

"I do," she said automatically, because the Lord was still a fact, more or less. "But it's got nothing do with him." She nodded toward her son. There. She was afraid to say it, but that was the truth. She snapped up straight, defying any of them to say differently. And just then she was taken by grief that pushed up in waves from the dead center of her. Each wave lifted her out of the chair and wrenched her voice from her throat, and that voice warned them: "I can't bear it." She couldn't open her eyes and inside the darkness there was a darker darkness, a weight like a ball, rolling against the back of her eyes. "I can't support it," she said and everything obliged inside her and fell in, and there was a quick glimpse of Beau the way he'd come home one time after a fight—tatters of blood in the sink, too much blood to be coming out of his nose and no way to stop it—and she was falling, tumbling over and over. Someone shouted her name; hands held her face, her hands. They bobbed all around her, corks on a dark water.

And when finally she opened her eyes, she glared at them as if they'd waked her from a deep sleep. She looked at Beau's face: they had messed with it somehow till it looked almost rosy, and chalky too, dusted with powder. His hair was washed straight back as though a wave had combed it, so silky and fine. He'd taken to dyeing his hair—the roots were dark and a soapy cloying smell rose through the organdy—and she said on the last receding wave of grief: "Lord, don't I wonder what's keeping him company right now."

"Now don't you go wandering off there all by yourself," Mae Ruth said. Her eyes were inches from Ruby's own. Ruby looked at her sister and almost laughed in spite of herself at the funny veiny nose, more like a beak than a nose, the eyes like her own, two flat dark buttons. Now Mae Ruth's life was hard too, but it didn't fit her so tight. She made room in it. She could tell funny stories, then turn around and tell somebody off just as neat and they'd stay told off. Once they'd both gone to a palm reader out by Doraville and the woman had scared Ruby, and Mae Ruth had said, "Lady, far's I'm concerned you get your jollies out of scaring people half to death." That was Mae Ruth for you. Just then her face looked like she was about to imitate the way the woman had looked. Mae Ruth could pull her face down long as a hound's and say "Doom" in this deep funny voice and you'd have to laugh.

Someone new had come into the room. She felt it in the stirring among the crowd around her chair, the way they coughed and got quiet. "Dan?" she said. He'd left the room after the coffin was carried inside and had gone to stand outside with the men on the porch. She looked up, expecting to find Dan's narrow brown face, and there stood Charles Clinton and his new wife, looking cool in spite of the heat. "Well, look who's here," she said, "look who's showing his face around here again." The welcome in her voice would have chilled you to the bone. "Look who's come back to the well," she said. "Well's dried up, Charles Clinton," she said. Her breathing turned down like a low gas flame. His new wife tried to get in her line of vision, but Ruby kept ducking around her in order to keep an eye fixed on Charles. And doesn't it always happen this way? When she was most in need of the mercy of for-getfulness—just then, she remembered everything.

She was sixteen, up from Atlanta to Gainesville for the Chicopee Mill picnic. He stood apart from everybody, working a stick of gum, his eyes all over her every time she moved. The lights inside the mill had come winging out through the hundreds of small windows. Like stars, they'd winked on the water of the millpond. And the roaring of the mill barely reached them across the mild night, and it was no longer noise that could make you deaf. The air was clean of cotton lint and clear, and the mill glittered. Everything glittered that way. Oh yes, she remembered that glittering very well. He had eyes like dry ice. She should have known; she should have turned and run with what she knew instead of thinking she could sass and sharp-tongue her way out of everything. He said: "You're Ruby Nelson from Atlanta, aren't you?"

"How'd you know?" she said.

"I have my ways," he said. And thinking about those ways had made her shiver.

She should have bolted for sure. She was supposed to have married Hudger Collins, and she had no business forgetting that. But Hudger was dull next to this one who had hair like corn silk, a sloped and angled face that reminded her of an Indian, and slanted eyes that watched and watched.

"I take you for a soldier," she said. And he smiled that smile that rippled out across his face and was gone so fast you couldn't catch it.

"Now you're a right smart girl," he said, wrapping one hand around the top of her arm. "It just so happens that I was in the Navy. You're real smart."

Later that night as they lay over near the edge of the woods where the grass was dry and patchy, he said her name again and again as if he wanted to drive it into her. Now when she saw him again a pit opened inside her and all the fiends let fly. She looked at Beau jealously, as if he might rise up and join his father and together they'd waltz away into the night. She said: "Charles Clinton, why don't you come over here and look at your boy. He's dead, he isn't going to get up and worry you now. You don't have nothing to be ashamed of anymore." She hated her voice when it got quavery like that. She heard a dry crackling sob burst out of Charles's throat and nose and she leaned her head back and smiled at the ceiling. "Why don't you come closer?" she said. "You know me and him both." She patted the edge of the coffin.

"Ruby," Mae Ruth rasped in her ear, "everyone's suffering, let him be."

Ruby hooted and smacked the arm of the chair. "Who's suffering?" she said. "How can you tell when Charles Clinton's suffering?"

"Oh, Lord," someone said from the corner of the room, "there's just no end to it."

He stepped closer, and for the first time she looked directly into his eyes. She was afraid to do it because she believed in what she saw in people's eyes. Halfway into another bitter word she saw his eyes and bit her lip. His eyes were washed out, drained, the color broken. His mouth turned down, and something elastic was gone from under his skin. He'd lost a tooth, and though his powder-blue leisure suit was clean, the backs of his knuckles looked grimy, like soot had been rubbed in under his skin. And those were the very eyes I searched and searched, she thought, the ones where I tried to see myself for so long. And those eyes stared at her, void of anything but a steady pain that threatened to break from him. It scared her so much she couldn't speak, and she leaned over and fussed with the net over Beau's coffin.

She didn't love Charles, never had, she'd known that from the start. But it acted like love, like a horse colt kicking inside her whenever he laid her down. And it was time—Ruby saw that in men's eyes when she passed them by on the street, and she saw it in her mother's eyes—time to start that kind of living and hope that she came to love him down the road. Hope that they'd come to be like Pappy and Mama had been before they'd moved to Atlanta to work in the mill, standing together in the field with their long burlap cotton sacks trailing behind them, picking cotton together and filling those sacks till the whole length of them was stuffed with their time together. That's what she'd seen could come of a married life. That's what she'd believed.

She wore a tight dress of lilac-colored imitation linen all the way to Jacksonville on the bus. It was their honeymoon trip, but all the while she had the sense that she was riding along beside herself. Away over there was the girl who was wild crazy in love, but she, Ruby, couldn't get to her. All the while she waited for the special feeling to come up in her throat, the way a spring starts up out of the ground. She wanted that feeling, but it didn't come. She didn't love him, but she shut that knowledge away. That was her secret. She always believed it would be different, and that was her secret. And her faith, and her shame.

So, love or no love, and faithful to another law, Beau was born barely moving, hardly breathing. His lips stayed blue for the longest time. And both times—after the birth when the doctor had come in peeling off his rubber gloves, talking about some little something in Beau's heart that wouldn't close right, and now—Charles had stood there looking like something broken, his face taking on no more expression than the dead boy's. Only his eyes still spoke, and his hand trembled like an old man's hand as he lifted it to wipe his mouth. Why, I'm better off than he is, she thought. For all this, I'm better off. It was cold, proud comfort. The sweet vengeful cry she'd hoped for, the bass string she'd hoped to hear singing inside her at the sight of him broken by the death of his only son, wouldn't sound. She grabbed for Mae Ruth's hand because the falling sensation was creeping in behind her eyes again.

The fact of the boy had stuck in Charles like a bone in his throat. She spent her days sitting in the Grady Hospital clinics with Beau's heavy head lolling over one arm, because there had to be an answer. You'd have thought the boy was contaminated the way Charles's hands had stiffened when he picked up the baby. You'd have thought the boy was permanently crippled or contagious the way he held him away from his body. "Lots and lots of people's born with something just a little off," she said. "Lord, some of them never even know it," she told Charles pointedly. Of course, as things had gone on, the depth of the damage had been revealed, as it always is. By the time Beau had surgery on his heart at the age of five, Charles wouldn't even come up to sit with him. He said it was too humiliating to sit in the charity ward, where people treated you like you were something to be mopped off the floor.

And after Beau had managed to grow up and after he started coming home with pockets full of dollar bills, Charles could only say "What's going on?" She could almost see the words forming on his lips as he looked at his son in the coffin. Charles never understood a thing; that was his sorrow. She didn't want him near her.

She remembered her own sorrow, how it had struck so deep it had seemed to disappear inside her the first time Beau got caught in Grant Park in a car with a rich man from the north side of town. He was nothing but a baby, twelve years old. The police cruiser brought him home because the other man was not only rich, he was also important, and he didn't want trouble on account of Beau. Her son smelled like baby powder and dirty clothes. He was growing a face to hide behind. His lips were swollen as though someone had been kissing them too hard, and she stared and wondered whether that brand was put on his mouth by love or by hate or by some other force too strange to be named. She had to drag Charles into the room. "It ain't the money," Charles had shrieked at his son. "I know it ain't just for money." That was as much of the discovery as he could force out of his mouth; the rest was too terrifying.

"Why?" she asked her son. Her voice bored into him. She held onto his skinny arm and watched the skin blanch under her fingers.

"They talk nice to me," Beau said.

"Honey, those men don't care about you," she said, watching Charles turn away, watching Beau watch him turn away.

When Charles left, he said their life wasn't fit for human beings, and he moved out to Chamblee. He'd never lifted a hand against her. By Cotton Bottom standards that made him a good man. But she felt that violence had been done to her; there was a hardness and a deadness inside that made her swerve away from people as though she might catch something from them.

During that time, she went to Dan Malvern. It was right: he was her pastor as well as her friend, and together they'd puzzled over that deadness and prayed endlessly for forgiveness for her. She was never quite sure for what sin she needed to be forgiven, but she'd kept quiet and prayed anyway.

Now, sitting beside Beau's coffin, she'd come a whole revolution: she felt like asking for forgiveness about as much as she felt like getting up and walking to New York City. Forgiveness belonged to another lifetime, to people like Dan who had a vision left to guide them. Once, Dan had seen armies of souls pouring toward heaven and hell while he stood at the crossroads, frantically directing traffic. From that day on, he said, his cross and burden was to stand there until the Lord called him home. Now Dan stood just outside the door with his big black shoes sticking out of his too-short pants. You had to be gentle with Dan; he always had to be invited, so she said: "Dan'l, you're always welcome here." He crossed the room with one long country stride and grabbed her hand and rubbed it and said: "Are you holding up all right in the care of the Lord?"

"Getting by," she said. His eyes looked old. She took his hand more warmly and said: "Dan, bless you." But when she took her hand away it hung in front of her, bare and powerless. And there was Beau, dead, his life full of violence in spite of that hand, and she said "Oh," and bit her knuckle. Dan hauled her up, pulled her into the kitchen, and shut the door behind him. He rested a hand on her shoulder and threw back his head, and the tears squeezed out through the lashes like beads. She moved to embrace him but he stopped her. He was maneuvering into the current, setting his back to the wind. He shifted and hunched his shoulders: "Kneel down with me, sister," he said.

"Oh, all right, Dan," she said, sighing. She knew this part of the ritual, when they had to forget each other's names in order that God might hear their prayers. She knelt down facing him. She had to endure this because when Dan wasn't busy acting like God's own special riding-mule, he was one who shed a steady light onto her life, a light in which she could stand holding her shame and be loved, shame and all. Mae Ruth was another, only her light was barer and warmer. Dan remembered her and could remind her sometimes of ways she'd been that she could hardly recall. He knew her practically all the way back. She could go to him feeling small and cold, the way lights look in winter, and come away after talking about nothing for a few hours, with her feet set squarely on this earth again.

But something happened when he talked about God, when he started to pray. They didn't have much in common then. He became hard, he saw things in black and white and spoke of them harshly through his gritted teeth. His jawbone tried to pop through the skin, and his black hair began to tremble with indignation, and he jerked at the words as if he were chewing stringy meat. He strained after the words as though he could pull them from the air: "Lord, help her to see that sin is there," he began, "that sin has taken away her son. Help her to see the sin, to look on the *wages* of sin and to ask forgiveness, and help this woman, your servant, to know in her HEART the sin and to call OUT to the Lord in her hour of need."

She would have laughed had she not felt so lonely. Dan could let himself down into it anytime and drink of the stern comfort there. She envied him that plunge. She imagined that the relief must taste hard and clean as water from a deep well sunk through rock. She closed her eyes and tried to pray, to sink into that place. It would be so good to believe again in the laws, she thought, because those laws named the exile and the means of coming home in such clear ringing tones. First there was sin, a person drifting in some foreign land, then confessing the sin, then redemption, then hallelujah, sister, and welcome home. She felt for her heart, for its secret shame, and found only a sort of homesickness, a notion that there was some place that she'd forgotten, a place where there were no such people as foreigners, a place big enough to hold sin, grief, ugliness, all of it.

But forgetfulness, that was the sickness, the worm in the heart. Words like *good* and *evil* and *death* simplified things and rocked you and lulled you and split things apart. There was something else moving back there; she could barely feel it but it was there.

She watched his face move through the prayer, laboring against a current, and when he came back to himself with a great bass "Amen" she said "Amen" too, and a sob broke from her at the sound of that blank word. Her shoulders shook and her head wagged from side to side and she said: "Dan, I'm gonna tell you something. It must tire out the Lord himself to listen to all that talk about sin all the time. There must be some wages due to you for that, wouldn't you say?"

"Ruby," he said, "don't blaspheme now, don't go piling sin on sin."

At that, she labored to her feet and shook herself. "The way I understand it," she said, "we're all born fools, ain't that right? Nothing we can do about that. What's the sin in that? Seems like everything we do has got wages." The man of God with thunder and sword faded, and his face was restored to him, and the Daniel she knew came back, looking sheepish, pulling on his bottom lip. "So where are you going to look for better wages is what I want to know?"

"I know you're under a terrible strain," he said, "but I don't know where you get such talk." But by then she was halfway into the other room. And seeing her son in his coffin again, she felt she was coming on him fresh, and she saw how much Beau's face looked like her own— much more like her own than like Charles's face—and it scared her. The life he'd led showed in the set defiance of the chin, in the squint-marks around the eyes that the mortician's powder puff couldn't erase. That look was stuck there for all eternity, and he was only sixteen years old.

It was the same look he'd given her anytime she'd asked him about those men and why he went with them. She'd fought for him for so long and the fatigue of that fight caught up with her again and she was tossed up on a fresh wave of grief. She began to sob and twist, turning this way and that, trying to escape from the people who pressed in from all sides, suffocating her. Strong hands gripped her and shook her, and she recognized Dan and Mae Ruth, though neither of them spoke and her eyes were squeezed tight. "Get it out," Mae Ruth said. "You go on and get it all out, then you come on back here with us."

"I think I want to sleep for a while now," she said, opening her eyes.

"You want a nerve pill?" Mae Ruth asked. She shook her head. She stopped beside the coffin.

"Well, now," she said softly, "don't he look sweeter without that harsh light on him?" During the minute that she'd had her spell of grief, the light had shifted, softened to gray, pressing in at the windows. As the light softened in the room, her son's face softened too; he looked younger and not so angry at the air. He hadn't looked that way since he was a baby, and she loved him with a sweetness so sharp she felt she might be opened by it.

And what became of that sweetness, she wondered, as she pushed through the curtains into her bedroom. By what devilish sly paths did it run away, leaving the harsh light that never ceased burning on him? It took too much effort to remember that he was not just that strange being who'd thrashed his way through her life and out, leaving wreckage in his path. He was also another thing, but it made her head hurt to think of it. She pulled off her slippers and unhooked her slacks at the waist. It was easier to think that the march he'd made straight to his grave was the sin, to call that life ugly and be done with it. But the changing of the sweet to the ugly was the most obvious trick in the book. Anyone with eyes could see through that one. There was a better trick. She thought how much she wished she could still believe that the Devil dreamed up the tricks. That would explain the ashes around her heart.

But never mind: the better trick was that the soft curtains of forget- fulness dropped so quietly you did not hear them fall. It was forgetfulness that made things and people seem strange: that was sin if ever there was sin. Still, remembering things made you so tired. Better to live blind, she thought.

Once she'd begged Beau to remember who he was. She'd meant *her* people, the Nelson side, dignity and decency deep enough to last through two or three lifetimes. But they were as strange to him as the whole rest of the wide world. "Sure," he'd said, "I know who I am. I'm a Nelson from the cotton patch and a Clinton straight from hell." Seeing her shocked, with her hand pressed to her throat, he'd laughed and said: "Well ain't I? You're always saying 'Goddamn your daddy to hell.'" The way he'd imitated her, his mouth drawn back like a wild animal's, had terrified her. "That means I come from hell, don't it, Mama?"

She shook her head in frustration and eased herself down onto her bed. She wished that he were there, given back to her for just one minute, so that she could collect, finally, all she'd needed to tell him, so that she could tell him in words he'd have to understand, that if one person loved you, you were not a chunk of dead rock spinning in space. That was what she'd tried to tell him all during the long winter just past.

That was the winter when the mill had stepped up production again and had taken on everyone they'd laid off. She'd gotten a job in the sewing room. All day she sat there sewing, while her mind worked to find an end to the business with Beau. It was quieter there than in the weave room and she could forget about everything but one seam running under her needle, one train of thought going through her mind. Last winter he was gone more than he was home, and his face was pale and sunken around the cheekbones. Every so often she'd start way back at the beginning and come forward with him step by step, puzzling out the way and ending always in the same spot: the place she'd seen him staring into. She turned it over and over like the piece-work in front of her, looking for the bunched thread, the too-long stitch that would give, the place where her mind had wandered and the machine had wandered off the seam.

Once she'd taken half a sick-day and had gone home to find him staring at nothing. She'd barely been able to rouse him, and when she'd bent over him she'd been repelled by his sweet sick odor. But it was the way he'd looked that stuck in her mind: tight blue jeans, a black shirt, a red bandanna wound tightly around his neck. And his face, when he'd finally turned it up to her and smiled dreamily into her screaming, was sly and serene as the face of a wrecked angel. It was the smile that made her blood shut off. When he smiled that way, there was a shudder in the room like the sound that lingered in the air if the looms shut down, and she knew that he was bound to die, that he was already looking into that place. She saw it in his eyes all winter.

The cotton came in bailed through enormous doors and was pulped, twisted, spun, woven, mixed with polyester and squeezed and pressed and dyed and made into sheets and blouses and printed with tulips, irises, gardens of blowing green.

It wasn't right that she should worry herself the way she did all winter. She was up all hours of the night waiting for him, but half the time he never came home. Then one day she just went into his room and nailed the window shut, and when he went into his room that night, she locked him in and sat in the living room with arms folded, crying, as he bumped and crashed around and screamed awful names at her. It was for his own good and because she loved him. And if you loved somebody, she told herself, you had to make a stand and this was her stand. In the morning she'd explain to him, in words he'd have to understand, that she did it out of love.

Afterwards she was ashamed, and she never told anyone, not even Mae Ruth. She felt that she'd been in a dream, a fever dream, where crazy things made perfect sense and everything hung suspended way up high in clear air. But it didn't matter anyway because when she unlocked the door to set him free in the morning, he was gone. Glass all over the floor and the window kicked out.

She woke up after dark, groping around with one hand, looking for something on the bedspread. She'd been dreaming of black rocks looming over her, and at the base of the rocks, hundreds of people scrambling around, picking up busted-off pieces of the largest rock and holding them up in the moonlight. She groped her way out in to the living room, and people patted her and helped her ease down into her chair again.

All night she slept and woke. Whenever she woke, one pair of hands or another reached for her, and once she tried to say: "I want to thank you all for being so good." But her voice broke when she said "good," and someone said: "Hush, you'd do the same."

The voices went round and round her, a soothing drone that filled the room. Then the sun was up, the day was up bright and blazing. She looked at her son beside her in his coffin, and the thought of his going broke over her like a wave. And as the day rushed back at her, so did her memories of Beau, which were as sharp as if he were still alive. In fact, they were hardly memories at all, they were more like the small sightings we keep of someone's day-to-day life.

This is how he came in: her body had threshed with him for two days and a night. Then his sickness: she walked him day and night, while over on Tye Street Granny Brassler and the others went down almost to their knees, taken by the spirit, shouting: "Devil, take your hands off that baby."

He was never full of milk and quiet; he was long and gangly and he never fleshed out. And all the while he was growing a man's mind. By the time he was twelve, right after Charles left, he'd stay gone for days, nobody knew where. Then, last June, he and his friends had started sticking closer to home, robbing the men in the park nearby. That's when she'd set herself against him in earnest. The last time she'd smacked him good had been right there in the kitchen just as she was setting supper down on the table, when he'd come busting through the door yelling how someone was a nigger motherfucker. She'd grabbed his face and squeezed and said: "Don't you never let me hear you talking like trash again. You are not and never will be trash, and don't you forget it."

"Everybody calls me trash," he said. "What makes you any different?"

"Cause I'm your people," she said. "Cause you're mine."

"Ain't that funny?" he said. "That's what they say too."

Every time, somebody else was holding the gun, but the next time, or the time after that, she knew it would be Beau, and then he would be tried as an adult and sent away to the real prison up at Alto, and that would be that. Last June they'd only taken him as far as the jumping-off place, the *juvenile evaluation center* they called it. But it was a prison as surely as Alto where he'd end up someday, looking out with the others at the blue mountains beyond the high wire fence.

She wasn't like the other mothers, the ones who wept or pleaded or shouted. That time was long gone, and she knew it. She was there for another reason but it had no name, only a glare, like the harsh sunlight on the white walls of his room. She listened. He beat time on his thigh with the heel of one hand and talked, and sometimes he looked up and said: "Ain't that right?" And with knees spread, elbows resting on her knees, hands loosely knotted and fallen between her knees, she looked back at him and said: "No, that isn't right, Beau, not as I see it," in the strongest voice she could muster.

Staying, listening and staying, was a habit she'd had to learn. The first visit to the evaluation center had ended with her reeling out of the room, driven back by his words that were so ugly they seemed to coil like tar snakes out of his mouth. But she went back, *she did go back*, and she knew she must never let herself forget that. She went back and she listened to every word, and she had never felt so empty, so silent. The city, the room turned strange around her, and the only familiar face was the one just in front of her, the one with the mouth that opened and said: "You ought to see their faces when Roy shows them the gun."

She looked up quickly, hearing that voice again just as clear as if it were still ringing off the walls of the jail. She looked at his dead face, and her head began to tug with it, and she stood and bore down on him while all around her the dark closed in as it does when a person's about to faint. Only she was far from fainting. The dark narrowed around her until she stood inside a dark egg looking down at her son, the stranger made up for his grave, who rested in a wash of light that lingered at the core of the outer dark shell. And as she watched and listened—watching and listening with every cell—the stranger's face dropped away and the whole harsh chorus of his life tangled in her and sang again, and she remembered what she'd seen in the jail, what she'd seen a long time before the jail and had forgotten and carried with her the whole stubborn way and had never wanted to believe, and had believed: he was lost, and he had always been lost. His hands were folded, his face eternally still. Whatever he had been, he was now, forever. She gripped the coffin's edge while the fury rose up her legs and belly and chest and gathered inside her skull, a familiar pressure, and she wanted to strike or curse someone over what had become of this child. From the moment he was born, he was lost, *her own child*, lost. For a long time she'd believed that he was two children: one hers, the other possessed by another power. All his life, she'd worked to pull or wrestle *her* child free from the hold of his lost brother, to love the one, rage against the other and drive him out. She touched the wing of his nose where it flared out so pretty, then pulled her fingers away quickly and slipped her hand into the pocket of her dress. But it was too late. When she touched his skin, everything collapsed and ran together again, and there was no such thing as love apart from rage or this child freed from his own lost self. Nothing could be untangled, nothing pulled apart. Not then. Not now. Not ever. The roots all went down deep—the root of love, the root of fury, the root of the child—like the roots of the oaks that grew on the hill in the old cemetery on the border of this place. Down they went, and down, and mixed with the bones until the bones were roots and the roots, bones, and the trees grew tall over everything.

She stood very still, looking at his pinched white face. For the first time, she understood a Bible verse that people had always quoted at her. Dan had used it, everybody used it to tell her how to feel about trouble but she, Ruby, understood it for herself now, and no one could take it from her. *I will lift up mine eyes to the hills*, she thought. She looked and she saw the crowns of the oaks brushing the sky, and below the trees she saw the tangled maze of the roots running through the hill of the dead. That was all the comfort there was.

She sat down in her chair with a moan and began to rock herself and to pat the edge of the coffin in time with her rocking. She saw the panic start up on every face, and she pressed a hand to her chest to quiet herself. "Things should slow down," she said, "so that a person can have time to study them."

As though they'd been held back, people crowded into the room again. The air got sticky and close, and the smell of flowers and sweat and not quite clean clothes and the soapy smell that hung over Beau's coffin began to make her dizzy. So she focused on Charles and a prickly rash began to spread over her neck and arms and her vision began to clear. Finally she said, in a lazy kind of voice—lazy like a cottonmouth moccasin stirring the water—"Charles, you and your wife's taking up more than your share of air in here. Why don't you just step out onto the porch?" They ignored her. But Mae Ruth clucked her tongue.

"Ruby, shame, he's still the boy's father; you can't deny him that," she said.

"I know that," Ruby snapped. "Don't I wish I didn't."

She closed her eyes and wished for the old way, the old law that said *the ones that give, get back in kind.* She wished that the weight of that law might lie in her hand like a rock. She wished for some revenge sweet enough to fit his crimes, the kind of revenge that came from a time before people were condemned to stand linked to one another. She could make him order the tombstone and have Beau's name drilled there, yes, and be gone before the funeral started. She tried it out on herself but the little cold thrill the thought gave her wasn't enough to satisfy. Oh me, she said to herself, there isn't no country far enough away where I could send him. She opened her eyes and searched the room for a single unfamiliar face on which to rest her eyes, and found not a one. And she felt the whole dense web of love and grief descending, settling over her shoulders as it had before, in the prison. "This don't ever stop," she said out loud. And she thought of how she had never loved Charles, not in the way that a woman loves a man, and how, still, he was part of the law that turned and turned and bound them all together, on each turn, more closely than before.

Then there was the vault out under the strong sun without a tent to cover it, and the flowers were wilting under the sun, and Mae Ruth's strong voice led off a song. Then Daniel spoke of dust, and of heaven and the Redeemer for a long time. They were in a new cemetery and the lots were parceled out of a flat field. Through the thin soles of her shoes, Ruby could feel the rucks and ripples of once-plowed ground.

She wore a dress of hard black cloth that trapped the heat inside and made the sweat trickle down her sides. Charles stood on the edge of the crowd, his chin sunk onto his chest, and he looked faded under the light that seemed to gather into a center that was made of even whiter and hotter light.

Ruby barely listened to the resurrection and the life. She saw her son's face: surrounded by darkness now, closed in darkness forever. Those words Dan said, they weren't the prayers, she thought, not the real prayers. The prayers rested in the coffin, in the dark there. Her eyes followed its deaf, dumb lines. The prayer was his life that she couldn't save, and the prayer was her own life and how it continued. And the prayer never stopped; lives began and ended, but the prayer never stopped. She looked at the ground and had the sensation that she'd been standing there for a very long time, trying to memorize each one of the scrappy weeds that had begun to grow again out of the plowed-over land. Those weeds were like the threads; she watched them in the same way. The threads flew toward her like slender rays of light and twisted spool to spool and disappeared through another door toward the looms beyond. The sound of their coming and going made one continuous roar.

Because she wanted it that way, they all stayed as the coffin was lowered into the hole. She stepped up to the side of the grave and saw her own shadow, thrown huge, on the lid of the vault. It startled her so much she stepped forward instead of back and the edges crumbled under her shoes. Then there were hands on her arms, and she looked down again and saw Mae Ruth's shadow and Dan's beside her. It was as though they were in a boat together, looking over the side. And the sun beat down on them all: on the living, and into the grave, and on those who had lived and died.

HARBOR HOUSE

Emily Ellison

Jayne Mateson
25

I t's like this every morning at about this time, between three o'clock and four, that time when everyone is finally asleep and no one has started stirring. *I* should be sleeping, there's no other time. But my eyes won't close. So I sit up and look at my babies and all the others around the room on cots and bunks. What's to become of us?

Another girl and I take turns watching each other's children and we take opposite shifts waiting tables at Denny's. I've got the dinner hour and all the while I'm serving patty melts and chicken fingers to other people's children I'm wondering what that girl, Vera, is feeding Tommie and Lee Ann.

They bring in speakers sometimes, "experts" they call them, that give us tips on getting out on our own. This one woman, she's from the county, she comes and tells us we've got to change our lot in life. We've got to get some training she says, some education. And this black girl, Leeta, she don't even raise her hand but yells out, "Yeah? When you think we gonna get us a education, honey? While you tending our kids?"

I was brought up right, wore little white gloves trimmed in lace to Sunday School, patent leather shoes that slipped over the wooden floors. I was taught manners and morals and all the Golden Rule and Ten Commandments. Not to steal or lie. Cheat or kill. Now I stuff anything from Denny's that will fit in my pockets or purse. Crackers, desserts, foil-wrapped baked potatoes. Things off the salad bar. I bring it back and give it to my children at night in case they didn't get enough to eat or in case I have to leave here and there may not be anything for the next night's supper.

I was going to be a teacher. Can you imagine? I was going to inspire our nation's youth. I have two of my own now, pale and timid, two I steal for, would lie for, beg for. And if I had to, I'd pull a gun on somebody too. That's all that matters, all that my eyes point to, that

thin black line that shows the way to where my kids will be safe and
sleeping where nobody can take what they don't have away.

Carter Jones
42

My mother was so small there was rarely a chair that allowed her
feet to touch the floor. Her face was small, too, like a tight hard nut,
chestnut. I don't mean to imply *she* was hard, because of course she
wasn't. Only her quick, small, overworked body was hard and efficient,
never missing a step or making unnecessary movements. My father,
my namesake, was the opposite. Tall, limber-limbed, with hands and
feet the size, it seemed to me as a child, of rug beaters. What an odd
pair they must have made to strangers, and yet those who knew them,
and during their time that was almost everyone in Atlanta (for the Atlanta
of the fifties and sixties was not much more than a town, really), thought
of them as perfectly suited, a perfect unit. They were the ones who
started Harbor House, in the basement of the Unitarian Church and later
in an old two-story clapboard off Moreland Avenue.

Those were more prosperous times but even then there was always
a family or a single mother who temporarily needed help. And my
parents were there to give it to them. There was a steady stream of
people—young women, children, an occasional bum—who filled the
rooms, and, although there was rarely an empty bed, there always seemed
to be a place for whoever needed it.

Now, now there are never enough beds, never enough rooms, never
enough spoons or sheets or toilet paper. Never enough anything. Liz
and I started working at Harbor House, at the old place off Moreland,
before my parents died. And later we kept going, first to a larger house,
and a larger one, and then finally to an abandoned warehouse that we
have converted into a refuge against the last days of the twentieth century.

It is a weak refuge, this ten-thousand-square-foot hole of steel and tin
and concrete and linoleum, cheap paint and curbside furniture. We beg,
borrow, and maybe more for these green plastic plates, hand-me-down
everything, twenty-gallon cans of potatoes, frozen turkeys. There was
a time when we used to be able to get a family back on the right track.
We'd get the husband sobered up, the children clean, both parents good
jobs. We'd find them a decent place to stay, shoes on their feet, soap
in the shower, flour and sugar and coffee in the cupboards. We did
it all the time, one after the other. A very few would end up back on
the street again. But not most of them. Most would come back in a
year or two, bring us a gift, a mess of turnips or a chocolate pound
cake to thank us. We'd see we'd made a difference, that maybe a life
or lives had been changed.

Now if someone came back, I doubt if I'd remember them. Now there is no time to single out a family or even one person, to help a guy make a contact and get him on a payroll and his name on a health insurance policy. We're too busy shoveling stew, washing pillow cases, scrubbing johns, begging bakeries for their stale bread and restaurants for leftovers, asking the city or the county or the state or Uncle for one more thousand. *When will it end?* I can see Liz asking with her stares at the endless flow of down-and-out, shirtless, shoeless, chemically dependent, stoned-out-of-their-gourd, layed-off, sold-out, washed-up, unmarried, left-behind, abused, used, pained humanity.

I used to think this was the right way, maybe the only way to raise children. To show them the way the other half lives. But, because we could not stand the thought of buying dining room chairs or a new set of matching towels when there wasn't space for that one more woman and her shivering kids, we've little by little sold most of our personal possessions. Furniture, any little art we had, the books, records, wedding china. The house. We live here too now, upstairs. We, my children, *we* are the other half. I have no more, sometimes not even more spirit, than the rest of them except for my fifty-thousand-dollar northeastern education. Sometimes that's one of the things that keeps me awake at night, what I could do with all that loot that went to Harvard. And the rest of the time I'm thinking, What have I done? What have I done to Liz and my boys? Where will the money come from when it's time for *them* to go to college? But we can't leave it, can't turn our backs on what we know will be wave after wave after wave of needy.

And so we stay. And late at night like this, way after midnight, I thank God that that little tight spring of a woman and her rubbery-boned husband are not here to see it. She had a photograph of a lighthouse she hung on a wall in the front room of the old house. So they could all see their safe harbor, she used to say. Yeah. I wonder.

Hanks Morgan
33

They don't like nobody hanging round here later than seven A.M. in the morning, least ways not the men, so R.W. and me go to the Public. It don't open to nine. Sun out, we take our time and walk on over there. It's raining we still walk but we do double time. Maybe an old 'Lanta Journal held up over our heads.

There's nothing they can do becausing it's a public library but they don't like it you can tell. I get me a *People* magazine. I hear R.W. call it that, and the next time I pick one up that looks the same way I call it *People* too and he never gets a clue that I'm not taking in the words. I just drifted, see, over reading the little bit I was in school and nobody seemed to think it amounted to anything one way or the other. One or two words here or there I might know. *Run. Stop. Boy.* I hold the magazine up in front of me and it looks like I'm reading because I look at the pictures so slow. Most times I carry a newspaper under my arm. Sometimes R.W. will say, "How many times you going to read that, son?" but he still don't know.

He is snoring by ten and I have to nudge him. You're reading they can't say anything to you, but you start sleeping they start looking like they're going to be waving their thumb at the door.

It's quiet in there, just that little fast clicking from people on them computers. Maybe some pages turning, a chair scraping the floor. But so quiet compared to the way it is at the House. There's noise here even in the dead of night. Men and children crying, loud snoring, some old woman hollering out. But at the Public it's as neat and clean and still as one of them shelved books. Cool in the summer, warm on cold days like this, and the most comfortable chair I'm ever going to find. Chemical smells like new carpet and hard plastic and metal. Not the way you'd think books would smell. But I like it, *clean*, and I breathe it in and try to take clean with me back here at nights in my lungs. It's ours, the Public, R.W. says, our tax dollars pay it. And I laugh at him and say, "Yeah, how would you know, son?"

Benjamin Bolt
61

White men, colored. Women. Babies. They're all the same. Faces, faces, all these same faces. But not me. Not me with my own place. Curtains on the windows, deadbolt on the door, five little jars of dried beef in the cupboard. Boxes of macaroni. Beans, peas, Green Giant creamed corn. That one can of pink salmon that cost me almost two dollars. Collecting *dust*.

Me! Me with my own shoe stand, and probably now some colored fellow's got it, proud as a screeching peacock, flinging *my* soft rags over a fat man's shoes. All left behind. All over a woman who never meant me a minute's harm.

The softest cheeks you ever felt. Oh, little crisscross lines, little x's, a thousand wrinkles hanging on the sides of that face but the softest wrinkles you ever felt. And the softest words, never once Ben, you shouldn't have, Ben, you can't, Ben, don't you dare. It was like saying Ben with lamb's ear for breath. *Ben?*

Oh, why are we fools? Why do we stay across the street, watching at such distance, jumping back and hiding every time she opens the door, hiding for fear our loved one will see us and call us home?

I eat this salty food with the twisted metal spoon, sleep on this three-inch mattress that smells like dirty hair and scalp. I take a pee at eleven and four at the McDonald's, my shoes making black tracks on that wet tile floor. All out of chickenshit fear of softness.

All these same, same faces. Same. So same, misery. But not me. Not ever me. I am *different*. You son-of-a! I've got somewhere to go.

Caroline Undset
36

In the beginning I was critical. I thought most of these people were only asking for handouts, were doing nothing but sponging off Carter and Liz. I mean where I come from, if you're out of a job, you call someone. Your father or uncle knows someone who knows someone and a call is made and you take over a résumé, talk a little about each other's families, where you went to school, what clubs you were in, where you go in the summer, who your neighbors are. You *get* a job. I had little empathy, to be honest. Even after a year or so, I was more full of scorn than concern.

And then Bea Wallace's husband lost his job. He was an executive with one of the larger insurance companies that had been downtown forever. The Wallaces had a weekend place at Big Canoe near my parents, and a nice big Tudor house right down the street from us near Brookwood Station. There were four children either in or on their way to college. He was mid-fifties, I suppose, not as old as my father but a good deal older than we are. No one ever expected it of Mr. Wallace. And even after it happened no one ever expected them to lose their house.

They *must* have had savings, but after eight or nine months of paying tuitions and making the mortgage there wasn't anything left. My mother said they called in Clements Auction House from Tennessee and sold everything off piece by piece. Even Bea's Audubon prints and her collection of cloisonné and ivory figures.

Where do you stay? That's what I've heard so many of these people ask. Not where do you live, but where do you *stay*? Because they're always staying with someone I guess. Or maybe because what they're doing doesn't seem like living. I saw one of Bea's long-legged children outside Kroger a few months ago and I caught myself almost asking, "Where do you stay?"

Now I come three or four times a week and help Liz out with the lunches. I've pulled old highchairs and toys out of the attic and basement—Tinker Toys and Mr. Potato Head, an old box of shells from Sea Island my children used to like to play with—and hauled them over in the back of my station wagon. Joe and I go through our closets every season and I bring over boxes of shirts and jackets, shoes, sweaters, some of my old dresses. I know a lot of their names and have held their children. But it's more than that. It's like insurance. Maybe if I keep putting in, I'll never have to use it, like making the payments on a big umbrella policy against disaster.

Sarah
Age Withheld

Come on, have a seat, have some lunch with me, hon. Sure, I know what you want: My Story. That's what they all want, those who come in thinking they can change a few scrambled lives with some donated books, a couple of sermons, and a lesson on proper dressing. Dignity 101: We give you dignity and you give us your story. Except they go spread that story around like it's storebought icing: nothing.

Okay, how's this. My father was a neurosurgeon, my husband a veterinarian. I was once a foreign correspondent. Sure, write it down. Let me give you a pencil. And some paper, honey. Now don't miss this, we're just getting started. I did TV weather. Sure, prime time, network. Designed my own line of clothing. Did some chiropractory. Taught for a while, advanced composition. Later chemistry.

Let's see, what else? I raised seven children, sent them all to college and graduate school by cleaning houses. Walked ten miles to do it. Ten miles there, ten miles back. Cooked every meal they ever ate, ironed every stitch of school clothing. Sure they all come see me, hon, every one. All eight of them.

Here's more. I once put a hot iron, after thirty minutes on the cotton/linen setting, down on my first husband's arm. Did time for slamming the second one in the forehead with a cast-iron skillet. Shot old number three through the knee while he was sleeping. Yeah, we're on the best of terms, all five of us.

Oh, and there's this. Tell a little girl to sit pretty. Tell a little girl to mind her manners. Tell a little girl she doesn't have to worry about a thing because daddy or the next man can fix it.

What's the matter, hon? Don't you have an appetite? Sure, go on, but how about leaving that baloney and macaroni on the table? Come back now. Come back anytime, we'll go on with the rest of it.

Stubbs Calloway
54

I've had all kinds of jobs in all parts of the country. My favorite was this time I worked for a few months up in Kentucky. I worked around horses for this woman who owned some stables. Kept fresh shavings in the stalls, fresh water and oat mixture in those rubber buckets. I painted this wet stuff that looked like paper cement all around on their hoofs to keep them from drying out and cracking. Braided their manes, hosed them off and brushed them, walked them out to the pastures when people got through riding.

Another time I worked as a groundskeeper at a country club. I helped sew the bent grass on the greens, Bermuda on the fairways. Kept it all mowed down just so, like outdoor carpet. Kept flowers blooming round all the different seasons.

My one regret is not having a education. I know just little pieces of this and that. Not the whole ball of wax like that woman who owned the stables. She knew everything that had to do with horses, every strap and buckle in the tack room, all about diet and diseases, how to ride them proper. Those big tall animals followed her around like gnats on a mayonnaise sandwich. I just picked up bits from her and some more from the head gardener at the golf course, some more from a fellow that owned a restaurant. Some here about stripping furniture, some there about painting and sheetrocking. A little this, a little that, what pieces people showed me. But I'm no expert on nothing. That's your safety net, having a education. Being master of the facts on something or another.

Liz Jones
39

It's quiet this time of day, three in the afternoon, about the only time it is quiet. Most everyone out on the streets, looking for work or the next high, some of the women washing clothes, children at school or sleeping, my two boys not yet home and Carter out somewhere, at a bank maybe, or with a city councilman, holding out that short-lined hand one more time.

Sometimes I think, No, that's it, I've had it, I have no more to give to these people, I don't *want* to give to these people, I can stand no more. I think of going to Carter and saying, Babe, we've got to live like a normal family. We need a home, a savings account, maybe a new coat this winter, Christmas for the children without having to borrow from my mother. But I would never say it. Because the truth is, he would never go. He can't, no more than I could leave him or the boys.

They're predicting the first frost tonight. Temperatures down in the thirties. From now until early March we'll be at our absolute limit, not one spare pillow or blanket. The worst is always mid-February for me, the time it seems the bleakest, when everyone is fresh out of holiday generosity and frozen pizza. When families are tired of taking a cousin in or even a daughter. It's the time I always think I'm least able to do it.

This is quicksand we're in, and we both know it. Maybe we'll drown or maybe we'll get thrown a rope. But there's one thing for sure: there's no *walking* out.

Mrs. James L. (Rose) Rowley
50

I know her mother, lovely woman. She's older than I am, of course, but we work together on the Hostess Committee at St. Phillip's.

Look at Liz. It's hard to believe she was once a Morgan, the way she has let herself go. Working twenty hours a day in this dreadful place. Oh, everyone should do their part, I believe. It's why I come down every Tuesday to teach painting and paper art such as origami. But this is ridiculous, their living upstairs with those children. Such fine-looking boys.

They've got Harbor House divided into three sections. One for the single women (mostly unwed mothers). Another for the men. And a row of rooms out back for families. It's too much, I tell Liz, you're too scattered, running yourself ragged, dear. You need to concentrate in one area. Just the young women maybe. But no children. She's holding a six-week-old baby at that moment, which is of course bad timing on my part. "Which would you suggest I turn out first, Rose?" She nods at the baby. "Maybe Lucinda here?" And she hands me the child and slowly walks to the office to answer the phone.

Well, she hasn't lost one thing—that same straight spine as her mother's.

Jasper O. Burke
48

I never heard nobody talk to youngins that way.

Miz Liz's youngest boy, I one time seen him break a window with one of them Frisbee things. Sliced slam through that window in her office where she sitting, right above her head, about this time of the afternoon. She go out there to him, he just as skinny as his daddy, those arms a hanging, legs long as Oil Can Boyd's. I thought she going to hit him upside the head. But what she say is, "What happened here, Allen?" He comminces to telling her that that old circle just slipped right out his fingers and went a flying in the wrong direction.

"You have the money to fix it?" she say.

"How much will it cost?" he want to know.

"That's a big piece of glass. I imagine twenty or thirty dollars."

"No ma'am," he say. He don't have it.

"Well there's plenty of ways around here to earn it. Why don't you start by moving that pile of bricks from the back exit around to the side alley. And then sweep the parking lot."

She start back to her office then turn around. That's it, I figure, she going to jerk a knot in his tail. Knock some teeth on the ground. She say, "I believe this belongs to you." She fixing to hand him that purple circle but stops and slides it back and forth in the air. "Need a little more wrist action, don't you?" she say. And she curl her arm in, flick the wrist, and that old Frisbee has a curve on it like something thrown by Blue Moon Odum, just glides, up and over the parked cars and come back long and smooth and land right in the boy's hand.

I rolled the wheelbarrow round to the exit sign and propped that big sweeper broom by the door. But I don't help him none.

Jasper O, she call me. Nobody ever talked to me that way before either. Jasper O. My good man.

Tommie Mateson
5

There's that man that keeps the squirrel in his pocket. He's here everyday at dinner time and gives it little pieces of food when nobody's looking. He said that if I don't tell anybody, he'll let me touch it. He said he might get me a squirrel someday too. He said we could think up a name for it together and I said, "We could call it Ninja Squirrel," but he didn't hear me.

Mama said not to talk to him anymore, that he's strange. She says that pretty soon we're going to have our own house and I can get a bird feeder and we're going to get another TV.

I'm five and a half. I weigh forty-nine pounds. See—*muscles*. I'm her big man.

I might put some peanuts on the bird feeder so I can catch me a squirrel.

Lee Ann Mateson
4

Tommie says for me not to cry when Mommy goes. Tommie says that only babies cry. Tommie says that if I'm quiet he'll let me give a piece of my sandwich to the squirrel. But I don't want to give any of my bread to that squirrel.

I want to go back to that motel room, and put my clothes in that drawer.

Jewel McFee
51

One time me and my children lived out of a car. It was years and years ago and it was only for a few days. But you don't forget it. Washing them up with cold water in the service station bathroom in the mornings before school. Driving around hunting for the safest place for sleeping. Willard just up and said he'd had enough, started staying with another woman.

First I had a sister took us in. Then we stayed a while with the preacher and them. But people get to looking a certain way at you every time you come through the door or start walking toward the refrigerator. You gots to move on.

Sold that car somewhere along the way. Last one I ever had. The way I fed my children was by raising somebody else's. White babies, girls mostly. I liked girls best since I only had the three boys. I like to put them in their little starched dresses, put ribbons in their hair. Willie's a good boy, my best, never gave me a peep of trouble. He finds me every now and then and brings me something. My worst one was my middle child, Cabb, about worthless. Fonzo was my baby. Got with the wrong crowd too but he's not bad as Cabb.

Somebody threw my teeth out. I was staying with my nieœy. Came home one night dead tired and the place a wreck, chicken boxes everywhere like they had a party. I didn't have the strength to bother with any of it. Next morning I see they took to cleaning. Somebody tossed out that paper cup I had my dentures soaking in. "I didn't do nothin with yo teef," her boyfriend say. Niecey helps me look out in the dumpster, but we don't find that set of dentures.

I used to love hats. I had one one time that had the prettiest satin ribbon on it and a pheasant feather. I was always dressing up for Sunday, had my boys in them little short britches and bow ties, pretty as a picture.

You see nice-dressed women coming in here, bringing in donations, helping with the food line. They have shiny fingernails, earbobs the size of plums and peaches.

I hate it most when they serve something chewy, like that French bread or pizza. I hope Willie don't find me. I always said to *them*, "Speak up. Take your hand away from your mouth when you're talking to me, son."

Carter Jones, Jr.
13

Mom's got me cutting out pumpkins and witch's hats. They had a run on construction paper at Big Lots and she bought two cases. Now she's worried about the cost, said she could have bought a blanket for the same price. So we're going to make use of this she says, and I've been cutting and pasting orange and black circles for two days. All up and down the halls and in the dining room, even in the bathrooms, we've got sharp-toothed pumpkins, ghosts and goblins, skeletons for Halloween. Make it scary, Mom says yesterday standing outside her office. What's scarier than this, I want to ask her.

When she finally comes upstairs tonight at nine she looks tired. I'm looking at her through two holes I've cut out of an old sheet she said I could use to make a ghost costume for one of the little kids. One of the holes hits too close to my nose, but I can still see her and I think for the first time that maybe she's old and I didn't know it. Or maybe there's something wrong with her. Maybe she and Dad aren't going to live much longer. And that scares me so much I don't answer when she asks me if I'm about finished. All I can think to do is grab on to the sides of the sheet and holler, "Boo!"

Ray Thompson
29

One day at a time. I read that sign how many times a day when I sit on the front row at every meeting? I go to the seven A.M., noon, 5:45 and eight o'clock. They've got a AA meeting just about every hour of the day in this city. I know. I've been to all of them. I'm a fucking graduate student of the Twelve Step program. Ninety meetings in ninety days, that's the suggestion to AA newcomers. Since I picked up my white chip I'm busting the national average, I figure. How about 372 meetings in ninety days? Fifteen hundred meetings per annum. Shit, I need a Salem. "Does anybody have a goddamn Salem?"

This is the worst time of the day, when the old skin really starts crawling, toes squirming. Knuckles busting. Ten-thirty at night and not enough time to get to a meeting and back here before the doors are closing. Too much time left before I'm sleeping. Read the Big Book. What does Dr. Bob say? Page . . . page. What the fuck page did somebody tell me? "Hey! Cut off that bugaboo music, will you!"

Okay. Okay. Easy does it. Easy does it. I think about Shirley. Tipping Buds with Shirley. Taking hits off a toke with Shirley. Getting slugged in the gut over Shirley. Don't think about it. Don't, just don't. Maybe later when I'm sure I'm not going to walk into Crown Liquors instead of the 5:45 meeting. "You touch me one more time, bub, and your butt's going to go through your nose and land on the floor."

Okay. Okay. Serenity prayer. Serenity prayer. They ought to tag on a line that says, Oh, yeah, God, and how about granting me the good sense to fall asleep before daylight, will you?

"No, man, I'm shutting up. Not causing no trouble. Right. Right. One more peep and I'm out of here. I got'cha." Okay. Okay. Easy does it. Easy does it. Easy . . . *Easy.*

Fucking easy, Shirley.

Allen Jones
11

Dad nailed a sign up outside on the doors that says no one is admitted after eleven P.M. and no one leaves before five-thirty in the morning. But some nights someone will come and bang on the door anyway.

Last year it was snowing and you could hear this guy banging away. He stood out there forever, kicking and yelling.

I got up and went into the kitchen. Dad was still dressed, sitting with his elbows on the table, rubbing his head back and forth in his hands. When I said, "Dad?" he looked up at me and his hair stuck straight out between his fingers.

He said, "Just who I was looking for. Someone to help me listen to my favorite music." He clicked a cassette into the old tape player and I lay back against him in the big chair and I fell asleep listening to The Moldau. It wasn't until the next day at school that I remembered him putting the headphones over my ears and I realized (*stupid!*) that only one of us could have been hearing music.

Avery Potts
47

People like to read two things: about ordinary people doing extraordinary things (a forty-some-odd housewife who becomes a marathoner) and about extraordinary people doing ordinary things (Candice Bergen walking around in her house shoes and opening up a can of chili for her daughter's supper). The first category helps readers believe they can achieve anything too, and the second helps confirm their notion that the rich and famous aren't so different from all the rest of us. But the ordinary doing ordinary and the famous doing superhuman shit, readers have no interest in it. I have a second sense about what a person likes to see in his newspaper.

I started out on the copy desk and then became a slot man, handing out headlines to guys on the rim, and ended up as city editor. I was a damn good newsman, *knew* what made fair copy. But I couldn't get any of those little pissants to see it. Watergate killed newspaper people in my opinion. After that every college kid who came through the door thought he was going to be Woodward and Bernstein. *Investigative* reporting, they all wanted to do. Half of them wouldn't know how to get to the press room, wouldn't know what a slot man *is*.

This is the time of night we'd be putting out the bulldog, the edition that went to all the outside counties. Just before midnight the proofs would come back up and we'd look for errors. There were some humdingers, damn *brilliant* headlines. My favorite was a cutline under a photograph of that Polish bishop who got promoted to the Vatican: FIRST NON-CATHOLIC EVER ELECTED POPE, it said. *Italian*, you idiot! First non-*Italian*. You can laugh about it later, after you've knocked the crap out of some poor jerk. But, at the time, you want to bust him one and start in on the Old Granddad.

Truth is, it just didn't make sense anymore what they were putting in newspapers. *Color*, that was foremost on a lot of people's mind. Color on the front page instead of writing a decent news story. And obits. About the only time in his life a guy will get his name in the paper and these kids can't get his name spelled right in the damn obituary.

Something snapped, I guess. Maybe some smart-ass kid writing an epic when I needed a ten-inch sidebar to fill a hole on page eleven. Maybe an ambiguous headline. Maybe a brain-shrinking hangover. Whatever. One afternoon while on deadline I took out a pistol from my top drawer and started shooting up computer terminals.

The squirrely bastards let me know how generous it was of them not to press charges, to give me that six-month severance and an extension on the insurance to cover a month and a half in a treatment center. Damn good of them after twenty-three years without a sick day.

I've got no gripes. With them or Helen. She put up with enough more than enough years. Kids grown and educated, house in her name, I don't blame her. Take it. This place isn't as bad as a lot of people say. It helps you see the truth of things, in my opinion. There's a guy here, new one, who shakes so bad I think he's going to knock something loose in his head, lose a tooth or something. He's a wreck that boy, scared to death he's going to start drinking. He'd camp out at the AA building if they'd let him. Every other day I say, "Hey, Ray, you going over to Triangle?" And he and I'll catch a ride or walk to the bus stop together. The whole way he's blithering like an idiot. Watch that and it'll keep you sober, let me tell you. Beads of sweat popping out on his head like marbles.

I can look at a man like Ray and tell you what he'd like to read, if he could keep his hands still long enough to hold a newspaper: Joe Blow with a wife and job and twenty years of sobriety; how many times Hemingway busted *his* skull falling against a table leg. That's what a man like that wants to read, the ordinary doing the extraordinary. Etcetera.

from KING OF THE ROAD

Paul Hemphill

In the gift shop of the restaurant, before going to his room the night before, Sonny had discovered a rack holding a score of original paperbacks published by OK Press. The books were fanciful little dramas, half-fact and half-fiction, about a bountiful array of masculine heroes connected with the South and the Southwest: Davey Crockett, Geronimo, Sam Houston, John Wayne, even Louis L'Amour himself. Sonny had bought a dozen of them, including slick photographic albums on rodeo cowboys and truckers, and spent the evening hours perusing them in his room after the call to Charley. He had to admit that they were no more and no less than E. J. Hardison had advertised, loose on facts but high on drama, and he figured he might be able to produce a fifty-thousand-worder on the obscure Seminole chief Billy Bowlegs over the rest of the summer were he so inclined. OK Press's authors, so far as he could discern, were the dime novelists of their time.

When he awoke at seven o'clock the next morning, to the wailing of children and the slamming of doors and the cranking of station wagons, he slipped into his jeans and a T-shirt and sneakers, not knowing whether Jake had tried the door during the night, and stepped outside into the broiling sun to track him down. More than half of the rigs of the night before were gone, including the Freightliners sandwiching Redball, and those that remained were being tended to by their drivers as Sonny walked across the hot pavement. When he reached Redball, he slapped his palm on the cab and shouted for Jake through the half-opened window.

Jake was a wreck: eyes bleary, hair akimbo, T-shirt sopping wet. He literally rolled out of the sleeper, becoming entangled with the curtains as he descended and the gear shift when he landed, and he swung open the door gasping for air. A pile of crushed beer cans littered the floorboard. "I thought it was Truck Stop Annie again," he rasped, sitting sideways on the wide truck seat, blinking and cradling his head in his hands.

"At your age?"

"Them gals ain't particular, far as I can tell."

"I wouldn't go home bragging if I were you."

"Nothing to brag about. We just talked."

He had persuaded one of them to join him in the cab around midnight after her business slowed, he said, simply because he had never talked to a hooker before. She was a waif from Tulsa, eighteen years old, already with a vivid tale of abandonment and wandering and drugs and various degradations. They had sat up in the cab for an hour, swapping life stories and drinking beer and listening to the all-night truckers' show over WWL in New Orleans, "The Road Gang," about the only place on the dial where one could hear the country music of the forties and fifties anymore.

"Name of Darlene," Jake said. "She was a right spunky little thing."

"I can imagine. Christ, Pop, you should've come and gotten me."

"You ain't *that* horny."

"Call it research. Americana."

"Then that'd make two of us with the wobblies this morning. Now's when I wish I'd taught you how to drive a truck. Don't know how far I'm gonna get today."

Jake took his time preening himself and the truck, and it took forever for them to get breakfast in the motel cafeteria, something Jake reluctantly agreed to only because the "only way a body can screw up grits and eggs is out of meanness," so it was nearly nine o'clock before they got on the road that day. It was a Friday, and it was going to be a scorcher as they headed for the high plains of western Kansas in hopes of making it to the cooler air of Colorado before they fried. They would pass the halfway point of the trip in the early afternoon, about the time they picked up U.S. 50 at Dodge City, putting them on schedule to reach the mine in Nevada on Monday afternoon. His bursting head aside, Jake's only concern seemed to be how Redball would take the heat that was in store for them that day.

Jack rabbits and black racer snakes, not as quick as their reputations, replaced skunks and turtles as the prevailing dead-on-the-roads once Jake had wiggled back onto U.S. 160. They were on the pure Kansas plain now, imperceptibly gaining altitude as the telephone and power poles clicked off the miles, rocking through tiny crossroads farming communities with their flat midwestern names of Milan and Danville and Harper painted on silver water tanks gleaming in the blistering sun of early summer. The view through the windshield was a split screen, an artist's rendering, of golden wheat on the bottom and endless blue sky on the top, with a horizon broken only by windmill-operated water pumps and stark white grain elevators known as Kansas skyscrapers and skeletal praying mantis-like contraptions on wheels spraying the fields with water so precious that men kill for it out there. And that is precisely what the country was called, Out There, by those who had been overwhelmed by its sheer breadth and emptiness. Counties named Comanche and Kiowa. Ruts meandering over the horizon, the Chisholm and the Santa Fe trails, just as the lumbering Conestogas had left them one hundred years earlier. Alfalfa, wheat, corn, soybeans. A lone farmer aboard an air-conditioned thresher, raising eddies of dust, seen from three miles off. A little yellow biplane crop duster, looping the loop and coming in at ten feet off the ground, trying to beat the grasshoppers to the wheat. The words "Keep Out" whitewashed on tires affixed to a barbed wire fence surrounding a spread the size of a whole county in, say, Georgia. And the heat; the relentless breath-sucking heat, ninety-seven degrees according to a digital bank sign at midmorning as Jake and Sonny cruised through Medicine Lodge.

Sonny had never experienced such heat. In Tallahassee there was the breeze coming up from the Gulf, swimming pools everywhere, and the air conditioning at both his apartment and the college; but here there was no escape. He had tried to tame the hot wind rushing into the cab of the truck, first by cracking the window an inch or so and then by rolling it all the way down, but either way it was like sitting beside a blast furnace. He had begun to strip, one article of clothing at a time, until soon he was down to his jeans and a bandanna tied around his forehead to keep the sweat out of his eyes, with his bare feet propped on the dashboard to escape the heat pounding up from the engine well. Since they had found nothing of interest on the radio at this time of day, and the CB frequency seemed to have been discovered by kids and housewives and jackleg preachers, he absently watched Kansas roll by and skimmed through the stack of OK Press paperbacks he had placed beneath his seat.

Sweating himself but preoccupied with staying alert for stray livestock and the occasional eastbound cattle rig coming at him on the narrow highway, Jake seemed to want to talk. "Geronimo," he said. "That got something to do with your teaching?"

"It's just an interest of mine."

"Saw a movie on him one time. Kirk Douglas did him, I think it was."

"Jeff Chandler."

"Believe you're right." Like a one-armed juggler, steering with his elbows and guessing where his cigar was, Jake lit up. "Who wrote the book?"

"It says Jesse Dalton, but that's got to be a *nom de plume*."

"'Nahm-day-ploom.' That's a good 'un. Saw it in a crossword one time. Means 'pen name,' don't it?"

"You got it."

Sonny told Jake all about E. J. Hardison and OK Press and the proposal that he crank out an original paperback on Billy Bowlegs, and Jake seemed astonished that Sonny would hesitate. "It ain't exactly like writing for the *Reader's Digest,* you understand, but it beats being on somebody's payroll."

"You might be right, Pop. I don't know."

"Don't know? Hell, coming back, we could run right through Sallisaw and make the deal."

"This guy sounds like a Hadacol salesman on the phone. Which reminds me. I owe you for a phone call."

"Might turn out to be the call that makes you a free man, son. Since that bitch is off your back and your kids are growed up, looks like you can do anything you want to now."

"I want it to be right, though."

"Hell, one thing leads to another. Take me and the coal, now—"

"This is different, Pop."

"Ain't that much difference."

"It sounds degrading, a book like this."

"You want to hear about 'degrading'? During the Depression, I had my choice. I could go off and work on one of them damned CCC camps that Roosevelt dreamed up, or I could dig my own coal out of my own hole in the ground and deliver it in my own truck. Wasn't near the money I could've made, working for that rich sonofabitch Roosevelt, but by God it was mine. And then, because I had me a truck when the war came, here I am. There's plenty to be said for being your own boss."

"I appreciate your sentiments, Pop."

"It takes a lot of guts to try it now."

"Right. The old nerve again. Uncle Zeb and the bus driver and them."

"Might be a little off to say it, son, but you could be running the risk of turning into another Lee Riddle."

"Wait a minute, Pop."

"Like I said"—Jake waggled his cigar in a manner that had begun to unnerve Sonny—"we can do Sallisaw coming back."

"Goddamn you." Sonny muttered it, bit if off, but he had spoken loud enough to make himself heard over the rush of wind and the roar of the engine.

Jake looked stunned, as though he had been slapped in the face. The cigar was poised, like a question mark. "Say what?"

"You heard me. I said God *damn* you."

"What's eating on you?"

"You're a fucking cowboy, just like Phyllis said."

"Doubt if she said it like that." Jake cackled in falsetto. "Yippy-ti-ki-yo, I'm a lonesome—"

"Cut out the bullshit and listen to me for a change, Pop. I'm not some guy you ran into at a loading dock. I'm your son. I've already heard your stories."

"That mean you don't want to better yourself?"

"See there? That's what I'm talking about. 'Better yourself.' 'Where's your nerve?'"

"Well, hell's bells, son—"

"You think life's a country song, don't you? No grays, just black and white. Good guys, bad guys, simple solutions to everything. 'If you can't stand the heat, just get out of the kitchen.' Damned if you don't have a homily for everything."

"'Homily.' Got a nice ring to it."

"Dammit, Pop, stop the clowning and listen to me." Sonny wondered why this had taken forty-five years. "Phyllis wasn't that far wrong when she said cowboys are fine on the movie screen but they're hell to live with. She and Mama have sure paid the price, cleaning up your messes. But, by God, so have I."

"I don't know what you mean by 'messes.'"

"It's been a psychic thing for me, Pop, and I may have suffered as much as anybody."

"That mean I ain't been a good father?"

"Ah, shit"—*how do you say it?*—"yes and no. You're honest and hard-working and a hell of a truck driver and all of that."

"Looks to me like that'd be enough."

"No, it's not, dammit. I told you yesterday after you'd pulled that crap at the motel with the bugs that you're a tough act to follow. You think there's just one way to live, and that's your way. 'Everybody off the streets, Jake Hawkins has arrived.'" Jake kept trying to cut in, but Sonny wouldn't let him. "I'm talking now, Pop, and I'm going to finish. The mess you've left *me* to clean up is one you can't see. What you're doing is asking me to live my life, which turns out to be words and ideas, like it was just another load of tires. You're trying to tell me that it don't amount to shit if you can't weigh it, load it, haul it, and unload it."

"It's been good enough for me—"

"Yeah, yeah, and there ain't nobody starving."

"Well, it's the truth. If you'd been a trucker, you'd o'—"

"I'm not a trucker, Pop. Maybe my life would've been simpler that way."

"You might've been a good 'un."

"We'll never know. All I'm asking is for you to quit equating earthmover tires with Shakespeare."

Jake cleared his throat and finally stuck the cigar in his mouth. "Like I said, we can do Sallisaw coming back."

"Let's see how it goes. I got plenty of time to think about it." Sonny tucked the book beneath the seat with the others and looked up in time to see them being welcomed to Coldwater, elevation twenty-one hundred feet, where the highway abruptly made a ninety-degree turn to take them through Greensburg en route to Dodge and U.S. 50. "Jesus Christ," he said, changing the subject, "this must be what it was like, working at the Sloss Furnace."

"I usually did Kansas at night," Jake said, rolling his shoulders and flexing his hands, still trying to straighten out the kinks from spending his night in the cab. "It ain't so bad when the sun's gone down. Gets downright airish, in fact."

"How long since you've been out here?"

"Western Kansas? Might be ten years. Redball IV was brand new."

"Looks to me like you would've paid a little more and gotten air conditioning," Sonny said.

"Too damned expensive. I didn't come out here that much, anyway, after I bought this one. You just got to tough it out."

"Well, air conditioning would be nice."

"A lot of things would be nice."

Jake, even while they talked, had been keeping a close eye on his gauges, frowning and muttering to himself during lulls, and when Sonny leaned over for a glance at the dials he saw that they hadn't been making fifty miles an hour; not even on the flat stretch of forty miles that had run from Medicine Lodge to Coldwater without a single town between the two.

"Trouble?"

"Hard to tell," said Jake.

"From the way the wheat's bending, it's windy out."

"We've been running right into a twenty-mile-an-hour headwind. It's always like this."

"We seem to be climbing, too."

"Seems I heard you climb about five feet a mile out here. It adds up." Jake double-clutched and grabbed the next lower gear, but nothing happened. "Come on, dammit," he said.

"Redball okay?"

"Probably needs some looking into. I'm hoping to make Minnie-Lou's without stopping."

"Who's Minnie Lou?"

"It stands for Minnie and Lou Dahmer."

"A truck stop, then."

"Minnie-Lou's is more than that," Jake said. "They're about two of the best people I ever met. Back when I was running refrigerated to California, I was known to drive all the way across Kansas without stopping just so I could make it in time for supper."

"I hope it's coming up soon."

"It's still four more hours if Redball don't act up. Right near the Colorado line."

"Please tell me," Sonny said. "Air conditioning."

"Got them big floor fans anyway."

"The kind that sound like jets taking off?"

"Same ones," said Jake. "Steaks as thick as your arm, and Lefty Frizzell on the jukebox. And ol' Lou knows his trucks about as good as Junior Wages does."

The prevailing rule-of-thumb about gaining five feet in elevation for every mile of roadway headed west was holding true. At Greensburg, where the water still came from a 109-foot-deep well dug by hand in the 1880s, the town limits sign gave the elevation as 2,240 feet. Steadily rising, pushing toward the sky, seeing more traffic now as they neared Dodge City, they began to pass giant feed yards where as many as four thousand cattle were being fattened for slaughter in mucky corrals that could be smelled from five miles away. More wheatfields, more grain elevators, more jack rabbits; now running beside the Arkansas River and the railroad tracks. Dodge City: old Fort Dodge barracks, major railyard teeming with cattle cars, tourists in Bermuda shorts swarming all over Boot Hill and a tacky "restoration" of Dodge with their cameras and credit cards, El. 2,500. And, finally, at Dodge City, they rolled onto U.S. 50.

It was around three o'clock in the afternoon, now Mountain Daylight Time, the sun at its hottest, when Jake spied the rusted old blue-and-white Pure Oil sign being buffeted by the wind of the high plains less than ten miles from the Colorado line: Minnie-Lou's Truck Rest. Those signs were collector's items now, Pure Oil having become Union 76 some years earlier, but he knew Minnie and Lou Dahmer to be cantankerous enough not to change it for the very reason that some corporation said to. Clucking and smiling at the sight, still a mile ahead of him, Jake checked the mirrors and began the process of bringing Dixie Redball IV to heel: hitting the turn signals, tapping the brakes, gearing down, slipping on the air brakes, blasting the air horn in case there were any doubts as to his intentions, finally easing off the highway onto the shoulder and then rolling into the empty gravel parking lot that once had held as many as twenty big rigs at a time.

Puzzled by the stillness, changing into his cowboy boots and a pearl-buttoned long-sleeved shirt, Jake slid from the cab and surveyed the place. Where once there had been four gasoline islands, each sheltered by its own corrugated tin roof, now only two pumps sat mutely in the searing heat. The Pure Oil sign rocked and squeaked in the wind whistling down from the distant foothills of the Rockies. Nestled in a grove of trees, like a slain dinosaur, there was the low-slung white abode building that since the early fifties had beckoned truckers like an oasis, no matter the time nor the weather: steaming coffee, great gobs of heavy food, loud country music, sassy waitresses, telephones, bunkhouses out back, Minnie and Lou Dahmer themselves.

Jake tugged the bill of his Graddick Tire cap, motioned for Sonny to follow, and slumped across the gravel to the twin plate-glass doors. They, like the picture windows that stretched all across the front of the place and wrapped around the sides, were caked with dust. Wiping a circle clean with his shirtsleeve, Jake peered inside to find a sea of white bedsheets covering the long counter, the tables, the jukebox, the coffee urn, the cash register, and the floor fans in every corner of the place. Beside the doors was a handprinted note, "Restaurant Closed— Ring for Gas Beer," signed by "M. Dahmer." Jake pressed the buzzer and stepped back, lighting the stub of his cigar, turning to watch a Kenworth diesel smoke past on the highway with a reefer rocking in tow. Sonny toed the gravel with his moccasins and squinted into the sun to see a hawk soaring on the thermals.

"What'll it be, boys?" They were startled to hear a voice in the stillness of the plains, and when they spun they saw a woman in tight jeans and a man's blue work shirt and cowboy boots. Her face burned and freckled from the incessant wind and sun, her steel gray hair secured in a ponytail by a bandanna, she had come around the west side of the building and was trudging toward them. With her was a German shepherd dog on a leash strapped to her wrist.

Jake took the cigar from his mouth and stared at the woman, a cockeyed smile playing on his face. "We was hoping for the works," he said.

"About all I got these days is beer, ice, and gas."

"Won't your Wurlitzer play no more?"

She paused. "Lord, no. Can't you see we're closed up now?"

"Be damned. And here I've come all the way from Alabama."

She gasped. "I don't see no banjo on your knee."

"Well, you wouldn't happen to have none of them big El Productos, would you?"

She came to them now, the German shepherd growling and straining at the leash, and when she got close enough to Jake, she stopped and cocked her head and looked directly into his eyes. "Jake?"

"Me and Dixie Redball are thirsty, both."

"It *is* you. You old rascal."

"I come a thousand miles to see y'all, Minnie."

"Lou would appreciate that, Jake. He sure would."

"Well, where's he at?"

"Out back, Jake. What was left of him."

Over the next hour, Sonny felt like an outsider, a friend of a friend of a friend, who had been invited to a family reunion. Stories of people and places and events flew back and forth between Jake and Minnie Dahmer as the three of them sat in the darkened living room of her adobe bungalow, cooled by a window air-conditioning unit, sipping iced tea, stuck back under the trees behind what once had been Minnie-Lou's Truck Rest. From the way they carried on, touching and eyeing each other long after their laughter had run its course, Sonny had a fleeting thought that perhaps there had been more than just highway friendship between his father and this tough woman of the plains; one whose life was a world away from that of Evelyn Hawkins, "the only woman this old man ever loved," with its churches and sewing circles and begrudging acceptance of his life as a man of the road.

Later, beneath sycamores behind the house, they sat on stone benches around a grotto whose centerpiece was a stone cross marking the grave of Louis Grist Dahmer. Grasshoppers and locusts played in the trees and the tall brown weeds as Minnie told of what had transpired in the ten years since Jake's last stop. They had closed the truck stop soon after, when the serious long-haul truckers began favoring I-70, which crossed Kansas some one hundred miles north of U.S. 50, and at the age of fifty-five Lou had bought his own rig and taken to the road as he had always wanted to do in the first place. He died five years later, at the bottom of a canyon at Four Corners on U.S. 160, leaving Minnie to get by on insurance and her own Social Security checks and what income came from dispensing gas and beer from what remained of Minnie-Lou's Truck Rest. She was now sixty-six years old, alone, her children long ago established in Kansas City and Denver.

Using Lou Dahmer's tools, stored in one of the six motel units affixed to the rear of the place, Jake spent the afternoon under the trees tinkering with Redball. Fine-tuning was about all it had needed, he said, making adjustments on the carburetor and the water pump, changing a fan belt and replacing the air and oil filters while he was at it. Sonny sat in the relative cool of the grotto, aimlessly watching the grasshoppers and reading about Geronimo, as Minnie kept Jake company or fetched iced tea for them or waited on the random customer who rang the bell out front.

"So tell me about yourself, Sonny." Minnie had just sold some gas to a local in a pickup, and now she sat on one of the benches near Lou Dahmer's grave. "Married? Kids? What do you *do*? All I know is that one time he told me and Lou that he'd raised an educated fool."

"Sumbitch said that about me?"

She smiled. "When he quit bragging on you."

Sonny filled her in about himself, and about Jake's adventures in retirement. "I feel more like an enforcer than anything else."

"I can't say I'm surprised," Minnie said. "These fools get the road in their blood and there's no stopping 'em. I ought to know something about that. I knew the minute Lou got a truck that it was gonna be his coffin."

"So here you are."

"Here I am. The Widow Dahmer."

"Couldn't you have stopped him?"

"Why, Lord no." Minnie seemed surprised that anyone would ask such a question. "Why would I want to?"

"So you wouldn't be left alone like this, for one thing."

"That would've been selfish, for me to try and stop him."

"It seems like he was the selfish one."

Minnie said, "Let me tell you about these boys, Sonny. They *are* selfish, the good ones. They have to be, to do what they do. Seems like I read where fifty thousand people get killed in traffic every year, and I never saw a trucker yet who thought he was gonna be one of 'em. They aren't much different from test pilots and these tightrope people at the circus. They work alone, and they can get killed doing it, and in their mind that makes 'em special. They've got to be selfish to survive. That's why no trucker ever walked into my place after driving all day across Kansas and said, 'If it's not too much trouble, could I please have a little coffee?'"

"Well," Sonny said, "I thought maybe you could help me."

"Help you do what?"

"I was going to ask you to reason with him."

"Reason with Jake Hawkins? Hah."

"He's causing an awful lot of trouble back home. I told you about the alcoholic place and about Mama. My sister gets slapped around by her husband every time the old man acts up, and I'm still not convinced that he won't do something that'll get Mama kicked out of the retirement home even in her condition. Me, I've got ambivalent feelings about the whole thing. On the one hand, I understand how he feels about trucking and I hate like hell to see him dry up like he's been doing. But, on the other hand, I wish he'd start thinking about other people for a change."

"Well, it's too late for that."

"He's already had his career. It's time to quit."

"Truckers don't quit, Sonny. They just die."

"But he's almost seventy years old, Minnie. He can't even see to read a menu anymore. We didn't cover three hundred miles today, but he's a wreck. There's all that trouble he's left back home. Can't you say something to him?"

"About all I can do is make today a good one for him." Minnie arose from the stone bench, tugged the knot of her bandanna that held her hair in a ponytail, and sidled over to where Jake was humming

and working on the truck. She said, "Jake? I was thinking about reopen-
ing the place. What do you think?"

Jake raised up from the opened hood of Redball and said, "You won't
even be able to pay your power bill, Minnie. Nobody stops here anymore."

"I'm talking about for one night only."

"What do you mean?"

"For old times' sake, Jake. Please."

"I don't know. Me and Sonny ought to be moving on. We could
make good time and it'll be cool."

"You got plenty of time, Jake. You need rest. Come on, I'll cook
up some steaks and clean up a couple of rooms for you to stay the
night. Look at Sonny. He's no more used to this than you are."

Around nine o'clock at night, with the blinds closed and an improvised
sign saying "Private Party" taped to the front doors, the three of them
sat in the middle of the restaurant finishing off a dinner of chicken-fried
steak and mashed potatoes and sawmill gravy and biscuits. Jake and
Sonny had showered and changed in the tiny rooms, last rented in the
spring to a crew of highway construction workers, and Minnie had dressed
up in a cowgirl skirt and pearl-buttoned blouse. While the two men
were lifting the bedsheets from one table and the jukebox and the floor
fans, Minnie had done the cooking in the kitchen at her house. Now,
with the fluorescent lights and the fans causing the white sheets to billow
and glare, they dined as though on a cloud.

"Kinda pie you got, Minnie?"

"Sliced."

"Still sassy as ever, I see."

"Among friends, Jake. Among friends."

The Wurlitzer, rigged especially for the evening, required no quarters
as it ran through Bob Wills and Lefty Frizzell and Webb Pierce; music
of another time, another place: "There Stands the Glass" and "San Antonio
Rose" and "Movin' On." Plates pushed aside, cold six-packs of beer
on the red Formica table, cigar smoke clouding the stark lights, jukebox
pounding, Jake glowed like a man furloughed from prison. Sonny, full
and content himself, chanced a beer as he silently watched Jake and
Minnie parry like lovers reunited.

On the jukebox, "Faded Love," Bob Wills and the Texas Playboys.
"Jake," Minnie said, "dance with me."

"Lord, Minnie, I can't dance."

"Anybody that can drive an eighteen-wheeler can dance."

"What would my wife think?"

"Promise I won't tell her if you won't."

"How 'bout Lou, then?"

"This is for Evelyn and Lou and every trucker that ever came through that door, Jake."

While the fiddles played, Minnie took Jake by the hand and led him to the jukebox. She in her denim bolero skirt, he in cowboy boots and polyester slacks of hideous green, they held each other close and danced. Across the road, the new moon and the stars high in the Kansas sky glistened on the lazy Arkansas River. On the road itself, the loneliest road in America, big rigs thundered into the night, rattling the windows as they passed.

NOTHING TO FOOL WITH

Rebecca Hill

H ere is something I ought to have known: nobody gets to be forty-two years old and still has things organized loose in their life.
Let me tell you the first thing he ever said to me. Not the very first thing—which must have been hello or maybe excuse me four months ago in a Howard Johnson's full of people I didn't know, and him among them—but practically the first thing that fell out of his mouth the minute he got me (or I got him) to that motel room just off exit four of Highway 985 to Atlanta. That was more recent.

He picked up my left hand and stared at the ring and said, "I have sure done some running around in my life, but one thing I have never done before is make love to a married woman."

Plainly this was bothering him. And marriage is nothing to fool with, I was with him one hundred percent there. But what I couldn't get over was the pride he had, like he was saying the running around he did wasn't being done to a married woman, namely his wife. For he was married, he was very plain about that, and wanted no trouble. I had already agreed to that.

He raised up on one elbow—we still had our clothes on, and he was wearing a plaid perma-press shirt and blue jeans and in fact that was what I was wearing. He said, "I have never in my life ever made love to another man's wife."

Well, that was just the wrong thing to say to impress me. I've been married to Stuart these seventeen years, and one thing I am not is some man's wife. Or at least that is not the end of it, not the whole story about who I am. The wife part, and Stuart would be the first to say so, is nothing I ought to brag about. Anyhow I thought this over for a minute and decided to keep my mouth shut as nearly as I could. If this fellow was more worried about bothering my husband than he was me, I didn't like it one bit. But I wanted to like Clary Gaines. So I didn't say anything. Some people are like that, and maybe you have met some of them too: they will tell you the very worst thing they can think of about themselves first off. It's almost like a dare, like they are saying, first jump over this. Then let's see.

We didn't start off talking about husbands and wives. The way we started off that very first time was by looking at one another, sideways and in all the ways you do when you're playing it cagey and don't want to get caught too far down the road too soon. He was by himself and so was I, and he walked right in between the little space between my table and the chair that belonged to the next one there in the Howard Johnson. I felt his eyes slide over mine, and I let mine ease away. He told me in the motel room later, "I took one look at you that morning and thought, 'When was the last time I saw a woman who looked like that?'" Him saying that made me feel so good that I didn't even want to ask him, "Looked like what?" The blue jeans I had on that day were ordinary as could be, an old pair, and the top was not new but one I have got used to pulling out of the closet when I feel like I was feeling that morning when I started out. I had to get my clothes on to take Shannon her lunch over at the high school, since she had forgot it and was spending her quarter for ice cream to call me on the pay phone and tell me she would starve to death. The shirt I had picked out was my old buff-colored flannel, all softened up with washing. I bought it back when I thought Stuart and me would be fishing buddies, and that was a long time ago. Long before I had two children. The way this shirt goes on, it makes me think of nothing so much as baby blankets; that is the feel it has on my skin. I never thought but what that's what it might look like on my skin, too.

"When was the last time I saw a woman who looked like that?" he said, and I took it at face value, since he was talking about that very first time when we had just sat and ate breakfast and got acquainted in a way that seemed not to have any harm in it. Except what is there between two people that can be guaranteed not to have any harm? He told me he was a salesman for farm tractors and parts, and how often he traveled that old highway between Atlanta and Greenville, and how often the other way down to Mobile and Baton Rouge. I had no way of knowing what he was thinking at the time, and so to hear this coming later, when things were different—I just was happy hearing it, the way he said it made me feel special in the world, and I hadn't felt like that in a while. I didn't want to talk to Clary about Stuart. Not that time, or to tell the truth, any other time. Maybe people do talk about the people they are married to when they get set up in motel rooms with people they are not married to. Maybe it's just the thing to clear the air and let everybody know how it stands between them. Two strangers who mean to keep on belonging to other strangers. Why drag the others into it? Not that I can claim to be experienced in these matters after seventeen years of faithful marriage, but my opinion was that two of us in that motel room seemed like all our situation required. But the way Clary Gaines kept looking at my hand with the ring on it, and talking like he did about this other man, meaning my husband, the total kept coming out to three. And his wife made it four. He called her by name, too, though I hadn't said Stuart's name yet.

"Melissa and me, we don't have children and we don't have parents, none that we count anyway since Melissa's daddy divorced her mama and her mama's dead now. So Melissa and me, we have to be everything to one another. That's just how it is with us."

This was exactly the fifth time I had laid eyes on the man. In some ways that was way too quick, but at the time it seemed like a slow killing on TV. I can't explain that, but I know the things he was saying were making it slower. He had the snaps undone on my plaid shirt, and there I was laying next to him. Him saying the name so much made her sound like somebody we both knew, somebody right in the room with us. If he was wanting to talk about his wife I felt like I ought to do my snaps back up.

Then he stopped still himself for a minute and said, "Let me tell you what I'd do if somebody was fucking *my* wife. I'd go get my gun and shoot the son of a bitch, not even think twice about it."

I slid my fingers under his and held my shirt together. "You would what?"

"I would without giving a hair's chance."

Now we had five people in the room and one of them shot dead. Except I knew when he said this that the man Clary Gaines was thinking about was himself, because that's how people's minds work.

"My husband doesn't carry a gun," I said.

"What's his name?"

He asked me, so I told him then.

"Well, if he does or if he doesn't," he said back, "I do. Got it right in my rig." I had seen the big John Deere suitcase he had with him in back of the Dodge he drove, and I thought about him carrying that case into and out of tractor showrooms all over the South and Southeast. What did he need a gun for, with tractor people?

I said, "And if my husband did carry one, and if there was any shooting done, it'd be me shot and not you." I did up two of the snaps. "You can bet on that," I told him. And I have to say that I liked Stuart for it at that moment, that he'd know where to point a gun if it came to shooting. Because it was me that walked into this motel room on my own two feet. Now Clary I could tell didn't see things that way. For him the men were the only ones in it, and where that put me I don't know. It was a moment to put you off what was in front of you. Maybe it should have. The plain truth was it made me mad, and I forgot what I told myself before and had to open my mouth.

"Let's hold it a minute," I said. "Let's say somebody *was* doing your wife. In the first place, let's just turn it around and say it was her idea, *she's* with some other man because she wants to, because we're not talking about being hit over the head, which would be something else. And in the second place, let's give some credit and say this man probably means something to her, or she wouldn't be in the room with him at all. Now *you* walk in with a gun and put a hole through him, what do you see happening next? You see her falling right into your arms to say Thank you so much, thank you?"

Clary was laying flat on his back staring up at the ceiling. None of this was going through his brain. That was the morning we had sat and had breakfast together for two hours in the Howard Johnson's, getting late enough into lunch that he bought us ice cream cones on the way out. Clary says he can eat ice cream any time of the day or night. He wouldn't listen when I said I didn't want one, and by the time I got it he was right.

About his wife and another man, I could tell when he was listening to me and when he wasn't, these things aren't hard to know. He was surely not letting that picture in his mind right then on that bed. He was laying there with his eyes gone little, and all he could see was a notion he intended to shut out. His mouth got set with the bottom lip pooched out.

"I'd shoot him without giving a hair's chance," he whispered.

I have noticed how the brain can quit working when there is a matter of feeling involved. I have been there myself, and to tell the truth, why else was I where I was except that I had stopped worrying about plain facts and the snaky little trains of thinking about what might happen, for the sake of what I am feeling. What I am feeling on that bed looking at Clary's stubborn mouth is a strong singing in my ears that tells me all my thinking for the day has got over and done with. And when I pay attention, the feeling rushes out all over me, and I want to see what Clary's mouth, which is looking tight and carved, that wide seagull bow spread thin across his narrow jaw, might taste like.

I give out a sigh and shift on the bed, and Clary's quick eyes go bright. He is a hunter, he has told me. He was never one for fishing the least way. He is a hunter, and this helps all the talk of guns make some sense. Also he is not one to miss signs. The dead hand on my back comes to, and he uses it like a spade to carry me tight to his chest. We are done talking.

I called home from the motel room at three-thirty, knowing my kids had got home from school and I was wanting to check on things. This is a habit, but you have to think about it. This morning's paper had a news story, "Fire Kills Three." You can read anytime about fires that sweep through a household just when a parent has stepped around to the grocery store, and have thought they were safe leaving a nine-year-old in charge. Not that I had done that. Stuart Junior is seven but Shannon is fifteen. Then all that business of accounting for exactly why those parents thought such a thing then, and retracing their footsteps for the newspapers and explaining their motives.

With her innocent voice on the motel telephone Shannon said, "God, Mom, you sound so happy!" I was fuddled that it showed right through like that. I couldn't think what to say next since I had already used up the only lie I had ready, and she said, "Keep right on shopping if it cheers you up that much. Stay till the stores go slam shut."

Fifteen years old and she was writing me an open ticket, making me feel bad at the same time. How does she know so much? And am I so hard to live with? These are things I wanted to ask Clary right then and there, if he could have told me, but of course he wasn't the one to ask. It never in the world occurred to me that I might be unhappy enough to have it show, and maybe it really doesn't or maybe Shannon didn't have a name for it until she heard something different in my voice.

It surprises me that she would listen to anything I said with any attention at all. We used to be close but this teenage is something else. She's more likely to tell me than listen—tell me how nobody wears Levis anymore, especially not at my age (which is thirty-seven), and how she wouldn't be caught dead looking like I look. When Bruce Springsteen wore his Levis on the cover for *Born in the USA* I thought I'd won something. But in Shannon's school Bruce Springsteen means less than I do.

Still she's a good girl, with a heart for her little brother. Yesterday the two of them were hobbling around the TV room with their shoelaces tied together for a three-legged walk. But today it could just as well be Shannon would get to bullying him or Stuart Junior would get into some of her makeup and I'd have the devil to pay when I got home. These things change quick and you never know how it will snap from one minute to another. I got off the phone feeling uneasy, feeling free too, but the way a convict on the run might feel free. In that way I guess Clary might be right and I might be wrong. Maybe two people never get to be just two people in a room.

With two more hours left before Stuart would get home, I went out with Clary in his car to a steak house on the highway where nobody would know me. I sat with my back to the door, just in case, and watched him put away a sixteen-ounce T-bone. I felt hungry myself but I just couldn't keep my mind on my business. Clary would look up from his plate and wipe his mouth, or push his knee over next to mine. With these things going on I got filled up quick, and Clary ended up finishing what I ordered. We talked some too, but it was about nothing, songs we liked in high school, dances we used to do.

"I like your company," he said to me, standing at the cash register. "So many women, you can't talk to them, they don't know what you know. You and me came out of the same pod, I like that."

I knew Clary would be on the road to Atlanta by five o'clock the next morning, and standing there next to him I was half-wondering about me sneaking out of the house from two till five. I know how crazy that sounds. But I could picture the stars out, and me rolling the car down the dark driveway till I could start it down the hill. Would such a scheme work? Could I do it? Thinking those things all the way back to his motel, my heart raced like it was going somewhere. But then I took my own car home, and stayed there in my own bed next to Stuart till six-thirty, and time to get the kids up.

It wasn't till days later that I got around to thinking in a hard way about what we said that time. I spent those days on the cloud of my choice, trying to keep from shuddering at the breakfast table or forgetting the hot iron on one of Shannon's wide skirts. This is because of certain thoughts that come over me now: of the way Clary fisted on to the motel bed headboard to hold back. Or changes that came over his face and made him look so many different ways—like an Indian on one of those old buffalo nickels, or one time (though who would have thought it about a chiseled-looking man like Clary) like a pretty child.

I told him one time when his hands were running over me light as feathers, "You have such a way with your hands. Your mother must have raised you right."

That was me adding extra people to the room, and I was sorry because for a minute his hands came to a halt. "I guess that must be where anybody learns loving," he said.

And I was glad when the thought passed on.

Here lately I stand around with my hands in dishwater and can't help but recall how my mother was the one who loved us when we were children coming up, my father so awkward with his hands that any loving from him would more than likely turn into a slap or a knuckle rub. It seemed to embarrass him. He didn't know how and couldn't seem to learn, and so a loving touch probably always would surprise me in a man.

"Am I hard to live with?" I asked Stuart this at the supper table after we had dessert last night. My family is not much for sugar, and I'm glad of it, but it was me that wanted the ice cream.

"Hell, no," Stuart said, wiping his face with a napkin. "Sweetest woman the Lord ever put on this earth," he said. He winked at me and took a look to see where the kids were, and they already had stuck their heads back in the TV so he reached out and pinched me on one breast. I mean light, not hard.

"Stuart, quit," I told him. What would he think if I ever said anything else?

"Except for that lip," he said, turning red and grinning. "The Lord never had anything to do with the lip on a woman."

He wasn't telling me anything I hadn't heard a thousand times.

And when he got up I stood at the sink and brushed my other nipple kind of rough with my own hand, to make myself feel balanced again.

Since Clary has gone on, and I have got to thinking it all over, what he said about shooting a man keeps coming back to me. I can't feel settled with it. It has all the marks of something he hasn't thought truly about—how his wife might be flesh and blood, real as I am, who finds somebody to show her a side of herself she hasn't seen in a while. And how just that very thing might be worth a risk to her. And how his coming home killing that somebody would not make her less lonely when he's out on the road. She wouldn't be grateful. And even if she was or said she was, he'd be in jail and not the one to enjoy her gratitude.

These things seem so plain. I thought for a time that I would just check up and see if he might have thought about all that, the next time I saw him. Just see if any of it had sunk in.

"You will see my face again, you can bet on that," he had said at the last. "You take care of your sweet self."

I have said those words over and over, at first just to have the pleasure of them, and lately to see if there was something I didn't hear. It's been five full weeks and it didn't take me too many Tuesday mornings of going out to the Howard Johnson's and sitting there by myself for it to come to me that I won't be getting to make this check on his thinking, or anything else I might have had in mind to do.

I have had time to make up my mind to other things that are plain. You don't get to be grown without doing things on purpose, and what looks loose to somebody else is just their mistake. Since I was thirty I have had friends tell me to leave Stuart, but divorced women always think married ones are unhappy. I've got it all buttoned down tight in my mind how women of a certain age with children just don't up and find happiness that also gets the bills paid and the children raised. Besides which the only reason to put up with children sometimes is purely for the reason that they are yours, and this is a fact. Stuart says it often enough, and I have no use whatever for people who say different.

And Clary Gaines had no use for me to tell him about his own wife. He has got that buttoned down too. If he has told her about this killing plan, it would be a good reason for her not to go off with anybody she cared about. It would be doing both men a favor, is one way she might look at it.

I think it must make an easy life for Clary, having Melissa home scared to move while he does what pleases him, and then her to come home to, all safe and private. And I know what that must mean he thinks of me, which is not much, for endangering his life, or my husband's. And wouldn't it be easy, making love to women who are not married so that he could give them a call anytime from Atlanta or Mobile or Charlotte, wherever he was working and at any time of the night or day. He might just pull into the parking lot of the apartments they live in, or into their driveways if they are divorced women, and take his chances. It would cost him so little. With no other man's mailbox to consider it could be he might drop these quiet women a friendly postcard and say when it was he might be coming through that way next.

MOTHS

Mary Hood

It had taken since Easter to cut this much. It would be another two weeks till they had pulped all the way back through the thousand acres to the lake. They worked hard, from early breakfast till late supper, as the year turned toward summer. It was just the three of them, Cheney and two green kids, cutting and loading onto Mr. Anderson's old truck.

Mr. Anderson wanted the oaks left standing, but he had said Cheney could have the sweet-gums and poplars for his own woodpile—just don't cut firewood on wages. That meant Cheney had to come back in the evenings to gather it. Every night he would fill his pickup truck bed with the day's rounds and haul them home. He would split them later, when some of the sap had dried out. The days were getting longer, but it was always dark night when he gave the last log a kick and it rolled from the truck. Sometimes he sat on the steps, too tired to wash, or eat, or sleep.

Mr. Anderson wanted the pines cut no lower than waist high to leave the dozers something to push against. They were going to tear the stumps out and grade the acres into lots. They had already begun piling the pinetops, limbs, deadfall, and stumps to burn. The smoke rose high in the dry, still air. The light had a strange yellow look to it, and the flames and heat cast their own shadows.

They were going to clear the land and build houses—not Cheney and the boys who worked with him, but another crew. Mr. Anderson had plans. He and the surveyors stood by his fine car, talking, looking at blueprints, pointing, nodding. Mr. Anderson was the boss now, but he had started out just like Cheney and the boys, harvesting pines for someone else.

When they had stacked the truck with the morning's cutting and chained the logs down, it was almost time for lunch. They would take the load to the pulpyard and on the way back, get something to eat. The boys always stopped at Mama Red's for lunch. Cheney told them they were wasting their time working so hard if all they did was spend the money on food. "Besides, all that grease'll kill you before you're twenty," Cheney warned.

"You're getting old," they ragged him.

"I'll die rich," he said.

He brought his lunch from home—a mayonnaise jar of tea and rattling ice, corn bread and a sweet potato, slab meat in a biscuit. While the boys drove the truck to the pulpyard and stopped by the hamburger joint, Cheney stayed behind. After he had eaten, after he had sharpened the saw-chain for the afternoon work, he would lie down in the shade and sleep till they got back.

Once when Cheney had slept past their return, the boys woke him up by dropping peanut hulls on his face. So today when the crunching noise woke him, he thought it was the boys sneaking up on him to play a trick. He opened his eyes and sat up, quick. There was no one around. The truck wasn't back yet.

Again he heard it, that slow crunch, crunch, like dry cornflakes being broken one by one. A squirrel? Cheney yawned. He couldn't see any squirrel. The sun was directly overhead. He squinted up at the limbs above him, listening. When he put his hands to his mouth and gave a squirrel call, no squirrel sassed back. The crunching noise came again, not up in the tree, but on the ground.

"Something's getting itself ate like corn on a cob," he said. He took up his file and gave the saw a last lick, tightened the chain on the bar, checked the oil and the gas. He was ready to work. If the boys didn't get back soon he was going to start without them. As he knelt to crank the saw, he heard the crunching again and noticed the dry leaves move.

With the file he flipped the leaves over. He thought he would see a mouse—or a snake—or something . . . He didn't see anything. There was no hole. Nothing had escaped, yet nothing was there.

"I don't care," Cheney said. He didn't like tricks. He didn't like not knowing what. He was going to kick the leaves around, just stomp whatever it was out of business and be done with it, when he noticed the moth on last years's dead goldenrod. The wings were silver-green, like two dogwood leaves. Cheney leaned low to look, and his laughing breath made the weed sway. The moth held still.

So that was it—he had been right about it being a trick. The noise was probably some little gadget the boys bought at Bully's store, something rigged up with fishing line and a spoon lure, wired to the paper moth, then wired to the twig. The paper legs looked like chocolate. Cheney knelt closer. The feelers were two dusty little feathers of angel gold, and the wings were outlined in pink.

But when Cheney reached for it, it flew—it was real, not paper! It left green chalk on his fingers. It flew low, as if he had hurt it, as if it were about to crash. Gliding more than flying, it didn't go far. When it lit on the next weed, it crawled out on a twig and hung itself straight flat open, like wash on a line.

Now Cheney reckoned it wasn't a joke unless it was a wonderful one, and this time when he reached for it, it shuddered away from him. It kited off in that same heavy-tailed way back to the first weed and clung, motionless. Cheney went to get his tea jar. He was going to clamp the moth inside. It was a quart jar and the moth would about fit. When he bent over to pick up the jar, though, he saw something trembling in the dry leaves with that same crunching noise that had waked him. It was papery, brown, no bigger than a cigar stub. Cheney took it in his hand and watched as one little gold feathery feeler stuck itself out the hole. It looked just like the feeler on the green moth.

The case was crumpled on one side as though it had been stepped on. Maybe the truck had run over it. Cheney shook it. Inside, the moth struggled. He could feel it. The moth butted at the frayed end of the case, trying to be born. It had worn a hole with his head, trying to escape. One strand blocked the exit, caught the moth across the head, between the feelers, tangling the one already free in the air. Cheney took out his knife, but before he could make the hole larger, the moth stuck out the other feeler and began pushing its way out into the day. Its eyes were rubbed dull, and there was white dust where the moth had scrubbed itself bald trying to escape the crumpled case. The hole wasn't large enough, but the moth wouldn't wait. It freed itself in stops and goes, and each struggle brought more of it to light. The wings were tiny and folded, like young pea leaves. The body was soft and covered with white plush, which the hard labor was scouring off.

When the moth was all the way out of the case, it was bigger than Cheney's thumb, bigger than the case itself, as though it had fattened on sunshine and free air. It walked all around on Cheney's hand, always climbing upward. When Cheney touched it, to feel that soft plush, it squirted mud water on him, the color of raw land being cleared. "You little beau gator!" Cheney said, almost slinging the moth away in surprise. It was more active now.

It climbed up Cheney's arm, across his sleeve, onto his shirt front, up his chest. When it tickled Cheney's throat, he lifted it off, more gently this time, and let it start all over again, climbing up his arm. It seemed to be seeking. Cheney told it, "Settle," the way he would speak to his own baby.

He held up his arm, and the moth climbed as far as it could and hung from Cheney's busted thumb. Hung motionless like the one already unfurled on the goldenrod. Cheney was still holding his arm up, watching for the moth's wings to fill out, when the boys got back.

He showed them. They had never seen anything like either the flat moth or the crumpled one. Cheney thought he could see the little wings begin to grow—if he looked away, then looked back, he thought they seemed a little larger.

Nobody knew how long it took. Cheney fingered the moth onto a gum sapling. It clung to the bark of the trunk, hanging straight, the crumpled wings slightly raised. It didn't look to be busy doing anything. Neither did the other one. Donnie said, poking at the freshly hatched one with a pine needle, "Maybe he's dead." The moth raised a feisty foreleg. "Huh, nope." He kept tracing it with the pine needle to watch it make those little warning lifts of this leg, of that leg, but still it held its place.

Cheney said, "Now y'all leave my pets alone," and they laughed.

Ward said, "Something's wrong with him, he ain't never gonna be right," and Donnie said, "You mean Cheney?" and after that, they went back to work.

Cheney could gauge as well as any woodswalker how many trees to cut for a load. He'd been at it for long enough, but it was more than experience. There was pride in it too, not to leave too much timber lying cut at the end of the day, making it easy for poachers.

Cheney was the one who cut. He didn't like felling timber too near another saw. But once the trees were down, Ward took the second saw and helped limb and top and walk off the lengths. Donnie stood on the truck, running the hoist.

When lunch wore off, when the afternoon began to cool and everyone was glad the day was about over, they took a break. Cheney and Ward smoked. Donnie washed his candy bar down with Pepsi left over from lunch. They had forgotten the moths. Cheney remembered.

Even now, hours later, the crumpled one was clinging to the sweet-gum, its wings still stunted. The other moth hung straight on its weed.

"I bet they's a book about them, telling their name and everwhat else about them," Cheney said.

"What's to tell?" Donnie asked. "They just hang around." He stripped off his T-shirt, dried his chest and under his arms, and turned his back on the sun, hugging himself, enjoying his rest. His feet kept time to an inner radio.

Ward said, "Mama Red asked about you."

Cheney lit another cigarette. "Me?"

"Said why didn't our good-looking boss stop by."

"I ain't no boss," Cheney said, pleased. "Musta meant Mr. Anderson." He lay back on the ground.

Donnie said, "Didn't say 'boss'—said 'the old man'. . ."

That was when Cheney caught on—they had made it up to tease him. He sat up. "Tell Mama Red I got me a good cook at home. I don't have to hire it."

"Whoooeee!" Donnie said.

Ward kept on. "I told her that. And you know what she said? Said you was the first married man she knew who enjoyed it."

"What'd you say?" Cheney studied his cigarette.

"Said you enjoyed it a couple of times a month—rest of the time you too tired."

Donnie gave his great huh-huh laugh.

"Check this," Cheney said. He dusted himself off, ran to the truck, and swung lightly up. On the crane he chinned himself, again and again. Ward kept count aloud, then lost interest.

Donnie said, "Any monkey can do that," and tossed a pine cone at him. Cheney ducked. He stood rubbing his palms on his jeans.

Ward climbed up. He wanted to try. He wasn't very good. Cheney said, "Your laigs'll get you wherever you need to go, but your arms'll make your fortune, boys. Them and knowing what five A.M. looks like every day but Sunday." He jumped to the ground and said, "Let's get this one finished. Two hours more ought to do it right."

Just that little break gave them energy. They started back to work, cheerful. Ward was whistling. Not thirty minutes later the hoist chain snapped as they loaded the truck, and the whiplash laid open Ward's scalp and took out his front teeth.

Donnie yelled, "No!" and jumped down, crying, "Jeez oh Jeez, Cheney!" Cheney was already there.

"It looks worse than it is," he said. That's the first thing he said when anything went wrong. He pulled the younger boy back. But Donnie swung around on him, wild.

"That's my brother! You fix it!"

Cheney said, "Son, you can help. Find the teeth."

The boy stood staring. Cheney said, *"Find the teeth."* The boy dropped to the ground, patting the dirt. Cheney said, "They can put them back. I saw it on TV. He don't have to go courting looking like me."

Ward's eyes flickered. He looked around. "God, I hope not," he tried to say. He turned his head to spit. "Blood," he said.

Cheney had taken off his shirt and was tying it around Ward's head. "You ain't pretty right now, that's a hundred percent sure." All the time he kept fixing the bandage. "Nurses going to drop dead right and left at the sight of you."

"That bad?" Ward coughed.

Donnie was crawling around under the truck, trying to find the teeth. "I got three. How many more?"

"Smile," Cheney said, trying to count Ward's gaps.

"You look like Halloween," Donnie said, helping count. He was red-eyed and sniffing, but he managed a huh-huh, and was steadier now.

"Aw, hell." Ward sat up. "I'm okay. Let's go back to work."

Cheney said, "First time I ever heard you say that. It must be the blow to your head." He and Donnie got Ward up and into the cab of the truck, and then they tightened down the load they had. The chains were rusty. Donnie rubbed that off his hands as if it were Ward's blood. They rode toward Deerfield, Ward between them. Donnie held Ward steady with one hand. In his other hand he still had the three teeth, all he ever found.

Cheney said, driving fast, "They can put them back in."

Donnie wanted them to go faster. "Put your hassle lights on and lean on it—he's my brother, man."

Cheney clicked on the emergency lights, but he didn't use the horn. The road was all theirs. He took the curves down the ridge in the middle, letting the loaded truck drift, then easing it back in bounds. He would get them there.

Deerfield was nine miles. When you got there, there wasn't much to it—one block of stores facing the railroad. But it was closer than anywhere else. And there was a dentist. He had a big plastic tooth for a sign, and a billboard at the city limits, needing a coat of paint.

"Dentist first," Ward mumbled. "I'd rather bleed to death than live looking like Cheney. Damn! I cain't even whistle up my dogs."

But at the dentist's, the nurse, seeing they were strangers, said, "All emergencies are cash," and left them to talk it over. Cheney rang the bell again. They had eleven dollars among them. He held out the teeth and showed her. "They can fix this."

She said, "I'll ask the doctor." She didn't touch the teeth. While she was gone, the patients looked at Cheney and the boys. When she came back, the nurse said. "If you have *proof* of insurance, of course we'll take that. Otherwise, cash." She smiled. "That's our policy for non-appointment emergencies. It's posted," she added, pointing. She wouldn't look at Ward, who sat forward so he wouldn't bloody the wall. He kept his handkerchief to his mouth, from time to time spitting into it.

Cheney said, "It was on TV, how they can put a man's teeth back, so he don't have to gum along empty." The nurse swung her chair to the typewriter and began to work. There was music coming down from the ceiling. Donnie was hunkered in front of the fish tank, looking at the deep-sea diver.

Ward pushed up from his chair and said through his stained handkerchief, "C'mon." He went out.

On the steps, Cheney said, "Maybe there's another dentist."

"Not this end of the county. Forget it. C'mon."

But Cheney went back in. He told the nurse, who looked frightened now, "My boss is Mr. Anderson . . . He'll pay. You call him?"

"We close in five minutes," she said.

"You could just call him—it's not long distance."

"*Look,*" she said, but that was all.

The waiting room was empty. There was a yellow umbrella hanging on the hat rack. It hadn't rained in weeks. Cheney could hear water running. He could hear voices and the mosquito noise of the drill. The fish tank's filter hummed and the treasure chest's lid bubbled open and shut, open and shut. Cheney left.

Donnie said, "I think he needs stitches."

Cheney looked. "Yeah, I guess."

"Aw, hell, they'll shave my head." Ward sounded weak.

"He paid thirty dollars for those curls," Donnie said.

"They'll only shear half of that wool," Cheney said.

Donnie didn't want Ward to hear. He said, "You reckon they'll take us to the hospital?"

Cheney shrugged. "If they don't, my old lady'll do it with spool thread and a darning needle."

"Momma's gonna have a fit," Donnie said.

The hospital was across the tracks. Cheney had to ease the truck over the rails. The side road was washed out. Donnie looked back, worried, but the load didn't shift. "That's all we need," he said.

It wasn't much of a hospital. Private, hardly larger than the dental clinic. "Maybe they're dog doctors," Ward said.

"An idea," Cheney said. "If they don't take you here, we'll drop you off at the pound. They'll feed you for a couple of days, and if nobody wants you, they'll put you out of your misery." They got him to the door, up the ramp, sagging between them. He was leaning hard when Cheney told the nurse at the desk, "My buddy here's been hurt. Got his skull busted open. We got eleven dollars. Maybe we can give blood or something for the difference." The nurse looked at them.

She rolled a wheelchair over and helped get Ward settled. "There'll be a way," she said.

Cheney stopped at the pay phone while they went on to Emergency. He found Mr. Anderson's card in his wallet and thumb-flicked the grime off the Atlanta number and dropped the quarter in. After he dialed, he could hear the faraway noises as his signal crossed the exchange boundary at the river. A long time later it began to ring. Mr. Anderson didn't answer. Nobody answered. Cheney tried again, to be sure. Then he went to find the boys.

They were asking Ward how long he had been knocked out. He didn't know. Cheney told them two minutes, maybe. Not long. Maybe less than that. The doctor wanted to take an X-ray of Ward's skull, just in case. Then they'd stitch up his scalp. It wasn't serious, they said, looking at Ward's eyes with a light. The bleeding had about stopped.

They told him he was lucky. One of the nurses had filled a rubber glove with ice to hold on Ward's mouth. He wanted a cigarette—Cheney was out, and Ward's were lost. Cheney said, "I'm going to the drugstore, okay?" and left Donnie in charge of waiting. They rolled Ward down the hall to take pictures.

Cheney walked back to town.

Traffic on the state road was heavy. He finally took a chance and dodged across. On the sidewalk, he stopped at the phone and tried to reach Mr. Anderson again. He didn't know how much X-rays would cost. But Mr. Anderson always said, "Do what you have to," if the truck needed a tire, or something done to the engine. Whatever it was, do it, and get on with the job. So Cheney thought it was alright about the X-rays, but he would like to talk to him to be sure. Mr. Anderson still didn't answer.

Cheney bought two packs of cigarettes—one for him and one for Ward. He headed back up the street toward the hospital road. Next to the Rexall there was an empty store, and then a dry goods store. In the window of the dry goods store were all sorts of things for spring: cardboard rabbits, little girl dresses like lamp shades, and a basket filled with plastic eggs. They hadn't gotten around to changing the window display, though Easter was past. The patent leather shoes looked dusty. The plastic tulips had faded. One of the wings was broken off the paper butterfly. That made Cheney think of the moths, and when he went past the last building on the block, on the corner, where the bank had been, he stopped and read FARMERS AND MERCHANTS carved in the stone of the fake front. It wasn't a bank now; it was a library. Cheney walked by, then went back. He stood another minute after finishing his smoke, and then he went inside.

He was going to look up the green moths. He hadn't counted on there being so many books. He didn't remember from school days where to look. He just stood there. He didn't see anyone, but in back, between high shelves, he could hear quick footsteps coming his way. The door had a cowbell on it—that was what gave the alarm. When the woman saw him, she stopped. She had a watering can in her hands, and it dripped a little.

"Yes?" She came up and stood between him and the books. "And you want?" She was as clean as Sunday. Her hands were white enough to make bread.

Cheney didn't know. He wished he didn't have so much of Ward's blood on his undershirt. He wished he didn't have so much rosin on his jeans. He wished that he had washed his hands. He put his hat back on. "I come in the wrong store," he said. "Reckon I just didn't notice where I was." He went out.

He looked back as he crossed the street. She was already pulling the shades down, and locking up for the night. It was going-home time for everybody. He didn't worry about his wife, even though he might be going home late. She was used to just about anything. Some days it took him a little longer, and she knew to keep the supper warm. When he was going to be very late, he'd call her sister, and she'd run the message by home.

Cheney figured they'd let Ward go as soon as they had stitched him up. Then Cheney would drop him and Donnie by their momma's house, and head on to the pulpyard. After that, he could go home.

When he got back, they had finished with Ward. He was sitting on the porch, and Donnie was sitting beside him. They looked okay. Cheney tossed Ward his cigarettes. He had a pack of crackers for Donnie.

Cheney went inside to tell them about the billing. They took down Mr. Anderson's name and phone number. It would be all right, they said. Cheney said, "Much obliged."

Ward and Donnie were already in the truck. Ward was feeling better. He still held the ice to his mouth, but he didn't have to spit so much. The bandage on his head wasn't that bad. The place they had sheared off the curls looked like where Rural Electric had clearcut for the powerline right-of-way through deep woods. Donnie said it again, "Momma's gonna have a fit."

Ward said, "Doc says for me not to do much for a couple of days, but I'll be ready tomorrow. I'll be ready." He talked fast. His tongue didn't know what to do with the gaps. He was talking funny from the shot they had given him.

"I'll find me somebody," Cheney said, "for the rest of the week."

"Don't give my job away."

"You know me," Cheney said, "I don't give nothing away worth anything." He handed Ward his teeth. "Put these under your pillow," he said.

After that he went to the woodyard. They didn't say anything much about the short load. It was sundown when Cheney got home. The kids ran down to meet him, riding on the running boards, yelling in the windows at him. Cheney went slow, the truck wallowing up the rutty drive. When his wife came out, with the baby, he said, "Just don't ask me about where's my shirt. You'd a lot rather I lost it than to have to wash Ward's blood out of it, anyhow."

She looked at his undershirt and said, "Bad hurt?"

"He knows what a rusty chain tastes like. He'll be ordering soup for a while."

The baby was fretting. Cheney took the child in his arms and talked to her. "Got any new teeth yet?" He checked. "Looks about like Ward." The baby began to cry. "Ssshh now," he said.

His wife said, "She won't."

A redbird chuck-chucked and flew across the clearing, with food for its mate. Cheney said, "It ought to be like that, him taking care of her, her doing her part, everybody working to make things go." The birds were almost black in the twilight.

"You going back after supper?" she asked, taking the baby.

"Let me think," he said.

They headed on up to the double-wide. She had been planting flower seeds near the porch. The ground was all dug up and there was a hoe lying there. She was outlining the flowerbed in rocks. On the way past she picked up the hoe. "Put this up," she told the nearest boy. He rode it over to the shed, straddling it like a horse.

"Y'all already ate?" Cheney said.

"We waited . . . You hungry?"

"I could take nourishment," he said.

While they were eating, his wife asked again, "You going back tonight?"

"Every stick I cut now when it's cool'll save me some sweat in July."

"We'll come too."

"Baby's sick, ain't she?"

His wife laid a hand on the child's forehead. "Teething fever's all it is. You know how they fret. We won't hinder."

"I didn't think you would. I don't want you lifting a twig, though. You know what the doctor said."

"I'm better," she said. "I been digging like a field hand all day . . . The boys can help you."

"I wouldn't mind the company," he said.

They worked in the wedge of the truck's headlights. Cheney had a lantern, too. He set it on the stump and told the kids to leave it alone, and they mostly did. The boys helped him load. The baby chewed on the corner of a washcloth, watching them work. She started to fret and cry every time Cheney's wife tried to lay her down on the quilt.

His wife was willing to let the baby cry it out, but Cheney said, "Put something in that child's mouth." It got on his nerves to think the baby was unhappy.

"One thing she wants," his wife said.

"Everwhat it takes,"Cheney said.

His wife took the baby to the truck and sat nursing her in the cab.

The day's wood was mostly sweet-gum. None of the trees was very big. The boys could carry two rounds across their arms each trip. The truck bed slowly filled. Cheney would have cut some more stove lengths, but the baby was finally asleep—the saw would wake her for sure. She lay on the seat of the truck, but she still held to her mother's shirt hem.

His wife shrugged and smiled. Cheney said, "She been like that all day?" His wife looked tired.

She said, "It's harder on her than on me."

Cheney pulled his wife's shirttail out of the baby's fist, and the baby didn't wake. "Come here," he said. He took the lantern and walked over to the sweet-gum tree where he had left the green moth. It was still there. They both were there, on that tree. Cheney told his sons, "Don't mess with them."

The crippled moth was still shriveled, but the perfect one had found it. One of the perfect wings was broken now, as though there had been a fight.

"They's like a cup and saucer," his wife said, and pressed her right fist against her left palm, in a cup and saucer gesture.

The moths were completely still. They were joined at right angles, end to end. The boys said, "What is it?" and Cheney said, "It's a moth." He puffed the lantern out after lighting his cigarette from it. "It's hot," he warned, handing it to the boys. "Put it in the truck, safe, and both of you get in back, go on."

His wife told them, "Don't y'all wake her!"

In the beam of the headlights, dimmer and more faraway than the lantern's glare, the moths seemed to be one living thing, not two. Cheney's wife bent to see better. The moths were so still. "So that's how," she said.

Her shadow didn't disturb them. Nothing did. "You reckon they dead, Cheney?" She took a straw, the way Donnie had, earlier that day, and touched the one with the crippled wings. The little dark leg lifted, warning. She stepped back. "Looks like a spider leg," she said. She shook her head.

The flat, perfect one was belly up, but Cheney could remember how it looked topside. "It's got red around the edge. All around. And brown. And a sort of eye-looking thing on each wing," Cheney told her. Right then, before she could stoop to see the moth's back, they parted. The perfect one flew low and rested on some broken branches on the ground, then flew again.

Cheney could tell the other one wouldn't fly, couldn't fly. "Maybe it don't need," he said. "Maybe it just don't need to." He waited to see.

"We don't go soon, the battery's gonna run down." His wife looked around at the truck. The headlights were yellow and dim.

"Cut the lights off," Cheney called, and the boys wrestled to be the one to hit the switch. They flicked them back on again, playing. Cheney said, "Boys?" and then it got dark.

There was a little air stirring. The pines on tomorrow's cutting were tall against the first stars. Up toward Hammermill the sky was lighter.

Cheney could see, after his eyes got sharper, the glint of the mayonnaise jar he had brought his tea in for lunch. He had forgotten it when they left to take care of Ward. He picked it up. The lid was missing. Cheney tossed it—it hit on something and smashed. "I'm so goddamn tired of being poor," he said.

The smoke from the day's burning stumps drifted toward them across the acres. They walked back to the truck in the dark. The baby was still sleeping and the boys had settled down in the back, tired out, crouched on the logs, quiet, almost asleep.

Cheney steered home easy. The Ford rode home low in the back from the load, the headlights striking high on the passing trees and signs. There was all that wood to unload when they got home. His wife mentioned that.

"It looks worse than it is," Cheney said.

The baby was sleeping good—she liked to ride along. The boys used to be that way, sleeping till they got home, and he'd lift one under each arm like groceries, carry them up the steps into the house to their bunks. But they were too big for that now. They were growing fast.

NICKELS AND DIMES

Greg Johnson

I haven't been here ten minutes when she gives me that look. You'd think she'd know better, working here in Grady's ER, but she can't be more than twenty-two, skin fresh as a baby's, so maybe she's just out of school. Still clinging to her Florence Nightingale fantasies. My calling her Florence, trying to make a joke never mind that I'm hurting like hell—stabbing pains in left thigh and side, left arm surely broken—is what earned me that look in the first place.

Roughly translated, the look means something like this: How did you get in this fix, anyway? You don't seem to be drunk, you don't strike me as a moron or a psycho. I'm detecting a glimmer of intelligence now and then, and you look young and strong, and reasonably healthy. So what are you doing here? Would you kindly explain yourself?

Maybe I'm reading too much into just a look, but I've gotten enough of them, these past few weeks. Like I said, it's a rough translation.

"How fast was the car going?" she says now, gingerly touching my ribs.

"About twenty, twenty-five. He tried to veer off, but too late."

We're both looking down at my side. There's a visible gash, but to my surprise it's not bleeding. This may sound strange, but I'm disappointed. And that's not all. When we first came in here, Florence draped my shirt over the portable wall-on-wheels that divides us from the next cubicle, but if the smell hit her nostrils, she didn't show it. It's two months since the shirt saw a rinse cycle, almost a month since my last full-fledged shower. When she asks me to raise my left arm, I hesitate a second but not because of the pain.

"I don't think it's broken," she says, frowning. "Just a sprain, maybe. We'll get one of the docs in here . . ." She turns and peers beyond the partition. When she first led me in here, there was a big black Mama sitting next-door with a carving knife stuck in her head. Not her cheek or her neck—her head, just above one ear. It looked like some sort of weird Afro headgear, and I didn't see any blood. Even Florence was startled, but the Mama just smiled and said hello.

"It's a good thing you didn't pull that out," Florence had told her. "You'd have been in trouble then."

"I knows better," the Mama said. "I done been here befo."

Now I can hear Florence asking her, "Honey, has a doctor seen you yet?"

I don't hear the answer because I'm staring at Florence's rear end, so beautifully outlined by the starched white uniform as she leans around the partition. There's a swelling in my pants, so I guess I'm still alive.

Now Florence glances over and I think she catches me looking. She doesn't show it, though, so maybe she's savvier than she lets on. Which makes me like her even more. All the time I'm thinking this, I forget about the pain and about getting knocked into West Peachtree and hit by a three-ton red Buick.

"Honey," she says (and I'm thinking, how nice if I hadn't heard her call the black Mama that), "just wait for a minute, would you? I'm going to see what the hold-up is."

She hesitates, giving me that look again—it's brief but unmistakable. I'm not imagining it.

"Honey, I'm not going anywhere," I tell her, and I even manage a little wink.

The cops delivered me here, though I asked for an ambulance. "Those're mighty expensive, son," the older cop said. He was fat and friendly, though he never looked right at me. (I've had considerable trouble, lately, in getting the visual attention of other folks; I'm wondering if there's some new comic book idea here, *The Invisible Guy.*) "C'mon," the cop said, "I'll drop you off." Then he said, "Good luck, son," as we pulled up to the glass doors of the ER; his skinny younger partner hadn't said a word. I waited a second, all of a sudden feeling scared and wanting the big one to walk me inside. But I told myself that my daddy was dead and you do not get a replacement. I said, "Thanks, sir," and hobbled clear of the car.

When I get scared, I get jokey, so when I found the reception desk I emptied both my pockets' worth of change onto the counter. The young black chick working the desk was on the phone, but she watched from the sides of her eyes. There were four nickels and seven dimes, along with some pocket lint. There weren't any pennies and I was glad. Even the silver coins looked small and grimy under the bright fluorescent lights. "Ma'am?" I said, though she was still on the phone. "When you've got a minute, I'm interested in buying me some first-class medical care." And I laughed, which felt like a white-hot poker stabbing my side. I doubled over with the pain. "Sir," the receptionist said sharply, one palm over the mouthpiece. "Would you please sit over there and wait your turn?" I glanced toward one wall, where a row of the sorriest-looking critters you could imagine sat on bright orange plastic chairs. I straightened, and I guess the strain showed on my face; the receptionist's eyes softened a little. "I'll bring you some forms to fill out," she said. "In a few minutes." I nodded. "Sorry, I was just—" but even though it had been a joke, like I said, there wasn't any point in explaining. With the edge of one hand, I scraped my change back off the counter. I sat against the wall like I was told.

Seeing my little pile of coins reminded me of something Daddy used to say. When Rafe and I wanted to go to the movies, or to play pinball down at the A&W, he'd dig in his pockets and roll his eyes and complain how we were "nickel and diming" him to death. He'd be smiling, though; I knew he was proud that he had the change to give us. Unlike his "good-for-nothing" kid brothers who'd dropped out of school and wandered off, never to be seen again, Daddy held a good job in the tire plant until one morning when the plant machinery mistook his arm for a hunk of unformed rubber. By then, Mama had been dead six months and he'd been drinking quite a bit. Had he gotten drunk on the job, gotten careless? He never told, and after sitting up in the house for a while, getting his disability, he never said much of anything. Just stared at the TV. If you said something to him, he muttered answers nobody could interpret. So Rafe and I just decided to let him alone. One time we were at Daddy's house, a Sunday, all three sitting in front of a ball game, and Daddy muttered something about a beer. When I came back from the kitchen I said, "Okay, here it is, but, Daddy, you're nickel and diming me to death, you really are." I rolled my eyes just the way he used to do. Rafe laughed out loud, but Daddy's eyes stayed glued to the TV. It was that day when Rafe and I decided: just let him be.

My brother and I worked at the tire plant, too, but a few months after Daddy's funeral I got laid off. Rafe found out he was sick during that same week. I was over at Rafe and Marsha's, and I said, "Brother, we sound like a goddamned soap opera." Rafe laughed, but Marsha had been crying, and she gave me a look straight from hell and ran out of the room. Shoot, I knew what leukemia was, but I felt sure that Rafe could beat anything. Ever since we were kids, he'd been the calm and steady one, harder-working and better-liked, even though I did better in school and much better with girls. (Rafe looked just like Daddy, and I often wondered: did Daddy think I took after his vanished kid brothers, good-looking rascals who never did anything for the family? If he thought that, he never said it.) So I just let the word *leukemia* wash right past me; even after I'd gone flat broke and moved in with Rafe and Marsha, I tried not to think about it. But I saw he was getting sicker and sicker; I knew Marsha wasn't just being a hysterical woman, though I thought it to myself, what with all her worrying night and day (and out loud, really loud) about the plant maybe laying off Rafe, too, just to keep from paying his medical bills. I'd point out that they couldn't do that; it was surely illegal. Of course, I didn't know what I was talking about, and for opening my mouth I'd get further looks from the realm of Beelzebub.

Pretty soon, I figured, Marsha would be asking Rafe to kick me out. ("Has he looked at the want ads lately?" I overheard her asking, out in the kitchen one morning. "Is he even trying?" "Hell, yeah, he's trying," Rafe said, though I didn't hear much conviction in his voice. "You know how things are in this city nowadays, if you ain't finished college. Atlanta's just turned into a little New York, if you're asking me." This didn't sound like Rafe, and I wondered if it was something he'd heard from Daddy. "Besides," Rafe said, "he's still all riled about Cindy, you know? I know he don't say nothing, but—") That's when I closed the door to their little spare room and plopped back down on the bed. In fact, I *had* been reading the morning want ads—and Marsha knew it, while she was cooking Rafe's eggs I'd asked if I could borrow the paper—but now I stared at the newsprint and the little red circles I'd made and it all started to blur. I pushed the paper aside, kicking my legs until the sheet dropped to the floor. I decided that I'd have it out with Marsha. Rafe was her husband, sure, but he was my brother, and I intended to pay back every dime they'd spent on feeding me. We never had this airing-out, though, because Rafe took a turn for the worse that very day, and never came back from the hospital.

So, to answer Florence's sweetly puzzled and sympathetic look, that's how I joined the ranks of the great unwashed. She could read the form, if she liked, that I filled out for the ER receptionist. Age twenty-six, three years of college, 4.5 years of steady work experience, though granted I spent every check as soon as I got it. Marital status, single, though I came awfully close. Too close, maybe. For almost everything else, I put "none" (Employment, "none," Insurance Coverage, "none," Next of Kin or Other Person Who Will Be Responsible for Your Bill, "absolutely none—sorry!"), but maybe there's enough information that Florence could figure it out, if she tried; and who knows, maybe she will.

I was certainly glad, I'll tell you, when she came out between two cubicles and said, "Eustace, James," looking around her with a pleasant expression as though meeting Eustace, James, would be the high point of her life so far. I'd started to get depressed, sitting out there with my colleagues in the plastic chairs. There was a woman with a puffy dark-bruised face; she kept cradling her arm, and moaning. There was a tiny black man with bright yellow eyes and, it seemed like, no eyelids— not that I looked too closely. There were a couple of teenaged guys who mumbled to each other nonstop, high on something, but I couldn't see that either one was hurt. One of them coughed a lot, though. And soon after I filled out the forms, in came the black Mama with the knife in her head, looking calm as you please. They took her right inside, probably figuring she wouldn't do much for morale out in the waiting room. By the time Florence showed up, they'd brought in two women from a pretty bad car accident. One was unconscious, but the other was screaming to beat the band. They lay on gurneys in the hallway, and a black orderly had set up IVs, but after that they were pretty much ignored. The loud one kept calling for her mother, and for someone named Fred. The thin gurney mattress had soaked through, and her blood had started to drip onto the floor.

So I said to Florence, as she led me to the cubicle, "Now wait a minute, this is Disneyland, right? I must've taken the wrong bus stop, huh?"

She smiled and said, "Very funny." And it was.

Now, though, she's been gone a long while; the doctors here must be in short supply. My arm is throbbing, and my left side feels hot and raw, but what's strange is that I focus on my stomach. When I get in bad situations, it always acts up. Those last few times with Cindy . . . that day I understood I was really on the street . . . that fine morning a few weeks ago when some black guys rolled me in an empty parking lot over on Eighth, took my sleeping roll, watch, corduroy jacket, and my little stash of grimy pathetic wadded-up dollar bills. My stomach goes into heavy turmoil at such times, and good luck sneaking into some store or restaurant to find a bathroom. . . . But the good news, as they say, is that the doctor—his name is Ogilvy—turns out to be nice. His smile is really sweet, he calls me "Sonny," and he clicks his tongue while doing the examination. The bad news is that he looks to be about 112 years old, and I can feel his hands shaking as they move along my side. They're cool and papery, like a granddaddy's hands. But I guess I'm not in a position to be choosy.

"Did they get the driver?" he asks, writing some shaky notes on a little pad.

"No, but they'd probably like to give him a medal," and then I could kick myself for saying that. For it's then that he gives me the look, too. Who *are* you, Sonny. And Florence is hovering over by the partition, her usual sweet and puzzled self. These are the villains of my story, I'm thinking. I can't have Nurse Ratched and Dr. Mengele, oh no. Can't get any kind of break at all.

So now Dr. Ogilvy tries some grandfatherly humor. "You're too smart a boy," he says, "to be playing out in the street."

I have to smile at that one; it's then I understand that I haven't been smiling.

"You got me," I tell him. "So what's the news. Is it broken?"

"No, just a bad sprain," he says, "but I'd like to keep you overnight, Mr. Eustace." All of a sudden, he sounds serious; I liked "Sonny" much better. "I'd like to do some X-rays," he says, "and see how that side is doing in the morning."

"Overnight?" I ask. "Well, I could stay in Florence's room," and I glance toward the partition.

Dr. Ogilvy looks in her direction, squinting. He doesn't get it. He probably hasn't gotten it in quite some time, I'm thinking, but I guess I shouldn't joke with the old guy.

"Look," I tell him. "I can't pay."

He ignores this. He tears the top sheet off his pad and hands it to Florence. "See what you can arrange," he says, and then he gives me that sweet smile again. Now I see that it's his professional smile and that he probably knows what he's doing, after all. "See you in the morning, Sonny," he says, his clodhopper wing-tips shuffling along the tiles as he goes out.

"You're lucky," Florence murmurs, helping me with my shirt. "Doc Ogilvy's retiring next year, but he's still one of the best. He'll take good care of you."

I start to say something smart, but all at once there's a catch in my throat. I manage to say, "That's good news. I haven't had much of that, lately."

She steps back, watching me. "I'll be right back," she says, and she looks blurry, like some kind of white-dressed apparition.

She says, "I'm going to get you something for the pain."

When I wake up, it's pitch black except for some sort of droning, or buzzing. I blink my eyes, and gradually understand there's a TV up near the ceiling. My mouth feels dry, cottony. I start working my tongue, trying to keep my eyes open and understand where I am. I guess I'm really here, an official guest of Grady Memorial Hospital. Hot damn, as Decker would say. He's this black dude out on the street who told me he'd gotten thrown in jail this past winter to get himself out of the cold. Said Fulton County detention was safer than most of the so-called shelters, and not quite as smelly. I'd met Decker first thing when I walked out of the Y, where I'd gone after Rafe's funeral and stayed until my cash ran out. When I called Marsha to ask for a small loan, she said in a grief-thick voice that the movers would be arriving any minute and to call her new number in a few days. So I waited, then used one of my remaining quarters and dialed the number and learned it would be cool tonight, showers likely, low in the mid-fifties.

That morning, Decker had caught my stymied look. Even though it was mid-April, he wore a navy pea-coat and a knitted cap pulled down past his eyebrows. He could've been thirty, or fifty—I soon learned that guys on the street all look the same age. He was a light-skinned dude, with sharp features and one gold tooth. Looked at me sideways, that first time, and asked for a light; before long he'd gotten a buck out of me and given me a short introduction to life out here. That's what Decker always called it—"out here." He laughed when I said I was looking for a job. He said I was lucky I'd missed the winter, and told me to keep to the busy streets at night and avoid Piedmont Park. We never hung together, really, but as the days passed he seemed to be everywhere, lounging against a parked car or rummaging through a trash bin at the next corner. I'll admit that I was usually glad to see him.

His scowling, slit-eyed face keeps coming to mind as I watch the static-filled TV screen. I've been wondering who's on the other side of the partition, and I can hear myself asking, in Decker's snide voice, "What's a room here cost, anyway? A hundred a day, two hundred? And who the hell is paying?" But I've done better than Decker ever could with his petty jail time (vagrancy charges, usually), and the big chip he carries on his shoulder. . . . It's then I catch myself. I'm thinking like one of them. And I catch myself again. One of *them*? I don't seem to fit anywhere, exactly, as if I'm waiting for someone to tell me which side I'm on, just who or what I am.

Like a three-ton red Buick, maybe. Splat, kid, here's what you are. Dead meat.

But not quite yet. I'm lying afloat in the Never-Never Land of a hospital late at night. Vaguely I remember them bringing me up here, and helping me out of my clothes. Some black guy—for a second I thought it was Decker—gave me a sponge bath. He laughed whenever I said anything, showing huge white teeth. What was I saying? The shot they gave me had sent me high as a kite. I remember eating a little something, I remember stumbling into the bathroom, but mostly I drifted in and out of sleep as though my brain were filled with heavy fog. The pain was gone, sure enough. My worries too, for a while, all except that vague nattering about who or what I was, the way half-remembered dreams will tug at your mind in the middle of the day, like a pull at your sleeve, to tell you something you don't want to know.

Somewhere around dawn a nurse comes in and these vague thoughts scatter like confetti. I've begun to hurt, and hurt bad. Arm and side throbbing, a burning in my left thigh as if jabbed by a red-hot needle.

The nurse isn't Florence and my insides deflate like a kid's balloon. I guess she went home, or else is still down in ER and has forgotten me by now. What's that song?—oh poor, poor pitiful me. That's the one.

This new nurse—an older gal with iron-gray hair—bends to my ear. "I'm here to change the bandages. How are you?"

"Okay, I guess, but all of it hurts."

She asks if I want more medication. She says it's allowed.

"Yes, thanks, if it's all right."

"I'll let it take effect," she says, "before I start pulling on those bandages."

"I appreciate that, ma'am," I say sincerely. I'm lying here thinking to myself how wrong Decker was. When we'd shuffled through Midtown together he'd whisper sideways in my ear about the prosperous folks passing by us, how they didn't give a shit about us and didn't even see us any more. Businessmen with their silk ties flapping in the wind, dressed-up women carrying briefcases and using their free hands to keep their hair in place—all of them in a rush, staring down at the sidewalk. I didn't see that they were particularly heartless, just hurrying, but it didn't do to contradict Decker. He'd raise his screechy voice and repeat himself until he'd worn you down. He had evil things to say about the police, lawyers, doctors, just everybody. Now I'm looking forward to telling him about Florence and Doc Ogilvy, though I know he'll think of some way to put them down. I guess it's the main difference between Decker and me: he's given himself over to being on the outside, whereas with me it's just a run of hard luck. I'm thinking that when I'm back on my feet and have a job, I'll drive through Midtown and look for Decker and offer to help him somehow, if only to make him eat all his ugly words.

By eight o'clock the pills have kicked in, my bandages are changed, and I've had some oatmeal and juice. The guy in the next partition—I still haven't seen him—has turned on the *Today* show, where this black movie star is talking about his latest action-adventure. Behind his glossy smiling face I can see Decker's sly dirty one, mocking everything the movie star says. I'm in the midst of this daydream when Doc Ogilvy touches my shoulder.

"How we doing, Sonny?"

"You're a sight for sore eyes," I tell him, and he's grinning while he pokes at my arm and ribcage.

"Say doc, is there some way I could take a shower?"

He thinks a minute. "Make sure you face the water with your right side," he says, "and then just sponge on the left, around the bandages. You'll need to be careful for a while, you know."

"Gotcha," I tell him, and for some reason I start talking again about the money. "Listen, is there some way I can help out around here? I hate being a charity case."

"Down on your luck, are you?" he asks. "Got a place to live?"

"Not right now, but . . ."

"You're young, good-looking, and smart," he says, like he's talking to himself. "It doesn't make sense, does it?"

"No sir," I say, starting to feel embarrassed. "But it's just a temporary thing. I've had some college, you know. I'll be working before long. I mean to pay back what I'm spending here."

"Never mind that," he says. Finished with the exam, he pats the sheet around my chest and adjusts his spectacles and fixes his little blue-gray eyes on mine. I can see that he's a smart and shrewd old guy. His eyes aren't smiling but he says, in a kind voice, "Why don't you stop by personnel on your way out this afternoon, ask for Michelle. You could get something permanent, I'm pretty sure. I'll put in a word for you."

My heart is pounding so fast I can feel the first glimmers of pain come back to my ribcage. "Thanks, doc," I tell him. "I appreciate that. You know, there's this guy I met out on the street, and he thinks—"

I break off when I feel the crisp bill against my palm. I open my hand to see that it's a fifty.

"This should help till your first check," Doc Ogilvy says. "Pay it back whenever you can. And don't worry about the hospital bill, the government will pick that up. I'm sure you've paid some taxes before, haven't you?"

"Yes, sir," I tell him, but I don't say anything else because I'm feeling so grateful. I figure he sees it in my eyes.

A little before noon the older nurse comes back with a small kit of bandages and ointments, and instructions for the next few days. From what she's saying, I can tell she doesn't know I'll be out on the street, and I'm glad of that. Maybe I'll use the fifty to check back into the Y, and then ask personnel for an advance on my first week's pay. I'm thinking fast and only half-listening to the nurse, but when she says, "Would you like another Percodan before we check you out?" I tell her yes, and I also tell her that Doc Ogilvy has okayed a shower. She watches me swallow the pain pill, and then she says, "Okay, I'll come back in half an hour, and then we'll get you out of here." I say, "Sounds good," wondering how she'd react if I told her I'd like to stay another week.

By the time I get in the shower, the pill is taking effect. I can move my arm better now, and those hot jabs in my leg are dying down. For some reason I'm excited and happy, keyed-up, and have to keep reminding myself not to get the bandages wet. Before stepping into the tub I glimpse myself naked in the bathroom mirror and of course that gets me thinking of Cindy, how we used to shower together and afterward watch in the mirror as we dried each other off, so slowly, sometimes laughing, other times serious and quiet, of all things I'd have to remember that now. But I can't help feeling hopeful, I feel like this past day or two is a turning point, maybe I needed that Buick to knock some sense into Eustace, James. (Didn't one of my high-school teachers say, laughing, "You're smart Jimmy, but you haven't got a bit of common sense"? No, nor common cents, either, but let's recall that she's the same teacher that made a pass at me, in her office, when I was still a sophomore, so maybe common sense isn't so common, after all?) But, in effect, Cindy said the same thing. I took her for granted, she claimed. We weren't going anywhere, she claimed, just drifting, whereas she wanted to build something with a man and not just drift from week to week, paycheck to paycheck. She didn't want the same life her mother and aunts had lived— the life *my* mother and aunts had lived, for that matter—there was more to life than sex and laughter and cuddling in bed on Sunday afternoons, God knew I'd been valuable for that, she said laughing, about to cry, about to turn and walk out for the last time, but no, she said, she just couldn't invest any more time in this. She didn't want—and now she spat out the words, making them as ugly as possible maybe (who knows) so I'd be able to say, Good riddance—she said, in a low queer whisper, I don't want to be the wife of a factory worker, James. I want more than that.

So she did walk out, closing the door gently behind her. No slamming doors for her. No raised voices. Just cutting her losses, you might say.

Okay, I'm thinking, so it was like that Buick crunching a few bones, knocking the breath out of me, only Cindy had knocked the will out of me. For a while, anyway. Who's to say her new white-collar boyfriend hasn't walked out on her by now, who's to say he isn't a loser in bed and she's wishing like hell she knew where to reach me? She'll know soon enough, I'm thinking. Two, maybe three months at the Y, then enough saved for first and last months' rent on a nice apartment, and the phone deposit, and the utilites deposit, and so on, and then one quiet summer night I'll give her a call, I'll set candles around the tub, have the champagne chilled, who's to say all this isn't within my reach, here in the land of opportunity known as the U.S. of A.?

Okay, I'm letting the pain pill and this lovely hot water make me goofy, I'm smiling up into the shower nozzle and letting the water stream down my face like happy tears, I'm thinking of being in that tub with Cindy and yes I'm getting myself tremendously horny in the process (how long since I've felt horny, by the way?—for a while, I just let the street unman me), but the remedy's quick enough, two or three hard pulls, that's how long it's been, oh Cindy Cindy here I come, and I moan thickly into the streaming water like a wounded animal and stand there a few seconds with eyes closed, catching my breath, and I twist the faucets to *Off* and stand there dripping, panting, never mind that the bandages are ruined and maybe I'm bleeding a little, never mind that I've lost my family and girlfriend and have fifty bucks and change to my name, everything has turned around and I feel so clean and warm, that deep glow in my belly branching out in all directions, I'm healing, I'm getting well, I'm going to be all right.

I remember one of Decker's favorite phrases and murmur aloud, smiling, "Thank you, Jesus!"

But not in Decker's bitter chortling voice.

Well, the nurse gives me a *tsk-tsk* while she redoes the bandages, but we joke back and forth, talking about anything, everything, I'm so happy that it seems to be contagious. "Good luck, Mr. Eustace," she says in the lobby, once the paperwork is done. "You follow those instructions, now!" I tell her that I'll surely do that, and I have the weird idea that I ought to tip her or something, but that's ridiculous, I push the thought away. All at once I'm out on the street in the bland May sunshine, feeling wonderfully clean and naked under my clothes. Even the clothes are clean, courtesy of hospital laundry while I was in bed. When I see the bus approaching from the next block, I dig in my pockets for the change and count it up—ninety cents, exactly the right amount. I take this as a sign and I'm glad, I didn't want to break the fifty yet.

I get off at the Arts Center, and it's not ten minutes before I see Decker, over on the other side of Peachtree. He's leaning up against one of the white stone walls at Colony Square, hunched and bitter-looking, his knitted cap pulled down across his eyes. The noontime lunch crowd crisscrosses the walkways in front of him, well-dressed, chattering, but Decker stands there motionless, his arms folded. He's dark-clothed and grimy here in the warm sunlit air, his very posture a rebuke to the shoppers and office workers streaming by. Not that they see him, of course. But I see him, and I'm so intent on getting over there, lurching across Peachtree against the light, that I earn a few horn blasts from the heavy traffic and almost get myself knocked flat again.

"Hey Decker, how's it going?" I call when I get close enough. I'm determined to be friendly.

"Man, you got any money?" he says, but he still doesn't move, as if he's conserving energy. I'm not sure he even remembers me.

"Sure," I tell him. "Just got out of the hospital, though. Folks there were nice as hell."

It's then my stomach lurches: I forgot to stop by the personnel office and ask for Michelle, whose name alone made me want to meet her. So damned high on the pain pill that I forgot all about it.

"That right?" Decker says, with a nasty grin. "Folks just so nice, was they?"

"Listen, Decker, you've got it all wrong," I tell him. "Come on, I'll buy you some lunch. You want a burger?"

"Man, that Buick like to made *you* into a burger—that's how nice folks is." He laughs, but so deep in his chest you can hardly hear it.

"That was an accident. Nobody meant to—"

"What the fuck you talkin about, man?" Now he does move, shifting his weight from foot to foot. Uneasy. Furious. "Man, you done forgot that you got pushed into that street? Ain't you recalled that I was there and seen the whole thing?"

I stand there for a moment, stymied. Yeah, I could remember that the street was crowded, and somehow I'd gotten knocked off the sidewalk . . . maybe, now that I think of it, I can even remember a hand in my side, a hard and deliberate shove . . . but no, it had just been an accident, I wasn't going to be tainted by Decker's evil thinking.

"You're full of shit," I tell him.

"Better than shit for brains," he says, "walkin round talkin 'bout how *nice* folks is. Man, you gettin hit in the street was a big show for these folks, somethin to see on the way home from work. Shit, to them, that's all you're good for—something to shove in the street, and watch it get splattered all to hell."

"They treated me good at the hospital," I tell him. For some reason I'm breathing hard. "They gave me money."

"Sure they gave you money," he says. He looks away, coolly.

So I dig into my pocket and pull out the fifty. I know it's still the pain pill and I'm acting like a fool but all of a sudden I don't care, I wave the fifty in front of his veiled black eyes and then I grab his scabby dry hand and close it around the money.

"There you go, shithead, and don't say nobody ever did anything for you," and with that I turn around and start walking. It's half a block before I understand I'm walking in the wrong direction—I don't have a dime, literally, so I'd better be heading toward Grady. Turning, I can't resist glancing back toward Decker, needing to see the look on his face. But he's long gone, and I'm standing here like a fool. All around me are strangers, and my side's hurting again, so I duck my head and keep walking, starting to limp a little, thinking that some time must pass before something good can happen.

THE MEMORIAL

Terry Kay

It was a practice of each morning for Seth Pennefeather and Whitman Robart to meet at seven-thirty in the Corner Cafe for coffee. At five minutes before eight, each man would place two dimes beside his empty cup, one for coffee and one for Beatrice Allen's perfumed service, and they would then walk directly across the street to begin their business day. Seth's furniture store and Whitman's department store were side-by-side, joined by a brick wall that fused them like an attachment of Siamese twins.

Seth's and Whitman's early morning conversations were rehearsals for the roles they would inevitably perform during the day. It was an exercise in mood-setting and though the mood was most often one of languor in the habitual exchange of greetings and in trite compliments to Beatrice, Seth and Whitman were easily influenced by the effect of the external world on their ritualistic twenty-five minutes together. They sat always in the same place, at the second table in a row of booths, close to the window, and stared at the external world through the slats of venetian blinds, like aging scholars reading prophecies in obscure nuances. Seasons. Habits. Fidelities. All passed before the windowseat occupied by Seth and Whitman in the Corner Cafe and all were judged in monosyllabic agreements. The agreements were important. The agreements meant harmony and harmony was the bond between Seth and Whitman. They could not risk imbalance by an irritation as needless as argument. Seth and Whitman had achieved (reached, discovered, lucked upon) the sublimity of perfect tolerance, and the fraternal trust of that high attainment sustained them against haphazard assaults of chance and change. They enjoyed childish slander and accusations and even the most insignificant heroics dazzled them.

Still, there was an importance to their mornings that not even Seth and Whitman realized: their agreements emitted a signal that rippled throughout Edenville like the voice of sovereign authority. It was the electric spark that drove the heart pump of Edenville and, in its mysterious way, provided energy for the great and small parts of the town's body.

Though both belonged to the three-man City Council (had for years), Seth and Whitman did not make decisions; they refined the half-sentences of attitudes and reached comfortable compromises, and because they knew they were in agreement, it was easy to promote their judgments, without deliberate intention or even their awareness, to other people. It had become part of their character to use the collective "we" and when they spoke individually to other people of their opinions, the discussions were always prefaced with, "We was talking . . . " Everyone in Edenville knew who the "we" was, and it was that qualification, that quick overture into their thoughts, that gave Seth and Whitman credibility and made them more important than they imagined. To Seth and Whitman, their morning coffee habit was nothing more than homage to friendship, a private quietness. They had no idea that Edenville was eavesdropping.

And on July 12, 1954, Edenville waited eagerly for Seth and Whitman to agree on a rumor that none of them could believe: Cy Hall, the great baseball player, was coming home.

"Could be right," Seth said, sugaring his coffee.

"You think so?" Whitman asked.

"Could be," Seth said again. "Cleveland was saying he'd talked to him personal."

"Could be, then," Whitman said. "Sure could."

"Town ought to be proud, him coming back, if he does."

"What I was thinking," Whitman said, nodding. "He made a name for himself."

"And the town," Seth added, peering through the opened slats of the blinds as two boys on bicycles crossed the street lazily. "Can't forget the town. Saying you live in Cy Hall's hometown means something."

"It does. Sure does. What old Ben Phelps been saying all these years."

Seth sighed a laugh and sipped from his coffee. He said in a whisper intended only for Whitman, "I bet old Ben's about to pee in his pants. He's been saying Cy'd come back someday."

"Been saying it for fifty years, I guess," Whitman agreed. "Long as I can remember people been laughing at him."

"Well, maybe old Ben can have the last laugh. I'd guess he was right about Cy coming back. He does, the town ought to be proud to have him. That's the way I see it."

"Me, too," Whitman said. "Ought to be real proud."

By the end of the day, July 12, 1954, everyone in Edenville was preening with the joy of the news of Cy Hall's return. Seth and Whitman had confirmed it, or almost confirmed it, and it had become an exultation of gossip by older citizens, a confetti of words shredded from the speculation that Cy Hall planned to buy a select tract of land and build a fine, expensive home that would be a monument to Edenville. He had corresponded with Cleveland Prichard by mail about the house, had even included designs clipped from magazines or sketched in his own hand. Cleveland Prichard was the most accomplished builder in Edenville. If anyone could construct a home for Cy Hall, it would be Cleveland. Besides, someone—Seth Pennefeather or Whitman Robarts—had speculated that Cleveland's recent absence from Edenville was due to a trip made to California to talk to Cy Hall. Cleveland refused to talk about the rumor. If he had met with Cy Hall, it was a private matter. And the people of Edenville said, "He's met, all right."

"Ought to be something," the people said.

"It'd have to be. Cleveland's keeping quiet about it and that ain't like Cleveland. God knows, it ain't. He'd brag on building a hogpen."

"Cleveland won't even talk about it. Not a word. He just turns away, without saying nothing."

"That proves it right there. He's been to California and I'd bet my last dime on it."

In the days that followed, Seth's and Whitman's morning agreements about the latest news of Cy Hall's return to Edenville left the Corner Cafe with them and became distorted and circled back to Seth and Whitman with an embellishment so gaudy that it had the sound of a new truth, and Seth and Whitman were astonished each morning by the additional speculations. They said to one another, in innocence, "Wonder where such things get started?"

Those who knew, or said they knew, told of Cy Hall's obsession about returning to the South. He had been away all those years, living in the sun of California, perpetuating the legend of his name by his relentless zeal for financial achievement. But in his sixties, his body had begun to ache from old scars and bruises that he wore as ugly medals on sagging pink-white skin. His muscles were no longer rock-hard. A cataract film clouded his eyes like a spider's web and he blinked constantly to wipe away the haziness. His eyes had been his pride and his talent; clear, bright eyes with the peripheral sweep of a hawk. He had been able to see more than the movement of a baseball; he had been able to see the aura of other men, into them, through them, with some gift of cubistic sight more mystic than astral wanderings. It was the failing of his eyes that drove him from the game of baseball. When he could no longer see the aura of other men, he knew he was common, and he would not be common.

"Sad, what people say about Cy's eyes," Seth said to Whitman.

"It is. It sure is. I read in a magazine that he might be going blind," Whitman replied.

"Yeah, now that you mention it, I think I did, too."

Those who knew, or said they knew, whispered that Cy Hall had become morose, often sitting for hours with the shades of his home closed to the sun of California. But a stirring had begun in him and it was the stirring of an ancient animal, brooding with primeval instincts, his mind circling the wind drafts of time like a pterodactyl with membrane wings and a leather body, yearning to touch down and stay and be swallowed into the coloring of the landscape. It was nature's way of dealing with wanderlust. Each man, each creature, had a God-planted homing instrument in the brain and that instrument picked up spiritual signals of ultra-frequency no one had ever been able to understand. All you had to do was study the habits of birds, how they would migrate from place to place, leaving and arriving as precisely as a clock, a floating net of wings lapping in the wind against a sandbar of clouds, the sirens of their squealing answering the cry of a homing instrument in a place too far to see.

"Maybe there's something to it," Whitman said to Seth. "Him being homesick, thinking what it was like when he was a boy. Maybe he's just got to come home, like Ben Phelps has been saying."

"What I was thinking," said Seth. "Maybe it's something he can't help. Ben's right about that. I remember him saying something about it the night we had the little dinner for him."

"He did. Yes, he did."

"You don't suppose Cy could be dying, do you?" Seth said. "I've heard that people who are dying get homesick."

"I don't know," Whitman said seriously. "It could be. It could be just that. I've heard the same thing."

Cy Hall's return to Edenville, fifty years after he had left for professional baseball, was not surprising to those who knew—from good sources, they said: "It's something he can't help. He's coming to his end. He wanted to come home, to be where his real folks are." It was an observation that pleased the curious of Edenville. It was sensible and reaffirming. A wandering man is expected to return home. You could find that in the Bible. The Prodigal Son. And what about the Jews? They wandered around for forty years, didn't they?

The impressions circled back to Seth and Whitman.

"Don't know how such talk gets started," Seth said to Whitman. "I didn't know he was dying, but maybe he is, like everybody's been saying. Maybe its something he can't help, coming back now. Lots of people want to die where they was born."

"I was thinking about the same thing on the way over here this morning," Whitman said. "Tell you the truth, Seth, I never did think he'd come back, but I never thought about him dying, neither."

"Don't guess I thought he'd come back, neither," Seth admitted. "Don't guess nobody did, except for Ben Phelps."

"Old Ben," Whitman said sadly. "I hear he's beside himself, talking the ears off anybody that'll listen."

"Town ought to be patient with Ben," Seth said.

"That's right. Ben's all right. Just a little stubborn at times."

"Ben's a good man."

"He is. He sure is."

After he heard the rumor that Cy Hall would leave California and move, permanently, back to Edenville, Ben became nervously energetic. He slept restlessly and awoke early each morning, eager to be in the stores and shops of Edenville to hear the latest report of Cy Hall's return. And as he listened and moved from place to place, taking the reports—all fragments and speculations—with him, Ben enriched the gossip with stories that only Ben would know, or pretend to know.

It was in Ben's stories that Cy Hall became again young and powerful and gifted. It was in Ben's stories that Cy Hall again conquered other men with his incomprehensible superiority.

"Goda'mighty, Ben, I never heard that, not even from you," the people would say in astonishment.

"Lots about him you never heard," Ben would snap arrogantly. "That's because you didn't know him. You got to know Cy to know what he's done. I saw him do things down in Augusta that nobody playing ball today could do. Not one damn one of them."

"Well, I knew he was good," the people professed, "but I just never read about some of them things you're talking about."

"Most of the things he's done nobody ever wrote about," Ben would argue. "That time I was up in Boston, I saw him put three men out of one game. Got to where they wouldn't even try to tag him out when he was on base. He'd yell out, 'I'm coming down,' and then he'd light out and they'd jump out of the way. I mean, I saw that with my own eyes. Heard him yell out. Everybody in the park did."

Ben's stories of Cy Hall had always been mildly tolerated; now the stories were urgent and the townspeople begged to hear them. Cy Hall was returning home. Edenville needed to be proud of him. Seth Pennefeather and Whitman Robart had been saying that Cy Hall had given Edenville a good name and Seth and Whitman were right.

"When's he coming home, Ben?"

"Don't know. I called Cleveland two or three times, but he ain't never home and he don't call me back."

"You ought to go over there and kick his ass, Ben."

"He don't call me in a day or two, that's what I'm doing."

Cy Hall arrived, unexpectedly, in Edenville on the morning of July 20. He stopped at Byron's Motel and Restaurant on Highway 29 and asked Byron Hayes if a room was available to be rented for a few days.

"Just about take your pick," Byron said pleasantly. "Not much business these days."

"The quietest one you got," Cy Hall told him.

"That'd be number fourteen, down at the end," Byron replied. He slipped a registration card and pen across the counter and watched as the man picked up the pen and turned it carefully in fingers swollen at the joints. Arthritis, Byron thought. He wondered why an old, arthritic man was traveling alone. The man was frail and seemed tired, perhaps hungry.

"Got a restaurant right next-door," Byron said cheerfully. "Good country food. They still serving breakfast if you hungry."

The man did not reply. He pushed his hand slowly over the registration card.

"You want, I could bring you something down to your room," Byron said.

Still the man did not reply. He put the pen down across the registration card and stared at Byron as Byron turned the card and read from it.

"All right, Mr. — " Byron read the name: Cy Hall. He looked up. "Cy Hall?" he said. "You're Cy Hall?"

"I am."

"Yes, sir," mumbled Byron. "We—we heard you might be coming back. Yes, sir."

"Can I get the key?" The voice was hard and annoyed.

Byron reached for a key beneath the counter. He said, "Everybody's real glad about you coming home."

"Where's the room?"

"I'll show you," Byron said quickly. "Let me get your things."

Cy Hall turned and walked through the door and stood outside beside his Cadillac and looked at the small shopping center across the street.

"Changed a lot since you been here, I guess," Byron said.

"Everything changes," Cy Hall said. He pulled the keys to his car from his pocket and handed them to Byron. "It's all in the trunk."

"Yes, sir."

"You know Ben Phelps?" Cy Hall asked bluntly.

"Sure do," Byron answered. "Ben's been talking a lot about you coming back. Don't guess nobody in the world knows as much about you as Ben does."

"We grew up together."

"What Ben says."

"You know Cleveland Prichard?"

"Yes, sir."

"Call him and tell him I'm here. Tell him to come over at two o'clock."

"Yes, sir."

The first person Byron called was Ben Phelps.

"He asked about me?" Ben said in a quivering voice.

"Sure did, Ben. Right off the bat. Wanted to know if I knew you."

"He say anything else?"

"Nothing much," Byron replied. "Wants me to get Cleveland over to see him this afternoon."

"He want me to come over?" Ben asked anxiously.

"No. No, he didn't say nothing about it," Byron told him. "But he looked tired. Must of drove in from Atlanta this morning. He's got a new Cadillac. Looked like he needed to take a nap and I guess he's got business with Cleveland to talk about that house."

"That's the story," Ben said. "I been telling everybody he was coming back, by God. Everybody just thinks I'm a crazy old man who don't know nothing about nothing. Well, he's there, ain't he?"

"He's here, Ben. You're right about that."

"I guess I'll be seeing him before long," Ben said, "but I better let him get his business with Cleveland out of the way and get him some rest. That's a long way from Atlanta."

"That'd be best, you ask me," Byron agreed.

"Tell him I asked about him when you see him," Ben said. "Tell him I'll be around to see him or he can give me a call. Maybe Rachel can cook a meal for him."

"I'll tell him, Ben."

At noon, Ben went to Byron's restaurant. The restaurant was filled with townspeople who had heard the news (quickly circulated) of Cy Hall's arrival. They were jubilant, their mood giddy and loud-talking, and they ate noisily and waited for a chance appearance of Cy Hall. But Cy Hall did not appear and the crowd left and Ben sat alone in a booth near the window where he could see the Cadillac parked in front of room fourteen.

Ben had not seen Cy since the three days in Boston in 1918. Thirty-five years, he thought. So many years, but not so many years, not in memory. His memory was vivid with the heat of the excitement of Boston. He had lied about it to his family and to the people of Edenville, but it was only a part-lie: he had seen Cy, at the games, but he had not been with him. Each day he had called for Cy at the office of the Red Sox, leaving his name, but his calls were not answered. He had dutifully attended the games, reveling in the splendor of the great players at play (at war). And he had walked through the city of Boston, watched the trespassers on the Commons, stared in awe at the ships in the harbor where the Boston Tea Party had defied England. He had gone by rail to Harvard University and mingled among the students, pretending to be one of them. But he had not been with Cy Hall. It was not Cy's fault, he had reasoned. It was the fault of the office, protecting Cy.

The messages had not been delivered: Cy would have called. Cy would have taken him to dinners and to see the attractions in Boston. He had gone to the dinners and the attractions alone and then, by invention, had placed Cy with him. It was easy enough to do. Invented words were more lasting than real ones. Being in Boston did not seem so long ago to Ben. Thirty-five years was only a flicker of time in memory.

Ben took more iced tea from Byron Hayes's wife and stared at the Cadillac and remembered his pride in telling the men sitting around him at the stadium in Boston that he had grown up with Cy Hall and had played baseball with him. The men had regarded him with amazement, but they had believed him because he sounded like Cy Hall. Ben wiped at his eyes and drank from the tea. He had meant to see Lottie Parker on that trip, he thought. Lord, God. Lottie. Maybe she was dead now. He thought of the letter from Lottie about Foster and about their son, Ben. No one had ever seen the letter. It was safe in the locked attic of his home. He thought of the letters he had written Lottie each year, informing her that his planned trip to Boston had been postponed, and of the answering letters from Lottie with stories of her son. He had not stopped in Kentucky in 1918 as he had promised and after that year he had never again written Lottie. He wondered about Lottie's son, his namesake. The boy would be—how old now? Born in 1907. Ben did the subtraction with his fingers. Forty-seven. My God, Ben thought. Forty-seven.

At two o'clock, Ben saw Cleveland Prichard's pickup truck pull into the parking lot of Byron's Motel and Restaurant and stop beside the Cadillac in front of room fourteen. He saw Cleveland get out of the truck and go to the door and knock and stand waiting. And then Ben saw the door open and a figure step into the doorway. The figure was old and thin. He was wearing a robe. His hair was white. Ben could feel his pulse quicken with surprise. "Cy," he whispered aloud.

At dinner, Rachel Phelps asked her father, "Did you see him, Daddy?"

"Who?" Ben asked sharply.

"Cy Hall," Rachel said patiently. "I understand you went out to the motel, where he's staying."

"I had me a bite to eat out there."

"Why didn't you come home?"

"Maybe I wanted to eat somebody else's cooking," Ben snapped.

"You always come home."

"That's a lie. I eat downtown a lot."

"You always let me know when you do. I had lunch ready today."

"Rachel, how old are you?" Ben asked bitterly.

"I'm forty-two, Daddy. You know how old I am."

"How come you never got married?"

"Nobody ever asked me, Daddy."

"How come?"

"Maybe they knew I liked it so much at home, taking care of things."

"Well, you can get married anytime you want to, to anybody you can find," Ben said. "I can take care of myself."

Rachel smiled and picked up her father's plate, still filled with food, and placed it on the counter. She had never been away from home, had never done anything but care for her parents and teach dance to restless children. Since her mother's death, she had become more impatient with her father. He was demanding and rude and unfeeling.

"You didn't answer my question, Daddy," Rachel said. "Did you see him?"

"Wadn't looking for nobody," Ben replied.

"I heard you on the telephone with Byron Hayes today," Rachel told him. "You wanted me to cook a meal for Mr. Hall. I think that's a good idea."

"Just talk, nothing else," Ben mumbled. "Don't know why he called me in the first place."

Rachel poured coffee and placed it in front of her father. She said, "He called you because you know Mr. Hall better than anybody in Edenville. I think it was nice of him."

Ben looked up angrily at his daughter. "Why don't you go marry Byron Hayes and live out there in the motel?" he hissed.

"He's already married, Daddy," Rachel said gently. Then: "I'd like to have Mr. Hall over for dinner. Why don't you ask him?"

Ben pushed back in his chair. "I run into him, maybe I will," he said harshly. "I ain't looking to run into him. It's been thirty-five years since the last time I saw Cy Hall. People change."

Rachel stared evenly at her father. "Yes," she said quietly. "Some people do, I suppose."

JUST BEFORE DAWN

Warren Leamon

It was something like this:

Rimley came around the corner of the building, half-walking, half-running. He stopped, stood first on one foot, then on the other. He was outside the Redrock Building and he could see, when he looked in one direction, the Athletic Club and all the rich people in overcoats going in and out. And if he looked in the other direction, he could see the Greyhound bus station and all the rednecks and bums and winos and soldiers going in and out.

"Please. Not another social conscience story."

"Look, you asked me to tell a story."

"Yeah. But I wasn't expecting that stuff. I mean, I thought you were . . . And Rimley. What kind of name is that? Nobody is named Rimley. You made it up."

"Give me a chance, will you?"

I was there because my uncle's office was in the Redrock Building and I was going to see him. That's why I saw Rimley that day. I knew Rimley. He worked for my grandmother as a kind of yardman/ handyman. Or rather he *had* worked for her. He showed up drunk once too often and she fired him. Nobody told me, of course. I wasn't old enough to be told anything. I overheard everything.

"How old were you?"

"I don't know. Eleven or twelve, I suppose."

"Then all this happened . . . what? Fifteen, twenty years ago."

"I guess. 1950 or so."

"And what the hell were you doing downtown alone at that age? I mean, a nice little suburban kid like you. This is all a lie. A goddam twenty-year-old lie."

"Back then you could go downtown alone when you were that age. The city was different back then. Everything was different. It had to be a work day because my uncle was in his office. And it had to be winter because it

was cold as hell. So it must have been some kind of school holiday because I never played hooky. And how do you know I was a nice little suburban kid?"

"Jesus. Is this your autobiography or something?"

"You're the one who doesn't believe anything, who wants proof."

"Okay, okay. Go on."

I called his name and he looked and at first he didn't know who I was. Then he recognized me. I asked him what he was doing and he said he was going to see my uncle. I asked him what for. I was still little. I didn't know what questions might embarrass him. "I'm going to see if he can find me a job," he said, and I said, "Come on. I'll go up with you," and he said no, told me to go on, that he'd wait and I started to argue with him. God, I was . . .

My voice trailed off. I was lost in the darkness that truck was traveling through, but I could feel all around me the endless flat stretches of land. It would be morning soon, I could feel that, too. But now I could *imagine* what was out there, could imagine what I was moving through. I think if it had been light I never could have told him that story. By which I mean, I never could have told myself that story. And I wouldn't be able to tell it to you now. Not even in a letter.

"Come on. The deal was, you'd keep me awake, not put yourself to sleep."

"I'm not asleep."

"Well, I almost am. So get on with it."

I went up to see my uncle. Whenever I went to see him, he gave me some money, so I never missed a chance. He was a rich man, I think. Everyone said he had made a killing in cotton.

"What is this, Gone with the Wind?"

"Cotton waste. He bought and sold the waste products of cotton mills. I don't know where it came from. Probably Texas. Or maybe right here in Arizona. But this was in Georgia. Atlanta."

"I know Atlanta. Go through it all the time. The traffic's a goddam disaster. Say, what are you doing way out here?"

"As a matter of fact, I'm coming to that if you'll stop interrupting me."

Before I left I told my uncle that Rimley was waiting to see him. He groaned and said, "He's looking for a handout."

I—who had just received a handout—was outraged and told him that Rimley *said* he was looking for a job.

My uncle said that he always said that and anyway there weren't any jobs, "At least not for Rimley," and he went on to point out that even if there were, Rimley could never hold one because of his drinking. So I asked him why he didn't just say no and send him on his way.

Uncle Walter smiled and said, "I know. That's what you've heard all of us say."

"*All of us? Who's all of us?*"

"*The family. My mother (his sister) and my father and my grandmother, my uncles, aunts, cousins. Don't you have a family?*"

"*Yeah. Somewhere or other.*"

"*And it was true. That's what I'd heard all of them say: 'If you give them money, they'll just spend it on liquor.'*"

"*Damn right. It's why they're bums. They spend all their money on liquor. And drugs these days. It's getting to be more drugs than liquor. I'll bet you Rimley—if that's what his name was—was a nigger.*"

I cringed there in the truck in the dark—cringed at the word. I was only twenty-eight and it was 1966 and I hadn't learned about words, how they conceal as much as they reveal. Words tell us much about the people who use them, but the people tell us much about the words, and it never occurred to me back then that I knew far less about that truck driver than I knew about Rimley. But as you can tell, I had almost everything upside down because I was scared. That's why I ran, because I was scared. And I suppose that's why I lied and said, "No, Rimley was white," I told myself I did it because I didn't want to reinforce his prejudices when actually I didn't want to admit my own. And I thought it was all right to lie if it was for a good cause.

"*Well, maybe he wasn't a nigger.*"

"*Black. He wasn't black.*"

"*All right, black. Just get on with it.*"

Naturally, I got the feeling, even when I was eleven or twelve, that my uncle was being . . . ironic. I would have said sarcastic. Same thing. So as I was leaving I asked my uncle if he wanted me to tell Rimley to go away and he said no, just tell him to come on up.

Now even though it was cold and I probably wanted to get back home and I was going to have to wait at a bus stop, still, I hung around, waiting for Rimley. It wasn't long before he came out the door, half-walking, half-running. "Did he get you a job?" I asked before he saw me, and he jumped before he said yes and then I noticed that he had something in his hand, something balled up in a fist. "But it's up in Gainesville," he said, "so Mr. Walter gave me the bus fare. That's where I'm going, to the bus station." I stood there, amazed, and watched him walk to the bus station where he became another one of the bums disappearing inside.

And then it was my turn to jump when a voice said, "You still here? You'll freeze to death," and I turned and saw my uncle in his heavy grey overcoat and jaunty hat with a maroon feather stuck in the band. I told him I had waited to talk to Rimley and he had told me about the job. "I thought you couldn't get him one," I said and my uncle said, "I happened to think of something." Then he smiled and said, "Went to the bus station, did he?"

I suppose I knew right then what had happened. My uncle started off in the other direction from that of Rimley and soon he disappeared too, into the Athletic Club, where he always ate lunch. I went to the bus station and, sure enough, Rimley wasn't there and there hadn't been a bus to Gainesville since early that morning.

I knew my uncle would go back to his office after lunch so I waited in the bus station for over an hour. Sat on a wooden bench and kicked my feet and watched people come and go and began to realize that most of the people weren't coming and going. They were just sitting. Like me. Keeping out of the cold. Finally I went back to my uncle's office.

"Boy, you were a stupid little bastard, weren't you? Even a kid should have been able to figure it out."

"No. I told you. I had figured it out. I wasn't stupid. I was something worse. I was a self-righteous little prig."

But that wasn't right either. Or rather, it wasn't the most important thing, which was: why was I, at the age of twelve, already a self-righteous prig? Sitting in the truck, running away, I was still too young to realize anything but that I wasn't what I once was. It never occurred to me that I might be running away from you for the same reason that I was a prig at the age of twelve. And how could the truck driver know that? I don't mean that he couldn't know it because he was a truck driver, because he wasn't educated. No. Twenty years ago when I was riding in that truck I might have thought that and felt sorry for him. Now I don't think it and I don't feel sorry for him. Or rather, I don't feel anymore sorry for him than I do for anyone else.

"Well, go on. What happened when you went back?"

I told him that Rimley hadn't gone to Gainesville. And when he said, "Oh, is that right?" or something like that, I blurted out, "You didn't find him a job, did you? You just gave him money. A handout. I know. It was still in his hand." I remember what I said, word for word. I can see myself, standing there, not even wanting to sit down in that office. My uncle only asked why I thought that Rimley hadn't told me the truth and I said because he was . . . but I couldn't find the word or couldn't say it and my uncle supplied it. "Ashamed," he said, and I said, "That's right, ashamed," and went on. "Why didn't you tell me? I'll tell you why!" I was shouting now. "Because *you* were ashamed. That's why."

"*Jesus. There must have been something wrong with you, boy. I can't imagine anyone twelve years old . . .*"

"*Don't you think I know that! Don't you think I know! What the fuck do you think I am!*"

You know, sometimes even now I wake up in the middle of the night and my right hand aches and I feel it squeezing the door handle of the truck. And when I realize there's no truck driver to tell a story to and I'm much farther from "home" than I was then, I squeeze so hard that the dull edge almost cuts me. Even as I write this letter, in the darkness just before dawn, I can feel something of the pressure in my fingers. That kind of pressure—that kind of pain—it can only come from fear, fear that's almost but not quite panic. Because when you panic you don't feel anything but trapped. Outside there were the endless dark stretches of land and I was in the cab, closed in, moving through something I couldn't touch, smell or see. But I was moving through it. The truck driver looked at me. I couldn't see his eyes but I could see his head turn. Maybe he was scared, too, afraid he had a lunatic on his hands. I don't know. All he said was "All right, calm down. Take it easy." And waited.

My uncle said yes, that I was right, that he (this is, my uncle) was embarrassed, ashamed. But not because he had lied. He paused and looked away. "I was scared," he said. "Afraid. That's why I gave him the money. And then . . . I didn't want you to know I was scared." He paused again. Then stumbled on. "Not because I thought you'd think I was a . . . coward . . ." And he trailed off. Stopped.

But it was too late. I knew what he meant. It was something I had lived with since I knew I was living with anything at all other than people and things. We—my family on both sides—had all come from dirt poor farms that I often had to go back to for funerals and reunions and every time I saw what I almost was, what I could become again at any moment if it was only a matter of luck. So I . . .

"*What do you mean, luck? What are you talking about?*"

"*I had to believe that Rimley was the way he was because he was no good. Sorry. It couldn't be just luck. Because if it was then . . .*"

Why couldn't I tell him? Because I knew—no, intuited—that the truck driver was like me, one generation removed from the dirt. No more. Only the thinnest line between us and what we came from. The thinnest

line. That's how I'd started the story, after all, with me standing there
by the Redrock Building with the bus station the same distance from
me as the Athletic Club. And so beginning my story that way was kind
of intuition. I thought I was only setting the scene, not beginning with
the end, with what I was trying to face, to come to grips with. I know
what you're thinking. Let the story tell itself. But this isn't a story,
it's a letter. And explanation. When I was in that truck, rolling through
the Arizona darkness, far away from those Georgia sharecroppers' shacks
and the slums of Atlanta—back then everything was a story I was writing
or going to write. That's what I was doing in the truck, writing a story.
Or rather, I *thought* I was. But now I'm a hell of a lot further away—in
time and distance—than I was then. It seems strange that our life together
should come down finally to a letter that may or may not make it over
the ocean. And then across a continent. Across Arizona, all the way
back to Atlanta.

"Then what? You keep swallowing things. Anybody can be unlucky."
"I mean . . ."
"Oh, nevermind. Just get on with it."
I don't know what else my uncle said. Maybe nothing. All I remember
is that, as I was leaving, he suddenly asked, "Why shouldn't I have
given him the money?"
I said, "Because he'll only spend it on liquor." It wasn't my voice,
of course. It was my mother's, my father's, *his.*
But before I could open the door, he asked, "So what?"
"Well . . . What did you say? This ain't much but I guess it beats all
that noise on the radio."
"I didn't say anything. I couldn't answer his question."
"What do you mean, you couldn't answer it? I can. It's wasted money.
Time. Blown on whiskey. Believe me, I know. And what's more, it keeps
him from ever stopping. Long as you give him money, he'll drink. Be a bum."
"So what?"
"So what? Who wants to be a bum?"
"He did maybe. Maybe not."
"That's crazy."
"No. Don't you see? It was a profound question. It was the ultimate
profound question, the question that all other questions go back to."

So there it is. Come and gone. Can you believe it? One moment
I'm cringing in fear, on the verge of panic, gripping the door handle,
maybe about to jump out. So close to the truth that I could have squeezed
it as I was squeezing the handle. And the next moment—a pretentious-
academic-would-be artist, thinking I had found in the simple folk the

final mystery of existence. Still the self-righteous little prig. And I was twenty-eight. Not twelve. Not twenty-one. Twenty-eight. It's no wonder the truck driver got his back up and went cold on me. He thought I was trying to impress him, to convert him to something. He was right. After all, my uncle had only meant, "If he gets drunk and is happy for a little while, isn't that worth something?"

"That's your story then? Christ. Oh well, it'll be . . ."
"No. There's more."
"Well, I hope . . ."
I saw Rimley again nine years later. I know it was nine years because I had just finished my freshman year in college and I had come home for the summer to work. I had to earn money because my father had lost all his and had had to take a job that made him travel. He was gone all summer, in Texas or somewhere, appraising damage done by tornadoes. One evening the police called and asked if I knew someone named Rimley. At first I said no. Then I remembered and said yes. The policeman told me he was dead—at least they thought it was him—and they needed someone to identify the body. They had called my uncle but he was in the final stages of emphysema and was almost dead himself. I asked if Rimley didn't have any relatives, and the voice—the tone saying, "Look, buddy, if he did would we call you?"—said no, they couldn't locate any. So I said I'd come in before work the next morning and hung up before I thought to ask how they knew about me.

Well, I'd seen plenty of dead bodies—like I said, I'd been going to funerals ever since I could remember—but they had all been painted up and laid out in nice clothes in coffins. So I was . . . scared, I guess. And when they showed him to me—laid out under something, not a sheet exactly—it took me a minute to really look at the face and be able to say, just barely, that it was Rimley.

"Just barely? What was wrong? Had he been in a wreck or something?"
"No. He was just . . . older. A lot more than nine years older, it seemed. His face was thinner and his skin had gone a bit . . . splotchy . . . I don't know. He'd changed a lot is all I can say."
Afterwards, before I left, I asked the policeman what had happened to him, and he shrugged his shoulders and said, "Who knows?" They had found him on a golf course, of all places, in the middle of a fairway, curled up and dead. Early in the morning. Golfers had turned a dogleg and there he was. I asked him how he knew to call me—or rather my home—and he said that Rimley had a piece of paper in his pocket with several telephone numbers written on it. They just went down the list. "An old woman said she'd never heard of him. Then—who was it?—your uncle, who told us to call you."

I wasn't so much afraid now as confused, bewildered, I guess, and I didn't think to ask what I should have asked—what were the other numbers? Who were they? I was already on the street when I thought of it, but before I could turn back, another thought came into my head, or rather an image, an image of my uncle, hooked up by a long plastic tube to an oxygen tank, hearing Rimley's name and . . . remembering. And then, as I was walking along the street to the bus stop, I saw him that other day, years before, heard him ask the question once again. And I knew why he'd given the police my name.

Later I asked my mother whether we should bury Rimley and she said, "Lord, son, we couldn't afford to bury *you* right now."

"*That's not all, is it? I mean, what happened to him? How did he die? You know.*"

"*That's all. I never found out what happened to him. It doesn't really matter, does it?*"

"*Course it matters. What good's a mystery if you don't solve it?*"

"*It wasn't that kind of mystery.*"

But of course it was. And is. Knowing how he died would tell me how he lived those last nine years. But I really didn't care about Rimley then. I was too busy pretending that the story I was telling the truck driver was the same story that I was telling myself, that why I was running away from you was embodied in the story of Rimley. Now I want to know what that truck driver wanted to know: what happened to . . . Calhoun? (That was his real name, but in those days I was embarrassed to think that a black man might actually be named that.) I can guess, imagine, make up stories, but nevertheless something *did* happen to him. After all, I saw the ravaged face, the dead body. And it was *his* face and body, not *all* faces and bodies or the symbol of a certain class of people or the expression of an age or culture. That's what you know—intuit—when you're young and one generation away from what he was and that's why I was running, because I thought I might could keep myself out of that police station, that morgue. But only so long as I was alone and could run.

I remember the truck driver saying, "Well, at least the fucking sun is coming up and I don't have to worry about falling asleep anymore. It's always that way. First rays of the sun and I'm wide awake." As he said it all that dark land I'd been imagining all night was beginning to take shape and it wasn't too different from what I'd imagined. But it *was* different. Just as, if I tried to describe it now (or then), my description would be different from what it really looked like. And the same will be true when I start telling you what it's like where I am now. That's all right. Nobody, not even the most primitive savage, ever really thought that a word—a sound—was the thing itself, though most of my erudite young colleagues are overwhelmed by the discovery. But I come from a different time and place, from people often overwhelmed by how close words can come to being as solid as things. We may be doomed to live in a world we can never understand until we are out of it, beyond the ending. But we can come close, close enough to *feel* the reality. Close enough, if we're very lucky, to love it.

"First rays of the sun," the truck driver said. I didn't know exactly where I was, and I wouldn't know the place when I passed through it again that same day. But what took shape around me in the rising light was very beautiful indeed.

THE LIGHT

Judson Mitcham

"By a strange twist, the thought of God's anger only arouses love in me. It is the thought of the possible favor of God and of his mercy that makes me tremble with a sort of fear."

—Simone Weil

I have found a way to reach the woods near their home, unnoticed. From there I have watched the house like a thief—but what is it I would steal?—or like a voyeur trying to witness some passion in secret. That is what I am.

I have seen him sweep the driveway and take out the trash. I have watched her water the flowers. But mostly I stare at the house. It is across town from the one they lived in when I knew their son, so if there is a shrine inside, it is only a reconstruction, not the actual room left exactly as it was—where the angle of the guitar pick on the desk would have come to seem immutable with the last touch.

Yesterday, I saw him cut the grass, then rest for a while. I saw her come out the door with two tall glasses of what looked like lemonade. They sat on the front steps smiling and talking while they drank.

Today is the day.

When the doctor stepped through the door of the emergency room and told me Paul had died, I traveled into the smooth green shine of the hospital wall, gave the tenderest part of myself away to the surface, as if fascination could protect me; as if I could really journey off and leave my body—so awkward and stupid, so capable of error.

Believe me, you can stare at a thing until it almost heals you. You can listen to a noise until the quality of lullaby arises. You can travel endlessly into the most ordinary event or thought, if only you give your entire life over to it for a moment. And when you have lived this way, foraging for a particular kind of sustenance, each element may begin to fit, as in a dream—when the telephone rings and you realize you have been waiting, all along, for someone to call.

I can see the dirt road—red clay packed so hard that it gleams; deep ruts, ridges baked in their long molds, rigid as bone; a winding road rolling through the low hills of the piedmont, rocks rapping up against the underside of the car; here and there, stretches of loose sand challenging the tires, so the steering wheel turns in my hands.

We are riding out into the late afternoon one Sunday after a movie, down a road none of us is familiar with, the red dust billowing out behind us.

We have chosen this road for its remoteness, for the likelihood that at night no one travels it, and so a boy and a girl might drive out here to be alone. Fatigued by the long war movie, slightly queasy from the popcorn, happy to be almost lost, we are looking for places a car might ease off the road and not get mired in the mud, trying to find driveways leading to abandoned or burned-down houses. But we are bound for a place where we will each be touched in a way we cannot yet imagine.

I watch old couples.

An old man stands in line alone, buys two chili dogs, two soft drinks, and a single order of french fries. He sets the tray down in front of her on the table. They both keep their coats on, though it is relatively warm. They are clearly not in a hurry. The woman leaves the chili dog in the wrapping. The man flattens the paper out, and he eats leaning over it, bits of chili escaping the bun and falling with each bite. He keeps checking the front of his coat.

He is finished before she is, and wipes his mouth, sucking his teeth. He balls up the napkin, drops it on the tray, then looks around slowly, no visible emotion in his eyes as he watches the young people lining up for pizza. She does not look up.

When I awoke today, having made my decision, a quietness came over me. I made coffee, then sat on the sofa, looking out across the deck.

The dawn came in—a slow haze, mist between the branches—then the sky like a low blue flame, and the trees, in their stillness, like watercolors of trees.

"No, he's still alive," I heard her say—that woman I had never seen before and never saw again, who took it on herself to telephone Paul's parents. But within five minutes—or perhaps it had already happened when she hung up the pay phone and we walked back down the hospital hallway—he was gone.

I can summon no good image of that woman. I don't know if she was thin or stout or what color her hair was. I cannot offer the first detail about her face, but I would know her voice—would know it absolutely—that soft drawl with all the world in it.

I prayed in short breathless bursts of words not formed into complete thoughts or sentences. I said "God," and "please," and "no," groaned these words aloud as I ran down the dirt road, not knowing where I was, wild to find help. Somewhere behind me, Paul lay bleeding from his mouth—Raymond kneeling beside him, repeatedly making the sign of the cross.

In the days to come I would remember a story from Sunday school: how a man walked up to a bad wreck out of nowhere, and without a word to anyone, ripped off the car door, overpowered the crushed-in steel pinning the little girl and her mother—simply willed his muscles and bones to accomplish the impossible, lifted out the woman and the girl, then suddenly was gone. Days later he was identified as a man who had lost his own wife and children to an accident, and who finally, in his rage and sorrow, had given himself over to the Lord—whose instrument, Samson-like, he had become that day on the road.

And I was a lean sixteen-year-old, finely conditioned from year-round sports, able to run forever, I believed. But when I turned from the wreck, took my loafers and socks off and began to run, what could I do but start off fast, in a flat-out dash? I knew, my whole body knew, the wrongness, the obscenity, of setting a pace, of loping off over the hill with a measured, medium stride. I ran as hard as I could—sprinted, churned, knees high, arms pumping—as if trying to steal home or as though I could see a finish line.

So it came to me—my education in the heavy body. With a boy lying near death I felt the earth take hold, felt gravity drip its syrupy liquid into my limbs, so that no will, no force of thought, no panic, no prayer could stop them from slowing down. The June heat sucked the breath from my mouth, set the light melting and swarming near the edges of everything, turned the air busy with nothing, and I moved as if underwater. But I did not stop. I did not sit.

They are stranded on the median of I-75, trying to cross three lanes of holiday traffic and get back to their car, parked on the shoulder. They are inexplicably in the middle of the interstate. There is no clear reason why they should have crossed the highway—no service station or telephone on the other side, only another open field, no houses.

They are poised to make a dash when there is a gap in the traffic, their angelhair whirling and fanning back in the fumey wash of the trucks and cars, their faces looking the same—not worried, but studious, gauging distance and speed. They hold hands, but neither seems to be about to lead the other, both providing ballast, steadiness. They disappear swiftly behind me—a sudden mystery in the late afternoon, though I know with some certainty what it is that I have been to them.

Sometimes I stand in the door to my son's room and look around at the clutter—clothes thrown across a chair, books lying open, his guitar against the wall, tapes stacked precariously on a shelf—and I see it frozen like that, never to be shuffled into another chaos by his own hand again.

I stand there, and I stand there, and I stand there.

Sunday afternoons my family used to drive out through the countryside in our old blue Chevrolet. Over and over, my father proposed the same activity: we were to search for something worth noting, whether by virtue of its beauty or its ugliness, its size, disarray, or unexpectedness—the quality we focused on did not matter.

We soon learned not to take a scattershot approach, pointing at everything. In this there was no pleasure, no return. We learned to take our time. My father drove so slowly on those days, we used to joke that he was practicing to drive a float in the Christmas parade. I remember one afternoon when he wouldn't pass a tractor.

We all saw the flock of starlings rise like a black veil from a field milky and thick with unpicked cotton. We all saw the fence made out of bedsprings, the bird dog asleep underneath a pulpwood truck leaning sideways on a jack.

Once, soon after we had pulled back onto the main highway, traffic slowed almost to a stop, and as we approached the wreck, my father made it clear that we were not to look, that he would not have his children gawking and rubbernecking at someone else's misfortune. But late one night on a trip to Daytona Beach, when I saw the flashing lights, I pretended to be asleep. Then I raised my face to the window just long enough to catch another face staring back—a deep gash underneath the right eye, swollen shut, and the other focused hard on me.

My earliest memory is of anger and tears, upon awakening from a dream in which I had flown a small yellow airplane with short square wings and a boxy fuselage. Though I had piloted the plane, I see it above me, there in the bedroom, climbing—the left wing angled downward, its tail near the top of the door leading to the kitchen. I remember the disbelief I felt, that my toy—my only means of flight—had been taken away. It had evaporated after that brief moment when it seemed to stall near the ceiling, no one at the controls.

Last night I dreamed, again, of wandering through an old house as large as a hotel, though it is someone's home. In this dream I am always looking for the right room. What is in the room, whether it is mine or someone else's, I do not know. I have never found it. I have tried many doors. Usually they are locked, but sometimes they open onto the outside of the house, so that if I step through, I will fall and keep falling, since the house rests on the edge of a cliff.

Perhaps the strangest part of this remarkably consistent dream is the way the hallways are thick with weeds—the broomsage knee-high—and there is a breeze blowing down the halls, always—a rising breeze, as though there is a storm coming in the house.

The next day, my brother drove me home from the hospital, and when we passed the junkyard, as we had to, there they were, lined up at the fence, pointing at the car.

I suppose it was something worthy of note—a rolled Corvair, all its tires flat, no glass left in the windows.

Sitting in the row in front of me, she smiles at the old man next to her, who has dozed off halfway through the movie.

When he opens their front door, my name escapes softly from his throat—like a breath let go—and with a tentative sweep of his hand, he shows me in.

They have both been sitting on the couch, reading the newspaper. She does not move or speak or in any way acknowledge I am there. Her face is classical in its immobility—a weathered carving out of the ancient world.

He sits down again at her side, leaving me to negotiate the room on my own. I remain standing. He leans over and whispers to his wife, but she does not answer.

Thirty years of whirling in silent orbits around the same dense absence and now the stillness of this room . . .

"Mrs. Bennett, for a long time . . ."

At the sound of my voice, her face breaks, her lips starting to tremble, as if some deep fault which opened up inside her long ago had again begun to shift. "Why did you come here?" she asks, though her eyes evade mine, focus on something beyond and make me want to look behind me.

Suddenly he is on his feet, moving quickly. "There's something I want you to see," he says, pulling me by the arm toward the hallway leading to the rear of the house. As we pass, she lunges at me and I throw up a hand to protect my face, but she wrestles me into her arms, kisses me roughly on the cheek, then grabs me above the elbow, her fingernails digging into my skin, then relenting—though she does not let go—and they both guide me deeper into the house.

The light along the wall is so golden, there must be a window at the end of that hallway.

But there is nothing I want to tell them now, and nothing I want to see. I only want to run, but they are holding me.

THE WHITE LINE

Linda Chandler Munson

I always knew that I was a stupid sonofabitch, but I never thought I was a fool. But what else do you call a guy sitting on the side of the road, broke, smoking his last cigarette, with maybe, just maybe, enough gas in his bike to make it to the next town, Edom, or whatever the hell the sign said. I guess someday this is going to seem as funny as running over chickens, but right now I got a serious problem.

I stopped at a roadside bar last night after riding all day, three hundred ball-busting miles without stopping, except for gas, and I kept that motor humming so it filled my head. That way I didn't have to think about anything, and just to make damn sure I didn't, I had almost emptied the flask in my jacket pocket by the time I pulled in the parking lot. I didn't want to think about it anymore. Hell, I was tired of chewing on it.

I think I could of took that bastard Polonski setting me up as the fall guy for his fuck-up. I mean I hated that damn steel mill anyway, day after day, always the same thing. And after I caught him outside the gate, and thanked him personally for getting me fired, I felt better. Just the sight of that piece of shit, face down, snorkeling mud, made it worth losing the job.

But what I couldn't take was Wanda. After I got home, got me a beer, and sat down at the kitchen table, she came in from the bedroom.

"I hear you got fired," she said.

"I see the fucking phone must be working," I answered.

She didn't mention it anymore, and a little later, the kid came home from school, not my kid, but Wanda's, and the rest of the night went as normal as hell, except quieter.

The next morning Wanda woke me up. She was dressed for work, standing by the bed, but she wasn't looking at me. Instead, she was staring over my shoulder at the bare wall. When she didn't say nothing, I asked, "What's the matter?"

"I need my job at the mill," she said. "It's all I know how to do. I got a kid to take care of." She pulled her eyes from the wall and looked at me. "You know how they are. If you stay here, they'll get me too."

Her face looked pinched, like she was holding it real tight, and her eyes were red and swollen. "I got to keep my job," she said again, and walked out, letting the screen door slam behind her.

So how do you pack up five years? Well, you throw most of it in the trash, put the rest in a duffel bag, tie the bag on your bike, and follow the white line down the center of the road to something else.

Anyway, when I finally pulled over and parked last night in front of a flashing red and black 'Beer here' sign, the ride and the bourbon had me more strung out than any twenty-five-dollar trucker's massage on Route 3 had ever done. So I was pretty loose when I went in, and it looked good, everything kind of soft and hazy with a Pabst Blue Ribbon sign throwing red, white, and blue lights over the bar.

I don't know how long I had been there, drinking and smoking, when she came in. I don't even remember exactly how she looked, just slim, long dark hair, and light-colored blue eyes that darted away if you looked straight at her. And, hell, I was ripe for the picking. Who could of resisted? I might as well of had a goddamn sign pasted on my forehead that said "Sucker." When I woke up the next morning, all I remembered was following her to a room somewhere behind the bar, laying on a bed, then babbling and whining about Wanda, Polonski, and god-knows-what-else, like I was some little sniveling kid.

Jesus, I lost it, lost it all. And it took a long time for me to feel, really feel, her against me, for her to be more than just something warm and firm to hold on to. But when it finally happened, and I saw her, the white breasts and opened thighs, I found I still had it, and it was then I felt that day and all the days before drop away like the quarters she had dropped earlier in the jukebox, playing every sad song she could find.

So I woke up the next morning and she was gone. All my money was gone too, except for a five-dollar bill, and the door to the bar was locked up tighter than a constipated cat's ass. A thousand dollars shot to hell, and I knew there was no use looking for her. No one would know her or would of ever seen her, and the thought of them laughing at me being taken was more than I could stand, so what was there to do but leave. I got dressed and went out the back door.

I saw a pump on the side of the building, so I went over and put my head under it and pumped until the cold water forced my eyes open. Then I drank, swallowing huge handfuls of water, handful after handful, trying to wash out the shakes and fill up my heaving stomach. I drank until I threw it all back up again. Swishing my mouth out with the last drink of bourbon from my flask, I spit it out on the red dirt where it splashed on my boots.

"You stupid 'battery-acid-for-brains,' you're too stupid to live," I said to myself out loud. Then I got on my bike and left.

I made it to Edom, one main street, nobody in sight at ten o'clock on a Saturday morning. Christ, what a dead-ass place. I had some gas left in reserve, so I thought about trying to make it to the next town. Then I saw the "Help Wanted" sign in the restaurant window. As it turned out, the job wasn't there but outside town, in a backyard garage, the man behind the counter told me. The guy, he said, had lots of work from the pulp mill, and his regular mechanic had just quit last week.

The place was out of town all right, all by itself down a red dirt road covered with pebbles. Getting the bike over the pebbles was a bitch, and I did some fancy two-footed riding before I finally pulled up in the yard. The house was back under some large pine trees that all touched at the tops, making the yard shady but mostly dirt and pine needles. The house wasn't much more than a shack with a rickety porch sprawled across the front, and the garage was what had been the barn at one time. Two pulpwood trucks were parked out front.

A man, leaning inside the hood of one of the trucks, looked up when he heard my motor. I revved the engine up high before I got off the bike, just so he could enjoy it. He straightened up and wiped his hands on a rag that was a lot blacker than his hands.

"Help ya?" he asked through a large chaw of tobacco.

"I'm here about the job," I said.

He looked me over top to bottom, and then smiled at me like I was crazier than bat shit. He had large gaps in his teeth.

"Job? This here ain't no motorcycle shop."

"I can fix anything you got here." I tried to keep my voice level.

He was still grinning. "Oh yeah, then why ain't you mechanicking somewhere. What ya been doing?" He pointed to my head. "Been busy growing your hair?"

I stuffed my hands in my pockets to keep from smearing that shit-faced grin all over his face. "Look, pop, what's with the questions? I need a fucking job. Do you have one or not?"

He just grinned even wider. "Pretty touchy for a man that needs a job, ain't ya?"

I stared at him. He stared back. Then I almost laughed out loud. He looked like such an asshole standing there, staring out from a baseball hat that said "Trojan Field-tester" and smiling like he had just jacked off.

I gave up and smiled back. "Yeah, I guess I am. How about it?"

"See that truck over there." He pointed over his shoulder. "Pull the front wheels on it."

With that, he spit a long yellow stream on the ground next to my feet and went back to working on the other truck.

I took out my wallet and checked to make sure my money was really gone before I took off my jacket.

We worked until the sun was at the top of the sky. It was damn hot even with the shade from the tall pines. I had pulled off my shirt earlier and threw it over on the ground with my jacket, but I was still sweating buckets. At least I got both wheels off without having to ask the old coot anything. Not that he offered any help. After he put his head back under the hood of the truck, I didn't see him again until a voice called "Uncle Willie, you all ready for something to eat?"

He popped his head up at the same time as I stepped around the truck to see who it was. A young girl leaned on the porch railing looking towards the garage.

"Yeah, we're ready," Willie yelled back. "Come'ere, I got somebody for you to meet."

As soon as she got close enough for me to see her good, I knew it was her. Sure, her hair was different, pulled back from her face, and she didn't have on makeup, but it was her alright.

She stopped short when she saw me, like somebody had snapped her back on the end of a chain, and her eyes widened, those same darting blue eyes. She stepped back a little and shifted to look at the old man.

He motioned towards me. "Emmy, this is . . ." He paused. "I didn't catch your name."

I was still staring at the girl. I felt kind of strangled, and my eyes must of been popping out of my head. "I didn't throw it." I managed to say. "It's Gavin."

She shot me a sideways look and said "Hi" real low so I could hardly hear her.

"Emmy's my niece," Willie said, "keeps house for me."

She was already turned and leaving. "I'll get some sandwiches," she said over her shoulder, but she didn't come back. Instead she sent the food with a kid, Willie's boy.

All afternoon I tried to figure out what the fuck to do. If I told Willie, there was about a snowball's chance in hell he'd believe me, and I'd probably get canned for my trouble. If I went to the law, they'd never believe me either. I didn't have no witnesses, just my word against hers, and you can bet your last dollar, if you had one, which I didn't, that the people in the bar had all been struck blind, deaf, and dumb.

On top of that, the way my luck was running, I'd probably get locked up as a vagrant. Lots of these one-horse towns had a twenty-dollar-law, where if you didn't have at least that much on you, they can lock you up. I found out about it the hard way. So, what if I said nothing?

I'd have to face her every day with her knowing what she did to me, and me not being able to do a damn thing about it. Jesus, I could hardly stand thinking about it. Don't it just fucking beat all? Sometimes I'd like to take one of those bumper stickers that says "Shit Happens" and just paste it across my fucking eyes. I mean I walk around like I'm helpless as a goddamn blind man anyway, so what the hell difference would it make?

When it started getting dark, Willie pulled the chain on an overhead light mounted up next to the top of the garage door, and we worked about another hour before he said, "Quittin' time."

He walked over and looked at the work I had done. I had pumped jacks and turned wrenches like a maniac all afternoon, trying to straighten out my mind, and I had both wheels off, the rims out, and the new tires ready to go on. He nodded his head. "Five dollars an hour and meals. You want it?"

"Yeah, I want it," I said, like I had some kind of goddamn choice.

"How long ya looking to stay?" he asked.

"Long as you need me," I lied. Christ knows, as soon as I got enough money I was out of there.

Willie looked at me and smiled that stupid-ass grin of his. He pushed the Trojan hat back on his head. "What you really mean, son, is as long as it takes you to get enough money to scratch that itch of yours."

He laughed and pointed to a sink inside the garage door. "Wash up over there. I'm hungry."

At the table, the girl sat across from me. The kid sat beside her, and I noticed he wasn't as young as I had first thought. It was his face. It was kind of simple, a baby's face on an older kid's body, like he was probably not playing with a full deck. He didn't say anything except to ask for more food, and the girl quickly gave it to him every time he asked. As he ate, he stared out at me from under a hat just like Willie's. I couldn't help thinking that his hat should say "Trojan Failure" instead of "Trojan Field-tester."

Willie talked nonstop. I guess he had been saving it up all day, and he didn't let little things, like a mouthful of rice and gravy, interfere with his talking. Every so often, a piece of rice would find its way out onto his chin and cling there until Willie's flapping jaw sent it flying across the table. The boy was twelve years old, he said, and his wife had passed about three years ago. She had never been right since the boy was born so late in life, but they got along now that Emmy was with them. Emmy's mama was in the hospital, been there a long time. Not much chance she would be out soon.

The girl had her head ducked and was pushing food around on the plate. I thought she blushed when he said that about her mother, but it was hard to tell, not being able to see much but the top of her head.

I couldn't take my eyes off her. What kind of woman does that, lays and rolls a guy, and then comes home and acts as if nothing happened? I wanted to hear her talk. Except for the few words earlier, she hadn't opened her mouth. I wanted to compare her voice with the one I remembered from last night, the soft one that had floated all inside and outside my head, leading me on, and me following like a fucking moonstruck dog.

When Willie took a breath, I jumped in. "You in school?" I asked her, trying to keep the hard edge out of my voice. She flinched as if I had raised a hand to her. I glanced at Willie to see if he noticed, but he was deep in his turnip greens, bent over the plate so that anything that dropped out of his mouth wouldn't be lost.

It surprised hell out of me when she suddenly looked up and stared right at me with those strange eyes, eyes like the color of a summer sky right before a storm.

"I quit," she said in a flat voice and glared at me like she was daring me to go ahead and say something, to just get it over with, quit playing games.

"Emmy works most weekend nights as a waitress over at Jerry's place down on the highway," Willie mumbled over the pork chop bone he was gnawing.

She sure as hell does, I thought to myself, never taking my eyes off her. Emmy's eyes shifted to her uncle. She stood up.

"I got things to do in the kitchen. I'll clean up when you're done."

The kid followed her out, grabbing a pork chop and putting it in his overalls pocket.

"She's a good girl," Willie said, refilling his plate. "She's supported her mama for over two years now. All by herself with no help." I would of smiled at the no-help bit, but I was afraid my face might break. Willie went on while he spooned a river of gravy over his plate. "Every month she sends money to that hospital, like clockwork."

He lowered his voice. "Her mama's mental, you know. But don't say anything to Emmy. She don't like people to know. Course, everybody around here knows what happened, but Emmy acts like they don't, and nobody ever says nothing to her about it."

He paused and put about a quarter-pound of butter on his biscuit. "Her mama went off her rocker, crazy as a rat in heat. She shot every living thing on their farm, from the cats down to the cows. When Emmy got off the school bus, the poor kid had to walk through all those slaughtered animals to find her mama sitting at the kitchen table with the shotgun in her mouth. Emmy stopped her."

He shook his head, sprinkling crumbs from the biscuit stuck in his mouth and hanging out the corners all over the table.

"Never knew what happened, why she did it. She won't talk. Just sits in a chair all day. Been that way since it happened, two years ago last month.

I didn't know what to say. I never do when somebody tells me some shit like that. What do you say anyway. "I'm sorry" sounds as stupid as hell. I mean, what can you do about it? Nothing, nothing at all. I was glad Willie didn't bother to shut up long enough for me to say anything if I had wanted to.

"You got a place to stay?" he asked, peering at me from under eyebrows that threatened to cover his eyes.

Jesus, I hadn't even thought about that with everything else going on. I took a deep breath and leaned back in the chair. I felt like I had been run over by a couple of those pulpwood trucks outside. "No, I don't," I answered.

Willie shoveled a few uninterrupted bites into his mouth and then said, "You can bed down in the garage. There's a cot in the tool room. I'll have Emmy fix it up with some covers."

He squinted his eyes and considered me over his loaded-down fork. "If you don't mind me saying so, son, you look like stale shit." He pointed to the hall. "Bath's over there. Take you one and turn in."

"Thanks." I got up from the table.

As I eased myself into a steaming tub of water, I wondered what other goddamn perverted twist my life could take.

Later, out at the garage, I leaned back on a truck and smoked a cigarette from the pack I had bummed from Willie. Bugs were flying all around the light over the door, and every so often one would get too close to the hot bulb. I don't know why, but I felt sorry for them, the poor stupid bastards, groping for a little warmth and brightness and getting fried for their trouble. So I went over and turned the light off.

The night was nice, real nice. You don't see country like this in Pittsburgh, not where I was from anyway. The moon was out, all full and ripe like a peach about to bust, and the moonlight turned the tops of the pine branches a whitish-green while underneath the trees it was all dark and deep.

If I didn't think about how I came to be here, I felt good, and I hadn't felt good about working in a long time. But doing those wheels and rims had been damn satisfying, not like that assemby-line crap at the mill where your brain seeps down into your ass from boredom.

I was thinking about my daddy, before he died, and how I used to help him fix things, I mean he could fix anything, when I heard the screen door slam. I could just make her out in the moonlight, picking her way across the yard with a bundle in her hands.

When she got next to the truck, I said, "I'm over here."

She jumped and almost dropped the bundle. "What're you doing, standing out here in the dark?" she gasped catching her breath.

"Nothing, just looking." I didn't move, but stayed in the truck's shadow.

"I got your covers." Her voice sounded thin, and I could see her straining to see me in the dark.

Then I remembered what she had done to me and it pushed the good feeling away, and I hated how I couldn't help noticing how pretty she looked in the half-dark, holding that bundle in front of her like she was hiding behind it.

I pushed the thought out of my mind, crushed out my cigarette, and went in the garage, turning on the inside light. She used a key to open the tool room. It was small. Tools hung on all the walls, and along one side of the room they were stacked on racks and thrown on the floor. On the other wall was a cot and a small dresser with a cracked mirror hanging over it. The only light came from the bulb in the garage so it was kind of dim and shadowy.

I leaned against a tool rack and watched her make the bed. I don't know what I was thinking. I don't guess I was thinking anything, just watching her move, because when I heard her voice it surprised me. She was turned away from me, pulling a pillowcase on a pillow.

"I can't give it back to you. I don't have it."

I didn't say nothing.

She turned around, standing just inches from my face. "The money. I don't have it. I already sent it. I mailed it off this morning." She looked down at the floor. "I didn't mean you no harm. I didn't go there to do that. It just happened. I had to have money quick, and when I saw what you had . . . I don't know . . . I just took it." Her words were tumbling, one over the other. She stopped and waited for me to say something, but I didn't.

She looked back at me. "It's gone," she said again, like I hadn't heard the first time, "so there ain't no use in you hanging around here thinking you're going to get it back."

I lit a cigarette and took a long drag on it. "I don't believe you," I said. I don't know why I said that after what Willie had told me about her mama and all. I guess I wanted her to tell me more, to be sorry, to make me believe that she was something more than just a back-roads whore and thief.

I saw her face go hard. "I don't give a good damn what you believe," she said and walked out.

I followed her to the garage door. "Then it looks like you owe me a lot in trade," I said to her back as she crossed the yard.

She stopped and turned around. For a minute, she just looked at me, kind of sad-like. Then she said, "You need to put on a shirt to sleep. It still gets cold here nights."

I fell asleep like someone had hit me over the head with a tire iron, but I woke up again, wide awake, in the middle of the night. The room was as black as muddy water and the air as cold as a witch's tit. I didn't know where I was at first, and I laid there breathing real slow, waiting for it to come, and then I remembered where I was and why I was here. When my eyes adjusted to the dark and I could see a little, I lit a cigarette and leaned back against the wall.

I didn't know what the hell to think about Emmy, or how I felt about her now. If you'd asked me this morning, I could of told you. But not now. I kept telling myself that she stole from me, took everything I had, but when I thought about her, I kept seeing her standing in the moonlight, in cutoff jeans and rolled-down white socks, looking like a kid that's lost her last friend. And if I forced myself to remember her from the other night, it didn't help either, because I kept seeing her holding me like a baby while I got the Wanda and Polonski business off my chest.

When I finally dozed off, I was covered with sweat despite the cold air, and I tossed and turned, dreaming all kinds of weird shit about Wanda, the mill, and Emmy. It was all mixed up and none of it made any sense. The room was getting light when I finally quit dreaming and really slept, and it seemed like I was only asleep a few minutes when somebody was shaking me. I opened my eyes to see Willie's ugly grizzled face a few inches from mine.

"If you want breakfast, son, you need to get your ass out of the sack. We got lots to do. That pulp mill bastard Corbett will be here worrying us to death if we don't have those trucks ready by tomorrow."

Breakfast sounded good, but the prospect of seeing Emmy again didn't. It seemed like I had just confronted her, and I was confused about what to do or think. It was easier when I believed it was just a simple fuck-and-roll. Now I didn't know, and right then I didn't want to think about it anymore. I wanted to be alone, to forget it for a while.

"No," I said, shaking my head, trying to clear out the dreams, "I'm not hungry. I ate too much last night."

"You sure? Emmy makes a fine belly-filling breakfast."

I looked up at Willie and the thought of watching him eat grits and eggs was enough to convince me I didn't want any. "No, I'm okay. Just bring me some coffee when you come out. I'll get started out here."

I didn't see Emmy all day. The kid brought lunch out, sandwiches again, with homemade chocolate cake, and it was all just like the day before. About an hour after dark, Willie walked over, looked at my work, and said, "Quittin' time," and I wondered if he said that every night even if there wasn't no one to hear.

Supper was also a repeat of the night before. Willie talking, eating everything in sight, the kid staring at me from under his hat, Emmy looking at her plate and leaving the table early. I tried not to stare at her, but I couldn't help it. She had her hair down, like it was that night, and I remembered waking up one time during the night with it over my face, and being unable to breathe, it was so thick and heavy. I couldn't eat much. The food stuck in my throat. Not that it mattered. Willie and little Willie, as I had taken to calling him to myself, finished every morsel on the table.

After a bath I sat for a long time on the truck hood and smoked. The lights in the house went off after a while, leaving only the two windows facing the garage lit. I wondered which window was Emmy's, and what she was doing, and if she was thinking about me. I hoped she was, damn it, I hoped she was, and that made me madder than hell with myself.

I slept just as bad as I did the night before, sweating even in the cold, and pulling the sheets loose until they were in such a knot I had to get up and remake the bed.

Then morning came, and night came, over and over, and finally it was Friday.

At quitting time, Willie counted out three hundred dollars in my hand. He counted it carefully with tobacco-stained fingers, rubbing each ten and twenty to make sure they weren't stuck together. "That's six days, ten hours a day, at five dollars an hour."

I pocketed the money. Willie stood there like he was waiting for something. "Something else?" I asked.

"The cigarettes," he said, lifting one hairy eyebrow.

I reached in my pocket and got out a five-dollar bill. "Here, five packs, five dollars."

"Thanks," he said and put the money in the front pocket of his overalls. "You got to fend for yourself tonight. Emmy's working at Jerry's." He gave me a poke on the shoulder. "You ought to go over there yourself. You look kind of torqued up, like you need to loosen up a bit." He grinned. "You know what I mean?"

I smiled back and got my jacket and helmet. "Yeah, I know what you mean." I didn't have any intention of going there. The only thing worse than a damn fool is a damn stupid fool.

As I pulled out of the yard, I saw the kid swinging in a tire tied by a rope to a large pine tree. He waved to me. His hat was pushed back on his head and he was grinning from ear to ear. I waved back. All he needs, I thought, is a few missing teeth.

I rode for about two hours, just getting the kinks out and relaxing, taking roads as it struck me. Then when I got hungry, I went to that restaurant, the one I went in the first day I came in town.

The food was good and I took my time, drinking coffee and smoking after I finished eating. At three hundred dollars a week, I'd have my money back in about a month. Then I could hit the road again, go south. I always wanted to see Florida. Hell, I might go all the way to Key West, get myself a job on one of those shrimp boats. The thought of me, a city boy, out on the ocean working on a boat made me smile.

When I left there it was pretty late, but I didn't want to go back to Willie's yet, so I rode some more, and I don't know how it happened, I must of not been paying attention, but I found myself outside of Jerry's. The parking lot was full, and I could hear the music all the way out on the road. Pulling in, I saw Emmy through the window. She was leaning over a table and some jackass had his hand on her waist. I circled the building a few times and then went on down the road to a small bar where it was quiet and dark, and I drank there until my mind went numb.

Willie worked my ass off the next week. As quick as we turned out the trucks, they'd bring more in. Some nights I felt like my arms were going to fall off, but I liked it. I would be so tired that, at least, I would sleep the first part of the night even if I didn't sleep much the rest, and Willie and me worked good together. He left me alone, let me work my way, and at the end of the day, he would look at what I had done, nod his head, and say "Quittin' time."

The kid took to me and kind of followed me around, sitting over to the side and watching me work, handing me tools when I needed them, and even washing parts. Like Willie, during the day anyway, he didn't say much, just smiled a lot.

Emmy seemed to relax a little once she figured out I wasn't going to make a stink, but she made sure we wasn't ever alone and spoke to me only when she had to. But, sometimes, at supper, I caught her watching me with a strange look on her face, like she was confused or something. And one night, after supper, when I was sitting outside the garage smoking, like I did every night, I saw her come to the window, and it looked like she didn't have on nothing but a slip. She stood there for a moment, and if it hadn't been so dark, I would of swore she looked right at me. Then she pulled the shade.

I did a lot of thinking that week, and when Friday came again, and Willie counted out my three hundred dollars, I knew where I was going. There was no sense in denying it. I was going to Jerry's.

It was about ten o'clock when I pulled into the parking lot. The place was already jumping with every table filled. I took a seat at the bar and ordered a boilermaker. I didn't really know why the hell I was here, what I wanted to prove. The only thing that could happen was that I was going to make a fucking fool of myself again and probably get stomped in the bargain.

Emmy saw me, and I could tell me being here upset her because she rushed around ignoring me. One jerk-off kept making passes at her, and I swear he was the same stiff I had seen through the window with his hand on her. She tried to tell him in a nice way to get lost, but it didn't do no good. I had to hold myself in my seat to keep from explaining to him in terms he could understand exactly what she meant.

I stayed and drank, watching her, until the place began to close. People wandered out, one after the other, until no one was left except me, the jerk-off, and a couple that kept dancing to the jukebox even though they couldn't hardly stand up. The dancing twins finally staggered out after the bartender pulled the plug on the jukebox. If I thought at all about just leaving and giving it up, I changed my mind when I realized the jerk-off was waiting for Emmy to get off. I put out my cigarette, drained my beer, and got up. Emmy was clearing tables over in the corner. I walked over there.

"I'll take you home," I said. My voice sounded harsh to me, and I could hear the slur in it. I had been drinking a long time.

Emmy kept wiping the table. She didn't even look around. "I don't need a ride. I got my own car."

"Leave it. We'll get it in the morning. You're riding with me." I was watching the jerk-off out the corner of my eye. He was getting closer, trying to hear what we was saying. It made me angry. Then, suddenly, I was angry at everything. I wanted her to come with me. I didn't want to play around any more. I reached her and took the rag and tossed it on the table. She turned, swinging her hand at me. I caught it and held it. She looked like she was about to cry, and she struggled, trying to pull her hand loose.

First thing I knew, the jerk-off was in my face, pushing my shoulder, yelling for me to leave her alone. I dropped Emmy's hand, then dropped him at the same time with a fist in the stomach. When he didn't go all the way down, I gave him another to the side of the head. Jesus, it felt good. I had wanted to do that all evening.

I turned back to Emmy. "Let's go," I said. She looked uncertain, like she was almost afraid of me. Swallowing hard, I lowered my voice and said, "Please." And then I walked out without looking back.

On the ride back to Willie's, the night air beat cold and hard against my chest while Emmy pressed warm against my back. My head was beginning to clear, and I was calming down. I didn't know where this was leading, but at least I had done something.

"Hold on tight," I said to Emmy, and turned on the dirt road leading to the house. I guess I went a little fast over the pebbles, and the bike was sliding while I tried to stay up. By the time I reached the garage, I was laughing and Emmy was clinging with both hands to my jacket.

"Jesus H. Christ!" I said. I was laughing so hard I almost fell off the bike. "I hate that fucking road!"

I helped Emmy off. She was shaken a little, but all right.

"I'm sorry. It's like riding on glass, nothing to hold on to," I told her.

No sooner had she got off than she started up to the house.

I ran after her. "Hey, hey, wait a minute. Where you going?"

She turned back. "I'm going to bed. Thanks for the ride." Her voice sounded hard, but she looked small and nervous, standing there, kind of hugging herself, in the middle of the yard.

I went up to her. "Don't go yet. I want to talk to you."

"About what?" She looked like she might run at any minute. I took her hands and led her back into the shadows between the trucks and the garage. "I just want you to tell me why you did it, Emmy, exactly what made you do it. I want to know."

She pulled her hands away. "I already told you. I took it. Why do you keep after me? It's over. You can think what you want about me."

I lifted her chin so I could see into those strange blue eyes. "Tell me again. Tell me everything."

She leaned back against the truck, and I saw her take a deep breath. She looked up at the sky where the stars looked like a thousand holes punched in a huge black shade. I waited.

Finally, she started talking. She didn't look at me, but looked off into the dark under the trees, then up at the moon, half-covered with clouds.

She said her mama was sick, it was mental, and there was a new treatment, but she needed money before they would start it. She had some but not enough. Then she looked right at me, and it was that same clear defiant look she had given me that first night at the supper table. "When I went into that room with you, I went because I wanted to, because you looked sad, desperate for someone to hold on to, and because," she smiled briefly, "you have a kind face."

Then she was serious again. "So there it is. I saw the money. I thought what it could do for Mama, how you could always make more, but it was her only chance."

I moved over and leaned on the truck next to her and put my arm around her shoulders. She leaned on me, and we stayed like that for a long time. Then I pulled her around in front of me, holding her next to my chest, burying my face in her hair. It smelled just like I remembered, like green pines and warm spring nights.

"Next time, just ask," I said.

"You were too far gone to ask anything. Besides, you had troubles of your own." She wiggled closer and I could feel her relaxing against me.

"Ask me now," I said and held her away from me so I could see her face. "My eyes are wide open and my head's straight. So ask me now."

She studied my face. "Are you kidding?"

"No, I'm not. Say 'Gavin, I need a thousand dollars. Will you give it to me?"

She looked me straight in the eyes. "Gavin, I need a thousand dollars. Will you give it to me?'"

I bent over and kissed her, feeling her lips part. Christ, I thought, I feel like a kid getting his first kiss. Then I did it again, and I drew her close and did it again.

She pulled her head back. "Does that mean yes?" She smiled.

I didn't answer, but led her through the garage to the tool room. And it was better than last time. She was all light and dark, cool and warm, all pale skin and tumbling hair. Her breasts filled my hands, and she fit in every curve of my body, rising and falling, under me and then over me. I felt like it could last forever, but then I knew it couldn't, and when I finally clutched her to me, she said my name over and over.

Afterwards, she slept curled up under my arm, her head on my shoulder, her hand thrown across my chest. I reached down with my free hand and found my jacket on the floor. Getting a cigarette, I put it in my mouth and lit it, trying not to wake her.

Laying there, smoking, feeling Emmy's steady breathing, I wondered what more could you want except for the moment, the present, with no past or future, to be like this, where everything is all together, all straight dry road and no blind curves or slick spots. Jesus, it was going to be quite a month, and after that, who knows what's waiting down the road, down that white line.

from LIGHTHOUSE

Eugenia Price

Author's Note

Newly married James Gould, builder of the first St. Simons light tower at the turn of the nineteenth century, grew up in Granville, Massachusetts— a close friend and devoted pupil of the Reverend Lemuel Haynes. Haynes, educated by Deacon Rose, the man who kept him on as an adopted son after young Lemuel had worked out his indentured servant agreement, taught the boy, James Gould, not only about mathematics and engineering, but also about the absolute necessity to be free, no matter a man's race or background.

James is, in the fall of the year 1805, alone on the busy street above Savannah's waterfront, mulling over possible plans for where to settle his beloved young wife, Janie, and their infant son. He knew only one thing for certain: Whatever he did for a living, he could not—because of Lemuel Haynes's teaching, because of where James had grown up in Massachusetts—*ever* own another human being.

O n the south side of the Bay, near the corner of Whitaker, a crowd had gathered. Some sort of sale was in progress. He crossed the street to investigate.

Had he noticed the crudely lettered sign, he would have turned back:

AUCTION OF VALUABLE SLAVES

In Charleston, he had, when possible, avoided the slave market behind the Exchange, his stomach turning at the sight of human beings forced to stand inspection like cattle. Today, he found himself watching when a stocky mulatto, as light-skinned as Lemuel Haynes, stepped onto the rickety, foot-high platform.

The auctioneer, a modestly dressed, graying man with a pockmarked face, went about his business in a matter-of-fact way, gesturing from time to time toward the young man on the block.

"Gentlemen, I have the pleasure to offer a most unusual mulatto named Frank, aged about thirty-two. Has been in this country seven years, is an excellent coachman and hostler, understands perfectly well the management of horses and is, in every respect, a first-rate character, except that he will occasionally drink. Though, I hasten to assure you, he is not an habitual drunkard." He stroked the Negro's heavily muscled bicep with the back of his hand. "Now, ain't that the truth, Frank?"

James saw the mulatto lower his head.

"Well, I see the cat got Frank's tongue today," the auctioneer went on affably, "but now—what am I bid? For this splendid specimen, do I hear twelve hundred dollars?"

Bidding began at six hundred, the auctioneer droned on, and James moved to the edge of the crowd, where he could see the other slaves lined up. A child no more than five clung to its mother's tattered skirt; a young man in his twenties; a grizzled old Negro with deep white scars across his bare shoulders. Last in the straggly line, a little apart from the others, stood a tall young woman, her long, faded pink dress spotless and mended, her head proudly erect, her deepset eyes looking deliberately off over the small crowd of bidders and onlookers. James thought he had never seen a more noble-appearing woman, black or white. He stepped closer to wait through the sale of the others, for her summons to the block.

"All right, Larney!"

The woman moved with dignity, stepped up onto the box and stood looking toward the river. She was near Mary's age, James supposed, undoubtedly a house servant, capable, well trained, but he seemed to see more, and his head began to throb with hatred for the auctioneer. This slave was no longer black. *She was Mary* standing there, alone, unprotected—for sale.

"Yes, indeedy, my friends," the auctioneer was saying, "we have saved the best to the last. Larney will not be sold for pennies! She is here for sale only because her mistress died in Richmond a month ago and her master, old and infirm, went to live with his son. Larney, thirty-odd, born in Virginia, of fine sturdy stock, washes, irons, cleans, cooks—her rice pilaf would make your mouth water even before you taste! The perfect house servant, worth her weight in gold!" To prove his next point, the man casually ripped the neck of her dress to expose one brown shoulder and a breast. "Perhaps best of all, Larney is a proven, first-rate brood matron—look at that!"

James had pushed his way to the front of the group of men nearest the trading block, unable to leave until he learned the woman's fate.

"Ah, I see one interested gentleman," the auctioneer said, pointing at James. "Your interest only indicates your discrimination, sir. As further proof of Larney's worth as a breeder—note the width of the pelvis." He slapped her buttocks sharply. "No problem at all for Larney to increase your investment manyfold with little black pickaninnies. She's borne three fine sons already. All three brought a good price last year back in Virginia."

The woman had closed her eyes, but held her shoulders erect, her head high.

"See what I mean about her quality! Look at those wide, powerful shoulders. That chin in the air. You can't make Larney cringe and beg like other black wenches."

A sweating man with powdered hair shouted: "Nine hundred dollars!"

"For this excellent property? For this superb piece of black flesh? An insult! Let me hear a sensible bid, gentlemen!"

"Nine hundred and fifty," the man shrilled.

"Nonsense."

"Turn her around, so's I can get a better look. Maybe I'll raise it!"

The auctioneer turned the woman all the way around, touching her breasts with his gavel, her buttocks, noting again "the ample pelvis."

"One thousand dollars!"

James saw her open her eyes to look straight at the red-faced man who seemed about to buy her. She swayed slightly, shuffled one bare foot, then closed her eyes again and waited.

"One thousand and fifty dollars." The bidder's voice shook with annoyance. "No one in his right mind will go higher than that!"

"Eleven hundred!" James called out. She opened her eyes again. "Eleven hundred dollars," he repeated, to help her locate him in the crowd.

"Eleven hundred and fifty, by damn!"

"Twelve hundred dollars," James shouted. He heard the gavel bang three times against the platform where Larney stood, as the auctioneer began his detached explanation: "One half cash and the other half in notes at six months, drawn and endorsed to the satisfaction of the vendor, with special mortgages on the slave until final payment. Sold to the gentleman in the gray cape for twelve hundred dollars!"

James's profit from the hotel investment was in his pocket. "I'll pay cash," he said and began to count out the money. His head ached. He was still angry, but one relieving thought crossed his mind: Mary and Janie will be glad I saved her.

A minute ago, she *was* Mary, her eyes Mary's eyes: searching, wise, lonely, but somehow offering to help. Now Mary had turned into a strange brown woman named Larney.

A slave named Larney, who belonged to James Gould.

He paid for her, signed the necessary papers with as few words as possible, turned toward the woman, then whirled and sent the huckster sprawling to the ground. A few men guffawed. "You've got your twelve hundred dollars," James said, glaring down at the auctioneer, "and you've also got a tangible idea of what I think of a man who earns his living as you earn yours!"

Larney, who had not moved, stared at him.

For a moment, James wondered what to do. It was against Georgia law to free her. She was his legal property. His responsibility. People bought and sold Negroes every day. No one in all Savannah would think anything unusual had happened, he told himself.

His first impulse was to help her down from the block, but he realized what people would think, nodded instead and motioned for her to follow.

As he walked rapidly up Bull Street toward the Harris house, Larney a respectful distance behind, only one thing came clear: no matter how well he meant to treat this woman, he had sinned against the one person he had ever wanted to be like—Lemuel Haynes, son of a Scottish indentured servant and a black slave.

THE MANSION

Ferrol Sams

Lightning lived in a unpainted house that had three rooms. There was a bedroom for him and his wife and daughter, a lean-to for his sons, and the stove room where they cooked and ate and entertained whatever visitors who came around. It may have been a cabin, but it was not a shack. They covered the inside walls with cardboard to insulate against winter winds. Lightning's wife, in addition, plastered the stove room with layers of colored comic pages garnered from years of cleaning up and toting off at the Big House.

Lighting did not tolerate anyone's tearing loose boards off his house to start a fire, and his wife did not allow anyone to track mud across her floors. The house did not belong to them, but they lived in it for thirty years and thought it did. When something wore out, Lightning patched it. His wife was fond of saying, "Be neat. Be clean. And have a little talk with Jesus every day." She would scold a little and laugh a lot. The house responded.

It stood alone on the crest of the field. It was so near the Big House that Lightning kept his mule in the Bossman's barn; his wife's milk cow was likewise allowed to shelter there. The only outbuildings around Lightning's house were the well with its time-slicked log for windlass and the privy, which crouched well below the crest of the field on the edge of the sweetgum thicket and had a croker sack for a door.

Years of rain pouring off the tin roof of the house packed the red clay yard, and over time the drip line settled down and away from the foundation stones. The sills, in turn, canted toward the center, giving the impression that the house grew there, that it was rooted.

Lightning's folks all laughed more than they grumbled. There were plenty of things about which to do either, and they chose the high road. Instead of grumbling that there were no screens at the windows, they laughed about the old hen that flew in and laid an egg slap in the middle of Maw's bed. The entire family addressed the business of living; they worked hard enough never to fear hunger. Then they worked even harder hoping to get a little ahead, which was another matter altogether.

Every first Sunday they walked two miles to church. Lightning never owned a car, and they walked two miles through the woods. They left at ten and stayed all day. The children went to school from November through March and an additional month in August when the cotton was laid by but had not yet opened. The school went only through the seventh grade, and most children dropped out before then, either yielding to the pressures of puberty or fleeing the academic tyranny of Miss Willie, who was a stern disciplinarian and wore flowing scarves to hide the white spots on her neck. Lightning's children all finished the local pyramid of learning.

They grew up, married, farmed, visited their parents on Sundays, went to war. Lightning grew old and was able to plow only half a day and knock about a little. The Bossman helped establish his age and gave him a pension. Lightning died first and later his wife. One of their grandsons went to the University on a football scholarship and studied law. A great-granddaughter works in the bank. Lightning did not live to see either.

The house stood empty for years because the Bossman could not stand to see anyone else live in it. Even when the chinaberry trees grew up all around it, you could still tell that Lightning had lived there. Paint, when all is said and all is done, may be nothing more than a badge of privilege.

from A WHISTLING WOMAN

Louise Shivers

Author's Note

This novel takes place shortly after the Civil War in the American South. It is the story of two women, a young tomboy named Georgia Vick and her illiterate widowed mother, Mittie. At fourteen Georgia is impregnated by a married man. To keep the rural community from knowing about the disgrace, Mittie keeps Georgia out of sight, puts a pillow under her own clothes to appear pregnant, and shows up at the country church. Mittie is condemned as a fornicator and turned out of the church. The baby is raised as Mittie's child on the plantation where she works.

A few years later when Georgia marries a young man from Virginia, she moves her strange mother and "brother" to a town where no one knows any of them. The two families live side-by-side. Georgia "forgives" her own past and she and her husband open a store.

When Wilkes, the son, turns eighteen, Georgia wants to tell him who his real parents are. This brings about an explosion from Mittie, who is menopausal and very bitter. Because of her early life of poverty, illiteracy, abuse, and neglect, she has serious emotional problems. Georgia learns from the confrontation that Mittie has convinced herself that the boy is her own, the love child of her imagined affair with the Reverend Swann.

"You want to claim the only thing of my own I've ever had," she accuses Georgia. To her horror Georgia also learns that Mittie has much deeper problems. A year after Georgia was born Mittie killed her own tyrannical husband (who had forced her to have sex and had made her pregnant at fourteen), buried him under the outhouse, and led neighbors to believe that he'd been lost in the war. Understanding her mother as never before, Georgia feels great pity for her and decides to keep her own counsel and never reveal her mother's secret.

———

A whistling woman and a crowing hen never come to any good end.
                                          —Old Folk Saying

All my life I've been able to watch myself do things. See myself . . . stand off and look over at a chair or table and see myself there where I'd walked before . . . see the muslin sheets flap on the clothesline and see him stretched out on them beside me, or see the big oak tree by Contentnea Creek and see the other one push me against it and himself against me.

Right now I can see my whole life like that, some of the parts clearer than others, some real dim and shadowy.

The first thing I ever remember was when I was a baby. I had a bad dream; in it frogs were crawling in my bed, slithering right in it.

And then a few years later I remember us moving. It must have been 1867. I was about eight years old then. It was in the fall, I remember the cut hay in the fields. Mama piled our things in a big flat wagon and somebody drove us to a different house to live. It wasn't my papa that helped us. I didn't have a papa, never did that I knew anything about. I didn't even know him from pictures. The only thing I ever could get Mama to say about him was that he was a hard-luck fella from Fool's Bridge.

Before the man came to help us move, I remember that I played in the yard at Snow Hill with a ragdoll Mama'd made me out of scraps she and the seamstresses that lived there had left over. I don't remember much about those women, they were different ones that came and went. I'd gone to school there in Snow Hill so I could read good by the time we moved.

I remember sitting high up on the seat of the wagon when we moved. Mama sighed and said, "Ever stitch we own in the world," as she looked at the bedstead and the trunk and the old ballyhacked dresser. The bed shook from side-to-side as the horse clip-clopped along.

The places in the town looked so funny to me as we passed them with me perched up there. We rode and rode out into the country. Before we got too far out we passed the sandpit. There was a sorry-looking house near it. "Looka yonder at the limber-necked chickens," I called out, but Mama shushed me and sat up real stiff. I expect she knew the people that lived there, but she looked straight ahead as we passed.

"Sick chickens," she said after we were down the road. "That's Bad Alley down there." I peered down the lane trying to see what was bad about it. The colored man that was driving the wagon broke my thoughts.

"Mr. Fleeting's hoping you'll get there in time to give him a haircut befo' dinner."

"Well, I've got right smart to do to get settled in," Mama spoke up.

"I can hep with that," the man named Slender said. "Me and Maebelle are mighty glad to see y'all come. Mr. Fleeting hadn't had too much attention since his missus died three months ago. We've got just about all we can handle with the harvesting and all."

"Is Maebelle your wife?" I piped up.

"Yes, and my woman, too," he chuckled.

When we went around the hill, I sucked in my breath. There in front of me was Fleeting Plantation and I'd never seen anything like it.

It was a different world then than it is now. It wasn't long after that big war where everybody's lives had been changed around. Looking back to it now is like looking into a far place, as far as China in a hole if you'd dig deep enough.

When we rode up to that great big house and I saw it in front of me, it was a sight to behold. Mama said, "Not too many of these big houses left."

There was a house with long porches on both sides, and there were a lot of little buildings around it, some cabins, and a big round waterhole near the long grape arbor. We went on past the house and went down a lane. "Yonder where me and Maebelle live," Slender gestured with a sweep of his hand towards the woods.

We went on around for a ways and came to a little cabin with a big umbrella tree beside it. The way Mama got down off the wagon kind of nimble I could tell she liked it. The porch had a rail around it and a wooden shelf for the water bucket. In one direction there was the lane to the big house; in the other, a path to the river.

We unloaded our things from the wagon and placed them around in the two rooms. Then we walked away from our new house with its unpainted silver gray boards and went to meet Mr. Fleeting. Mama never had seen him, she'd just been sent for.

When we went through the door to the side porch, a big, raw-boned woman smiled at us from the kitchen. She called out welcome and nodded at us as she kept right on sifting cornmeal from the round sifter with one hand and turning the chicken frying in the black frying pan on the biggest wood stove I've ever seen in the other.

Mama nodded back at her and said, "Smells mighty good." I can still remember the smell of baking sweet potatoes and the wood smoke all mingled together.

"Maebelle, aren't they here yet?" It was a fine-sounding voice that called out from the front of the house—what I later learned to call an aristocratic voice.

Slender hurried us on into the room where Mr. Fleeting sat. He introduced us to the man. My eyes swept around that big sitting room. It was a grand room with sunshine coming in the long windows. Big-headed pictures hung on the wall, their eyes following me around.

When I set my mind to it, I can see Mr. Fleeting just like he looked that day. He was a medium-sized man and when he'd been young he must have had that kind of hair that they call strawberry blonde. He still had a lot of sandy gray-streaked hair and a moustache the same color. His skin was kind of pink and he had real light blue eyes. I remember noticing right away that when he'd try to talk a trickle of slobber would run out of the side of his mouth. You see, he'd had a little stroke before we came and he was shaky and addled. Mama said it sure could have been a whole lot worse. "He can walk and talk, and that's a blessing," she said.

I liked him right from the first. You don't know why you like some people the first time you see them but you just do. And some people you don't even want to like.

All of this was long before I even knew what the Ten Commandments were, let alone what they meant, and long before I pointed to the big framed copy of them in the hall and asked, "What does commit adultery mean?" and he had cleared his throat and said, "Mess around with bad women."

I could see that Mama was pleased by us being at the plantation. I'd hear her telling Maebelle in the kitchen about how glad she was for the work. "Sewing in town couldn't keep body and soul alive, especially these days. And with two younguns."

You remember about Mama's boy named Laffton. He was ten years older than I was. He was always real restless. When we'd come out to the country, he had headed for Virginia where he'd heard about some work. He said he was going to send us some money but he never did. Once in a while somebody would come through Snow Hill that had seen him and he'd send word that he was all right. Mama said that he'd always been up to something. I wondered if he was like our papa, the hard-luck fella from Fool's Bridge.

Soon Mama and Mae were thick as thieves, sewing and cleaning and thinking of things to tickle Mr. Fleeting's fancy. Part of the time Mae had to work in the fields. Slender and their grown children had all they could do. I'd help Mama in the big house then. I kept wanting to go back to school, but Mama said "Maybe after Christmas." Children came and went in school then, according to the work on the farms, so

I wasn't the only one out. So on those days I'd read to Mama and Mr. Fleeting. I made me a little book and I'd record some of the things I'd read to Mr. Fleeting on the days that he'd be feeling weak and Mama would be busy in the kitchen. He had a lot of books that he'd let me read.

During that time we didn't meet any of his kin. At Christmas time a package was brought out from his son, Mr. John Fleeting, who lived in Baltimore. That was the first time I'd heard of him.

It was at Christmas that I got to love old Mr. Fleeting. Santa Claus brought me a little birthstone ring. Looking back I don't know how Mama managed that as poor as everybody was back then. But she did, somehow. We all had a good time that day, Mae and Slender and their children all dressed up and happy. We all laughed and talked together and I showed off my ring with the emerald-colored stone.

But after sundown when they all went off and Mama had made Mr. Fleeting his toddy and put him to bed, I noticed that my finger was starting to swell. The more I pulled at the ring to get it off, the more my finger swelled. It started to ache and get red. That's when I started to get scared. I could tell that Mama did too. No matter how much soap we put on the finger trying to ease the ring off, my finger got redder and redder and throbbed more. Finally Mama set me down in a straight chair in the big kitchen and told me we were going to have to file it off. That's when I started to feel panicky and started to cry. Mama filed and filed. It felt like she was hacking as she ground back and forth with the big metal file.

I was so miserable that I slumped over and felt like I was going to die. Terror went through me as I thought of the things I'd heard of, like blood poisoning. Suddenly I felt a cool hand on my forehead and then a cool washrag, clean and sun-smelling laid across my eyes. When I opened them I saw that Mr. Fleeting had come in and was sitting in front of me. He was sitting on the round piano stool that Mama must have brought in and the light from the lamp shone behind him. He smiled at me and it was like I was seeing him in a kind of dream. He reached over and took my hand and wrapped it in a big cool white rag and we sat a minute. He kept dabbing it with icy water from the bucket outside. He said, "Now be real quiet and think of the best thing you know of." In a minute he said, "Now tell me what you're thinking about."

"Bananas," I said, and he smiled. We'd had some that day and it was the first time I'd ever seen any.

After we'd sat for a while he took a thin black file he'd brought from his room and slowly, very slowly, but with a hand so firm I couldn't believe it was his, filed until the ring broke in two and fell away from the sides of my finger.

We settled down at Fleeting Plantation. Before I knew it I was thirteen and then everything started to change.

I've always been able to step back and watch myself. Well, I can tell you exactly what I looked like then. I was tall and straight, taller than Mama even when I was just thirteen. When she'd go to tie a sash around my waist she'd laugh because it was so little. My legs were long and thin like bird legs. When I'd pull the black stockings on to go to school, they'd look even skinnier, and I know I was a funny sight. My bosoms were high and little. Mama said she didn't even see any need for me to wear a waist except to keep the cold air out. My face was long too, and my eyes were black, like muscadines Mae used to say. My hair was dark and straight.

I came in one day about that time, whistling and skipping, whistling up on the porch. Mama came out of the house, drying her hands on her apron, wringing her hands, looking anguished. "*George*, stop that whistling. Have you never heard that girls shouldn't whistle?"

"M'am?" I said.

"A whistling woman and a crowing hen never come to any good end," she said.

I looked at her, I could tell she was serious.

She went on in a lowered voice. "I don't want you getting on Mr. Fleeting's nerves. I need this job mighty bad, and men don't like to hear a big ole growin' girl."

After a while I did get to go back to school. I would walk about an hour and a half to that little building in the grove of trees. If it was too cold or icy, Slender would give me a ride in the wagon on his way into town. He was always going back and forth. But most of the time I walked. It gave me a chance to get off by myself and think things out. And I liked to investigate things. I'd collect different kinds of leaves and rocks. I had things I'd check on every day, ant beds and bird nests. In the fall I had a favorite thing, a big garden spider who'd spin a wide web every day, take it in at night after he'd caught his dinner, and then spin another one early the next morning before I'd even come by. I'd heard them called writing spiders, and people said that if they wrote your initial in the web you'd die. I didn't ever see a G, sometimes I thought there was a V, but then it would turn into something else. Some days I'd be so excited when I left the house for school that I'd wave my hands in the air. Mama would say, "Whatcha flittering for?" and chuckle at me.

On the trail that I walked in the winter I'd watch the trees lose their leaves. When they were bare and black, they laced against the sky like fans. I thought that was the prettiest sight I'd ever seen in my life. I still do.

Once or twice over those years when the leaves were all off the trees and I could see the road, I saw the man who would later change my life in a black-and-brown buggy hurrying by.

There were two main kinds of churches in Tar County: Methodist and Baptist. First, you'd see one, then the other. There was a Free Will Baptist one between Fleeting Plantation and town. The Fleetings had gone to the Episcopal church in town. Mr. Worth didn't go anywhere when he lived there. Mae and Slender went to their own African Methodist one, on the other side of the creek. Before we'd moved to Fleeting Plantation we hadn't gone to church, but out there Mama got a hankering to go.

It all started when Mr. Fleeting offered an announcement at supper one spring night. We generally all ate supper together. "There's a big Baptist camp meeting going on next week."

"A camp meeting?" Mama sounded vague, but my ears perked up. Something to do. Somewhere to go. But she didn't sound like it was going to have anything to do with us.

Finally, after a long quiet, she said, "I've heard tell of camp meetings all my life, but I never have thought to go to one. Do you feel like going?" she asked Mr. Fleeting.

"No, no, my churching's finished, but you and Georgia ought to go. If it's farther than you want to walk, Slender can carry you in the wagon, or he could get out the buggy."

It was settled then, and we did go. The meeting was outside, under a shelter they'd made. They called it a brush arbor because it was made out of little trees and branches put over a wooden frame, like a grape arbor, to make a tent.

It was the first preaching I'd ever been to. It was funny seeing folks from school and their families out there like that. That part was nice, being out of doors and all, but I didn't like the preacher from the minute I laid eyes on him. He was a real long-legged fellow with a sort of whinny laugh. "The ladies, God bless 'em, hey hey." He patted me on the top of the head when he walked by. I took my hand and brushed my hair all around to get the touch off. But the crowd got caught right up in the ranting and swelling and carrying on. When we got home, I heard Mama talking to Mr. Fleeting. "Georgia didn't seem to care much for the preacher."

He chuckled. "That girl never did suffer fools gladly."

But Mama was caught up in it, and it wasn't long after that before we started going to church at the regular church by the creek.

Contentnea Free Will Baptist Church was a pretty little white building, and the preacher that was there was as different from the evangelist as dark night is from bright morning. When I think back I realize that the preacher, Luke Swann was his name, must have been a young man, about thirty-five. But of course he seemed as old as the hills to me then. Still I enjoyed seeing the people and just the *going*. Afterwards I'd sit outside on a tree stump and eye everybody as they headed to their wagons while the mules whinnied and grazed in the corners of the churchyard.

Folks at that church dearly loved Mr. Swann's sermons. Mama and the other ladies would sit on the edge of the wooden pews just eating up every word he said. That's where I learned what it means when somebody says something is *gospel*. What Reverend Luke said was gospel. He was a fine-looking dark-haired man, tall and straight in his black suit, but when he walked he kinda drug one of his legs. From the way the women looked at him, that made them like him even more. "It was infantile paralysis," I heard a woman say to Mama.

He had a farm over near Eureka and came to our church on the second Sunday of every month. "He farms during the week," we heard, but we never saw him in his everyday clothes. We knew he preached at other churches too sometimes. In fact, before it was over, Mama got to wantin' to go other places to hear him. She talked about it, but she never did do it, no way she could have.

Mama changed after we started going to church. Her face kinda opened out. I'd hear her and Mae singing hymns about loving Jesus while they worked. Mr. Fleeting spoke out about it one day while she had him out on the porch sunning in the rocking chair. "Well, I don't see a thing wrong with it. It makes ladies feel good to go to church," he said.

Going out to that church gradually made Mama feel like somebody. There at Contentnea Church she could speak up and be a person. She'd fix her hair, and we'd be right there along with everybody else. It didn't even matter all that much that she couldn't read, a lot of the others couldn't either. She could listen to the Bible readings and learn the songs. The preacher wasn't one of the kind that looked down his nose at women. He would listen to what they had to say, each one of them, and seem to care. The women ran the church. There were three times as many women as men. I s'pect for a lot of them it was the only time they ever got to have any say-so about much of anything. I even got Mama to let me teach her some reading and writing, something she'd always been too ashamed to do before.

One day, after we'd been going there for awhile, I stood outside after the service and watched the women close in around the Reverend Swann. One of them nudged against his black sleeve like it was an accident.

I remember shutting my eyes and feeling and tasting moist wool in my mouth. I stood far back from the circle and heard, just slightly above the sound of the women's voices, a man behind me mutter, "Timothy I, Verse 2: Converse sparingly and conduct yourself prudently with women." I could see out of the corner of my eye one of the impatient husbands standing tapping his foot. But Reverend Swann talked earnestly on. Every time he ever stood in the pulpit he said, "All souls are precious in the sight of God." And it seemed to me that he meant those words with all his heart.

About the time the church going started, I woke up one day with a strained feeling between my legs. Waves of uneasiness moved through me from one bone to the other. My sharp hipbones stuck up when I lay down flat, and between them it seemed like a new ocean lapped with thin water. Something like an eggshell and egg white started happening when I stood up. After I had stood up for a while, I pulled down my drawers and saw weak pink stains in the egg white. I stood there for a long time. It didn't go away. I put my finger in and took it out. It came out sticky and red.

The air around my ears felt heavy. As I stared at the wall, little black specks like gnats flew between my eyes and the wall. Standing there, I could see a thin veil of myself leave and float out the window like a butterfly. The stains from the ripe mulberries that lay crushed on the ground turned the path that led to the creek red.

I'd told Mama when I went into the house. "I started," I said, and Mama had looked at me real strange and had given me a pile of clean white rags. She'd shown me how to fold them and pin them inside my drawers: "You'll need them every month, so keep them clean," she'd snapped. Then she'd slammed the door as she left to go to Mr. Fleeting's room. When I'd done what I had to do and gone up to the Big House, I could tell Mama had told Mae, because Mae put her big arm across my shoulder and leaned close so no one could hear.

"Don't wear the rag too long before you change it, it'll chap the sides of your legs. As soon as you take it off, take it way behind the house and soak it in cold water. And one more thing, Georgia, stay away from menfolks when the curse is on you. They don't like to have that around."

After that there were still a lot of long slow days. Days when we didn't see a soul but each other. Days when we made lye soap or boiled the washing and didn't hear a sound but the birds. Months would pass by like that, dusty days, moldy days, but Mama had different things to think on now, and she'd have me read from the Bible every night before we'd turn down the lamp.

But when spring came I'd go for long walks in the woods and across meadows. I'd watch the sweep of the fields just plowed. The curve would follow the line of the woods. The rows would make designs as pretty as ribbons, low and smooth, then ridging, washboarding. I'd want to go lie down in that sweet plowed dirt and wallow like a pig. At night sometimes that feeling would come over me when I was in my bed and I'd think of those sights and I'd feel like I was about to bust. I'd get so full of it that I'd bite the sheets and shake. I couldn't wait for the next morning—hated to take my clothes off at night because it just took time to put them on again the next day—only went to bed so that night would be over so that I could see what the next morning would bring.

One day Maebelle told my fortune. The main thing I remember her saying was, "Old, you're going to live till you're real old, and you're going to have two men, one light and one dark." Then she dropped my hand and looked at me hard. "And a secret, you're going to have a secret."

"A good one?" I asked.

"Good and bad, good and bad—now don't ask me no more," she said.

Later on she taught me how to read palms myself. "The main thing," she said, "is to be real quiet and you can feel something come out of the person to you, like a little whisper—it's more *that* than the lines." She also told me to be careful whose palm I read.

"Be careful reading men's palms. It's something you have to be careful about, it catches their soul—and it's a right smart *burden* havin' somebody's soul."

[Later in the story, after Georgia has become pregnant at age fourteen and told her mother about it.]

On a Sunday in October Mama took aholt of my elbow and we set out down the road to church. My throat was dry and achy. We didn't talk any all the way there. Mama's jaw was set. The only thing she said at all as we walked was, "I wonder what kind of thing Mr. Fleeting is harboring up for us to do next."

Now you may think by her saying that that he had something to do with what she was fixin' to do, but it wasn't like that at all. She just said that because she was still mad as a hornet about it all that had happened. We had no more than walked up into the churchyard before the women started staring and getting off in little bunches and whispering behind their hands.

Mrs. Owens came up to us and looked right straight at Mama and said, "Well, Mit, there must be something we don't know." Then she gave a little coy laugh. "Something you've been keeping a big secret?" Mama just nodded to her and held her head up real high and kept her back stiff as she walked into the church and took her regular seat in the middle.

The people already in the church rustled around and sucked in their breath and then it got so quiet you could hear a pin drop. The only sound at all was a hee-haw from one of the mules waiting outside. The preacher didn't notice a thing though and stood in the pulpit and went on and preached his sweet sermon.

Later, out in front of the church when he came to shake hands, he turned to Mama and the look on his face was like he'd been struck by lightning. His jaw dropped and he started stammering and blushing. Mama stood facing him, looking as bold as brass, her puffed-out belly there in front of her for the whole world to see. She just looked straight at him, her face set in such a way that the skin was pulled tight in the hollows under her cheekbones. Reverend Swann looked like he was about to spew. He turned abruptly and went back into the church, leaving the crowd in a circle around us. Mrs. Owens spoke up again.

"Tell us your news, Mit, speak up so that we can rejoice with you."

Mama looked her right in the eye and said, "We've not got any news to tell."

Well, you can just imagine the dither they all were in. The men started leading their wives to the buggies, getting on away. You could see that they were about to bust to start talking. There was no sign of the preacher; I guess he left the back way.

We went home and waited. We knew they would be coming pretty soon. Only the year before a brother had been excluded from the church for the sin of intoxication and attending a circus. Adultery and fornication wouldn't take long, it was right there in the Ten Commandments. It wasn't like the time Brother Aycock had been brought to trial for drinking French brandy. He had pleaded illness as an excuse and had confessed and begged forgiveness. There would be no forgiveness for this sin.

It took them three days to come out. It was a drizzly day, and I saw the covered buggy coming down the road. Mrs. Person sat up front beside the preacher, her little round bottom perched on the seat, her face saintly looking. The Reverend Swann looked like a mule had kicked him. In the back the three other members of the committee of honorable brethren appointed to investigate sat ready.

I don't know why at a time like that, when I'd been told to stay in the dark kitchen and hide behind the flour barrel and let Mama face them alone, I would think of such a thing, but a story Mama had told me when I was little came to my mind.

It was when she'd told me that my daddy was from Fool's Bridge and I had asked her how it got such a funny name. She'd said, "When the bridge was built across a stream there, with one end in a cemetery, the superstitious folks that lived near despised going through the cemetery at night to reach the bridge, and said only a fool would locate a bridge in such a hanty place."

I could hear some of the things they said, and some of the words would drift off. There were two women and two men besides the preacher. I guess they thought that was fair. I'd wondered before about how fair the people at the church were. Some of the things they did seemed mighty stern to me. But in this case I could see that they were trying to give Mama a chance there on the porch, a chance to say that she was married to Mr. Fleeting or somebody. But she just kept her lips tight together and snapped back at every question.

"No, 'tain't so."

I've never seen anybody more miserable than the Reverend Swann. He didn't ask any of the questions. Mostly it was Mrs. Person. "Well, what do you aim to do?"

"Take care of myself," Mama snapped.

It was dim out in the gray circle of the yard. Our dog got up and moved around and lay back down under the house. The trees around the house looked bare and lifeless like a winter deadening. There wasn't a sign of color or life anywhere. The leaves had already been blown away from our raked dirt yard, the unpainted house, the mud holes.

After about an hour of questions with nothing but bitter tight answers, with all of them standing on the porch in a little bunch, Mrs. Person said in a loud voice, "Well, at least you must come before the church and admit your sin and beg forgiveness." Then she whispered, "Is your husband come back? You can tell me."

"No, I'm not comin, and no, ma'am, I'm not begging anything. This is no one's doings but my own."

Mrs. Person sucked in her breath. "The Lord our Savior has something to say about it!" She sounded put out but gave it one more try and whispered, "But, Mittie, you have to confess if there is any hope of forgiveness, and name the man that sinned with you."

"No, ma'am," Mama said again and rared back so that her belly stretched the cloth of her dress. "I'm not doing any confessing."

"Then," Brother Sorrow, who had been quiet until now, boomed out, "the preacher will have to denounce you from the pulpit at the next meeting."

And he did. We weren't there, of course, but word got back to us quickly and with every detail . . . Reverend Swann stood there and said what was expected of him, "Caught in fornication and excluded from the church, the member Mittie Williams . . ." and then went on with a sermon about hellfire and damnation to all sinners while all the members sat wild with excitement, but holding themselves as still as corpses.

from OUTER BANKS

Anne Rivers Siddons

O n the Outer Banks of North Carolina there is a legend about the ships that have come to grief in the great autumn storms off those hungry shoals. Over the centuries there have been many; the Banks have more than earned their reputation as the Graveyard of the Atlantic. Most of them occur on Diamond Shoals, just off the point of Cape Hatteras, but the entire hundred-odd-mile sweep of coast has devoured its measure of wood and flesh. Myths and spectres and apparitions lie as thick as sea fog over the Banks, but one that I have always remembered is the one Ginger Fowler told us all . . . Cecie, Fig, Paul Sibley, and me . . . the September of my last year in college, when we were visiting her between quarters.

"They say that whenever a ship is going to go down you can hear something like singing in the wind," she said. "Bankers say it's mermaids, calling the sailors. Lots of them claim to have heard it. It's not like wind or anything. They say when you hear it, you have no choice but to follow it, and you end up on the shoals. A few of the sailors who've been rescued swear to it."

We were sitting on the front veranda of the Fowlers' house on the dunes on Nag's Head beach, watching the twilight die over the Atlantic. On either side of us hulked the great, black-weathered, two- and three-story cottages that made up what the Bankers call the Unpainted Aristocracy—a long line of huge, weather-stained wooden summer houses that had been built in the early days of the century by the rich. When they were first built, the houses reigned alone on that lordly line of dunes, owning by sheer *force majeure* the wild, empty beach. Now they are surrounded by flea-like armies of bungalows and timeshares and fishing piers and umbrella and float rentals, like mastodons beset by pygmies. But even now, when you are on the front porches or verandas, you have no sense of the graceless, idiot hoards nibbling at their skirts. Only of wind and sun and emptiness, and the endless sea.

I remember that I felt a small *frisson* that might have been night wind on sunburned flesh and reached for Paul's hand. He squeezed it but did not turn to look at me. He was looking intently at Ginger's sweet, snub face, stained red by the sun setting behind us over Roanoke Sound and by the long, golden days in the sun. Autumn on the Outer Banks is purely a sorcerer's spell: so clear you can see each grain of sand on the great dunes, and bathed in a light that is indescribable. We had stayed on the beach from dawn to sunset for the past four days, and all of us wore the stigmata on our cheeks and shoulders. But Ginger was the red-brown of cast bronze all over. The freckles on her broad cheekbones had swum together in a copper mask, and her eyelashes and towhead had whitened. She looked like a piece of Mayan statuary in her faded cotton bathing suit with the boy-cut legs, squat and abundant and solid as the earth.

I thought she looked almost perfectly a piece of the old house and the older coast, but in fact her father had only bought the house two summers before, from an imperious old widow who was going, most reluctantly, to live with her children in Wilmington. Before that Ginger had summered at Gulf Shores, on the Alabama coast, and lived with her family in a small north Alabama town called, appropriately, Fowler. It consisted of a huge textile mill, a mill village and store, and little else, all of which belonged to Ginger's father. The Fowlers were newly, enormously, and, to us, almost inconceivably rich. Ginger worked very hard to conceal the fact, and succeeded so well that, until we went to visit her on the Outer Banks and saw the house, we did not really comprehend it. Fig had told us when she proposed Ginger for sisterhood in Tri Omega that Ginger had a trust fund of her own approaching five million dollars; in those days, that was a breathtaking sum of money. But since none of us paid much attention to what Fig said, we either forgot it or discounted it. In the end, Ginger became a Tri Omega because we all loved her. It was impossible not to. She was as gregarious, sweet-natured, and simple as a golden retriever.

"And," Cecie observed thoughtfully, "looks not unlike one."

On the darkening porch that night at Nag's Head, Paul smiled at Ginger and said, "Have you heard the mermaids singing, Ginger?" and the little cold breath on my nape and shoulders strengthened.

"God, no," she said. "It would scare the bejesus out of me. I hope I never do."

"I wish I could," he said, and then he did look at me, and squeezed my hand again. "That would be something to hear. I think that would be worth just about anything."

I actually shivered; it seemed to me as if the very air around us had weight and meaning, and every whirling atom had particularity and portent. But I was so much in love with him by then that everything he said, everything we did, everything that surrounded us, our entire context, had resonance and purpose. Cecie looked at me and then at Paul, and said, "I think I'll go make some tea," and rose and padded into the house. I watched her out of sight, thinking once more how like a small, slender boy she looked in silhouette, wishing that she liked Paul better. For two years Cecie had been the friend of my heart, one of the two real loves of my life, and I wanted her to share this new love with me. I wanted the three of us, I think, to be a unit, a whole. But Cecie, who did not often or easily give her heart, was not about to accord it to Paul Sibley. From the moment she had met him she removed herself from him, physically when she could, emotionally when she could not. With another friend I might have thought it was jealousy, but what Cecie and I had went far beyond and deeper than that. I did not know what it was, and somehow could not speak of it with her, and she did not to me. Paul knew that she did not like him, but had been wise enough to simply let it alone. They did not often meet.

That week in September was, in fact, the last time Cecie ever allowed herself to be in his presence, but in the end it did not matter. I lost him that weekend to that old sea and Ginger's new money, but I did not know that until much later.

That winter I studied T. S. Eliot in a Contemporary Poetry class, and when we came to "The Love Song of J. Alfred Prufrock" and the professor read aloud those lines of ineffable beauty and heartbreak, "I have heard the mermaids singing, each to each./ I do not think that they will sing to me," I began to cry, suddenly and silently, and excused myself from class, and walked across campus to the Tri Omega house blinded by wind and tears, near suffocating with heartbreak and exaltation. I was still crying, intermittently, when Cecie came in from her history lab, and Fig and Ginger stopped by to see if we wanted to go to early supper.

"Who is it? Yeats? Dylan Thomas?" Cecie said, who had had the poetry course the quarter before and knew my penchant, that winter, for quick, rapt tears. It was mostly the helpless love for Paul that triggered them, a mature and obliterating and sometimes crippling thing, that left me flayed and vulnerable, as if I had no skin. An astounding number of things pierced me and brought tears in those days. But it was partly the poetry, too. Cecie and I often stayed up late into the nights reading poetry to each other, mostly the bitter, beautiful, sharp-edged poetry of the late nineteenth and early twentieth centuries, and if she did not, like me, weep openly, her blue eyes were sometimes liquid with tears. I never saw Cecie cry, but on those nights she often came close.

"Eliot," I snuffled. "About the mermaids singing, but not to him . . . I don't know. It reminded me of that thing Ginger told us up at Nag's Head, about the mermaids and the ships, and then . . . well, I just think that it's such a *sad* line. So sad, so sad . . . it's all of life. It's what ought to happen, but doesn't. It's . . . when you know it isn't going to . . ."

"What is?" Ginger said, her brow furrowed with perplexity. She and Fig shared a suite with us, connected by a bath, and often, in the mornings after Cecie and I had sat up reading poetry, Ginger would stick her shower-wet head into our room and say, "I hear there was a meeting of the Tri Omega Intellectual Society last night," and would grin and put out her tongue and slam the door as Cecie or I threw a book or a stuffed animal at her. Ginger was as slow to study as she was quick to laugh, and her grades, even in her undemanding major of elementary education, were in constant jeopardy. It took the entire sisterhood to get her through her pledgeship and maintain a grade average sufficient for initiation, but nobody minded. As I said, everybody loved Ginger.

I read her the lines from Eliot, and she said, "And that's what you're bawling about?"

"I think it's one of the most romantic things I ever heard," Fig breathed adenoidally. Her eyes, swimming myopically behind her thick lenses, looked like those of a rapt bug. She breathed through her mouth, audibly, as she did in times of transport. We hooted her down as we often did, and like a dog that is often threatened but not actually struck, she grinned gummily and tucked her short neck into her heavy shoulders, and looked at us slantwise.

"And sad," she added. "It's really sad." If I had said the poem was the funniest thing I had ever heard, Fig would have laughed heartily. Since we pledged her, Fig had had a kind of suffocating, sexless crush on me that was as obsessive as it was inexplicable. Very few things have ever made me so uncomfortable. Fig was a triple legacy, and National had threatened to put us on inactive if we did not pledge her. Otherwise, in those days of casual and killing cruelty, there is no doubt that she would have lived her years at Randolph in one of the independent women's dorms.

"If one of us were to hear the mermaids, who should it be?" she said archly. It was the kind of precious, off-balance, idiot thing she was always proposing: "If you were a flower, what would you be?" "If Kate was an animal, what animal would she be?" "If I were a famous woman of history, who do you think I'd be, Kate?"

"Grendel's mother," Cecie snapped once, and Fig trilled her laughter, by then disconcertingly like mine.

"That's good, Cecie, I'm going to put that in my diary," she said, and Cecie groaned. Fig's diary was infamous at the Tri Omega house. She wrote in it, furtively and ostentatiously, almost constantly. At chapter meetings you would end a heated discussion and look around and Fig would be scribbling in her diary. If you asked what she was writing, or made as if to snatch it away from her, she would pantomime fright and press it to her nonexistent bosom. Often, sitting in our room in one of the endless late night discussions that went on between us, I would feel Fig's eyes on me, and look over and see her staring at me, mouth open, and then she would smile mysteriously and drop her eyes and scribble in the diary. By that winter she had amassed four or five of them, big fake-alligator volumes she ordered from somewhere and filled with her tiny, cribbed hand. She kept them in a locked metal strongbox under her bed and hinted that they contained enormities. None of us felt anything anymore about the diaries but weariness.

I knew that she knew who Grendel's mother was, though. Fig was probably, in her own way, as brilliant a student as Randolph had ever had. Her grasp was intuitive and instant, her recall prodigious, and she studied like no one I have ever known before or since. Her point average alone, the sisterhood agreed, was worth the rest of Fig to the Tri Omegas. She was an English major, with a minor in history, and there was not a scholastic honorary she did not belong to. She meant to be a writer, and sometimes, when someone asked her again what she was writing in the diary, she would say, "I'm writing about all of you, and how proud I am to be a Tri Omega." And she would look so humbly, hand-dog grateful and smile so terribly coyly, that the questioner would turn away in embarrassment and distaste. Fig was so thankful to be one of us, and so relentlessly Pollyanna-cheerful and effusive in her praise of us, that we soon ceased baiting her and simply avoided her when we could. Most of us could, except Cecie and I and Ginger. Ginger is the only one of us I never heard say an unkind word about Fig. Ginger was, and is, incapable of malice. She came into Tri Omega as a sophomore pledge from Montevallo Women's College, having been sponsored, surprisingly and insistently, by Fig, who had lived her entire life in the shadow of Ginger's father's mill, in Fowler. It was, in fact, the Fowler-Kiwanis scholarship that sent her to Randolph. Fig's people were as spectacularly poor as Ginger's were rich. Ginger roomed with Fig, becoming our second suitemate, and went a long way in making the association bearable to me. I don't think it ever was to Cecie, not really.

Poor Fig. Her name was Georgine Newton, but I think she had probably been called Fig from birth. She was pale, puffy, squatty, spotty, frizzy-haired, sly-eyed behind the quarter-inch glasses, and had the constant, quivering, teeth-baring smile of an abused dog. She had sinus problems and asthma and snored so terribly that the dean of women made a rare exception and let her live alone. When we pledged her, we drew straws to see who would become her suitemates, and when we pledged Ginger and she moved in with Fig, we had a lottery going to see how long she could bear the fusillade of garglings and snortings. But Ginger was fortuitously deaf in one ear from a stray baseball, and so they simply arranged their beds so that Fig's snores fell on her deaf ear, and remained

roommates. It was Cecie and I who heard her, through a plaster wall
and a bathroom with two closed doors.

"Oh, *Lord*," Cecie would say, when Fig's name came up, and refused
to elaborate. But I knew that she disliked Fig with a pure and fastidious
animosity that was, for her, unusual. Cecie was censorious of few people;
she simply avoided those she did not like, but she could not avoid Fig.
It must have been an uncomfortable three years for her. We never talked
much about it, except that once in a while she cautioned me about Fig.
I had long since learned to smile and make light of Fig's heavy, cloying
adoration and her incessant copying of my voice and gestures and clothes:
I was myself a stranger in a strange land, and thought I knew how she
must feel, somewhere under all that Fig-ness. But I soon developed a
fine-honed skill at mimicking her, and I confess that I often used it in
the late nights when Cecie and I lay in our beds with the young moon
shining in on us, talking, talking.

"Shhhh," Cecie would gasp through her laughter. "She'll hear you.
She's got her bed jammed right up against the wall opposite yours."

"How can she hear me through a bathroom and two walls?" I would
scoff. "And so what if she does?"

"I wouldn't get on her bad side," Cecie said. "She's not what she
seems."

"Lord, Cecie, she's just Fig. What is she, if she's not that?"

"I don't know. But whatever, it's not what you think," Cecie said.
"Where's your famous intuition?"

"You're nuts," I said, and went on being polite to the lurking, adoring
Fig in her presence, and laughing helplessly at her in the nights.

And Cecie went on bearing her in silence, going away inside her
head when Fig was around. It was an astonishing talent; I have seen
her do it many times. You would be looking at Cecie, perhaps talking
to her, and all of a sudden you realized you were looking at the diminutive,
kitten-faced, red-haired outside of Cecelia Rushton Hart from the Virginia
tidewater, but that the essential Cecie was simply not in residence at
the moment. She could even converse while she was doing it, nodding
and murmuring the right things. After a while she would slip back
in behind her eyes and Cecie would be there again; I often wondered
what inner world she had made for herself that so seduced and comforted
her, and what she did there, and with whom. For all our bone-closeness,
there was a door very deep inside Cecie through which I could not follow,
and I knew it was there she went when Fig stumped too intrusively
into her consciousness.

"Who would it be?" Fig insisted with that terrible, lumpen playfulness,
on the day I discovered Eliot. "Who would the mermaids sing to? I
think it would be you, Kate. You'll be the one who hears the mermaids.
I bet you already do."

Cecie snorted.

"Maybe it'll be you, Fig," I said, thinking it would please her. And it did. She blushed an unbecoming magenta and said, "Do you really think so? I'd love that. But I'm sure it would be you. You look like you hear mermaids sometimes . . ."

"No," Ginger said, surprising us. We looked at her.

"It'll be Cecie," she said. "Don't you see? It has to be Cecie."

And I smiled, involuntarily, because of course she was right. It would be to Cecie to whom they sang. Behind her harlequin glasses and dry Virginia drawl, Cecie was smoke and will-o-the-wisp light, sea spray and flame. It would be Cecie who heard the mermaids singing.

And maybe she did. Maybe they all did, for all I know.

But I know that they never again, after that year, sang to me.

ROSELILY

Alice Walker

*D*early Beloved,

She dreams; dragging herself across the world. A small girl in her mother's white robe and veil, knee raised waist high through a bowl of quicksand soup. The man who stands beside her is against this standing on the front porch of her house, being married to the sound of cars whizzing by on highway 61.

we are gathered here

Like cotton to be weighed. Her fingers at the last minute busily removing dry leaves and twigs. Aware it is a superficial sweep. She knows he blames Mississippi for the respectful way the men turn their heads up in the yard, the women stand waiting and knowledgeable, their children held from mischief by teachings from the wrong God. He glares beyond them to the occupants of the cars, white faces glued to promises beyond a country wedding, noses thrust forward like dogs on a track. For him they usurp the wedding.

in the sight of God

Yes, open house. That is what country black folks like. She dreams she does not already have three children. A squeeze around the flowers in her hands chokes off three and four and five years of breath. Instantly she is ashamed and frightened in her superstition. She looks for the first time at the preacher, forces humility into her eyes, as if she believes he is, in fact, a man of God. She can imagine God, a small black boy, timidly pulling the preacher's coattail.

to join this man and this woman

She thinks of ropes, chains, handcuffs, his religion. His place of worship. Where she will be required to sit apart with covered head. In Chicago, a word she hears when thinking of smoke, from his description of what a cinder was, which they never had in Panther Burn. She sees hovering over the heads of the clean neighbors in her front yard black specks falling, clinging, from the sky. But in Chicago. Respect, a chance to build. Her children at last from underneath the detrimental wheel. A chance to be on top. What a relief, she thinks. What a vision, a view, from up so high.

in holy matrimony.

Her fourth child she gave away to the child's father who had some money. Certainly a good job. Had gone to Harvard. Was a good man but weak because good language meant so much to him he could not live with Roselily. Could not abide TV in the living room, five beds in three rooms, no Bach except from four to six on Sunday afternoons. No chess at all. She does not forget to worry about her son among his father's people. She wonders if the New England climate will agree with him. If he will ever come down to Mississippi, as his father did, to try to right the country's wrongs. She wonders if he will be stronger than his father. His father cried off and on throughout her pregnancy. Went to skin and bones. Suffered nightmares, retching and falling out of bed. Tried to kill himself. Later told his wife he found the right baby through friends. Vouched for, the sterling qualities that would make up his character.

It is not her nature to blame. Still, she is not entirely thankful. She supposes New England, the North, to be quite different from what she knows. It seems right somehow to her that people who move there to live return home completely changed. She thinks of the air, the smoke, the cinders. Imagines cinders big as hailstones; heavy, weighing on the people. Wonders how this pressure finds its way into the veins, roping the springs of laughter.

If there's anybody here that knows a reason why

But of course they know no reason why beyond what they daily have come to know. She thinks of the man who will be her husband, feels shut away from him because of the stiff severity of his plain black suit. His religion. A lifetime of black and white. Of veils. Covered head. It is as if her children are already gone from her. Not dead, but exalted on a pedestal, a stalk that has no roots. She wonders how to make new roots. It is beyond her. She wonders what to do with memories in a brand-new life. This had seemed easy, until she thought of it. "The reasons why . . . the people who" . . . she thinks, and does not wonder where the thought is from.

these two should not be joined

She thinks of her mother, who is dead. Dead, but still her mother. Joined. This is confusing. Of her father. A gray old man who sold wild mink, rabbit, fox skins to Sears, Roebuck. He stands in the yard, like a man waiting for a train. Her young sisters stand behind her in smooth green dresses, with flowers in their hands and hair. They giggle, she feels, at the absurdity of the wedding. They are ready for something new. She thinks the man beside her should marry one of them. She feels old. Yoked. An arm seems to reach out from behind her and snatch her backward. She thinks of cemeteries and the long sleep of grandparents mingling in the dirt. She believes that she believes in ghosts. In the soil giving back what it takes.

together,

In the city. He sees her in a new way. This she knows, and is grateful. But is it new enough? She cannot always be a bride and virgin, wearing robes and veil. Even now her body itches to be free of satin and voile, organdy and lily of the valley. Memories crash against her. Memories of being bare to the sun. She wonders what it will be like. Not to have to go to a job. Not to work in a sewing plant. Not to worry about learning to sew straight seams in workingmen's overalls, jeans, and dress pants. Her place will be in the home, he has said, repeatedly, promising her rest she had prayed for. But now she wonders. When she is rested, what will she do? They will make babies—she thinks practically about her fine brown body, his strong black one. They will be inevitable. Her hands will be full. Full of what? Babies. She is not comforted.

let him speak

She wishes she had asked him to explain more of what he meant. But she was impatient. Impatient to be done with sewing. With doing everything for three children, alone. Impatient to leave the girls she had known since childhood, their children growing up, their husbands hanging around her, already old, seedy. Nothing about them she wanted, or needed. The fathers of her children driving by, waving, not waving; reminders of times she would just as soon forget. Impatient to see the South Side, where they would live and build and be respectable and respected and free. Her husband would free her. A romantic hush. Proposal.

Promises. A new life! Respectable, reclaimed, renewed. Free! In robe and veil.

or forever hold

She does not even know if she loves him. She loves his sobriety. His refusal to sing just because he knows the tune. She loves his pride. His blackness and his gray car. She loves his understanding of her condition. She thinks she loves the effort he will make to redo her into what he truly wants. His love of her makes her completely conscious of how unloved she was before. This is something; though it makes her unbearably sad. Melancholy. She blinks her eyes. Remembers she is finally being married, like other girls, women? Something strains upward behind her eyes. She thinks of the something as a rat trapped, cornered, scurrying to and fro in her head, peering through the windows of her eyes. She wants to live for once. But doesn't know quite what that means. Wonders if she has ever done it. If she ever will. The preacher is odious to her. She wants to strike him out of the way, out of her light, with the back of her hand. It seems to her he has always been standing in front of her, barring her way.

his peace.

The rest she does not hear. She feels a kiss, passionate, rousing, within the general pandemonium. Cars drive up blowing their horns. Firecrackers go off. Dogs come from under the house and begin to yelp and bark. Her husband's hand is like the clasp of an iron gate. People congratulate. Her children press against her. They look with awe and distaste mixed with hope at their new father. He stands curiously apart, in spite of the people crowding about to grasp his free hand. He smiles at them all but his eyes are as if turned inward. He knows they cannot understand that he is not a Christian. He will not explain himself. He feels different, he looks it. The old women thought he was like one of their sons except that he had somehow got away from them. Still a son, not a son. Changed.

She thinks how it will be later in the night in the silvery gray car. How they will spin through the darkness of Mississippi and in the morning be in Chicago, Illinois. She thinks of Lincoln, the president. That is all she knows about the place. She feels ignorant, wrong, backward. She presses her worried fingers into his palm. He is standing in front of her. In the crush of well-wishing people, he does not look back.

from ALL THE WESTERN STARS

Philip Lee Williams

I don't reckon Lucas will mind me telling about us, at least he never told me not to. Sometimes now when I wake up early and look out of the house and see that prairie stretching out brown and blowing, I can't believe how I managed to end up here. But it's a peaceful satisfaction. I'll walk down to the creek there where Lucas used to come to hide and I can almost see him coming up through the morning fog.

Lucas would talk all the time about how we're in this ruined world for no reason. I never did believe that, but then I never did much thinking before I met Lucas and by then I was seventy-three years old. I never met a man who could go from plumb giddy to sulky as a child in such a short time. But I've had my own faults pointed out to me a few times, and I've always tried to reserve judging others as long as I wasn't a pearl either. So far, I'm not getting to be much better of a person, but you can always hope.

That was two years ago now I first met Lucas Kraft. Of course, I'd never heard of him and never read any of his books. I think the only poem I'd ever read then was something about a girl from Nantucket, but you picked up that sort of thing when you wandered around much as I did.

I didn't think I was getting feeble, but by comparison with what I used to be, I reckon it seemed that way to my niece, Belle. She's a nice girl but doesn't have a lick of feeling for anybody that might cost her and that boy husband of hers any money. My house was getting a spell run down and we were standing on the back porch looking out over the woods and the meadow when she told me she'd got a place for me in Fieldstone.

"It's a really good place for you, Uncle Jake," she said. "And I had to pay good money to get you a place. They had an old lady from Eatonton ahead of you and I bribed the director into letting me get you in first."

"I ain't going," I said, with what I thought was enough spit to end it right there, but it turned out she was more stubborn than I was. And

I was sick. I knew I was sick but that cross-eyed doctor I always went to kept telling me it was only my nerves, and I said, hell, my nerves never failed me yet. I started telling him about the time I worked steel and stood up on top of the Allied Consolidated building in Chicago, but he needed that fifteen bucks from his next patient too bad to listen to me. I hear he wound up an alcoholic at home babbling and shaking, and I'm sorry for his family, but I can't summon up much pity for him.

Anyway, in the middle of arguing with my niece, I passed out. Just slap fell out on the porch like I was going to sleep, and that was just what she needed to convince me she was right. A few days later, in a moment of weakness, I allowed her to shove some paper in front of me and I signed it and didn't find out till later I'd given her power of attorney. Not one month later she sold my house to a developer who wanted to build retirement condominiums. Lucas later explained to me the meaning of that word *irony*, and I had to admit this situation seemed full of it.

Like I say, I was sick, and the day they came to take me away, Belle and her husband, I had been up since dawn looking out over the pasture and wondering if I'd ever see it again. I'd built the house with my own hands thirty years before, back when I could work any man into the ground, back when Betty and me had just got married and spent all night huddled up beneath the sheets giggling like children and touching one another in all the good-feeling places God put on a body.

Well, she'd left me about six years after that and run off with a taxidermist from Monroe who had made a lot of money after deer season. I followed them around for a while, since I once spent two years working for an insurance company in New Jersey doing the same kind of work, but when I caught up with them, the taxidermist was scared I was going to kill him and Betty was clinging to him like she'd been sewed to his body, and I felt sick inside and went off by myself like a wounded old bear and got stupid drunk for a couple of days and found I was over her.

But that day Belle came for me, I still loved that house and I remembered what Betty looked like the day I'd finished it. The wind was blowing and her hair kept coming up in her face, and when she'd push it back there was a smile on her face that wouldn't go away. I don't reckon I've ever made anybody as happy as I did that one day, and it was worth every busted finger and cuss word I gave the place while it was going up. It wasn't much of a house, but ever since Betty had left, I'd come to fit it like a foot fits an old boot. I figured Belle and her boy husband would store all my gear, but damn if they didn't sell it off, too, just like I was already dead and that stuff didn't mean much to me.

It meant more to me than I want to remember now. I told Lucas one time about an old hand mirror that I'd inherited from my mama that I'd lost there, and he wrote a poem about it. I didn't understand it until he explained it, but then it made me feel like weeping a little, though I didn't do it.

Anyway, I was standing there when I heard their car come up, this ugly little foreign car that looked like a rolling outhouse turned on end. I knew I might never see the place again, and as I was standing there, a hawk came swooping down from somewhere and went flying across the field, claws down like a plane about to make a landing, but then it just touched the ground, like it was making sure it was still there, then it went up into the rising sun and flew off. When Lucas and I met up with Old Buffalo out in Texas, the Indian told me that it was what's called an omen, and now I can see that, but then it just struck me as being something right pretty.

"You ready, Uncle Jake?" Belle asked. I'll have to admit that even though she was my sister's girl, Belle looked like a bored horse, with a jaw long as a sack of grain. I was still sick then (they didn't find out what was wrong with me until later), so I just nodded and got my grip, in which I'd snuck a quart of liquor, and went on out the door. Her husband drove like he couldn't figure out which pedals made the car stop and go, and more than once I thought I was going to meet my maker on the way over to Fieldstone. Belle yelled at him the whole time, and he looked so miserable I guessed it was best not to make him feel any worse than he already did by telling him he couldn't drive worth a shit. Anyway, I reckon he knew it.

The town I lived in was called Branton, a nice little stop in the road in north central Georgia, which reminded me so much of my home town in Mississippi that I'd just stopped the car and settled down there years before. My being there was the reason Belle and her husband had moved to the country, them being hippies in the early seventies and me being agreeable about letting them live on a piece of the land I'd been buying. In those days, they lived in a tent and ate nuts and berries and I didn't mind if they did, though some of my neighbors told me they were Reds, but I don't think either one of them had ever read past Classic Comics.

Branton was a clean little town with wide streets and plenty of dog-woods and old water oaks, the kind of things that make you say this is a place that will last. That was what I was looking for when I came off the road, I reckon, a place that would last since hardly anything in my life had lasted for more than a few months. I picked up work here and there.

That day, though, as Belle's husband drove me through Branton, it looked like any of those places I'd passed through for a day or two when I was a boy, nothing special anymore, and I was amazed that I'd thought anything could last even as long as I had.

Fieldstone wasn't a new place. It was a long, flat brick building on the outskirts of town that looked out over a pasture that reminded me of a cemetery without any gravestones. Belle parked in front on a circular driveway and a big colored fellow came pushing a wheelchair out. I got out and looked real mean at him and ambled up to the doors, and damned if they didn't flap out like the wings of a vulture and nearly knock me on my ass.

"Is this your idea of a joke?" I shouted. I realized by the way the colored man reacted that I was acting like a crazy old man, which was what they figured I was anyway. Well, to hell with it, I thought. I went on inside with Belle on my arm while her husband was trying to park the car without destroying anything. There was a small check-in station and the place smelled like alcohol and school cafeteria food. While Belle was filling something out, I shuffled into a big room to the left and it was full of folks with at least one foot in the grave, some of them all but laid out with daisies in their hands.

I stood there for a minute trying to figure it all out. Four or five men and women were watching television, some game show, but their mouths were hanging open and I wondered if they ever caught flies that way, horrible as it sounds now. It seemed funny to me at the time. I was thinking about dead people and the smell of the place when I realized a tiny little fellow was standing at my left elbow.

"Who are you?" he asked. I'm six-two, least I was when I was a man, and he looked like something from *The Wizard of Oz*.

"Jake Baker," I said. "Who are you?"

He said, "Comer Bird, Jr."

"Comer Bird, Jr.?" I said somewhat sourly. "Is your paw here, too?" He did something I didn't think he'd do: he cackled like a hen, and his laughter going across the room was about as useful as hubcaps on a tractor.

"Don't eat any of the food," he said, whispering like it was some kind of secret. His put his knobby fingers around my arm and sort of pulled me off to one side. His fingers felt like they had scales and I had the awful feeling he was really a lizard. Women in white uniforms came wandering through, heading down the tiled halls, but I didn't see a one that appeared to enjoy being there any more than I did.

"How come?" I asked.

He said, "They put dog food and poison in it. They will try to kill you first thing. Don't eat anything but seeds. My daughter can bring you seeds." I never ate any seeds, but I figured if things ever got that bad, Belle and her husband, being former hippies, could advise me on which ones were good.

"Seeds," I said, trying to think of something to say.

"And don't let them give you a shot of any kind," he said. "They're drawing your blood out and putting it in the ones who die and making them come back to life." I've been around my share of fruitcakes and this guy, Comer, Jr., seemed like he came right out of the box. I gave him my "don't screw with me" look and got away from him.

I backed up a couple of steps and turned around, and a woman who looked about two hundred years old was standing there holding on to a walker and growling at me like a dog.

"How are you this morning?" I said. My daddy always made me be polite to people and often times now I'll do it without thinking, which surely must be making him happy where he is.

She growled at me again and bared her teeth, which were too ugly to be store-bought. Belle came and got me then, along with a tall man in a suit. His name was Mr. Denny, and he was the manager. He looked remarkable like a gravedigger I'd once known in Ohio, which was funny to me, so I laughed a little and they looked at me that way. The woman was still growling.

"That one got off her leash," I said.

"Let's not be unkind about others' infirmities," Mr. Denny said. His voice sounded like it was being poured out of an oil can and he worked his fingers together like he was trying to weave a rug out of them.

"Uncle Jake, please," said Belle. About that time, her husband came through the front doors, looking like a sheep heading for the slaughter-house. "The people here will look after you and you will love it so much. All the people here are so happy they've come and it's a blessing for them all." I wanted to ask her about who was supposed to bless me, since she'd once tried to convince me somebody named Krishna was running things, but I just kept my mouth shut. Comer, Jr., stood up and started waltzing by himself and singing something I couldn't catch.

Being sick, I didn't want to do anything but lay down, so I just shrugged and one of those women wearing white clothes and squeaky shoes came and took me down the hall until we got to a room on the right, and there was my name beside the door on a little piece of paper, and when I saw it, I felt really defeated and down about everything.

Belle and her husband came and said a few things, but to this day I don't recollect what they were. There was another bed in the room and there was a man in it who looked like he'd died some time before. Belle finally left and I sat and looked out the window at the pasture, snuck out the bottle, had a few drinks, and figured it was only a matter of time before I got the hell out of there.

Because Belle was my own flesh and blood, I didn't go over to her house and give her a tongue-lashing. Them being ex-hippies, they'd come to cuddling up with money late, and I figured I'd never be able to reason with them.

"Let's go break her knuckles," Lucas said helpfully while I stormed around yelling. We walked on down to the house and went behind it. Nobody had cut the grass in the weeks I'd been gone, and it was knee deep and wet as a river in the darkness.

"She's my niece," I sighed.

"Let's break his knuckles!" Lucas yelled. I knew what he was thinking. With my car gone, we were in pretty miserable shape for getting out to the Great Plains. "They have fouled their own nest."

"Aw hell," I managed to say. I broke out the back window next to the door and reached in and opened the door. The inside of my house was quiet as a tomb as we followed the flashlight beam around. Belle had had the electricity cut off, too.

"There's not a speck of stuff left," I said stupidly. "She just up and got rid of everything I owned."

"Let's break her thumbs," Lucas suggested, but he was starting to sound the way I felt, sad and disgusted rather than angry.

I stood there in the quiet for a right smart time. Lucas wandered into another room. From the light of the moon, you could see to walk. I just stood there, and I remembered Betty and how we'd get up in the middle of the night sometimes and make love on the couch because it was a different place, and the moon would come in on us and I could see her smiling under me. Lord, that was a thing. I just couldn't stand being there any more with the remembrances.

"Come on," I said, my voice hard and sort of cold. "We're getting the hell out of this dump." Lucas came back out, his heavy body creaking on the floorboards.

"Sue the bastards," he said like he was a king. "I think you should enter litigation, Jake. This is an abomination against your good name. Why, once I was sued by this jackleg son of a bitch who said I'd copied his novel and . . ."

"Would you shut up?" I said, turning to walk back out, and he could tell by my tone not to fool with me, so he just waddled after me. Lord, we must have been a sight.

I didn't really know what to do. The night didn't seem particular friendly any more, just damp and warm, and even the crickets and tree frogs sort of got under my skin. We walked back out to Highway 78, heading west. Lucas was breathing like he'd just finished the marathon, and once he tripped over an empty can of Budweiser and fell flat on his big rear end, cussing a blue streak. I grabbed his arm and helped him up.

"This enterprise has started like a herd of turtles," he said, and I started laughing and so did he, and we both felt better for a time. We walked down the highway, past the Purina Store, past Branton Memorial Hospital, past Mr. Colfax's hardware store where I bought most of the materials when I built my house for Betty. I had a powerful sense of leaving what had come to be my home, leaving it for the last time, and for no account I felt as blue as I had in ages.

We went on past the furniture plant. They'd had a strike there four years ago and the management had just shut the damn plant down, and now it looked like a monument, floodlights on it at night. There was always rumors they'd open it back up, but they hadn't yet. When I was a boy I belonged to a labor union in Chicago, but I've come around to believe now they're just about the worst thing ever happened to this country. We passed a fertilizer plant, and then a gas station that was closed down for the night, and then we came to the intersection with Highway 96, and the last spot with any light before you got out of Branton completely.

"I think we should go back to Fieldstone," said Lucas, whining like a child. Well, it had crossed my mind, too, but I knew I was gone from this land now, a feeling like I hadn't had in years, that feeling of leaving everything, making a break and going on the road.

"I'm heading on out," I said. A few cars came by. Nobody paid us much attention. "I'm going to Texas. If you hear they've found me dead along the road, drink one for me." I put my thumb out.

"You can't leave me!" he yelled. He put his hands in his pockets and started circling me. "I don't have anything to do now. I am in pain, goddamnit! Living here in this land is a pitiful thing, let me tell you. I had just as soon be on a commune somewhere in the wilds of Siberia."

"Nobody's holding you," I said.

He said, "Go to hell, Jake!" I knew what he needed, but I'd kept from it for a while. He was hopping around now, just wild from being cut loose of his bonds and afraid of it all. So I just stepped up to him and slapped the holy shit out of him. He didn't even make to hit me back, just started shaking and then he cried a bit and then quit.

"You okay?"

"Yeah," he said. "I suppose we are out on our own now, just living by our wits."

I said, "I reckon we are."

Contributors' Notes

Raymond Andrews is the author of the widely acclaimed trilogy about the lives of rural blacks in the Georgia Piedmont region: *Appalachee Red* (1978), winner of the first James Baldwin Prize for Fiction; *Rosiebelle Lee Wildcat Tennessee* (1980); and *Baby Sweet's* (1983). Recently he published his memoirs, *The Last Radio Baby* (1990), about growing up in the South. A native of Madison, Georgia, Andrews now lives in Athens, Georgia.

Tina McElroy Ansa is the author of the novel *Baby of the Family*. Ansa, who is currently at work on a second novel titled *Ugly Ways*, lives on St. Simons Island with her husband, filmmaker Jonée Ansa.

Michael Bishop is the author of *No Enemy But Time*, winner of the Nebula Award presented by the Science Fiction Writers Association. His forthcoming novel is *Count Geiger's Blues*. He is currently working on a novel about baseball called *Brittle Innings* and lives in Pine Mountain, Georgia, with his wife and two children.

David Bottoms, winner of the Walt Whitman Award for his first book of poetry, *Shooting Rats at the Bibb County Dump*, was also awarded the Levinson Prize, an Ingram Merrill Award, a fellowship from the National Endowment for the Arts, and an Award in Literature from the American Academy and Institute of Arts and Letters. *Easter Weekend* is his second novel; other titles include: *Any Cold Jordan*, *In a U-Haul North of Damascus*, and *Under the Vulture-Tree*. He lives in Marietta, Georgia.

Judith Ortiz Cofer was born in Puerto Rico and raised in New Jersey. She is the author of two volumes of poetry, a novel, *The Line of the Sun*, and a collection of essays, *Silent Dancing*. She is the recipient of the Witter Bynner Foundation for Poetry fellowship and the Bread Loaf poetry fellowship, and Fred Chappell selected her for the Georgia Poetry Circuit Tour. In 1989 she was awarded a writing fellowship by the National Endowment for the Arts. She lives in Louisville, Georgia.

Pam Durban is a graduate of the University of North Carolina at Greensboro and the Iowa Writers' Workshop. Her awards include the James Michener Award, two Ohio Arts Council fellowships, the *Crazyhorse* Fiction Award, and the Whiting Writer's Award. She lives in Atlanta, Georgia, where she teaches fiction writing at Georgia State University.

Emily Ellison is the author of *The Picture Makers, Alabaster Chambers* and *First Light* and, with Jane Hill, editor of *Our Mutual Room: Modern Literary Portraits of the Opposite Sex*. She lives in Cartersville, Georgia.

Paul Hemphill is the author of eight novels, most recently *The Sixkiller Chronicles, Me and the Boy*, and *King of the Road*. He has been a Nieman Fellow at Harvard, a newspaper columnist and a magazine editor, and is currently Writer-in-Residence at Brenau College. He lives in Atlanta with his wife and children, and, in addition to writing novels, also writes for several magazines.

Jane Hill is the author of *Gail Godwin* and *Cobb County: At the Heart of Change* and the editor of *An American Christmas: A Sampler of Contemporary Stories and Poems, Street Songs 1* and *2: New Voices in Fiction*, and with Emily Ellison, *Our Mutual Room: Modern Literary Portraits of the Opposite Sex*. She is winner of the Frank O'Connor Prize for her fiction and the recipient of fellowships from the Syvenna Foundation, Villa Montalvo, and the Georgia Council for the Arts. She lives in Marietta, Georgia.

Rebecca Hill is the author of *Blue Rise, Among Birches*, and, with Judith Guest, *Killing Time in St. Cloud*. A native of Mississippi, she now lives in Gainesville, Georgia.

Mary Hood makes her home in Woodstock, Georgia, and takes her characters from the changing landscape of that area. Her first collection of short stories, *How Far She Went*, won the 1984 Flannery O'Connor Award for Fiction. Her second collection, *And Venus Is Blue*, received the Townsend Prize for Fiction in 1987.

Greg Johnson lives in Atlanta and teaches creative writing and American literature at Kennesaw State College. He has published critical studies of Emily Dickinson and Joyce Carol Oates; his most recent book is a collection of short stories, *Distant Friends*. Johnson's work has appeared in more than fifty American magazines and anthologies, including *The Georgia Review, The Southern Review, Virginia Quarterly Review, Prize Stories: The O. Henry Awards,* and *New Stories from the South: The Year's Best.*

Terry Kay is the author of *To Dance with the White Dog.* Previous works include the Emmy-winning screenplay, "Run Down the Rabbit," and the novels *The Year the Lights Came On, After Eli,* winner of the 1982 Best Fiction Award from the Georgia Council of Authors and Journalists, and *Dark Thirty.* His forthcoming book, *To Whom the Angel Spoke,* is for children. He lives in Lilburn, Georgia.

Warren Leamon is the author of *Unheard Melodies.* He lives in Athens, Georgia, where he teaches at the University of Georgia. His work has appeared in numerous literary and commercial magazines and has won the Borestone Mountain Award.

Judson Mitcham is an associate professor in the Department of Psychology at Fort Valley State College. He was awarded a Creative Writing fellowship from the National Endowment for the Arts in 1988 and a Pushcart Prize for poetry in 1989. His chapbook, *Notes for a Prayer in June,* won a national competition sponsored by State Street Press and was published in 1986. Mitcham's forthcoming collection of poems, *Somewhere in Ecclesiastes,* is the winner of the Devins Award. He lives in Macon, Georgia, with his wife and two children.

Linda Chandler Munson is the author of *Heat Storm.* She is a former policewoman in metropolitan Atlanta and currently teaches creative writing at Mercer University in Macon, Georgia.

Eugenia Price is the author of eleven novels and twenty-six nonfiction books and is currently at work on her twelfth novel. Her latest is *Bright Captivity.* She is the recipient of numerous awards and lives on St. Simons Island, Georgia.

Ferrol Sams, a country doctor from Fayetteville, Georgia, has charmed a generation of Georgians with *Run with the Horsemen, Christmas Gift!, The Passing,* and *Whisper of the River.* His forthcoming novel is *When All the World Was Young.* Dr. Sams, his wife, and two of their four children practice medicine in Fayetteville.

Louise Shivers is the author of *Here to Get My Baby Out of Jail*, named Best First Novel by *USA Today*, and made into the movie *Summer Heat*. A native of North Carolina, Shivers has lived for many years in Augusta, Georgia. A recipient of a National Endowment for the Arts fellowship, she is currently Writer-in-Residence at Augusta College and Senior Editor of *Augusta Magazine*.

Anne Rivers Siddons has had a string of best-selling novels, starting with *Heartbreak Hotel*, *The House Next Door*, *Fox's Earth*, and *Homeplace*. More recent works include *Peachtree Road*, *King's Oak*, and *Outer Banks*. She lives in Atlanta, Georgia.

Alice Walker is the author of *The Temple of My Familiar*, *The Third Life of Grange Copeland*, *Meridian*, and *The Color Purple*, which won an American Book Award and the Pulitzer Prize. She is also the author of two short story collections, *In Love & Trouble* and *You Can't Keep A Good Woman Down*; four volumes of poetry; two volumes of essays; and two children's books, *To Hell with Dying* and *Finding the Green Stone*. A native of Eatonton, Georgia, she now lives in northern California.

Philip Lee Williams is the author of five novels: *The Heart of a Distant Forest*, *All the Western Stars*, *Slow Dance in Autumn*, *The Song of Daniel*, and *Perfect Timing*, and is working on a new novel, *Final Heat*. His other writing projects include screenplays, documentary scripts, newspaper and magazine articles, and poetry. A past winner of the Townsend Prize, in 1990, he was Georgia Author of the Year in Fiction for the Council of Authors and Journalists. He lives in Watkinsville, Georgia, with his wife and son.

Permissions